OKANAGAN COLLEGE LIBRARY
03688108

D1732785

the **kip** *brothers*

THE

WESLEYAN

EARLY CLASSICS

OF

SCIENCE FICTION

SERIES

General Editor

Arthur B. Evans

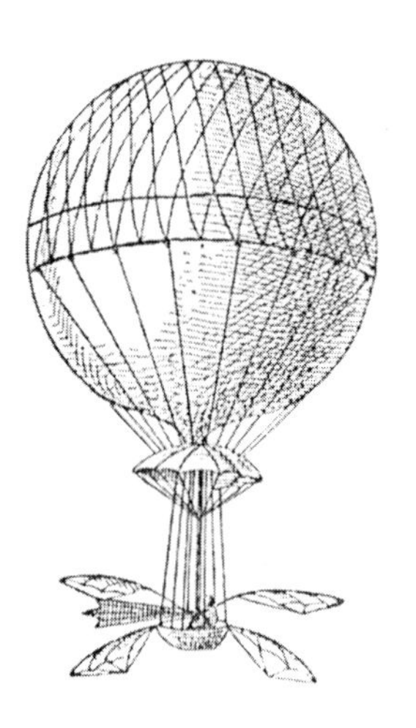

The Centenarian
Honoré de Balzac

Cosmos Latinos: An Anthology of Science Fiction from Latin America and Spain
Andrea L. Bell and Yolanda Molina-Gavilán, eds.

The Coming Race
Edward Bulwer-Lytton

Caesar's Column: A Story of the Twentieth Century
Ignatius Donnelly

Subterranean Worlds: A Critical Anthology
Peter Fitting, ed.

Lumen
Camille Flammarion

The Last Man
Jean-Baptiste Cousin de Grainville

The Battle of the Sexes in Science Fiction
Justine Larbalestier

The Yellow Wave: A Romance of the Asiatic Invasion of Australia
Kenneth Mackay

The Moon Pool
A. Merritt

The Twentieth Century
Albert Robida

The World as It Shall Be
Emile Souvestre

Star Maker
Olaf Stapleton

The Begum's Millions
Jules Verne

Invasion of the Sea
Jules Verne

The Kip Brothers
Jules Verne

The Mighty Orinoco
Jules Verne

The Mysterious Island
Jules Verne

H. G. Wells: Traversing Time
W. Warren Wagar

Star Begotten
H. G. Wells

Deluge
Sydney Fowler Wright

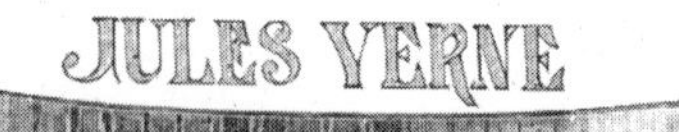

LES FRÈRES KIP

COLLECTION HETZEL
18 RUE JACOB:18
PARIS

the kip *brothers*

JULES VERNE

Translated by STANFORD L. LUCE

Edited by ARTHUR B. EVANS

Introduction and notes by JEAN-MICHEL MARGOT

WESLEYAN UNIVERSITY PRESS Middletown, Connecticut

Published by
Wesleyan University Press, Middletown, CT 06459
www.wesleyan.edu/wespress

Printed in the United States of America

The illustrations in the novel appeared in the original French edition of *Les Frères Kip;* the ones that are unattributed in the captions are by George Roux.

Verne, Julies, 1828–1905.
[Frères Kip. English]
The Kip brothers / by Jules Verne ;
translated by Stanford L. Luce ;
edited by Arthur B. Evans ;
introduction and notes by Jean-Michel Margot.
p. cm. — (The Wesleyan early classics
of science fiction series)
Includes bibliographical references.
ISBN 978-0-8195-6704-8 (cloth : alk. paper) —
ISBN 978-0-8195-6838-0 (pbk. : alk. paper)
I. Luce, Stanford, 1923– II. Evans, Arthur B.
III. Margo, Jean-Michel. IV. Title.
PQ2468.F74E5 2007
843'.8—dc22
2006046114

CONTENTS

INTRODUCTION

Les Frères Kip (*The Kip Brothers*) is one of those rare Jules Verne novels originally published as part of his *Voyages extraordinaires* that has, until now, never been translated into English.[1] Why? Some Verne scholars have suggested that British and American publishers refused to translate these works for political and ideological reasons, reacting to the growing number of anti-British and anti-American passages in them.[2] In the case of *The Kip Brothers,* however, the reason was more likely commercial. Since it did not conform to the Anglo-American stereotype of what a Jules Verne novel *should* be about (i.e., a Victorian sci-fi tale with intrepid heroes exploring the far-flung corners of the world and beyond, often with the aid of advanced technology), its market potential was probably deemed too low to justify the costs of translating and publishing. Otherwise, these same publishers would have no doubt opted to do what they had done for so many earlier English-language editions of Verne's works—that is, simply delete or rewrite the offending passages in question.[3] It is interesting to note that, even in its original French edition, *The Kip Brothers* is quite rare. In the words of a contemporary biographer of Verne, it "is among the least likely of all the books in the Verne cycle to be found today, for it was seldom, if ever, reprinted."[4]

It is therefore fair to say that *The Kip Brothers* represents a unique novel in Verne's oeuvre. Written soon after the death of his brother Paul, it celebrates more than any other the fraternal bonds of brotherhood. As a detective story that foregrounds themes of vision and perception, it resonates with Verne's own life as he struggled with his progressive loss of eyesight from cataracts. And finally, published during a time when the Dreyfus Affair was deeply perturbing and polarizing French society, it offers a strangely similar story of judicial error and social injustice.

COMPOSITION AND PUBLISHING HISTORY

In January 1902, Jules Verne's new novel *The Kip Brothers* began to appear in serial format in the popular French periodical *Magasin d'Education et de Récréation.* Episodes of the story continued to be published throughout 1902, concluding in the December issue of that year.

The *Magasin d'Education et de Récréation* was founded on March 20, 1864, by Pierre-Jules Hetzel, with a new issue appearing every two weeks. Quite successful, the journal offered an entertaining blend of fiction and nonfiction, and one of its educational goals was to teach geography and science to middle-class French families. Hetzel himself was arguably one of the most important book publishers in France during the nineteenth century.[5] And Jules Verne was, for more than fifty years, Hetzel's star writer. As a rule, most of Jules Verne's novels were first published as serials in Hetzel's *Magasin d'Education et de Récréation.*[6]

Exactly when Verne wrote *The Kip Brothers* has been the subject of some debate over the years. Many—including Christian Porcq—have traditionally assumed that it was during 1901,[7] whereas Olivier Dumas has argued for a much earlier date, 1898.[8] And the question of whether or not Verne's son, Michel, had a hand in the composition of this novel (as he did in most of Verne's posthumous works) has also been raised. To set the record straight, *The Kip Brothers* is among those last novels of the *Voyages extraordinaires* to be written wholly by Jules Verne,[9] and the date of composition was indeed 1898. How can we be sure? In 1892 Verne began to maintain a log in which he recorded the beginning and end dates of composition of each volume (a volume corresponding to a book "part"—*The Kip Brothers* is, thus, a 2-volume novel). In this log Verne reported the following: "Frères Norik (15 juillet 98—16 9bre), 2e vol. (16 9bre 98—fini 30 Xbre 98)."[10] As a result, we know that he began writing *The Kip Brothers* (whose first title was *The Norik Brothers*) on July 15, 1898, finishing the first volume on November 16; he then began the second volume the same day and finished it on December 30, 1898.

Nearly three years later, on September 2, 1901, Verne wrote to

Hetzel fils (Louis-Jules Hetzel), "I am sending you today by train, registered, a manuscript [first part of the *Kip Brothers*]. Please confirm by telegram your receipt of it so as to put my mind at ease." And on October 26, 1901, he wrote, "The second part of the Kip Brothers will leave tomorrow, Monday. You will receive it on Tuesday, and I ask you to please let me know of its safe arrival by telegram."[11] It does appear—and other letters of the same time period confirm this assumption—that Verne selected this novel to be published the following year from among several manuscripts he had already completed. From the mid-1880s onward, Verne was ahead of schedule with his writing and produced more than the minimum of two volumes[12] per year required by his contract with Hetzel.[13] In 1900 and 1901 Verne had a sizable stock of manuscripts from which he could draw to supply Hetzel with his two volumes for 1902.[14]

Hetzel received the first volume of *The Kip Brothers* in September 1901.[15] Most of the month of September was devoted to typesetting the novel. Verne received the proofs on September 28, and on October 7 Verne wrote to Hetzel, saying: "I am returning the text of the *Kip Brothers* to you little by little as I correct it."[16] These corrections and copyediting revisions were done directly on the printed proofs. Between the manuscript and the final printed versions, long sentences were divided into shorter sentences, the rhythm of the action became more active, and the descriptions gained in clarity. The modifications included word rearrangements in sentences and changes of wording that did not change the meaning of the text but made it more readable and improved the style.

After receiving the corrected proofs during the last months of 1901, Hetzel began to print the novel. As mentioned, the "pre-original" edition of *The Kip Brothers* was first published in serial format in the *Magasin d'Education et de Récréation* from January to December 1902, and it was illustrated with drawings by George Roux.[17]

The second printing was in book form and is called the "original" edition, two small in-octodecimo volumes, with few illustrations. The first volume was ready July 21, 1902, and the second was put on the market November 10, 1902.

The third printing was the famous octavo volume with full illustrations, often referred to as "the Hetzel edition" or (wrongly) as "the Original Edition." This edition was available on November 20, 1902, in three versions: paperbound, "demi-chagrin" (half leather), and deluxe fabric with red-and-gold covers.

Sales of *The Kip Brothers,* it seems, were generally disappointing. Like other novels published late in Verne's career, it had difficulty selling out its initial print run of 4,000.[18]

ILLUSTRATIONS AND PHOTOS

During the latter decades of the nineteenth century, as photography became increasingly popular, many publishers (including Hetzel) began to use photographs, photolithography, and two-toned lithography to illustrate their books. These new technologies gradually replaced the older woodcut-engraving methods because they were cheaper, faster, and less labor intensive.

To see a kind of historical "snapshot" of this technological (r)evolution in the publishing industry, one need only to examine some of Verne's later *Voyages extraordinaires* from 1890 to 1905 to see a fascinating mixture of old-fashioned woodcuts, halftone illustrations (some in color), and photographs.

The illustrated edition of Verne's *The Kip Brothers* constitutes an excellent example of this trend. One discovers therein four different types of illustrations:

1. Forty drawings by George Roux, engraved by Froment.[19] Twelve of the drawings, which appeared as black-and-white illustrations in the *Magasin,* were reproduced in color in the in-octavo edition (described on the title page as "grandes chromotypographies," full-page chromotypographs—a kind of early color print). The frontispiece and the title page illustration are also new in the in-octavo edition.
2. A dozen illustrations "borrowed" from other books. Seven, for example, were recycled from the nonfiction works of Jules Verne himself—his three-volume *Histoire des grands voyages et des grands voyageurs* (*History of Great Voyages and Great*

Navigators)—and one was taken from a book called *Voyage of the Griffin* (identified as "adapted by P.-J. Stahl" [a pseudonym of Hetzel] and, one assumes, published by him). But three other illustrations in *The Kip Brothers* were borrowed (should we say copied or stolen?) from a British four-volume work of geography,[20] and one—a mosaic of three woodcuts depicting Dunedin, New Zealand, along with a local volcano crater and a geyser—is not credited (although it too probably came from the same British work).

3. Six reprinted photographs.[21] The source for two of these photographs was a German book published in 1902, the same year that *The Kip Brothers* itself was published. It is somewhat ironic that though the text of *The Kip Brothers* dated from years before, such was certainly not the case for some of the photographs that Hetzel chose to illustrate the book—they were often last-minute selections.
4. Two maps[22] of the areas visited in the novel—New Zealand and the Bismarck Archipelago—engraved by a certain "E. Morieu." The first one was recycled from Verne's *Great Navigators of the Eighteenth Century* (volume 2 of his *History of Great Voyages and Great Navigators*).

SOURCES AND INFLUENCES

As a general rule, all of Verne's novels are derived from two types of sources: one for the science (broadly defined to include not only physics, chemistry, and biology but also geography) and one for the fiction.

Verne's sources included those many nineteenth-century dictionaries and atlases of which he made constant use, such as Privat-Deschanel and Focillon's *Dictionnaire général des sciences théoriques et appliquées*[23] and Reclus's *Nouvelle géographie universelle*.[24] He also consulted and quoted from a variety of reference books written in layman's language with the goal of teaching the natural sciences to the general reader—such as Figuier's *Les Merveilles de la science*[25] or Flammarion's *L'Astronomie populaire*.[26] Verne was also very well read in the published travelogues and histories of exploration of his time, such as Arago's *Voyage autour du monde,*[27] Agassiz's *Voyage au Brésil,*[28] Chaffanjon's *L'Orénoque et le Caura,*[29] and Charton's *Voyageurs anciens et modernes,*[30] along with similar accounts published in magazines like *Le Journal des voyages* and *Le Tour du monde.* Finally, Verne was also a voracious reader of scientific journals and the bulletins of scientific societies such as Malte-Brun's *Nouvelles annales des voyages, de la géographie, de l'histoire et de l'archéologie* and the *Comptes-rendus des scéances de l'Académie des Sciences,* from which he often gleaned ideas for his novels.[31]

So what were Verne's principal scientific sources for *The Kip Brothers?* Clearly, an important one was the author's own multivolume history of world exploration, *Histoire des grands voyages et des grands voyageurs* (*History of Great Voyages and Great Navigators,* 1878–1880), from which, as mentioned above, a number of illustrations were reprinted. And three other works that helped to provide much of the geographical and historical documentation for Verne's descriptions of the South Seas islands in this novel were Bougainville's *Voyage autour du monde,*[32] Dumont d'Urville's *Voyage au pôle sud et dans l'Océanie,*[33] and Duperrey's *Voyage autour du monde.*[34]

As for the discussions of retinas and ophthalmology presented in the surprise ending of the novel, Verne scholar Marcel Moré and family biographer Jean Jules-Verne have both indicated that Verne probably consulted the *L'Encyclopédie française d'ophtalmologie* by Lagrange and Valude[35] for details about such "optograms" (retina-photos). But these claims seem rather dubious since this nine-volume encyclopedia appears to have been first published in 1903, one year after Verne's *The Kip Brothers* came into print and five years after the story was written. It seems more likely that Verne read about the various retina experiments done in the 1870s and 1880s by scientists such as Félix Giraud-Teulon (1816–87) in Paris, Franz Boll (1849–79) in Rome, or Willy Kühne (1837–1900) in Heidelberg. Accounts of these experiments were published in journals that Verne perused on a regular basis such as the *Comptes-rendus* of the Academy of Sciences of Paris, the *Musée des familles,* or the *Revue des Deux Mondes.*

There exist at least two other possible (nonscientific) sources for this idea of optograms used by Verne. One, also mentioned by both Moré and Jean Jules-Verne, is a short story called "Claire Lenoir," first published in 1867 by Villiers de l'Isle-Adam (and later reprinted in 1887), a copy of which was found in Verne's personal library. Interestingly, in Villiers's narrative, the fictional protagonist supposedly reads an article describing optograms published in the minutes of the Académie des Sciences de Paris.[36] The other possible source is Jules Claretie's novel *L'Accusateur,* published in 1897. This detective novel features a sleuth named Bernardet who, having read Boll's and Kühne's articles, photographs the eyes of a victim whose murder he is investigating. He finds inscribed on the dead man's retinas the image of one of the victim's friends and promptly has him arrested. It is eventually discovered, however, that the incriminating image is a small portrait that the murdered man was staring at when he was killed. It is interesting to note that Jules Claretie, elected to the Académie Française in 1888, was also responsible for one of the first books of literary criticism on Verne (*Jules Verne,* Paris: A. Quantin, 1883), so it is quite likely that Verne was familiar with his work.[37]

From beginning to end, *The Kip Brothers* stands as one of Verne's more explicitly *visual* novels. References to perception and sight abound in the text: from the opening Zolaesque scene in the *Three Magpies* tavern where the villainous characters Vin Mod and Flig Balt are on the lookout for new recruits; to the trial where the fate of the Kip brothers hangs on the testimony of various eyewitnesses; to the efforts of Mr. Hawkins who "sees" the goodness in the heroes despite the visible evidence against them; to the "eye-opening" conclusion where only an enlarged photo of the victim's retinas ultimately proves they were framed.[38] Again and again, the twists and turns of the plot hinge on what can be seen, on what is hidden from view, and on what looks to be but is not. Given this thematic focus, it is significant that, during this time of his life, Verne was suffering from vision problems—severe cataracts, especially in his right eye. He described his condition in a 1901 letter to his old friend Nadar, saying, "I'm almost blind, and will remain so until my cataract operation. I no longer recognize anyone in the street, barely see what

I write, and live in a fog."[39] Verne also frequently refers to his condition in his correspondence with his publisher Hetzel fils. In 1902, for example, during their discussions about adding a subtitle to each of the two volumes of *The Kip Brothers* (the second volume would be subtitled, interestingly, "The Eyes of the Dead"), Verne writes, "I still have not undergone that cataract operation, and I won't decide on it until I can no longer read. . . . But up until now, my left eye has been sufficient."[40] Whether because of doctor's orders or because, as Verne himself claimed, he did not wish to risk surgery so long as he could see enough to continue reading and writing, the cataract operation would never take place.

The main source for the plot of Verne's *The Kip Brothers* is the true story of the Rorique (sometimes spelled Rorick) brothers whose trial became a highly publicized news story in France in the mid-1890s. On June 20, 1894, Verne wrote a letter to his brother Paul in which he confides: "A story that has always touched me is the one about the Rorique brothers, [whose death penalty is] now commuted. There is perhaps something to think about there."[41] Thus, the idea of fictionalizing what came to be known as the "Rorique Affair" was clearly on Verne's mind as early as 1894. During the final decade of his life, Verne had an Italian correspondent named Mario Turiello and, in three letters to him (written on January 15, May 25, and November 24, 1902), the French novelist links the Rorique Affair directly to *The Kip Brothers,* saying: "My new novel, *The Kip Brothers,* which was inspired by the story of the Rorique brothers, has two volumes"; "It's the story of the Rorique brothers that inspired *The Kip Brothers,* of which the first volume will soon be available"; and "You say that you didn't grasp what I meant about the story of the Rorique brothers. Obviously, you don't read a lot of newspapers. About ten years ago, these fine gentlemen were judged in France and sent to prison for having murdered their captain."[42]

Here is the story of the Rorique/Degrave brothers, as summarized by Marcel Moré in his *Le Très curieux Jules Verne* (120–23):

In July 1892 in Ponape, Micronesia, two brothers from Ostend, Belgium, Léonce and Eugène Degrave (sometimes spelled Degraeve), but better known under their assumed name of Rorique, were accused of having fomented a mutiny on board a French schooner named *Niuorahiti,* belonging to a Tahitian prince. After having allegedly killed the captain, at least one passenger who represented the cargo company (a certain Mr. Gibson) and several of the crew, the brothers then took command of the ship, modified her, and used her for piracy in the South Seas. Their principal accuser was the (mulatto) cook aboard the vessel named *Hippolyte Mirey,* a very suspicious character himself and one who was probably involved in the mutiny. After their arrest, the Rorique/Degrave brothers were transferred to France where they were put on trial for murder and piracy.

During the proceedings, it was discovered that, earlier in their career, they had once been recognized and celebrated as true heroes: during a storm at sea, they had single-handedly saved the captain and crew of a Norwegian three-master called the *Pieter.* But there were also reports of their having lied about having been castaways while in the Cook Islands in 1891. To the charges against them, the Rorique/Degrave brothers repeatedly proclaimed their innocence, saying that the murders had indeed been the result of a mutiny among the crew but one that they had helped to put down. As for the charges of subsequent piracy, they refused to confess to any wrongdoing. Many French citizens who followed the case, including Verne, believed them innocent. Their conduct during the trial was deemed praiseworthy; the brothers remained stoic to the end and asked only to stay together, whatever their fate.

Despite the fact that the prosecution's case was based on highly questionable witnesses, on December 8, 1893, the Rorique/Degrave brothers were judged guilty on all counts. The tribunal condemned them to death—a sentence that was commuted a few months later by French president Carnot and changed to life imprisonment at hard labor. Léonce died in prison on March 30, 1898. Eugène, who was pardoned the following year, went back to France and wrote his memoirs, which were published in 1901 as *Le Bagne* (At Hard Labor).[43]

Perplexingly, a few years later, Eugène abandoned his wife and child and again took up a life of travel and adventure. In 1907 he was seen in Trinidad working as a local policeman. He died in 1929, murdered in a jail cell in Pamplona apparently after having become involved with smuggling a large number of Colombian emeralds out of South America. And, in a final bizarre twist to this tale, the French writer Alfred Jarry demonstrated that portions of his book, *Le Bagne,* were actually plagiarized from the *Adventures of Arthur Gordon Pym* by Edgar Allan Poe.[44] Here ends Moré's account of this tale.

Were the Rorique/Degrave brothers, in truth, the innocent victims of conspiracy and judicial error that Verne and others believed them to be? Probably not. But it is clear, not only from his correspondence but also from the strong similarities in plot, names, and characterization, that Verne patterned *The Kip Brothers* directly on their story, both idealizing and immortalizing them.[45] Of course, at the time of the novel's initial composition in 1898, Verne could not have known that Eugène would eventually be pardoned, return to France, write and publish *Le Bagne,* and then have his life end tragically amid very suspicious circumstances. But—and this point is crucial—Verne did revise his manuscript during the summer and fall of 1901 before submitting the first part (volume 1) to Hetzel fils on September 2 and the second part (volume 2) to him on October 27. And he was still correcting proofs as late as March 1902.[46] During both periods when revisions to the text were being made—along with changing its title from *Les Frères Norik* to *Les Frères Kip*—Verne no doubt updated his story in the light of contemporary developments in the case and perhaps even consulted Degrave's book, *Le Bagne.*

These 1901 updates and corrections made by Verne to his 1898 manuscript are also very important when considering another possible but less acknowledged source for *The Kip Brothers:* the Dreyfus Affair. As Cornélius Helling observed in 1935, "This book was written when the Dreyfus affair was causing a stir and [it] has the feel of its era."[47] In fact, if one were not familiar with the case of the Rorique/Degrave brothers or if one did not have access to copies of Verne's correspondence from the 1890s, one would naturally assume that

The Kip Brothers had been based—either partly or wholly—on this legendary case of judicial error and unjust punishment.

The problem is that, during the late 1890s, Verne was a staunch and very vocal *anti-dreyfusard.* In late 1898, as demands for a retrial of Alfred Dreyfus (in prison at Devil's Island since April 1895) began to heat up because of new evidence discovered by Lieutenant-Colonel Georges Picquart and by Emile Zola's inflammatory letter "I Accuse," Verne wrote to Turiello, saying: "As for the D . . . affair, it's best not to talk about it. For a long time it has, for me, been judged and judged well, whatever happens in the future."[48] In a letter somewhat later to Hetzel fils, Verne mentioned in passing "I who am anti-Dreyfus in my soul . . ."[49] And, finally, in December 1898, Verne agreed to became a founding member of a conservative, right-wing, anti-Dreyfus organization called the *Ligue de la Patrie Française* (the French Patriotic League), created in opposition to the *Ligue des Droits de l'Homme* (the Human Rights League), a left-wing political group that supported Dreyfus's cause. Throughout this period, Verne's pro-government position on the Dreyfus Affair was very clear and well publicized, a position no doubt reinforced by his own anti-Semitic tendences.[50]

In dramatic contrast to his father, Michel Verne was enthusiastically pro-Dreyfus and did not hide his feelings either. Jean Jules-Verne, Verne's grandson and family biographer, describes how his father and grandfather repeatedly clashed on the subject:

> From the outset his son, Michel, a so-called reactionary with royalist tendencies, was violently outraged by the injustice of the Dreyfus case. I remember that what upset him most was the deliberate procedural error whereby documentary evidence was produced in court without being shown beforehand to the defence—particularly since the document concerned turned out to be a forgery. Obviously, Michel's visits to Amiens at this time could not help being stormy ones. They might have resulted in a momentary breach with his father; but fortunately their affection for each other was by now such that their relationship emerged

> unscathed. In any case, Verne's judgment was too sound for him not to see eventually that his son's indignation was justified; but to admit that much he had to sweep aside a good many beliefs that he had always regarded as inviolable.
>
> This made him all the more disposed to listen to the opinions of his prodigal son, who had turned out to have a cultivated and alert mind with which Verne could communicate.[51]

Could it be that, between 1898 and 1901 when he was to revise the text of *The Kip Brothers,* Verne slowly began to "see" his son's point of view on this matter? Could it be that he began to acknowledge that there were profound similarities between Dreyfus's unjust imprisonment and that of the Rorique/Degrave brothers on whom his own fictional protagonists were based? Could it be that Verne, unable or unwilling to "sweep aside a good many beliefs that he had always regarded as inviolable," purposefully embedded in the text of *The Kip Brothers* certain clues that reflected his change of heart about the Dreyfus Affair as he was preparing the final version of the manuscript in 1901?

Such is the premise of Christian Porcq in a seminal two-part article on Verne's *The Kip Brothers* published in the *Bulletin de la Société Jules Verne* in the winter of 1993–94.[52] In a provocative analysis that ranges from the factual to the far-fetched, Porcq argues that Verne—a lover of riddles, puzzles, and cryptograms—hid in his text a host of references to the Dreyfus Affair. Some are lexical: repetitions of certain words such as "affair" and "proofs" (legal as well as photographic—where Dreyfus is a kind of "negative" for the Kip brothers) or phonological anagrams in the fictional characters' names (like KAR[L]KIP which could conceivably be an inverted PIKAR, that is, Picquart, the name of the French officer who investigated Dreyfus's case). Some are chronological: the fact that Karl Kip is thirty-five years old when he was arrested (the same age as Alfred Dreyfus at the time of his arrest) or that the three successive court trials portrayed in *The Kip Brothers* (that of Flig Balt in January 1886, that of the Kip brothers in February 1886, and the Kip brothers' retrial in August 1887) parallel the timing of the court trials in the Dreyfus Affair a dozen years later (that of Esterhazy in January 1898, that of Zola in February 1898, and Dreyfus's retrial in August 1899). And some clues can even be found in one of the novel's illustrations: the portrait of Mr. Hawkins in chapter four bears an uncanny likeness to Edgar Demange, Dreyfus's defense attorney. According to Porcq, despite Verne's overt anti-Dreyfus views during the late 1890s, the author nevertheless secretly patterned much of his story on the legal tribulations of the French officer. Porcq's reading of this novel is fascinating but, ultimately, not entirely convincing. Verne's anti-Dreyfus views toward the end of his life seem as strong as before he published *The Kip Brothers*.

Finally, another source for *The Kip Brothers* was Verne's own first-hand experience with the sea and the nautical life. As Jean-Paul Faivre has observed, *The Kip Brothers* is one of Verne's most "oceanic" novels.[53] And the Pacific Ocean is used as the fictional locale for many of Verne's *Voyages extraordinaires* (*The Children of Captain Grant, Twenty Thousand Leagues under the Seas, The Chancellor, A Captain of Fifteen,* and *The Stories of Jean-Marie Cabidoulin,* among others) as well as in some of the author's very first short stories.[54] From the earliest days of his youth exploring the docks of the seaport city of Nantes, Verne had a consuming passion for the sea. His grandson writes: "Undoubtedly, it was in Nantes that Verne's love for the sea made its first mark on him, a real love that many years later led him to remark: 'I cannot see a ship leaving port . . . but my whole being goes with her.'"[55] Verne owned three yachts during his lifetime: the first, a nine-ton built-to-order vessel launched in 1868 and baptized the *Saint-Michel I,* in which he sailed out of the port of Le Crotoy (and aboard which he wrote much of *Twenty Thousand Leagues under the Seas*); the second was the *Saint-Michel II,* bought in 1876, which he owned for less than a year; and the last, purchased in 1877, was the *Saint-Michel III,* a luxurious steam and sail yacht with a crew of ten, in which Verne sailed to various ports of call throughout the Atlantic, the Mediterranean, and the North Sea until early 1886. When Verne was writing about ships and the sea, he knew the subject well.[56]

Verne's nautical expertise is often reflected in the pages of *The*

Kip Brothers. For example, consider the following passage when Karl Kip takes command of the brig *James Cook* during a ferocious storm at sea: "The storm, although extraordinarily fierce, was less dangerous, since it now attacked the ship by the bow, and no longer by the stern. The crew managed to set up, not without great difficulty, a heavy-weather jib, capable of resisting the wind's blasts. Under its storm jib and its small topsail whose reef Karl Kip had unfurled, both of which were trimmed tightly, the brig held close to shore, while seaman Burnes, an excellent helmsman, imperturbably maintained the *James Cook* on its proper course." While penning this particular scene, the author was no doubt recalling some of his own early maritime adventures aboard the *Saint-Michel*. As Verne's grandson Jean Jules-Verne describes it in his biography, "There can be no doubt that the thoughts of his mariner heroes were his own. . . . Hence, the importance of the *Saint-Michel* in his life and works cannot be overstated. Even though he visited few of the faraway places frequented by his heroes, he was a sailor, well versed in sailing and broken to [familiar with] the dangers of the treacherous seas between Boulogne and Bordeaux."[57]

NATIONALITIES, REVOLUTIONS, AND BROTHERHOOD

Another interesting aspect of *The Kip Brothers*—and one that distinguishes it from most other novels in Verne's *Voyages extraordinaires*—concerns how certain nationalities are portrayed. The novel's plot unfolds in Tasmania and New Zealand, former British colonies, and in the Bismarck Archipelago, which belonged to Germany. Most of the main fictional characters are therefore Anglo-Saxons and Germans, with the two heroes of the novel, the Kip brothers, being Dutch. This particular configuration in his cast of characters is a very unusual one for Verne, for two reasons. First, the majority of the protagonists in Verne's works tend to be British, American, or French.[58] The only French and American characters appearing in *The Kip Brothers* are secondary and clearly minor: the captain and sailors of the French ship *Assomption*, who announce the wreck of the *Wilhelmina* to the passengers and crew of the *James Cook*, and the unsavory American seamen Bryce recruited in the

Three Magpies tavern at the beginning of the novel. Second, Verne depicts the British and Germans in this novel in a very sympathetic light. The Kips' tireless advocate and friend Mr. Hawkins; the governor of Tasmania, Sir Edward Carrigan; and even the warden of the Port Arthur penitentiary, Captain Skirtle, are shown to be fine and honorable British gentlemen.[59] And Mr. and Mrs. Zieger of New Mecklenburg as well as Mr. Hamburg of Kerawara exemplify the best of German warmth and hospitality as they welcome the captain of the *James Cook* and the Kip brothers into their homes during the ship's layovers in the Bismarck Archipelago.

These approving portrayals contrast sharply with Verne's more cynical representation of these same nationalities in several of his other later works. Note, for example, the many diatribes against the British in the pages of such novels as *The Mysterious Island* (their conquest and domination of India), *Hector Servadac* (their jingoistic "Gibraltar" mentality), *Lit'l Fellow* (their terrible treatment of orphans), and especially in his 1895 *Propeller Island* (the greedy English imperialists of "perfidious Albion" are "cursed down to their children and grand-children, until its detestable name is wiped from the memory of the world!" And Verne's depiction of Germans follows a very similar trajectory. During the decade immediately after the Franco-Prussian war, Verne's first truly evil scientist emerged in the person of the racist megalomaniac Herr Schultze of *The Begum's Millions*. Other anti-Germanisms punctuated many of Verne's subsequent novels, such as *A Drama in Livonia* (in which Germans brutally oppress the Slavs) or in *Claudius Bombarnac* (in which the contentious and crude Baron Weissschnitzerdörfer personifies most Germanophobic stereotypes of the fin de siècle). As Verne scholar Jean Chesneaux has explained, however, it is important to understand that Verne's

> hostility towards England hardly ever stems from simple national chauvinism; it is politically motivated. England is castigated as the oppressor of the Scottish, Irish, and French Canadian nationalists, or for being a great colonial Power. Verne's Anglophobia is directed towards a country regarded as typical of certain nega-

> tive political tendencies, much more than towards an 'enemy' nation. . . .
>
> In the same way, Verne's Germanophobia, with the exception of one or two casual and ridiculous characters, is invariably linked with political criticism. . . . Even in this case [*The Begum's Millions*], symptomatic of the extreme vengeful chauvinism widespread in France in the 1880s, the 'eternal German' Schultze is indistinguishable from Schultze the armament industry magnate, the master of a gigantic totalitarian and, so to speak, proto-Hitlerian complex, a scientist who uses his knowledge in the service of destruction.[60]

Although there exists no iron-clad correlation between an author's personal politics and those expressed in his fiction, it is nevertheless interesting that Verne's portrayal of the British and the Germans in *The Kip Brothers* recalls those of a much younger Verne—a Verne of the 1860s whose earliest works featured the courageous and resourceful British explorer Samuel Fergusson in *Five Weeks in a Balloon* and the delightfully eccentric German geologist Otto Lidenbrock in *Journey to the Center of the Earth.*[61]

But perhaps in *The Kip Brothers* it is less a question of nationalities and more of nationalism. Consider, for example, Verne's favorable portrait, late in the novel, of the Fenians, who have "the goal of freeing Ireland from the intolerable domination of Great Britain." They also play a part in his novel about Ireland published in 1893, *Lit'l Fellow,* in which Verne describes the British aristocracy in the following terms: "It is nevertheless important to note that the aristocracy, which is rather liberal in England and Scotland, has shown itself to be quite oppressive in Ireland. Instead of offering a helping hand, it jerks on the reins. A catastrophe is to be feared. He who sows hatred will eventually harvest rebellion."[62] Throughout the *Voyages extraordinaires,* Verne repeatedly expresses his sympathy for oppressed peoples and his support for nationalist movements. Captain Nemo of *Twenty Thousand Leagues under the Seas* (1870) aids the revolutionaries of Crete in their fight against the Ottoman Empire by donating to them riches taken from the sunken galleons of Vigo Bay. The French Alsatians' hatred of their post-1870 German occupiers is a leitmotif running through *The Begum's Millions* (1879). The heroic Greeks are shown battling for their independence from the Turks in *Archipelago on Fire* (1884). The efforts of Hungarian patriots to regain their country's freedom from the Austro-Hungarian Empire serves as the political backdrop for *Mathias Sandorf* (1885). Norwegian separatists occupy center stage in *The Lottery Ticket* (1886), set during a time when Norway is under Swedish rule. In *Family without a Name* (1889), the French Canadians struggle to free themselves from their British masters; in the preface to this novel, Verne even suggests that they are setting "an example that the French populations of Alsace and Lorraine must never forget."[63] And in *A Drama in Livonia* (1904), one of the last novels published before his death and another a novel of "judicial error" similar to *The Kip Brothers,* Verne focuses on the Slavic peasants and their struggle against the wealthy ruling classes, who are of German extraction. In novel after novel, Verne shows himself to be faithful to the republican ideals of the Revolution of 1848, which he experienced first-hand as a young man in Paris and whose precepts he adopted as his own. A strong believer in social justice, Verne continually embeds in his fiction a sense of brotherhood with the downtrodden peoples of the world who are fighting for their freedom.

But *The Kip Brothers* stands as one of Verne's greatest tributes to brotherhood not only because of how the author portrays the rapport between the novel's two heroes or his solidarity with certain nationalist political movements such as the Fenians. A strong sense of brotherhood also resonates throughout this novel on a more personal level—Verne's fraternal love for his brother Paul who died in 1897, the year before he began to write *The Kip Brothers.*

Paul Verne was a year younger than Jules, and the two had always been very close. In an interview with a journalist in 1894, Jules Verne described their relationship, saying,

> My brother Paul was and is my dearest friend. Yes, I may say that he is not only my brother but my most intimate friend. And our friendship dates from the first day that I can remember. What

excursions we used to take together in leaky boats on the Loire! At the age of fifteen there was not a nook or a corner on the Loire right down to the sea that we had not explored. What dreadful boats they were, and what risks we no doubt ran! Sometimes I was captain, sometimes it was Paul. But Paul was the better of the two. You know that afterwards he entered the Navy.[64]

Paul enlisted as a midshipman in the French Navy in 1850 and joined the merchant marine in 1854. He soon retired from the sea and became a stockbroker, but he and his brother continued their seafaring excursions. In 1867 they crossed the Atlantic together on the *Great Eastern* (a voyage that became the basis for Verne's 1871 novel *A Floating City*) and visited New York and Niagara Falls. And they often voyaged together aboard Verne's yacht the *Saint Michel III*—in 1881 traveling to Copenhagen, for example, a trip that inspired Paul to publish an account of their adventure, "From Rotterdam to Copenhagen," in the Nantes newspaper *L'Union Bretonne* that same year. Earlier, in 1872, Paul had published a similar travel chronicle in the same paper called "The Fortieth Ascension of Mont Blanc," which was later reprinted in Verne's first short-story collection, *Doctor Ox* (1874).

On many occasions, Paul Verne helped his brother with the technical aspects of the stories he was writing. For instance, when working on the manuscript of *Twenty Thousand Leagues under the Sea* in 1868, Jules wrote to his father, saying, "In three or four months, when I have the proofs, I will try to send you and Paul the first volume so that you can clean up some of its errors or imperfections. I really want this machine to be as perfect as possible."[65] And when working up the preliminary engineering designs for his "Standard Island" in *Propeller Island* (1895), Verne repeatedly consulted with Paul, asking for his technical advice. The following excerpts from their correspondence of this period are typical:

Amiens, 5 June 1893

My dear Paul, . . . Next year I will really need your help for my propeller island, so as not to make any stupid mistakes. The first volume is written. The second will be in 3 months. I'm much ahead of schedule. The island is large, 25 to 30 kilometers around. Do you think that it can be steered without a rudder by using two propeller systems on each side powered by dynamos run by machines generating a million horsepower of force? . . . Tell me when you can, as you're waiting for me to send you the proofs.[66]

Amiens, 8 September 1893
My dear Paul, I received your letter, which has crossed my own in the mail, and I will send you today the proofs of the end of volume 2, which you can return to me when you've looked them over. I have rewritten according to your corrections, which I am using verbatim.[67]

Amiens, 12 September 1894
My dear Paul, . . . I suspect that I have made many errors, and that's why I sent you the proofs. But it is not enough to point the errors out to me; you must indicate to me how to fix them.[68]

Amiens, [October?] 1894
My dear Paul, I have just received your letter and the proofs. I thank you for the huge amount of work you have done. Without you, I would have never been able to manage this.[69]

It has often been argued that the pervasive and sometimes pivotal influence of Verne's editor-publisher Pierre-Jules Hetzel in shaping the content of the author's *Voyages extraordinaires* has been underestimated. It seems that Paul Verne's contributions to the fundamental design of some of his brother's legendary "dream machines" is also a story that remains to be told.

But it was especially Paul who served as his brother's most trusted confidant during those often-traumatic years of the late 1880s and the 1890s when Jules was repeatedly beset with a host of physical, emotional, and financial problems. As the biographer Herbert Lottman has observed, "Family correspondence, which sheds so much light on the life of the young Jules Verne, is missing for the middle years when Verne gained literary renown. But there is another rich lode of letters, beginning in 1893 to draw upon. These letters were written to one of the few people in whom Jules never ceased to confide—his brother Paul, who was now turning sixty-four."[70] Foremost among Verne's concerns were the continuing difficulties with his son, Michel, whose repeated career changes and bankruptcies, costly amorous escapades, divorce from his first wife, and difficulties with the law caused Verne at one point to complain to Paul "the future frightens me considerably. Michel does nothing, finds nothing to do, has cost me 200,000 francs, has three sons, and their entire upbringing is going to fall on my shoulders. I'm ending badly."[71] Verne's growing financial worries had earlier forced him to sell his beloved yacht, the *Saint-Michel III,* and he would never again sail the open seas, with Paul or anyone else. Then, on March 9, 1886, he was attacked at gunpoint by his deranged nephew Gaston and shot in the lower leg; he would remain partially crippled for the rest of his life. Later that same month, his publisher and "spiritual father," Pierre-Jules Hetzel, died. Soon thereafter, in speaking with Hetzel's son, Verne confessed, "I have entered the dark period of my life."[72] The following year, his mother died. And during the ensuing years, in addition to having to walk with a cane, Verne was plagued by a variety of physical ailments, including severe gastrointestinal problems, recurrent dizziness, rheumatism, cataracts, and diabetes. In a letter to Paul in 1894, following the June marriage of his niece Marie, the author confides, "I see that the wedding was very jolly, but it is precisely this sort of merriment that is intolerable to me now. My character is deeply altered, and I have received blows from which I shall never recover."[73] When Paul Verne died of heart disease three years later, on August 27, 1897, Jules was grief-stricken, saying, "What a friend I have lost in him!" and "I never thought that I'd outlive him."[74] According to his grandson, Verne "was so crushed and so ill that he could not attend the funeral."[75] With memories of his deceased brother fresh in his mind, Jules Verne began work on *The Kip Brothers* the following summer.

Some of Verne's novels have been called "visionary" for their unusual scientific or technological prescience. *The Kip Brothers* might also be termed "visionary," but in an entirely different way. The strongly *visual* nature of its thematic content—from the initial sighting of the castaways to its strange ophthalmologic conclusion—underscores Verne's own worsening eye problems during the late 1890s. As reflected in the novel's plot, two real-life dramas of judicial error can also be easily *visualized* (one acknowledged by Verne and one not): the Rorique/Degrave brothers' trials and the infamous Dreyfus Affair. Finally, *The Kip Brothers* envisions—or, more correctly, *re-visions*—its author's personal past as Verne builds an idealized literary memorial to his relationship with his beloved late brother, Paul. It is ironic that one of Verne's most sight-oriented *Voyages extraordinaires* has become, since its publication, one of his least visible works. It is our hope that this first English translation of Verne's *Les Frères Kip* will help to remedy that situation and to show the Anglophone reading public a new and different Jules Verne from the one they had thought they knew so well.

Jean-Michel Margot

— VOYAGES EXTRAORDINAIRES —

LES FRÈRES KIP

PAR

JULES VERNE

ILLUSTRATIONS

PAR

GEORGE ROUX

12 *grandes chromotypographies*

NOMBREUSES VUES PHOTOGRAPHIQUES

DEUX CARTES

COLLECTION HETZEL

18, RUE JACOB, PARIS, VIe

LES FRÈRES KIP

PREMIÈRE PARTIE

Dunedin

Tavern of the *Three Magpies*

At that time—1885[1]—forty-six years after its occupation by Great Britain, which had made it part of New South Wales, and thirty-two years after its independence from the Crown, New Zealand, now self-governing, was still devoured by gold fever. The disorders created by this sickness were not as destructive as they had been in certain states of the Australian continent. It did, however, lead to certain regrettable incidents that affected the population of both islands. The province of Otago,[2] which constitutes the southern part of Tawaï-Pounamou,[3] was invaded by gold seekers looking to establish placer mines, and the Clutha[4] deposits also attracted a number of adventurers. Evidence of this can be seen in the fact that the output of gold mines in New Zealand from 1864 to 1889 rose to a value of 1.2 francs.

The Australians and Chinese were not the only ones to swoop down like a flock of hungry birds of prey on these rich territories. Americans and Europeans flooded in as well. It will surprise no one that the crews of the various commercial ships bound for Auckland, Wellington, Christchurch, Napier, Invercargill, or Dunedin[5] were not strong enough to resist this temptation once they reached port. In vain did captains attempt to hold back their sailors; in vain did the maritime authorities offer their assistance! Desertion was rampant and the harbors grew cluttered with ships that, for lack of a crew, were unable to leave.

Among the latter, at Dunedin, could be seen the English brig *James Cook*. Of the eight sailors making up its crew, only four had remained on board ship. The other four had left with the firm intention of never coming back.[6]

Twelve hours after their disappearance, they were probably already far from Dunedin, heading for the gold fields in the countryside. In port for some two weeks, his cargo already loaded, his ship ready to put out to sea, the captain had been unable to replace the missing crew members. Neither the lure of higher wages nor the perspective of only a few months' passage had attracted any recruits. In fact, he was unsure whether the men who had remained on board might not be tempted to join their comrades. As the captain continued to seek more sailors, the bosun of the *James Cook,* Flig Balt, searched the taverns,[7] the bars, and the inns for men to fill out their crew.

New Zealand[8] is composed of North Island and South Island—called by natives Tawaï-Pounamou and Ikana-Maoui respectively—which are separated by Cook Strait.[9] Dunedin is located on the southeast coast of South Island. In 1839, at the place now occupied by the city, Dumont d'Urville[10] had found a few Maori huts where today one can see mansions, hotels, parks in full greenery, streets lined with trams, railways, warehouses, markets, banks, churches, schools, hospitals, bustling neighborhoods, suburbs growing without end. It is an industrial and commercial city, wealthy and luxurious, the center of many railroad lines coming in from all directions. It numbers some fifty thousand inhabitants, a lesser population than that of Auckland, the capital of North Island, but greater than that of Wellington, the seat of the government of the New Zealand colony.

Below the city, arranged like an amphitheater on a hill, the port spreads out like a vast semicircle where ships of every tonnage can enter thanks to a channel that had been dug from Port Chalmers.

Among the numerous taverns in this lower quarter, one of the noisiest and most frequented, belonged to Adam Fry, tavern keeper of the *Three Magpies.* This corpulent fellow, of flushed complexion, was scarcely of greater worth than the drinks from his counter and no better than his usual customers, all scoundrels and drunkards.

One evening, two customers were seated in a corner, facing their two glasses and a half-empty bottle of gin that they would probably empty to the last drop before leaving the tavern. They were seamen from the *James Cook,* the bosun, Flig Balt, accompanied by a sailor named Vin Mod.[11]

"You're always thirsty, eh Mod?" asked Flig Balt.

"You're always thirsty, eh Mod?" asked Flig Balt as he filled his guest's glass.

"Always between meals, Mr. Balt," replied the sailor. "Gin after whiskey, whiskey after gin! That doesn't stop you from talking, listening, watching! Your eyes are all the sharper, your ears all the keener, your tongue all the looser!"

One may rest assured that, in Vin Mod's case, these various organs functioned with a marvelous ease in the midst of the hubbub in the tavern.

A rather short fellow, this sailor, some thirty-five years old, slender, agile, muscular, with eyes like a weasel and where an alcoholic flame seemed to flicker, a cunning face you might say, intelligent yet pointed and with teeth like a rat. Perfectly capable of assisting in evil doings, just like his companion, who was well aware of this fact. They were two of a kind and could count on each other.

"We just have to get it over with," said Flig Balt in a harsh voice, striking the table with his fist.

"We can just choose at random," replied Vin Mod.

He pointed at the groups drinking, singing, and cursing through the vapors of alcohol and tobacco that darkened the atmosphere of the room. Just breathing this air would have led to drunkenness.

Flig Balt, some thirty-eight or thirty-nine years old, was of average size, broad shouldered, headstrong, powerfully built. One could never forget his face, even after seeing it but once: a large wart on his left cheek, eyes of a frightening hardness, eyebrows thick and frizzy, a ruddy, American-style goatee with no moustache, in short the physiognomy of a hate-filled man, jealous, vindictive. For his first voyage aboard the *James Cook,* he had hired on as bosun a few months before. Born in Queenstown,[12] a port of the United Kingdom, his papers declared him to be Irish by birth. But he had been traveling the seas for twenty years, and no one could claim to have ever seen his family. And how many of those sailors have no other family than their shipmates, no other country than the vessel they are sailing! It seems that their nationality changes with the ship. As for his shipboard service, Flig Balt carried it out precisely, punctually; and while being only a bosun, he filled—on board ship—the duties of the second in command. As a consequence Captain Gibson believed he could rely on him as far as details were concerned, reserving for himself the command of the brig.

In truth, Flig Balt was but a wretch waiting to pull off some evil deed, goaded on by Vin Mod's detestable influence and incontestable superiority. And perhaps he'd get a chance to carry out his criminal projects . . .

"I'll tell you once more," said Vin Mod, "that in the *Three Magpies* tavern, you can just pick them blindfolded. We'll find the men that we need here, and of a mind to do business for their own profit . . ."

"Sure, but still," observed Flig Balt, "you have to know just where those men come from."

"Not really, provided they go where we want them to, Master Balt! . . . Given that we are recruiting them from the clientele of Adam Fry, we can trust them."

And, indeed, the reputation of this tavern of ill repute was no longer a matter of discussion. The police could cast their nets without any risk of catching an honest person or one with whom they had not already had quarrels. Although Captain Gibson was in dire need of rounding out his crew one way or another, he would not have turned to the patrons of the *Three Magpies*. So Flig Balt had refrained from telling him that he would hire from that source.

The lone room, furnished with tables, benches, stools, a bar behind which stood the barkeep, shelves cluttered with decanters and bottles, was lit by two windows fitted out with iron bars, on a street leading down to the pier. One entered through a door with a heavy lock and a heavy bolt, above which hung a sign where three magpies, daubed with color, pecked away at each other—a sign worthy of the establishment. In the month of October, night arrives by eight-thirty, even at the start of the good season, at forty-five degrees of south latitude. Some metal lamps, filled with smelly oil, were burning, hanging above the bar and the tables. Those that worked were left working; the ones whose wicks were almost entirely consumed and were sputtering were left to sputter. This dim light seemed sufficient. When you drink neat, you have no need of seeing clearly. Glasses have no trouble finding their way to the mouth.

A score of sailors now occupied the benches and stools—people from every country, Americans, English, Irish, Dutch, deserters for the most part, some ready to leave for the placer mines, others just returning to squander their last nuggets. They were holding forth, singing, shouting so loudly that gunfire would not have been heard in the midst of this tumultuous, deafening din. Half of these people were drunk with that sad drunkenness that comes from the consumption of hard liquor that the gullet thoughtlessly downed and whose bitter burning was no longer felt. A few tottered to their feet, staggered, fell back. Adam Fry, with the help of the waiter, a hearty native, got them back on their feet, pulled them along, tossed them into a corner, all in a jumble. The front door grated on its hinges. A few were leaving, stumbling against the walls, banging into the signposts, floundering into the gutter. Some came in and found a place to sit on empty benches.[13] They renewed acquaintances, and rough remarks were exchanged with handshakes that could break bones. Comrades met each other again after lengthy shore leaves searching through the Otago fields. There were offensive words as well, and crude stories, insults, provocations that burst out from one table to the next. The evening would probably not end without some personal scuffle, which would degenerate into a general brawl. That wouldn't be anything very new, of course, for the owner or the customers of the *Three Magpies*.

Flig Balt and Vin Mod continued to observe everyone with curiosity, before speaking of their need and the circumstances that led them to the tavern.

"After all, what's the big deal? . . ." said the sailor, propped up on his elbows in such a way as to lean closer to the bosun. "Just replace the four men who left us with another four . . . We can't worry about the others anymore . . . They wouldn't have stayed with us . . . Once more, I tell you, we'll find what we need right here . . . May I swing from the yardarm if one of these rascals would turn down the chance of working on a good ship, sailing the Pacific instead of returning to Hobart Town . . . That's still in the works, right?"

"In the works it is," replied Flig Balt.

"Let's count then," continued Vin Mod. "Four of these worthy lads, Koa the cook, you and me, against the captain, the other three and the cabin boy. That's more than we need to take over! One morning . . . we just walk into Gibson's cabin . . . nobody there! . . . We call the roll . . . three men are missing! . . . A sea swell must have carried them off during their night watch . . . That happens even during a calm . . . And then the *James Cook* is never seen again . . . It vanished with all hands in mid-Pacific . . . Nothing more is said about it . . . and under a different name . . . a clever name . . . *Pretty Girl,* for instance . . . it sails from isle to isle bearing its honest traffic, Captain Flig Balt, Bosun Vin Mod. It fills out its crew with two or three fine scoundrels that we can find easily enough in the eastern or western ports of call . . . And each will make a small fortune instead of a meager wage, which is generally drunk up before it's cashed."

The fact that the din sometimes prevented Vin Mod's words from reaching Flig Balt's ears was of little importance. The latter had no need of hearing him. Everything his companion said, he was saying to himself. His mind made up, he no longer sought anything but to ensure its execution. So the only observation that he made was the following:

"The four new members, plus you and me, six against five,[14] including the cabin boy, fine. But are you forgetting that in Wellington we have to take aboard the shipowner, Hawkins, as well as the captain's son?"

"Right. If we go to Wellington after leaving Dunedin. But suppose we don't get there?"

"It's a matter of forty-eight hours with a favorable wind," continued Bosun Balt, "but it's not a given that we carry out the plan in the crossing."

"What's the difference!" exclaimed Vin Mod. "Don't worry about it, even if the shipowner Hawkins and Gibson's son are on board! They will have been thrown over the rail before they can realize what's happening. The essential thing is to recruit comrades who are no more concerned about a man's life than an old worn-out pipe, brave men who do not fear the rope. And we must find them here."

"Let's find them," Bosun Balt answered.

Both started to examine more attentively the patrons of Adam Fry, few of whom were looking at them with a certain insistence.

"Take a look," said Vin Mod. "That fellow there, hale and hearty, like a boxer . . . with that enormous head . . . I suppose he has already done ten times what it takes to deserve hanging . . ."

"Yes," replied Bosun Balt, "I can see that . . ."

"And that guy . . . with one eye . . . and what an eye! . . . You can be sure he didn't lose the other one in a fight where he was on the right side . . ."

"Well, if he's willing, Vin . . ."

"He'll accept . . ."

"However," Flig Balt remarked, "we can't tell them beforehand . . ."

"We won't tell them, and when the moment comes, they won't sulk about the job. And look at that other guy coming in! Judging from the way he slams the door, you'd think he sensed the police at his heels."

"Let's offer him a drink," Bosun Balt said.

"And I wager my head against a bottle of gin that he won't refuse! . . . Then over there . . . that sort of bear, with his sou'wester askew,[15] he probably spent more time in the bottom of the hold than in the forecastle, and had his legs more often in chains than his hands free! . . ."

The fact is that the four individuals designated by Vin Mod had the appearance of determined rogues. If Flig Balt recruited them, one might well wonder if Captain Gibson would consent to take on sailors of such caliber! . . . Besides, it was useless to ask for papers: they would not produce them, and for good reason.

It remained to be seen whether these men were interested in hiring on, whether they had just deserted their ship, or whether they were preparing to trade in their pea jacket for the jacket of a gold digger. After all, they wouldn't make the offer themselves, and what sort of greeting would they get at the proposal of embarking on the *James Cook?* You wouldn't know until you had talked it over with them, and whetted their conversation with gin or whiskey, as they chose.

"Hey there . . . fellow . . . have a drink . . . ," said Vin Mod, who directed the new arrival toward the table.

"Two . . . if you don't mind . . . ," answered the sailor, making a clack with his tongue.

"Three . . . four . . . half a dozen . . . even a dozen, if your throat is dry."

Len Cannon, that was his name or the one he was using, sat down without further ado, as though to prove he could easily handle a dozen. Then realizing full well that they wouldn't try to quench his thirst—or even admit such a possibility—just for the sake of his beautiful eyes and handsome ways, he asked:

"What's up? . . ." a voice hoarse from the abuse of hard liquor said.

Vin Mod explained the situation: the brig *James Cook* ready to leave . . . good wages . . . sailing for several months . . . just simple trading from island to island . . . plenty of drink and good quality . . . a captain who depended on his bosun, Flig Balt here, for everything concerning the welfare of his crew, home port of Hobart-Town, all in all everything capable of seducing a sailor who likes a good time during his stopovers . . . and no papers to show the Naval Commissioner . . . They'd weigh anchor tomorrow at dawn, if the crew was full . . . and if a man had some friend in bad straits, looking to embark, just point him out if he happened to be here in the tavern of the *Three Magpies*.

Len Cannon looked at Bosun Flig Balt and his companion, a frown on his face. What could a proposition like that entail? . . . What did it hide? . . . Anyway, as advantageous as it sounded, Len Cannon responded with only one word:

"No."

"You're making a mistake! . . ." said Vin Mod.

"Possible . . . But can't embark now . . ."

"Why?"

"Gettin' married . . ."

"You don't say! . . ."

"To Kate Verdax . . . a widow . . ."

"Hey there," Vin Mod retorted, slapping him on the shoulder, "if you ever marry, it won't be to Kate Verdax, but to Kate Gibbet[16] . . . the widow gallows!"

Len Cannon set to laughing and emptied his glass with one gulp. Yet, despite the insistence of Bosun Balt, he stuck to his refusal, stood up and rejoined a noisy group exchanging violent provocations.

"We'll try somebody else," said Vin Mod, not discouraged by this first failure.

This time, leaving Bosun Balt, he went to sit at a table near another sailor[17] in a corner of the room. No better a demeanor than Cannon, this fellow, and seemed less communicative, no doubt preferring to talk with the bottle, an interminable conversation which appeared to satisfy him.

Vin Mod went right to the subject:

"Can you tell me your name?"

"My name? . . ." replied the sailor after a certain hesitation.

"Yes . . ."

"Well, what's yours? . . ."

"Vin Mod."

"And what's that?"

"Name of a sailor on the brig *James Cook* put in at Dunedin . . ."

"And why does Vin Mod want to know my name? . . ."

"Just in case I might sign you up on our new crew roster . . ."

"Kyle . . . is my name . . ." answered the sailor, "but I'm holding out for a better job . . ."

"If one comes up, my friend . . ."

"Oh, one always comes up."

And Kyle turned his back on Vin Mod, who was no doubt a bit less confident at this second turndown. It was like a Stock Exchange, this tavern of Adam Fry's, and demand exceeded supply by far, which left small chance of success.

Indeed, with two customers haggling over the payment for their last pint with their last shilling, the result was just the same. Sexton, an Irishman, and Bryce, an American, would hoof it to America or Ireland rather than board ship, even if it were on the yacht of His Gracious Majesty or the best cruiser of the United States.

A few attempts at hiring, even with the support of Adam Fry, did not succeed, and Vin Mod returned at a loss to the table of Flig Balt.

"No dice? . . ." the latter asked.

"Nothing doing, Bosun Balt."

"Aren't there other taverns besides the *Three Magpies* around here? . . ."

"There are some," answered Vin Mod, "but if we can't get recruits here, we won't get them anywhere."

Flig Balt could not refrain from swearing, followed by a hard blow of his fist that shook both glasses and bottles. Was his plan doomed then? . . . Couldn't he introduce four men of choice into the *James Cook* crew? . . . Would they be reduced to filling out the crew with worthy sailors who might side with Captain Gibson? . . . It is true that good ones were scarce, just like bad ones, and weeks would probably go by before the brig, short of men, would be able to put out to sea.

However, there were other places to check. Taverns for sailors are not scarce in the neighborhood, and, as Vin Mod said, they outnumbered churches or banks. Flig Balt set about paying the tab for their drinks when a disturbance broke out at the other end of the room.

The discussion between Sexton[18] and Bryce about paying their tab took a turn for the worse. Both had no doubt drunk more than the state of their finances allowed. Now Adam Fry was not a man to give out credit, even for a matter of a few pence. They were out two shillings, and they would pay the two shillings or the policemen would intervene and take them to where they had been lodged more than once for blows, insults, and misdeeds of various sorts.

The owner of the *Three Magpies,* forewarned by the waiter, was about to claim his due, which Sexton and Bryce could not have paid even if others had reached into the bottom of their pockets, which were as empty of money as the men were filled with whiskey and gin. Perhaps, on this occasion, the intervention of Vin Mod, money in hand, might be effective and perhaps the two sailors would accept a few dollars as advance payment on future wages? He tried it out and was promptly told to go to the devil. Torn between the desire to be paid and the annoyance of losing two customers if they were to embark the next day on the *James Cook,* Adam Fry did not even come to his assistance as he had hoped.

When he saw that, Bosun Balt understood that they had to be done with it, and said to Vin Mod:

"Let's go . . ."

"All right," replied the latter. "It's only nine o'clock. . . . Let's go to the *Old Brothers* or to the *Good Seaman* . . . they're just a few steps away and I'll be hanged if we go back aboard ship without anything to show for it!"

As can be seen, the word "hang," as a comparative or metaphoric term, was often used in Vin Mod's conversation, and perhaps he imagined that it was the natural end of one's existence in this world!

Meanwhile, from harsh demands, Adam Fry was now turning to threats. Sexton and Bryce would either pay or spend the night at the police station. The waiter even received the order to go fetch the police, who were not rare in that section of the port. Flig Balt and Vin Mod were getting ready to leave when three or four strapping fellows took a stand at the door, not so much to keep people in but to prevent others from entering.

Obviously, these sailors were ready and able to defend their comrades. Things would soon get worse, and the evening could turn nasty as so many others had.

Adam Fry and the waiter did not anticipate such an eventuality, and they were going to rely on the police, as they usually did when faced with these circumstances. So when they saw the doorway blocked, they tried to get out to the alley that ran along the rear of the tavern.

The guards did not give them time. The whole gang turned against them. It was Kyle and Sexton, Len Cannon and Bryce who intervened. There were only a few unable to join the struggle, just a half dozen drunken sots stretched out in the corners, incapable of standing upright.

As a consequence, neither Bosun Balt nor Vin Mod could leave the room.

"We've got to take off . . . ," said the first, "we'll only get beat up around here . . ."

"Who knows," the other answered. "Let's see how it goes . . . We may be able to profit from this brawl."

And since both, while wanting to gain from it, did not want to suffer any losses from it, they remained safely out of harm's way, behind the counter.

The fight began using non-lethal weapons, if that expression can be used to describe the vicious kicks and blows of the combatants. Soon they would probably resort to knives, and not for the first time—nor the last—blood would begin to flow in the tavern. Adam Fry and the waiter would have been overpowered by the attackers and reduced to helplessness if a few others had not joined up with them. Indeed, five or six Irishmen, with the hope of working out a future credit, came forward to repel the assailants.

It was turning into a full-scale brawl. Bosun Balt and Vin Mod, seeking the best shelter available, went to great lengths to avoid being struck by glasses or bottles flying everywhere. Men struck out wildly, shouted, howled. Overturned lamps flickered out, and the room was no longer lit except from the lanterns outside, recessed in the transom of the entryway.

In short, the four principal brawlers—Len Cannon, Kyle, Sexton, and Bryce—after first being on the attack, now had to defend themselves. In the first place, the tavern keeper and the waiter were not exactly amateurs in their boxing skills. Powerful counterattacks had just knocked down Kyle and Bryce, their jaws half smashed. Yet they got to their feet to help their companions, whom the Irish were backing into a corner.

The advantage favored one and then the other; victory could only be decided by some outside intervention. Cries of "Help! Lend us a hand" rang out in the midst of the fight. However, the neighbors seemed unconcerned about the goings-on at the tavern of the *Three Magpies;* such riots among sailors had become customary. Pointless, isn't it so, to risk oneself in such a scuffle? That's for the police since, as people say, they get paid for it.

The brawl gained momentum as the fighters' anger rose to fury.

The tables were overturned. They struck each other with the stools. Knives emerged from pockets, revolvers from holsters, and shots were fired in the middle of the dreadful tumult.

As the tavern keeper kept maneuvering to reach the outer door or the entrance to the rear, a dozen policemen stormed in through the back of the building. It had not been necessary for neighbors to run to their headquarters on the dock. As soon as the police were warned by passersby that there was a blowup in Adam Fry's tavern, they went there in some haste. And, with that official pace that distinguishes the English policeman, they arrived in great enough numbers to assure public order. Moreover, between those attacking and the others resisting, it is probable that the police would not notice any difference. They knew the one group was as worthless as the other. By arresting everyone, they could be sure of doing a thorough job.

And although the room was only dimly lit, the police recognized right off the most violent, Len Cannon, Sexton, Kyle and Bryce, having previously thrown them into prison. Those four rascals, anticipating what was awaiting them, tried to escape by crossing the little courtyard behind the building. But, where would they go, and would they not be picked up the following day?

Vin Mod chose to intervene at just the right moment, as he had said to Bosun Balt he would. And as the others were attacking the police unrelentingly in order to favor the flight of the guiltiest among them, he rejoined Len Cannon and said to him:

"All four to the *James Cook!* . . ."

Sexton, Bryce, and Kyle had overheard.

"When does it leave? . . ." asked Len Cannon.

"Tomorrow, at daybreak."

And despite the police, against whom, by common consent, the whole group turned, despite Adam Fry who was especially trying to get them arrested, Len Cannon and the three others, followed by Flig Balt and Vin Mod, managed to escape.

Fifteen minutes later, the brig's tender was transporting them on board, and they were safe in the crew quarters.

The brawl gained momentum.

The Brig *James Cook*

The brig *James Cook,*[1] with a capacity of two hundred and fifty tons, was a solid ship with strong sails and a deep hull that assured its stability. Boasting a slender stern and a raised bow, it handled excellently at all sailing speeds, and its masts were slightly inclined. Its sails set close to the wind in a fresh breeze, and, when avoiding heavy seas, the ship slipped through the waves effortlessly at eleven knots.

Its personnel—as is already known from the conversation heard before—included a captain, a bosun, eight crewmen, a cook, and a cabin boy. It sailed under the British flag, having for its home port Hobart Town,[2] the capital of Tasmania, due east of the Australian continent and one of Great Britain's most important colonies.

For some ten years now, the *James Cook* had been carrying out its trade in the western Pacific, between Australia, New Zealand, and the Philippines. Its voyages were both successful and profitable, thanks to the seamanship and commercial acumen of its captain, a good sailor who also doubled as a good trader.

Captain Harry Gibson, at that time some fifty years of age, had stayed with the ship since it came out of the shipyards of Brisbane.[3] He held a quarter interest in the brig, the other three-quarters belonging to Mr. Hawkins, shipowner from Hobart Town. Their business prospered, and the beginnings of this voyage also held out the promise of large profits. The families of the captain and the owner had been close for many years, Harry Gibson having always sailed for the Hawkins firm. Both lived in the same neighborhood of Hobart Town. Mr. and Mrs. Hawkins had no children. Mr. and Mrs. Gibson had a single son, age twenty-one, who was also going into commerce. The two women saw each other every day, which made their separation from their husbands less difficult, for the ship-

Scenes in New Zealand

owner was located in Wellington,[4] where he had just founded a bank with Nat Gibson, the captain's son. It was from there that the *James Cook* was to bring them to Hobart Town, after having taken on its cargo in the neighboring archipelago of New Guinea, to the north of Australia, in the vicinity of the equator.

The bosun was Flig Balt—no point in saying here who he was or what he was worth, nor what villainous plans he was contemplating. Suffice it to say that in addition to those instincts pushing him toward crime and the jealousy he bore the captain, he possessed a cunning hypocrisy that had allowed him to dupe the latter since the beginning of this voyage. Thanks to his references, which appeared to be authentic, he had been hired as bosun on the brig, at the same time that Vin Mod had embarked as seaman. These two men had known each other for a long time—they had traversed the seas together, passing from one ship to another, deserting when finding it impossible to perpetrate their evil deeds—and they hoped to carry out yet another during the last crossing of the *James Cook* before its return to Hobart Town.

Indeed, Flig Balt inspired great confidence in Captain Gibson, who was taken in by the bosun's pretense of zeal and his expressions of devotion. Constantly close to the crew, he managed to gain an influence over them. As for the navigation and the commercial matters, Harry Gibson relied only on himself. Not having had the chance to prove himself, perhaps Flig Balt was not the sailor he claimed to be, though he assured the others that he had already shipped out as the second in command. It is even possible that Captain Gibson held some doubts about his background. But Balt's service left nothing to be desired, and he had never had a reproach to make to his bosun. So the voyage of the brig would probably have been made under the best conditions if the desertion of four sailors had not held him over in Dunedin for two weeks.

A few of the crew members in no way followed the example of their comrades. Hobbes,[5] Wickley, and Burnes,[6] belonged to that category of worthy men, disciplined and courageous, on whom a captain could rely fully. As for the deserters, there would have been no reason to miss them, had they not been replaced by the scoundrels that Vin Mod had just recruited in the tavern of the *Three Magpies*. We know what they are, and we'll soon see them at work.

The crew also included a cabin boy and a cook.

Jim, the cabin boy, was a young man of fourteen years, from a family of honest workers living in Hobart Town. The family had entrusted him to Captain Gibson. He was a fine lad, who would make a good seaman one day. Captain Gibson treated him as a father would, though with no special favors, and Jim showed him a deep affection. In contrast, Jim felt an instinctive repugnance for the bosun Flig Balt. The latter, who had noticed it, was always trying to find fault with him—which led more than once to the intervention of Mr. Gibson.

As for the cook, Koa,[7] he was of the type of natives belonging to the second race[8] of New Zealanders, men of average size, mulatto in skin coloring, muscular and agile, with frizzy hair, the general makeup of that class of people among the Maori. After this first voyage with Koa serving on board the brig as head chef, Harry Gibson had it in mind to dismiss the shifty man, who was vindictive, nasty—and sloppy as well—and on whom reprimands and punishment had no effect. So Flig Balt was correct to place him among those who wouldn't hesitate to revolt against the captain. Vin Mod and he got along well, too. The bosun spared him, excused him, punished him only if he had no recourse. Koa knew that he would be discharged when he reached Hobart Town, and more than once he had threatened to get revenge. Flig Balt, Vin Mod, and he, assisted by the four newly hired seamen, made seven men against the captain, the three other sailors, and the cabin boy. It is true that Mr. Hawkins, the owner, and Nat Gibson were to come aboard the brig in Wellington, and the ratio would then be more equal. But it was possible that Flig Balt could succeed in taking over the ship between Dunedin and Wellington during the crossing, which was of very short duration. If the occasion presented itself, Vin Mod would seize it.

The *James Cook,* plying the coastal waterways for four months, had loaded up at different ports where it had replaced its cargo with more profitable freight. After having successively made port in Malikolo, Merena, and Eromanga of the New Hebrides,[9] then at Vanoua Linon in the Fiji Islands,[10] it would return to Wellington where Mr. Hawkins and Nat Gibson were awaiting it. Then it would set sail for the archipelagoes of New Guinea,[11] well stocked with showy but inexpensive goods for the natives, and he'd bring back some mother of pearl and coconut worth some ten or twelve thousand piastres, a handsome sum. From there they would make their return to Hobart Town with stopovers at Brisbane or at Sydney,[12] if circumstances required it. Two more months at sea and the brig would then return to its home port.

One can imagine how much the delays suffered in Dunedin had vexed Mr. Gibson. Mr. Hawkins knew what had transpired, thanks to the letters and telegrams exchanged between Dunedin and Wellington, and by which he urged the captain to reconstitute his crew. He even talked about coming to Dunedin, if necessary, even though affairs of business required his presence in Wellington. Mr. Gibson, as we have seen, had neglected nothing and had worked hard to get the job done, and we cannot forget what difficulties he had confronted, numerous other captains having been caught in the same dilemma. Finally Flig Balt had had some success recruiting, and when the four sailors in the tavern of the *Three Magpies* were aboard, he had the ship's boats hoisted up so they could not leave during the night.

That very evening Flig Balt told the captain how things had gone, how he had taken advantage of a squabble to drag Len Cannon and three others from the reach of the police. How valuable they were would soon be seen. Generally such rowdy men calm down once the ship is at sea. Roughnecks on a spree most often make good sailors. All in all, the bosun thought he had acted for the best.

Mr. Gibson said, "I'll see them tomorrow."

"Yes . . . tomorrow," replied Bosun Balt, "and better yet, let them sleep off their gin until morning."

"Of course. Besides, the tenders are up on the hoists, and unless they throw themselves overboard . . ."

"Impossible, Captain. I had them go down into the hold, and they'll stay there until departure."

"But, when daylight comes, Balt?"

"Oh! with daylight, fear of falling into the hands of the police will keep them aboard."

"See you tomorrow then," Mr. Gibson answered.

Night passed, and no doubt it would have been useless to lock up Len Cannon and his comrades. They scarcely dreamed of saving themselves and fell asleep noisily, the sleep of drunkards. At dawn the next day, Captain Gibson made the last arrangements for leaving port. His papers were in order, and he had no need to return to land. That was the moment he chose to meet the new recruits on the bridge.

Vin Mod opened the main hatch, and the four sailors climbed up to join the ship's crew. Perfectly sober, they showed no intention of flight.

However, when they appeared before the captain, Gibson was master enough of himself to hide the impression that the sight of these men produced—an impression that could not fail to be most disagreeable—he watched them attentively, then asked their names, in order to enter them in the log.

In giving their names, they also indicated their nationality: two Englishmen, an Irishman, and an American. For their residence, they had none but the taverns around the port, whose owners kept rooms for the patrons. As for their belongings and everything that is usually found in a sailor's bag, they hadn't been able to bring them. Besides, Flig Balt would make available to them clothes, linens, and utensils that the deserters would never come back to reclaim. So there would be no reason to send them after their bags. And they didn't insist.

When Len Cannon, Sexton, Kyle, and Bryce had gone up forward, Mr. Gibson, cocking his head, said:

"Tough customers, Balt. I don't believe you got a lucky hand with these."

"Remains to be seen, Captain; we can tell by their work."

"We'll have to keep an eye on them, and a close eye at that."

"Of course, Mr. Gibson. Yet they're fairly skilled according to what an officer from the *West Pound*[13] told me, who is here on leave."

"You had already seen them?"

"Yes, a few days ago."

"And this officer knew them?"

"They sailed with him on an ocean voyage, and, according to him, they were good sailors."

The bosun was lying outrageously. No officer had talked to him about these four men, but his assertion could not be checked, and Mr. Gibson had no real reason to suspect its veracity.

"We'll be careful not to place them together in the same quarters," said the captain. "The two Englishmen with Hobbes and Wickley, the Irishman and the American with Burnes and Vin Mod. That'll be safer."

"Understood, Captain, but do let me say, once at sea they won't balk at working. It's just when they're in port, especially in Wellington, that they'll need to be watched. No shore leave, take my word for it, or they might never come back."

"No matter, Balt, they don't inspire me with confidence, and in Wellington, if I can replace them . . ."

"We'll replace them," replied the bosun. Flig Balt did not wish to insist more than was proper, nor appear to favor those temporary sailors.

"After all," he added, "I did my best, Captain, and I didn't have a lot of choice!"

Mr. Gibson went aft, near the helmsman, while Flig Balt went forward to hoist and stow the anchor as soon as the sails were set.

The captain looked at the compass located in front of the helm, then at the weathercock at the peak of the main mast and the British flag that the wind deployed over the top of the brigantine. The *James Cook* was rocking on its anchor line in mid-port. The breeze, blowing from the southwest, should favor its departure. After descending the channel to Port Chalmers,[14] it would find a good wind blowing up the eastern shore of New Zealand as far as the channel that separates the two islands. However, after having raised anchor, it would have to avoid several ships moored at the entrance to the canal and run close to the dock bordering the port on the starboard side.

Mr. Gibson gave his orders. The two topsails, the foresail, the jibs

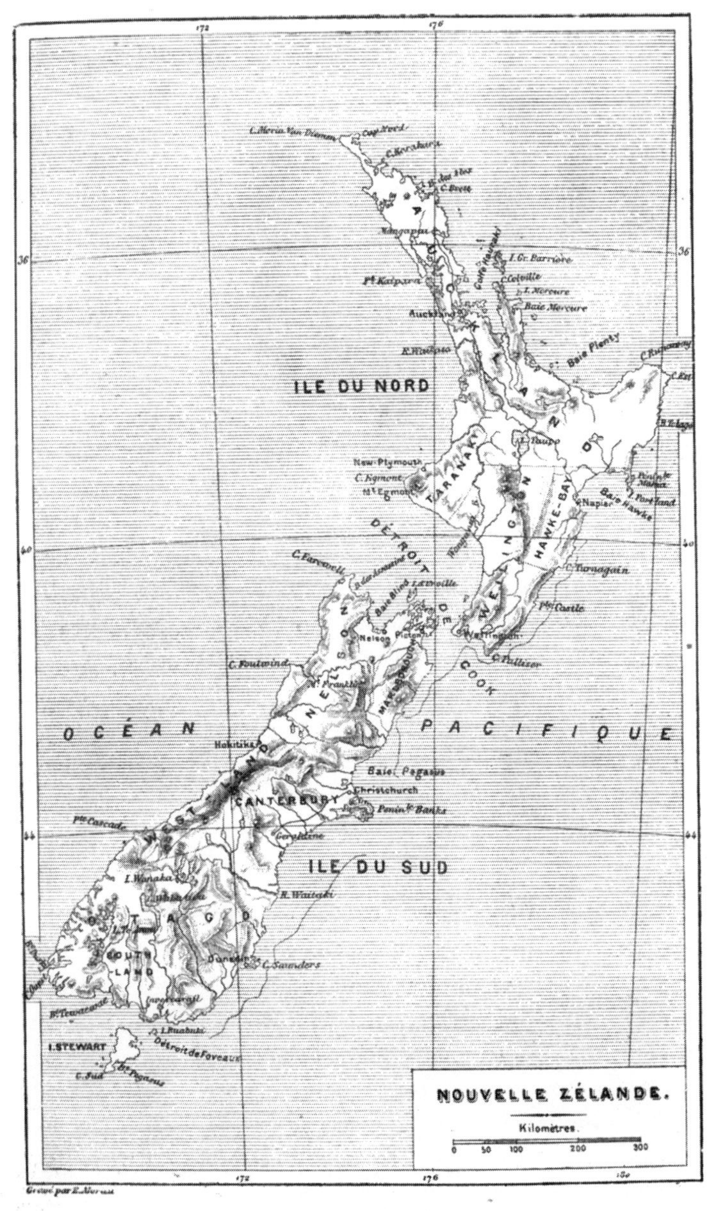

ILE DU NORD
ILE DU SUD
OCÉAN
PACIFIQUE
DÉTROIT DE COOK
TARANAKI
CANTERBURY
Auckland
New-Plymouth
Napier
Wellington
Hokitika
Christchurch
Baie Pegasus
C. Saunders
I. STEWART
Détroit de Foveaux
NOUVELLE ZÉLANDE.
Kilomètres.
0 50 100 200 300

New Zealand

and the spanker were set, one after the other. During this maneuver, it became clear that Len Cannon and his comrades knew the trade, and when they had to climb to the topgallant, they performed like men who have nothing more to learn about the setting of sails.[15]

The half-raised anchor was hoisted aboard the moment the sheets had stiffened to set the brig in the right direction.

Flig Balt and Vin Mod were able to exchange a few words during the maneuver.

"Aha!" declared the latter, "our recruits are working out well."

"Well enough, Mod."

"Three more louts of that sort and we'd have the crew we need."

"And our ship!" added Flig Balt in a low tone.

"And our captain as well!" Vin Mod declared, raising his hand to his beret, as though saluting his captain.

Flig Balt stopped him with a gesture, fearing that those imprudent words could be heard by the ship's cabin boy, busily engaged with the sail on the jib. Then he was returning to the deckhouse when Vin Mod asked him what Mr. Gibson thought of the four regular customers of the *Three Magpies*.

"He was somewhat satisfied," replied Flig Balt.

"The fact is that the outward appearance of our recruits works against them," replied Vin Mod.

"I wouldn't be surprised if he tried to disembark them in Wellington," said Flig Balt.

"To disembark them in Wellington," added Vin Mod, shrugging his shoulders, "you have to first get to Wellington. But I hope that we won't go to Wellington, and won't disembark anyone."

"Don't be imprudent, Mod!"

"Well . . . Flig Balt, the captain isn't happy?"

"No."

"What's the difference, as long as we are!"

The bosun came back to the stern.

"Everything ready?" Mr. Gibson asked.

"All set, Captain."

The *James Cook* slowly turned, approaching the dock where it would be within a half cable's length.

A group had formed there, sailors and onlookers, who were always interested at the sight of a ship under sail. And besides, for several weeks they had been deprived of this spectacle since most ships had not been able to leave their moorings.

Now in this group could be seen several policemen whose attention seemed particularly drawn to the *James Cook.* That could be guessed by their gestures and attitude. There were even two or three of these officers who had run to the far end of the dock, which the ship would soon be skirting.

Of course—neither Flig Balt nor Vin Mod had any doubt—these policemen were among those whom they had seen the day before in Adam Fry's tavern. Len Cannon and his comrades risked being recognized, and who knows if the *James Cook,* hailed in passage and ordered to stop, would not be given notice to surrender the sailors from the *Three Magpies?*

After all, Captain Gibson, at the risk of being held under strict surveillance, found it to his advantage to hold onto them, and he would have been extremely inconvenienced if he had been obliged to turn them over to the police. So, after a few words from Flig Balt, he approved Vin Mod's taking Len Cannon, Sexton, Kyle and Bryce below decks before they could be identified by the police.

"Get below . . . get below!" Vin Mod whispered to them.

They cast a rapid look toward the dock, understood, and disappeared down the hatch. Besides, their presence on deck was no longer necessary; the helmsman managed to direct the *James Cook* toward the entrance of the canal without any need to brace the sails.

The brig continued on its course approaching the end of the dock, even closer than usual for most ships, for it had to avoid an American steamship[16] whose loud whistles were rending the air.

The policemen thus were able to observe the sailors on board, and surely if Len Cannon and the others had not been sent below, they would have been recognized and forced to disembark immediately. But the police did not see them, and the brig was able to enter the channel as soon as the steamer had pulled out of its way.

There was nothing more to fear; the four sailors returned to the deck.

Besides, their help was needed. The channel, which goes from southwest to northeast, is rather winding, and one must let out or tighten the sails at every turn.

The *James Cook,* aided by the breeze, navigated without difficulty between the green shores strewn with villas and cottages, where along one bank runs the railway that connects Dunedin to Port Chalmers

It was nearly eight o'clock when the brig passed before this port and reached the open sea. There, on the port tack, it sailed along the coast, leaving to the south the Otago lighthouse[17] and Cape Saunders.[18]

Vin Mod at Work

The distance between Dunedin and Wellington, through the strait that separates the two large islands, is less than four hundred miles.[1] If the northwest breeze held steady and the sea remained calm along the coast, at the rate of ten miles an hour, the *James Cook* would arrive the next day in Wellington.

During this short crossing, would Flig Balt be able to execute his plan, taking over the brig after getting rid of the captain and his allies and sailing it toward the distant Pacific isles where he would find safety and act with total impunity?

We know how Vin Mod intended to proceed: Mr. Gibson and the men who were faithful to him would be surprised and thrown overboard before being able to defend themselves. But as of today, it was necessary to bring Len Cannon and his comrades into the plot—which would not be very difficult—in order to feel them out beforehand on this subject and be assured of their cooperation. That's what Vin Mod planned to do during the first day of navigation, and then take action that very night. No time to lose. In twenty-four hours, the brig, reaching Wellington, would take on Mr. Hawkins and Nat Gibson as passengers. So, that night, it was important that the *James Cook* be taken over by Flig Balt and his accomplices. If not, the chances of success would be substantially diminished, and a second opportunity might perhaps not be found.

As for the question of whether or not Len Cannon, Sexton, Kyle, and Bryce would consent to join them, Vin Mod did not worry much about it. He knew that such faithless and lawless individuals, who have neither conscience nor scruples, are always attracted by the prospect of profitable deals in these regions of the Pacific, where justice cannot easily reach them.

The southern island of New Zealand,[2] Tawaï-Pounamou, is said to resemble the form of a long rectangle, swollen in its lower part and somewhat obliquely laid out from southwest to southeast. On the contrary, the northern island, Ikana-Maoui, appears as an irregular triangle, its southernmost tip ending in a narrow tongue of land projecting out to the point of North Cape.

The coast that the brig followed is very jagged, banked with enormous rocks with bizarre shapes, which at a distance resemble gigantic mastodons fallen upon the shores. Here and there a succession of archways represents the periphery of a monastery, against which the waves, even in fine weather, hurl themselves furiously with a formidable roar. Any ship that was to find itself on the shore at high tide would be irredeemably lost; three or four rolls of the sea would demolish it. Fortunately, if it were seized by the tempest from the east or from the west, there would be a chance it might slip between the furthermost promontories of New Zealand. Moreover, there are two straits where it is possible to find shelter if you miss your entry into the ports: Cook's, which separates the two islands, and Foveaux's,[3] open between Tawaï-Pounamou and Stewart[4] Island, at its southern end. But one must beware of the dreadful reefs of the Snares,[5] where the waves of the Indian Ocean and those of the Pacific collide, an area that is abundant in maritime disasters.

Inland from the coast extends a powerful mountain chain hollowed out by craters and furrowed by waterfalls, which feed rivers that are sizable despite their limited range. On the mountain slopes rise tiers of forests whose trees are huge beyond measure, pines

Len Cannon and Bryce

a hundred feet tall and some twenty feet in diameter, cedars with olive-tree leaves, the resinous "koudy," the "kaïkatea" with resistant leaves and red berries whose trunks are bare of branches except at the top.

If Ikana-Maoui can be proud of the richness of its soil, the vigor of its fertility, and that vegetation which rivals in certain areas the most brilliant productions of tropical flora, Tawaï-Pounamou has less to be grateful for. At the most a tenth of the territory can be cultivated. But in some special areas, the natives can still harvest a bit of Indian corn, various herbaceous plants, potatoes in abundance, and a profusion of ferns, the "pteris esculenta," from which they make their principal food.

The *James Cook* at times approached so close to the shore, which Harry Gibson knew very well, that birdsong could be clearly heard on board ship, among others that of the "pou," the most melodious. There was also the guttural cry of various parrots, ducks with yellow beaks and feet of scarlet red, without mentioning numerous other aquatic species, whose most hardy representatives flew among the rigging of the ship. And also, when the ship's hull troubled their frolicking, with what rapidity fled those cetaceans, sea elephants, sea lions, and those multitudes of seals sought for their oily fat and their thick fur, two hundred of them producing nearly a hundred barrels of oil!

The weather held steady. If the breeze fell, it would not be before evening, since it came from land and, falling, would be blocked by the mountain chain.

Under a beautiful sun, the breeze blew through the higher zones and rapidly pushed the brig, which carried its staysail and its starboard studding sail. There was scarcely time to slacken the sails, to alter their course. So the new crewmembers could appreciate the sea-going qualities of the *James Cook*.

Around eleven o'clock, Mount Herbert, a bit before the port of Omaru,[6] showed its swollen peaks rising to five thousand feet above sea level.

During the morning, Vin Mod sought in vain to talk with Len Cannon, whom he considered, and fairly, as the most intelligent and influential of the four recruits from Dunedin. Mr. Gibson, as we know, had ordered his sailors not to stay together on the same watch, and it was better, indeed, that they be kept separated from each other. But, not having to maneuver, the captain now left to the bosun the surveillance of the ship and he was busy in his cabin, updating the ship's log.

At that moment Hobbes was at the helm. Flig Balt was strolling from the mainmast to the stern, on either side of the crew quarters. Two other sailors, Burnes and Bryce, were going back and forth along the rail without exchanging a word. Vin Mod and Len Cannon happened to be together downwind, and their conversation could not be heard by anyone.

When Jim, the cabin boy, approached them, they dismissed him rather curtly, and even, just to be safe, Bosun Balt sent him off to polish some of the copper instruments on the bridge.

As for the two other comrades of Len Cannon, Sexton and Kyle, they were not on duty and preferred fresh air to the stuffy atmosphere of their quarters. Koa, the cook, on the foredeck, amused them with his crude remarks and his abominable grimaces. This native was very proud of the tattoos on his face, torso, and limbs, this "moko"[7] from New Zealand where the skin is deeply furrowed instead of scratched, as is done by other people of the Pacific. This operation of "moko" is not practiced on all the natives. The "koukis" or slaves are not worthy of it, nor are people of the lower class, unless they have distinguished themselves at war by some feat of arms.

So Koa took extraordinary pride in them.

And—which seemed to greatly interest Sexton and Kyle—he was pleased to give them a detailed explanation about each of his tattoos; he told of what circumstances his chest had been decorated with this or that design; he pointed at his forehead, which bore his name engraved permanently, and which for nothing in the world would he erase.

Moreover, among such natives, their cutaneous system, thanks to these operations that extend over the whole surface of the body, gains a great deal in thickness and solidity. Hence their resistance to cold during the winter and to mosquito bites. How many Europe-

*A tattooed New Zealand native**

*Facsimile of an illustration published in the *Great Voyages and Great Navigators* by Jules Verne (Hetzel's note).

ans, at this expense, would thank themselves for being able to brave the attack of those accursed insects!

While Koa, feeling himself instinctively attracted by a quite natural sympathy toward Sexton and his comrade, was setting up the basis of a strong friendship, Vin Mod was working on Len Cannon who, for his part, was most happy to see him approach:

"Eh, Cannon, my friend," said Vin Mod, "so here you are aboard the *James Cook*. A pretty fair ship, isn't she? And she'll spin off eleven knots without your having to hold her hand."

"So you say, Mod."

"And with a fine cargo in her belly. Worth a lot . . ."

"So much the better for her owner."

"Owner, sure . . . or anybody else . . . In the meantime, all we have to do is cross our arms while she's running good."

"Today it's fine," replied Cannon. "But tomorrow . . . who knows?"

"Tomorrow . . . next day . . . on and on!" exclaimed Vin Mod, patting Len Cannon's shoulder. "But it's better than just staying on land, right? Where would you be, your friends and you, right now if you weren't here?"

"At the *Three Magpies,* Mod."

"No, Adam Fry would've thrown you out, after the way you treated him. Then the police would've taken you in, all four of you. And I suppose, since this wouldn't be your first appearance in court, they'd have favored you with one or two good months of rest in the Dunedin prison."

"Prison on land or brig at sea, all the same thing," answered Len Cannon, who didn't sound too resigned to his fate.

"Oh, come now!" exclaimed Vin Mod, "sailors talking like that! . . ."

"It wasn't our idea to sail away," declared Len Cannon. "If it wasn't for that miserable brawl yesterday, we'd already be off to Otago."

"To work, to slave, to die of hunger and thirst, of course, but what for?"

"To make a fortune . . . ," Len Cannon replied.

"Make a fortune! . . . by placer mining?" answered Vin Mod.

"Why there's nothing left to extract from there. Haven't you seen what they look like? The ones they've brought back? Just stones! All you want! And you can load yourself up with them, just so you won't come back with empty pockets! As for the nuggets, the harvest is over, and they don't grow back again from one day to the next nor even from one year to the next!"[8]

"I know men who don't mind leaving their ship for the deposits in Clutha . . ."

"Me . . . I know four who won't regret having embarked on the *James Cook* instead of taking off for the interior!"

"You saying that for us?"

"For you and two or three other gaffers like you!"

"And you're trying to make me believe a sailor earns enough for a good life, eating and drinking the rest of his days for taking care of a captain and an owner?"

"Of course not," replied Vin Mod, "unless he does it for his own account!"

"And how does that work? When we don't own the ship?"

"Someday you'll get to be an owner . . ."

"And you think that me and my friends have enough money in a Dunedin bank to buy a ship?"

"No, my friend. If you ever had savings, they passed right through the hands of Adam Frye and other bankers of that sort!"

"Well, Mod, no money, no ship. And I don't think that Mr. Gibson is of a mood to make us a gift of his own."

"No . . . but you know, misfortunes do happen! If Mister Gibson were to disappear . . . An accident, falling into the sea . . . that happens to the best of captains. One good wave, doesn't take more to do you in, and at night . . . without anyone noticing . . . and in the morning nobody's there . . ."

Len Cannon looked at Vin Mod, eye to eye, wondering if he understood.

The other continued:

"And then what happens? The captain's replaced, and in this case it's the second in command who takes over the ship, or if there's no second in command, it's the lieutenant."

"And if there isn't any lieutenant . . . ," added Len Cannon, lowering his voice and giving his interlocutor a nudge with his elbow, "if there's no lieutenant, it's the bosun . . ."

"As you say, my friend, and with a bosun like Flig Balt you could go a long way . . ."

"Not where you should go?" insinuated Len Cannon, tossing him a sideways glance.

"No . . . But it's where you want to go . . ." said Vin Mod. "Where real money can be made. Good cargoes . . . Mother of pearl, copra, spices . . . all of it in the hold of the *Little Girl*."[9]

"What do you mean . . . *Little Girl?*"

"That would be the new name of the *James Cook* . . . A pretty name, isn't it? It should bring us luck!"

In any event, whether it carried this name or some other—although Vin Mod seemed especially fond of the new one—there were definite possibilities here. Len Cannon was intelligent enough to pick up on the fact that this proposal was being addressed to his comrades of the *Three Magpies* and to himself. Scruples would certainly not hold them back. But, before getting involved, he needed to understand things thoroughly, and on what side his best interests would lie. So after several moments of reflection, Len Cannon, who cast his eyes about to be sure no one could hear him, said to Vin Mod:

"Let's hear it."

Vin Mod then informed Len Cannon of the entire scheme as Flig Balt had planned it. Len Cannon, quite ready to take on such a proposition, showed neither surprise on hearing the details, nor repugnance in discussing them, nor hesitation in accepting them. Getting rid of Captain Gibson and some sailors who would have refused to enter into rebellion against him, take over the brig, change its name and, if necessary, its nationality, traffic across the Pacific, equal shares with the profits, all that was sufficiently appealing to the rogue. Nevertheless, he wanted some guarantees, and he wanted to be assured that the bosun was in on this with Vin Mod.

"This evening at a quarter to eight, while you're at the helm, Flig Balt will talk to you, Len. Keep your ears open."

"And he's the one who'll take command of the *James Cook?*" asked Len Cannon, who would have preferred not being under anyone's orders.

"Ah, of course . . . devil take us! . . . ," replied Vin Mod. "You've got to have a captain, for sure. Only, it's you, Len, your friends and us who will be the owners!"

"It's a deal, Mod. Soon as I get a chance to talk to Sexton, Bryce, and Kyle, I'll tip them off to this affair."

"It's just that it's real urgent."

"As much as that?"

"Yes . . . tonight, and, once the new masters are in charge, we'll head out!"

So Vin Mod explained why the job had to be done before their arrival in Wellington, where Mr. Hawkins and the Gibson son would come aboard.

With two more men, the outcome would be less sure. In any case, if it weren't for the coming night, it would have to be for the next, no later . . . or there would be less chance of success.

Len Cannon understood those reasons. When evening came, he would tell his friends, in whom he had as much confidence as in himself. From the moment the bosun put out the command, they would obey him. But first, Flig Balt had to confirm everything that Vin Mod had said. Two words would be enough, and a handshake to seal the pact. And by St. Patrick! Len Cannon would not demand a signature. What was promised would be kept.

In short, just as Vin Mod had indicated, toward eight o'clock, when Len Cannon was at the helm, Flig Balt left the crew's quarters and headed aft. The captain was there at that time, and he had to wait for him to return to his cabin after having given out the orders for the night.

The northwest breeze held steady, although it had dropped a bit at sunset and it would not be necessary to change sails; perhaps they should only bring along the big topgallant and the little one. The brig would stay under its topsails, its low sails, and its jibs. Besides, it was less close to the wind, waiting to head toward the northeast. The sea promised to be calm until morning.

The *James Cook,* outside the port of Timaru,[10] was about to cross the vast bay that indents the coastline, known by the name of Canterbury Bight. In order to cut around the Banks peninsula that encloses it, the ship would have to alter the course by two points to the east and navigate close-hauled to the wind.

Mr. Gibson braced the yards and hauled in the sheets in order to follow that direction. When day came, provided that the breeze did not utterly fall, he counted on having left behind Pompey's Pillars to find himself abeam of Christchurch.[11]

After his orders were carried out, Harry Gibson, to the great frustration of Flig Balt, remained on the bridge until ten o'clock, sometimes exchanging some words with him, sometimes seated on the coping. The bosun, forewarned by Vin Mod, found himself unable to talk with Len Cannon.

Finally, everything settled down on board. The brig would not have to alter its route until three or four o'clock in the morning, when they would be in view of the port of Akaroa.[12] So Mr. Gibson, after one last look at the horizon and the sail spread, returned to his cabin, which let in daylight on the forward side.

The discussion between Flig Balt and Len Cannon did not take long. The bosun confirmed the proposals of Vin Mod. No halfway measures: they'd throw the captain overboard after surprising him in his room, and since they could not count on Hobbes, Wickley, and Burnes, they'd throw them overboard as well. Len Cannon had only to reassure himself on the cooperation of his three comrades.

"But when?" asked Len Cannon.

"Tonight," replied Vin Mod.

"What time?"

"Between eleven and midnight," replied Flig Balt. "At that moment, Hobbes will be on duty with Sexton; Wickley will be at the helm. Won't have to pull them from their post . . . And after we've gotten rid of those honest seamen . . ."

"Understood," replied Len Cannon, feeling neither hesitation nor a twinge of conscience.

Then giving up the helm to Vin Mod, he headed for the bow in order to let Sexton, Bryce, and Kyle know what was going on.

Arriving at the mizzenmast, he looked for Sexton and Bryce in vain; they were supposed to be on duty but neither was there.

Wickley, whom he asked, just shrugged his shoulders.

"Where are they?" Len Cannon asked.

"In their quarters . . . dead drunk . . . both of them!"

"Ah, those louts," murmured Len Cannon. "They'll be out of it all night long. Nothing to be done about that!"

Back at their quarters, he found his comrades sprawled out on their cots. He shook them . . . Real louts, for sure! . . . They had stolen a bottle of gin from the storeroom. They drained it, to the last drop. Impossible to drag them out of their stupor, they wouldn't revive until morning. Impossible to tell them about Vin Mod's plans! Certainly couldn't count on them to execute his plans before sunrise, and without them, the sides were too unequal!

When Flig Balt was informed, one can well imagine his rage. Vin Mod could not calm him down without great effort. He too would have sent both of them to the gallows, those wretched drunks! But anyway, nothing was permanently lost. What couldn't be done that night would simply be done the next. They'd keep an eye on Bryce and Sexton and stop them from drinking. In any case Flig Balt would be careful not to denounce them to the captain, neither for drunkenness, nor for stealing the bottle. Mr. Gibson would send them to the bottom of the hold until the brig reached Wellington, then turn them over to the maritime authorities, and disembark perhaps Len Cannon and Kyle as well, as Vin Mod saw it. It would be wise not to say a word. Moreover, sailors do not denounce each other. Neither Hobbes, nor Wickley, nor Burnes, nor even the ship's boy would talk, and the captain would have no cause to intervene.

The night went by, and nothing disturbed the calm aboard the *James Cook*.

When Harry Gibson went up to the bridge early the next morning, he noted that the men on duty were at their post, and the brig on a proper course at right angles to Christchurch after having passed the Banks Peninsula.

The day of the 27th was off to a good start. The sun broke above the horizon and promptly dissipated the haze. One could believe that the sea breeze would soon engulf the bay, but beginning at seven o'clock it came from the land and, no doubt, would keep to the northwest as the day before. By hugging the wind, the *James Cook* would reach the port of Wellington without changing its tack.

"Nothing new?" asked Mr. Gibson of Flig Balt when the bosun came out of his cabin, where had spent the last hours of the night.

"Nothing new, Mr. Gibson," he replied.

"Who's at the helm?"

"The sailor Cannon."

"You haven't had to admonish the new recruits while on duty?"

"Not at all, and I think those men are better than they seem."

"So much the better, Balt, for I believe that in Wellington as in Dunedin they must be short of crews."

"That's probable, Mr. Gibson."

"And, all in all, if I could work it out with these fellows . . ."

"It would be for the best," answered Flig Balt.

The *James Cook,* continuing north, went along the coast at just three or four miles an hour. The details came into view more clearly under the heat of the sun's rays. The high mountains of the Kaikoura,[13] which cross the province of Marlborough,[14] raised their capricious ridges to a height of ten thousand feet. On their flanks spread thick forests, gilded with sunlight, as streams of water flowed down toward the coastline.

Yet the breeze seemed to be calming, and the brig that day would make fewer miles than the preceding one. It was unlikely that they would arrive in Wellington that night.

Toward five o'clock in the afternoon, they could just make out the peaks of Ben More,[15] to the south of the little port of Flaxbourne.[16] It would take another five or six hours to reach the opening of Cook Strait. Since this passage runs from south to north, it would not be necessary to change the ship's speed.

Flig Balt and Vin Mod were thus assured of having all night to accomplish their plans.

It goes without saying that the participation of Len Cannon and his comrades was settled. Sexton and Bryce, their drunkenness dissipated, and Kyle forewarned, had made no real protest. With Vin Mod supporting Len Cannon, they just waited for the right moment to move. Here were the conditions called for. The plan was as follows:

Between midnight and one o'clock, while the captain was asleep, Vin Mod and Len Cannon would penetrate into his cabin, gag him, carry him to the rail and throw him off into the sea before he had time to utter a cry. At the same time, Hobbes and Burnes, being on duty, would be seized by Kyle, Sexton, and Bryce and subjected to the same fate. That would leave Wickley on lookout; Koa and Flig Balt could easily subdue him, as well as the cabin boy. Once the plot was carried out, the only ones left on board would be the authors of the crime. There would not be a single witness, and the *James Cook,* at full sail, would soon reach the Pacific east of New Zealand.

All chances thus favored the success of this wretched plot. Before dawn, under the command of Flig Balt, the brig would be already far from these parts.

It was about seven o'clock when Cape Campbell[17] was observed in the northeast. It was, properly speaking, the southernmost boundary of Cook Strait, matched by, at a distance of some fifty miles, Cape Palliser,[18] the extremity of the isle of Ikana-Maoui.

The brig followed the coastline within less than two miles, all sails set, even the studding sail, for the breeze fell with the evening. The shore was clear, bordered with basaltic rocks, which form the foundation of the interior mountains. The crest of Mount Weld[19] was visible like a point of fire under rays of the setting sun. Although the tides of the Pacific are of little importance, a current from the shore flowed northward and favored the progress of the *James Cook* toward the sea.

It was at eight o'clock that the captain would probably be in his cabin after having left the bosun on duty. They would only have to watch out for the passage of ships at the opening of the strait. Moreover, the night would be clear, and no sail appeared on the horizon.

Before eight, however, some smoke was sighted, astern and off the starboard side, and they were not long in seeing a steamer rounding Cape Campbell.

Vin Mod and Flig Balt were not put out. Surely, given its pace, it would soon have passed the brig.

It was a government mail carrier, which had not as yet shown its colors. Now at this instant a rifle shot was heard, and the British flag was unfurled from the yardarm.

Harry Gibson had stayed on the bridge. Was he going to remain there as long as the mail carrier was visible, whether it intended to cross the strait or head for Wellington?

That's what Flig Balt and Vin Mod wondered, not without some concern and even a certain impatience, as they were so late being alone on the bridge.

An hour stretched by. Mr. Gibson, seated near the crew quarters, seemed disinclined to retire. He exchanged a few words with the helmsman Hobbes and watched the packet, which was now less than a mile from the brig.

Imagine how disappointed Flig Balt was, along with his accomplices, a disappointment bordering on rage. The English packet was moving at slow speed, and little steam puffed out of its exhaust. It rocked to the undulation of the long swell, barely troubling the water from the wash of the propeller, making no more wake than the *James Cook*.

Why had this ship slowed down so much? . . . Had some misfortune befallen the engine? Or was it simply a reluctance to enter the port of Wellington at night, where the channel offered so many difficulties? In any event, for one of those reasons, no doubt, it seemed to have decided to stay until dawn under low steam and, consequently, in view of the brig.

That was enough to frustrate Flig Balt, Vin Mod, and the others and to make them somewhat anxious as well.

Indeed, Len Cannon, Sexton, Kyle, and Bryce all thought at first that the packet had been sent from Dunedin in pursuit—that the police, having learned about their embarkment and their departure on the brig, were now seeking to recapture them. Exaggerated fears and certainly unfounded. It would have been simpler to send by telegraph the order to stop them as soon as they arrived in Welling-

Mr. Gibson exchanged a few words with the helmsman.

ton. One does not send a government ship to round up a few rowdy sailors, when it is easy to jail them in port.

Len Cannon and his comrades were soon reassured. The packet made no signal to communicate with the brig, and put no tender in the water. The *James Cook* would not be the object of a search, and the recruits from the *Three Magpies* could rest at ease on board.

But if all fear was banished on this account, one can easily imagine the anger felt by Bosun Balt and Vin Mod. Impossible to act that night, and the next day the brig would be at its mooring in Wellington! Attacking Captain Gibson and three sailors could not be done in silence. They would resist, they would cry out, and their cries would be heard by the packet, which was but a few hundred yards away. The revolt could not begin in these conditions. It would have been quickly put down by the English vessel, which, in a few turns of the propeller, would have drawn alongside the ship.

"Damnation!" Vin Mod grumbled. "Nothing we can do about it! We'd risk being hoisted to the yardarm of this damned ship."

"And tomorrow," added Flig Balt, "the owner and Nat Gibson will be on board!"

If they had moved away from the packet, perhaps the bosun would have attempted it if the captain, instead of returning to his cabin, had not stayed the greater part of the night on the bridge. As it was, it was impossible to head out to sea. So, they had to temporarily abandon their plan to take over the brig.

The next day broke early. The *James Cook* passed Blenheim,[20] situated on the shore of Tawaï-Pounamou on the east side of the strait; then it approached Point Nicholson, which juts out at the entrance to Wellington.[21] Finally, at six o'clock in the morning, accompanied by the packet, it entered the port and moored in the middle of the harbor.

At Wellington

The city of Wellington is built on the southwest point of North Island at the far side of a horseshoe-shaped bay. Well protected from the sea winds, it offers excellent moorings. The brig had been favored by the weather, but such was not always the case. It was often difficult to navigate in Cook Strait, which is crossed by currents whose speed sometimes reaches ten knots, even though the tides in the Pacific are never strong. The seafarer Tasman,[1] to whom is credited the first discovery of New Zealand in December 1642, ran great risks of running aground and then being attacked by the natives. Hence the name "Bay of the Massacre,"[2] which figures in the geographic nomenclature of the straits. The Dutch navigator lost four of his men who were devoured by cannibals on that shore, and, a hundred years later, the English navigator, James Cook, left in their hands the crew of one of the ships in his fleet, commanded by Captain Furneaux.[3] Finally, two years later, the French navigator Marion Dufresne[4] and sixteen of his men met their death in an attack of the most frightful savagery.

In 1840, in the month of March, Dumont d'Urville,[5] aboard *Astrolabe* and *Zélée,* passed by Otago Bay of the southern island and visited the Snare Islands and Stewart Island at the southern end of Tawaï-Pounamou. Then he sojourned in the port of Akaroa, where he had no need to complain about the natives. The memory of this illustrious explorer's passage is marked by the island that bears his name. Inhabited only by bands of penguins and albatrosses, it is separated from South Island by the "French Pass," where the sea is so treacherous that ships do not voluntarily enter into its channel.[6]

Today, under the authority of the British flag, at least as far as the Maoris are concerned, every security is assured in the latitudes of New Zealand. The dangers that were of human origin have been warded off. Only those in the sea continue, and even so, they are of a lesser sort, thanks to the hydrographic maps of the area and to the establishment of the gigantic lighthouse built on an isolated rock in front of the Nicholson Bay,[7] where Wellington is located.

It was in the month of January 1849 that the New Zealand Land Company sent the *Aurora* to establish settlers on the shores of these distant lands. The population of the two islands counts no less than eight hundred thousand inhabitants, and Wellington, the capital of the colony, is itself home to some thirty thousand.

The city is pleasantly situated, solidly constructed, and has broad streets that are properly maintained. Most of the houses are built of wood (for earthquakes are frequent in the southern province) as are the public structures, among others the governmental palace in the middle of its beautiful park and the cathedral, whose religious character does not exempt it from such earthly cataclysms.[8] This city, less important, less industrial, and less commercial than its two or three rivals in New Zealand, will equal them someday no doubt, given the drive and colonizing genius of Great Britain. In any case, with its University, its Legislative House composed of fifty-four members, among them four Maoris named by the governor, its House of Representatives coming directly from popular suffrage, its colleges, its schools, its museum, its productive factories for frozen meats, its model prison, its squares, and its public gardens, where electricity is going to replace gas, Wellington boasts an exceptional standard of living, which many cities in the Old and the New World might envy.

If the *James Cook* did not tie up at the dock, it was because Captain Gibson wanted to make it more difficult for the men to desert.[9] Gold fever exerted its influence here as it did in Dunedin or in the other New Zealand ports. Several ships found it impossible to cast off. Mr. Gibson wanted to take every precaution to maintain his crew at full strength, even those recruits from the *Three Magpies* whom he would willingly exchange for others. Besides, his stopover in Wellington would be of short duration, scarcely twenty-four hours.

The first people to receive him on his visit were Mr. Hawkins

Wellington (photo: J. Valentine & Sons, Dundee)

and Nat Gibson. The captain had been brought ashore as soon as he arrived in port, and eight bells were striking when he presented himself at Mr. Hawkins's office, situated at the far end of one of the streets that ran down to the port.

"Father!"

"My friend!"

Thus was Harry Gibson greeted when he entered the office. He had arrived before the departure of his son and Mr. Hawkins, who were getting ready to go down to the dock, as they did each morning, to see if the *James Cook* might not be finally sighted by the semaphore lookout.

The young man flung his arms around his father's neck, and the shipowner hugged the latter in his arms.

Mr. Hawkins,[10] now fifty years old, was a man of middle stature, graying hair, no beard, bright and friendly eyes, good health and constitution, very nimble, active, knowledgeable in commerce, and bold in business. It was known that his business in Hobart Town was very successful, and he could have retired already with his fortune made. But it would not have suited him, after such a busy career, to live in idleness. So, with the goal of developing his fleet, which included several other ships, he had come to Wellington to set up an office with an associate, Mr. Balfour. Nat Gibson would become the principal employee and profit-sharer as soon as the *James Cook* had completed its voyage.

Captain Gibson's son, then twenty-one years old, had a lively intelligence, a serious turn of mind, and a deep affection for his mother as well as for Mr. Hawkins. It is true, the latter and the captain were so closely attached in his filial devotion that Nat Gibson could hardly distinguish between them. Ardent, enthusiastic, a lover of beautiful things, Nat was an artist who also had some talent for business affairs. His height was greater than average, his eyes dark, his hair and beard chestnut, his gait elegant, his attitude composed, his countenance friendly. He made a good impression straight off, and he had only friends. On the other hand, there was no doubt but that he would become, with age, resolute and energetic. With a firmer temperament than his father, he took after his mother.

Mr. Hawkins and Captain Gibson

In his leisure time, Nat Gibson dabbled with great pleasure in photography,[11] this art that had made much progress thanks to the use of accelerating substances, which bring the snapshots to the utmost degree of perfection. His camera was always in his hand, and one can imagine how he had already made good use of it during this trip: picturesque sites, portraits of natives, photographs of all sorts.

During his stay in Wellington, he had shot a number of views of the city and its environs. Mr. Hawkins himself took an interest in it. They were both often seen setting off, with their camera supplies strapped bandolier-style across their bodies, and returning from their excursions with new riches for their collection.

After having presented the captain to Mr. Balfour, Mr. Hawkins returned to his office, with Mr. Gibson and his son following him. And there, at first, they talked about Hobart Town. News was not lacking, thanks to the regular service between Tasmania and New Zealand. Just the day before, a letter from Mrs. Hawkins had arrived, and the ones from Mrs. Gibson had been awaiting the arrival of the *James Cook* in Wellington for several days.

The captain read his correspondence. Everything was fine at home. The women were in good health. It is true, the absence seemed long to them, and it was their hope that it would not be prolonged. But the voyage should soon be drawing to a close.

"Yes," said Mr. Hawkins, "five or six weeks more and we'll be back in Hobart Town."

"Dear mother," Nat Gibson exclaimed, "how happy she will be to see us again, just as much as we were, Father, in embracing you!"

"And that I was, myself, my son!"

"My friend," said Mr. Hawkins, "I have every reason to believe that the voyage of the *James Cook* will be of short length."

"That's what I think too, Hawkins."

"Even at average speed," replied the shipowner, "the voyage from New Zealand to New Ireland[12] is fairly short."

"In this season especially," answered the captain. "The sea is calm all the way to the equator, and the winds are steady. I think as you do that we'll have no delays to put up with if our stopover in Port Praslin[13] doesn't have to be prolonged."

"That won't be the case, Gibson. I've received a letter from our correspondent, Mr. Zieger, that is very reassuring on this subject. In the archipelago, there is a large stock of merchandise of mother of pearl and copra, and loading the brig can be done without difficulty."

"Is Mr. Zieger ready to take delivery of our merchandise?" asked the captain.

"Yes, my friend, and I repeat, I have been assured that there will be no delay on his end."

"Don't forget, Hawkins, that after Port Praslin, we'll have to go to Kerawara."[14]

"That will be only a day, Gibson."

"Well, Father, let's be clear on the length of the voyage. How many days will our stopover at Port Praslin and Kerawara be?"

"About three weeks in all."

"And from Wellington to Port Praslin?"

"About the same."

"And the return to Tasmania?"

"About a month."

"So in two months and a half, it's possible that the *James Cook* will be back in Hobart Town."

"Yes. Rather less time than more."

"Good," Nat Gibson replied. "I'm going to write to my mother this very day, because the courier to Australia raises anchor the day after tomorrow. I will ask her for two and a half months of patience. That's how much Mrs. Hawkins will have to have too, isn't that right, Mr. Hawkins?"

"Yes, indeed, my young man."

"And at the beginning of the year, the two families will be reunited."

"Two families will be as one!" replied Mr. Hawkins.

The shipowner and the captain shook hands affectionately.

"My dear Gibson," Mr. Hawkins then said. "We'll have dinner here with Mr. Balfour."

"Of course, Hawkins."

"Do you have business to take care of downtown?"

"No," replied the captain, "but I must return on board."

"Fine, then on to the *James Cook!*" exclaimed Nat Gibson. "It will give me great pleasure to see our brig again before bringing up our bags."

"Oh!" replied Mr. Hawkins. "It's surely going to stay a few days in Wellington?"

"Twenty-four hours at most," replied the captain. "I have no breakdowns to fix, no cargo to take off or bring on . . . Some provisions to renew, for sure, and an afternoon will suffice for that. I'll give orders to Balt to take care of this."

"Are you still happy with your bosun?" asked Mr. Hawkins.

"Still am," Captain Gibson replied. "He's a zealous man who knows his job."

"And the crew?"

"Veteran sailors, nothing to fault them for."

"What about those you picked up in Dunedin?"

"They don't inspire much confidence, but I couldn't find any better."

"So the *James Cook* is leaving?"

"As of tomorrow, if we don't have any incidents like at Dunedin. Nowadays it's not too good for captains of commerce to make port in New Zealand."

"You're talking about desertions that diminish the crews?" asked Mr. Hawkins.

Mr. Gibson replied, "More than diminish; out of eight sailors, I have lost four and haven't heard a word from them."

"Well, you're right, Gibson, be careful that the situation doesn't get to be in Wellington what it was in Dunedin."

"So I have taken the precaution of not allowing anyone to disembark under any pretext, even Koa the cook."

"That's wise, father," added Nat Gibson. "There are a half-dozen ships in port that cannot set sail for lack of sailors."

"That doesn't surprise me," replied Harry Gibson. "So I'm counting on raising sail as soon as we have brought on the provisions, and surely by dawn we'll have weighed anchor and already be on our way."

At the very moment when the captain pronounced the name of the bosun, Mr. Hawkins had been unable to keep from making a rather pointed observation.

"If I spoke to you about Flig Balt," he continued, "it's because he didn't make a very favorable impression on me when we hired him on at Hobart Town."

"Yes, I know," replied the captain, "but your misgivings are not warranted. He carries out his duties with zeal, the men know they have to follow him, and, I'll say it again, his service aboard ship has left nothing to be desired."

"So much the better, Gibson. I prefer to have made a mistake about him, and so long as he inspires confidence in you . . ."

"Besides, Hawkins, when it's a question of making command decisions aboard the ship, I depend on myself alone; for the rest, as you know, I willingly leave that to my bosun. Since our departure, I have had nothing to reproach him for if he wants to get back on the brig for his next trip . . ."

"That's your business, after all, dear friend," replied Mr. Hawkins. "You're a better judge of what measures to take."

It was clear that the confidence that Flig Balt inspired in Harry Gibson, an ill-placed confidence, was total, so well had this treacherous rogue played his role. That's why, when Mr. Hawkins asked again if the captain was sure about the four seamen who had not deserted ship, the latter replied:

"Vin Mod, Hobbes, Wickley, and Burnes are good sailors," he replied, "and what they didn't do in Dunedin, they wouldn't attempt to do here."

"We'll settle up with them when we get back," declared the shipowner.

"So," continued the captain, "they're not the reason I forbade the crew to come ashore . . . it's because of the four recruits."

And Mr. Gibson explained under what conditions Len Cannon, Sexton, Kyle and Bryce had signed on, out of their haste to escape the Dunedin police, after a fight in the tavern of the *Three Magpies*.

"So this was the most practical thing to do?" asked the shipowner.

"Assuredly, my friend. You know how hard pressed I was by this delay of two weeks. I was at the point of wondering whether I might not have to wait months to fill out the crew! What do you expect? You take what you can find!"

"And we part company with them as soon as possible," replied Mr. Hawkins.

"Just as you say, Hawkins. That's even what I would have done here, in Wellington, if circumstances had allowed it, and that's what I'll do in Hobart Town."

"We have time to think about it, Father!" Nat Gibson observed. "The brig will stay several months laid up, won't it, Mr. Hawkins? And we will spend this time as a family until the day I return to Wellington."

"That will all be arranged, Nat," replied the shipowner.

Mr. Hawkins, Mr. Gibson, and his son left the office, went down to the dock, hailed one of the small boats employed by the port service, and were brought out to the brig.

It was the bosun who welcomed them on board, as obsequious as ever, always busy, and for whom Mr. Hawkins, reassured by the captain's declarations, saved his good greetings.

"I see you're in good health, Mr. Hawkins," Flig Balt said to him.

"In good health, I thank you," replied the shipowner.

The three sailors, Hobbes, Wickley and Burnes, who had sailed for some three years aboard the *James Cook* without having given any cause for complaint, received Mr. Hawkins's compliments.

As for Jim, the shipowner kissed him on both cheeks, and the young man felt a great joy in seeing him again.

"I have excellent news from your mother," Mr. Hawkins told him, "and she really hopes that the captain is satisfied with you."

"Entirely," declared Mr. Gibson.

"I thank you, Mr. Hawkins," said Jim, "and you make me very happy!"

"And me?" said Nat Gibson. "There's nothing for me?"

"Why, of course, Mr. Nat," replied Jim, throwing his arms around his neck.

"And what a nice healthy appearance you have!" added Nat. "If your mother saw you, she'd be content, the fine woman! Also, Jim, I'll take your photograph before leaving."

"It'll look like me?"

"Of course, if you don't move."

"I won't move, Mr. Nat, I won't move!"

It must be said that Mr. Hawkins, after having spoken to Hobbes, Wickley and Burnes about their families who lived in Hobart Town, addressed a few words to Vin Mod. The latter showed he was quite sensitive about this attention. It is true, the shipowner knew him less than his comrades, and it was his first trip on board the *James Cook*.

As for the recruits, Mr. Hawkins simply greeted them with a "Good day."

There is reason to admit that their demeanor did not make a better impression on him than on Mr. Gibson. They could have, however, with no trouble, been permitted to go ashore. They would not have had the idea of deserting after forty-eight hours of navigation, and they would certainly have returned before the departure of the brig. Vin Mod had worked them over well, and despite the presence of Mr. Hawkins and Nat Gibson, they were quite sure that some occasion would present itself to take over the ship. It would be a bit more difficult. But what is impossible to people who have no faith, no law, and are determined not to back down from any crime?

After an hour, during which Mr. Hawkins and Mr. Gibson examined the books of the trip, the captain announced that the brig would put to sea the next day at dawn. The shipowner and Nat Gibson would return that evening to take possession of their cabin, to which they had already sent their baggage.

However, before getting back to the dock, Mr. Gibson asked Flig Balt if he had no reason to return to land:

"No, Captain," replied the bosun. "I prefer to remain on board. It's wiser to keep an eye on the crew."

"You're right, Balt," said Mr. Gibson. "Anyway, the cook will have to go pick up the provisions."

"I'll send him, Captain, and if needed, two men with him."

All was agreed upon, and the dinghy that had brought the shipowner and his two companions brought them back to the dock. From there they returned to the office, where Mr. Balfour was waiting. He joined them for lunch.

During the meal, they discussed business. Up to now, the voyages of the *James Cook* had been among the most lucrative, and it was showing good profits.

The great coastline trade had, indeed, developed remarkably well in this part of the Pacific. Germany, having taken possession of the neighboring archipelagoes of New Guinea, had opened up new opportunities for trade.[15] It was not without reason that Mr. Hawkins had established relations with Mr. Zieger, his correspondent from New Ireland, now Neu-Mecklenburg. The office that he had founded in Wellington was meant especially to build these relations through the attention of Mr. Balfour and Nat Gibson, who would be installed next to him in a few months.

Lunch out of the way, Mr. Gibson wanted to take care of the provisions for the brig that the cook could pick up that afternoon: canned goods, fowl, pork, flour, dry beans, cheeses, beer, gin and sherry, coffee and spices of various sorts.

"Father, you can't leave until I've taken your picture!" declared Nat.

"Not again," called out the captain.

"There, old friend," Mr. Hawkins added, "we are both obsessed with the demon of photography, and we give people no rest until they pose in front of our lens. So you have to submit gracefully!"

"But I already have two or three portraits at home, in Hobart Town!"

"Fine, this'll make one more," replied Nat Gibson. "And since we leave tomorrow, Mr. Balfour will take charge of sending it to mother in the next mail."

"Agreed," Mr. Balfour said.

"See, Father," resumed the young man, "a portrait is like a fish! It has no value unless it's fresh! Just think, now you are ten months older than when you left Hobart Town, and I'm sure you don't look like your last photograph, the one over the fireplace of your room."

"Nat is right," confirmed Mr. Hawkins, laughing. "I barely recognized you this morning!"

"For heaven's sake!" Mr. Gibson exclaimed.

"No, I assure you! There's nothing that changes you more than ten months of navigation at sea!"

"Go ahead, my child," replied the captain, "here I am ready for the sacrifice."

"And what attitude are you going to take?" asked the shipowner in a pleasant tone. "That of the sailor departing or of the sailor arriving? Will it be the commander's posture, his arm extended toward the horizon, his hand holding the sextant or the telescope, or the pose of the master second only to God?"[16]

"Either one you want, Hawkins."

"And then, while you're posing in front of our camera, try to think of something! That gives more expression to your face! What will you be thinking about?"

"I'll be thinking of my dear wife," answered Mr. Gibson, "of my son . . . and of you . . . my friend."

"So, we'd have a magnificent print."

Nat Gibson owned one of those portable cameras, top of the line, that produce the negative in a few seconds. Mr. Gibson's photo was very successful, so it seems, according to what his son said when he had examined the negative, and the print would be left in the care of Mr. Balfour.[16]

Mr. Hawkins, the captain, and Nat then left the office in order to buy everything needed for a voyage of nine or ten weeks. Warehouses are not scarce in Wellington, and one can find diverse maritime supplies: foodstuffs, sea instruments, tackle, pulleys, ropes, spare sails, fishing equipment, barrels of grease and tar, caulking and carpenter's tools. But except for replacing a few ropes and chains, the needs of the brig were limited to that of food for the passengers and crew. This was quickly bought, paid for, then sent to the *James Cook,* as soon as the sailors Wickley and Hobbes and the head cook had arrived.

At the same time, Mr. Gibson completed the formalities that are obligatory for every ship upon entry and departure. Therefore, noth-

*New Zealand dug-out canoes**

*Facsimile of an illustration published in the *Great Voyages and Great Navigators* by Jules Verne (Hetzel's note).

Maoris (photo: J. Valentine & Sons, Dundee)

ing would prevent the brig from weighing anchor, more fortunate than several other ships of commerce whose crew desertions held them in port at Wellington.

During his trips across the city, in the midst of a very busy populace, Mr. Hawkins and his companions met a certain number of Maoris from the surrounding region.[17] Their numerical importance has diminished greatly in New Zealand, like Australians in Australia, and above all Tasmanians in Tasmania, since the last specimens of this latter race have practically disappeared.

They number today but some forty natives on the northern island and scarcely two thousand on the southern one. These Maoris keep busy mostly with market gardening, principally with the cultivation of fruit trees, whose products are very abundant and of excellent quality.

The men are a handsome sort and boast an energetic character and a constitution that is both robust and healthy. In comparison, the women seem inferior. In any case, one must get used to seeing this "weaker" sex walk the streets, pipe in mouth and smoking more than the "strong" sex. It is also not surprising that the exchange of civilities with Maori women is very difficult since, according to custom, it is not just a question of saying "hello" or of shaking hands, but of rubbing noses.

These natives are, so it seems, of Polynesian origin, and it is even possible that the first immigrants into New Zealand came from the archipelago of Tonga-Tabou,[18] which is situated some twelve hundred miles to the north.

There are, basically, two reasons that this population is decreasing rapidly and destined to disappear in the future. The first cause is illness, especially pulmonary phthisis, which wreaks great devastation among Maori families. The second, still more terrible, is drunkenness, and it is to be noted that Maori women are first in rank in this dreadful abuse of alcoholic liquors.

In addition, there is reason to believe that the Maoris' eating habits have been profoundly modified. Thanks to the missionaries, the influence of Christianity has become dominant. The natives were cannibalistic in days gone by,[19] and who would dare say that such

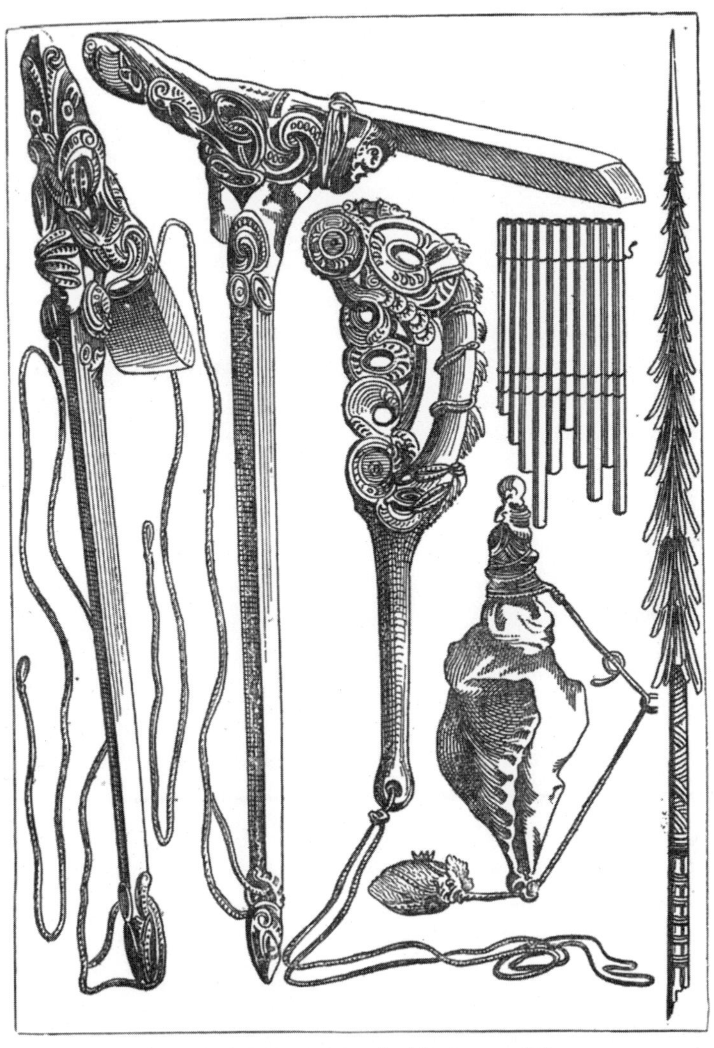

*Maori arms and musical instruments**

*Facsimile of an illustration published in the *Great Voyages and Great Navigators* by Jules Verne (Hetzel's note).

ultra-nitrogenous food did not suit their temperament? Be that as it may, it's better that they disappear rather than eat each other, "although," as a very observant tourist once said, "cannibalism never had but one goal, battle: devouring the eyes and heart of the enemy in order to become inspired by his courage and to acquire his wisdom!"

These Maoris resisted British invasion until 1875; it is at that time when the last Maori leader of the King Country region surrendered to the authority of Great Britain.

Around six o'clock, Mr. Hawkins, the captain, and Nat Gibson returned to the office for dinner. Then, after saying goodbye to Mr. Balfour, they had themselves brought to the brig, which would be ready to hoist anchor at the first glimmer of dawn.

A Few Days at Sea

It was six o'clock in the morning when the *James Cook* hoisted anchor and, with all sails set, began to get under way. The captain had to maneuver his way through the harbor and leave it through a narrow opening. After skirting Point Nicholson, thanks to much tacking, he found where the headwind was gusting and entered with the opposing wind blowing from the north. But when the ship reached Orokiva,[1] the sea breeze from the west allowed the captain to cross at close quarters the vast gulf along Ikana-Maoui's coast between Wellington and New Plymouth, beyond Cape Egmont.[2]

The *James Cook*, cutting diagonally across the bay, thus sailed away from land and would approach it again only at the latitude of the aforementioned Cape.

The distance to cover along the western shore of North Island was about a hundred miles. With a steady breeze it could be crossed in three days. Moreover, given the wind's direction, it would be impossible to remain in sight of the coast, whose hydrographic contours Harry Gibson knew perfectly. There would be no difficulty for the brig in maintaining its proper distance.

This first day went by under quite pleasant conditions. Mr. Hawkins and Nat Gibson, seated near their quarters, indulged themselves in the delightful sights and sounds that a ship at sea can provide. Leaning a bit under the wind, the brig rapidly cut through the long swells, leaving behind a frothy wake. The captain was walking back and forth, with quick glances at the binnacle facing the helmsman, and exchanging a few words with the passengers. Half the crew was forward on watch, the other half was resting in their quarters, after having received their morning rations. Several fishing lines had been cast off the stern and by lunchtime they would not be pulled in without bringing in some of the fish that were so numerous in these seas.

It is also well known that the localities around New Zealand are highly frequented by whales, which are hunted with great success. In this vast bay, a number of them appeared around the brig, and they easily could have been caught.

This led Mr. Hawkins to tell the captain as they watched these enormous mammals:

"I have always wanted to combine whaling with coastal trade, Gibson, and I believe the one would bring in as much profit as the other."

"It's possible," replied the captain, "and the whalers who reach these waters easily fill their hold with barrels of oil, fat, and whale bone."

"In Wellington they say," Nat Gibson observed, "that whales are easier to catch here than elsewhere."

"It's true," said the captain, "and that is based on the fact that they have less hearing ability than other species. So you can get within harpoon distance of them. By and large, any whale you catch sight of, you can catch, period. Well, unless bad weather takes over. Unfortunately, storms are just as numerous as they are fearsome in these seas."

"Agreed," Mr. Hawkins replied," someday we'll outfit for whaling . . ."

"With some other captain, then, my friend. Each has his own way, and I'm no whaler."

"With some other captain, fine, Gibson, and with some other ship too, for it takes a special outfitting that the *James Cook* wouldn't allow for."

"No doubt, Hawkins, a ship that can take on two thousand barrels of oil during some campaign that might last as much as two years, and longboats for pursuing the beasts, and a crew numbering as many as thirty or forty men, harpooners, coopers, blacksmiths, carpenters, sailors, apprentices, at least three officers and a doctor."

"Father," affirmed Nat Gibson, "Mr. Hawkins would not neglect anything that this type of outfitting requires."

"It's an expensive undertaking, my boy," answered the captain, "and in my opinion, in this part of the Pacific, coastal trade yields more dependable results. Some of these whaling expeditions have been ruinous. I might add that whales have sometimes been hunted out, so they tend to move toward the polar seas.[3] To find them, you have to go to the Bering Straits, the Kourile Islands,[4] or the Antarctic seas. These make for long and perilous trips, and more than one ship has never returned."

"After all, my dear Gibson," the shipowner said, "this is only an idea. We'll see about it later on. Let's just stick to coastal waters, since they have always turned out well, and then sail the brig back to Hobart Town with a good cargo in its hold."

Toward six o'clock in the evening, the *James Cook* crew came in sight of the coastline along the Waimah Bay and across from the small ports of Ohawe.[5] A few clouds appearing on the horizon made the captain decide to lower the topgallant sails and take reefs in the topsails. It is moreover a precaution taken by all ships sailing in this area, where the gusts of wind are as sudden as they are violent, and every night the crew pulls in the sails for fear of being surprised.

And, in fact, the brig was fairly well buffeted until dawn. It had to move out a few miles, having noticed the lights of Cape Egmont.[6] When day had come, the brig passed by the harbor of New Plymouth, one of the important cities of North Island.

The wind had grown during the night. It was now a stormy gale.

The crew was unable to use the topgallant sails, which had been tightened the day before, and Mr. Gibson had to be content to shake out the reefs from the topsail that had been drawn the night before. The brig was moving at a speed of twelve knots, leaning to starboard, rising slowly over the open sea. Sometimes the waves, striking its side, covered the bow with foam. The bow plunged so deep as to submerge the ship's figurehead, then immediately rose back up.

This pitching and rolling didn't worry Mr. Hawkins or Nat Gibson. Having many years of sailing experience, they were used to it. They breathed with gusto this air impregnated with the salty tang of the ocean, filling their lungs with it. At the same time, they took great pleasure in contemplating the infinitely varied sites along the western shore.

This shore is perhaps more curious than that of the southern island. Ikana-Maoui, meaning in Polynesian "The Maoui Fish," offers a greater number of creeks, bays, and harbors than Tawaï-Pounamou, a name that the natives give to the lake where green jade can be collected.[7] From a distance, one's view extends over the chain of mountains that are covered with green and where, in the past, volcanic eruptions had occurred. They constitute the skeleton or rather the backbone of the island whose average width is some thirty leagues. All in all, the surface of New Zealand is no less than that of the British Isles and resembles a second Great Britain owned by the United Kingdom in the antipodes of the Pacific. But if England is separated from Scotland only by the narrow stream of the Tweed, here it is a sea channel that separates North Island from South Island.[8]

From the time the *James Cook* had left the port of Wellington, the chances of the ship being successfully taken over had assuredly decreased. Flig Balt and Vin Mod often discussed this subject. And that day, at lunchtime, when Mr. Hawkins, Nat Gibson, and the captain were together in the officers' quarters, they discussed it once again. Vin Mod was at the helm, and they were not running any risk of being overheard by the sailors on duty up forward.

"Ah, that wretched packet . . . ," Vin Mod kept repeating. "That's what stopped our plan! For a whole day that confounded ship hung across our path. If its commander is ever sent up to the yardarm, I demand the right to haul on the rope that'll grip his throat! Couldn't he just have continued on his way instead of cruising along beside the brig? Without his interference, the *James Cook* would now be rid of the captain and his men! It would be sailing the eastern seas with a good cargo for the Tonga or the Fiji."[9]

"All that's . . . just words!" observed Flig Balt.

"We console each other the best we can!" Vin Mod replied.

"The question is to know," continued the bosun, "whether the presence on board of the shipowner and Gibson's son might oblige us to give up our plans."

"Never!" cried out Vin Mod. "Our companions won't ever listen to such a tune as that! Len Cannon and the others would have certainly figured out some way to slip into Wellington, if they had thought that the brig would just come back peacefully to Hobart Town! What they want is sailing for their own profit, and not for Mr. Hawkins's benefit."

"All that's . . . just words, I repeat," Flig Balt said, shrugging his shoulders. "Can we hope that the proper moment will turn up?"

"Well, of course," affirmed Vin Mod, angered at seeing the bosun's discouragement, "and we'll just have to take advantage of it. And if it's not today or tomorrow, then later on in the neighborhood of Papua[10] in the middle of those archipelagoes where the police hardly ever bother you. Let's suppose, for example . . . the shipowner and a few others, Gibson's son, two or three sailors don't show up some evening . . . We don't know what became of them . . . The brig continues on, right? . . ."

And Vin Mod, speaking in a low voice, whispered these criminal thoughts into Flig Balt's ear. Determined not to let him weaken, resolved to push him to the end, he could not restrain himself from uttering a powerful curse, when the bosun tossed out, for the third time, this less than encouraging reply:

"Words, words, nothing but words, all that."

Vin Mod shouted out another curse, which, this time, was heard as far as the officers' dining room. Mr. Gibson, having risen from the table, appeared at the after doorway.

"What's the trouble?" he asked.

"Nothing, Mr. Gibson," replied Flig Balt, "a sudden pitch that almost stretched Vin Mod out flat on the bridge . . ."

"I thought I was going to be tossed over the rail!" added the sailor.

"The wind is strong, the seas are unforgiving," said Mr. Gibson after having examined with a rapid glance the brig's sails.

"The breeze tends to pull to the east," observed Flig Balt.

"True. Pull closer in, Mod. No trouble about getting closer to land."

Then, that order being given and executed, he returned to his quarters.

"Ah!" murmured Vin Mod, "if you were in command of the *James Cook,* Master Balt, instead of letting the ship do the carrying, you'd let it luff."

"Sure . . . but I'm not the captain!" replied Flig Balt, heading toward the bow.

"He's going to be one, though," Vin Mod repeated to himself. "He has to be . . . should I be hanged!"

During the next day, they saw fewer whales than before, which would explain the scarcity of whalers in the area. It is rather along the eastern shore that crews try to catch them, toward Akaroa, and the bay surrounding the islands of Tawaï-Pounamou.[11] But the sea was not deserted. A certain number of coastal vessels were coming and going, sheltered by the land across and beyond the Bay of Taranaki.[12]

In the afternoon, still served by a strong breeze, having lost sight of the summit of Whare-Orino,[13] two thousand feet high and whose base rises out of the sea, the *James Cook* passed before the ports of Kawhia and Aotea, where a flotilla of fishing boats were heading in, unable to weather the open seas.[14]

Mr. Gibson had to reef in the topsails, while holding the foresail, the mainsail, the spanker, and the jibs. If the sea grew rougher, if the wind became a tempest, he would still have a refuge for the night, since around six o'clock in the evening the ship would be sheltered by Auckland.[15] So he preferred not to alter his route.

Supposing that the *James Cook* were required to seek shelter from the bad weather on the open sea, it would find it without difficulty in Auckland. The city occupies the back and north of a harbor that is one of the most reliable in this part of the Pacific. When a boat enters its narrow mouth between the Parera rocks and the "Manukan hafen,"[16] it finds itself inside a basin, protected on all sides. No need to reach the port. The basin suffices, and even entire fleets would find good mooring space there.

With such advantages for maritime commerce, it is not surprising that the city has rapidly achieved great importance. Including the outlying areas, it counts around sixty thousand inhabitants. Arranged in tiers on the slopes of the southern side of the bay, the city is quite varied in aspect. Superbly laid out with its squares and gardens, decorated with tropical flowers, its broad, clean streets, bordered with hotels and shops, this curious city, industrial and commercial, might be the envy of Dunedin and Wellington.

If Mr. Gibson had sought refuge in this port, he would have encountered a hundred ships coming and going. In this northern part of New Zealand, the attraction of gold mines was felt less than in the southern part of Ikana-Maoui and especially in the provinces of Tawaï-Pounamou. There, the brig could have rid itself—without much difficulty—of the recruits embarked in Dunedin and replaced them with four or five sailors chosen from among those dismissed from other ships. So little did he esteem Len Cannon and his comrades, the captain might well have made up his mind, much to the disgust of Flig Balt and Vin Mod, to cast anchor in Auckland. But to avoid further delay, he thought it best to remain under shortened sail during the night. Sometimes, even, he hove to and faced the waves from the west, only to pull away from the coast when lights seemed to close in on the starboard side.

In short, the *James Cook* behaved wondrously in the heavy winds, thanks to the capable hands on duty. It experienced no damage either in the hull or aloft.

The next day, November 2nd, under gentler gusts and a more manageable sea, the brig passed through an oblique wind at the opening of another harbor, more extensive than that of Auckland, the harbor of Kaipara,[17] at the back of which Port Albert[18] was founded.

Finally, twenty-four hours later, for the breeze had noticeably calmed, the heights of the Mannganni Bluffs, Hokianga Harbor, Beef Point, and Cape Van Diemen,[19] after a distance of seventy or eighty miles, also lay in their wake. They passed on their left the reefs of the Three Kings.[20] The sea then opened graciously before the bowsprit as far as the jumble of the archipelagoes of the Tongas, the Hebrides, and the Solomons,[21] which are located between the equator and the Tropic of Capricorn.

There was naught to do but set sail toward the northwest and New Guinea, still some nineteen hundred miles away, and to become acquainted with the Louisiades[22] and, beyond them, island groups that are today part of the German colonial domain.

If wind and sea remained favorable, Mr. Gibson counted on making that crossing without delay. Sailing up the equinoctial line, bad weather is less frequent, less dangerous than in the vicinity of Australia and New Zealand. On the other hand, it is true, a ship navigating by sail is exposed to calms that can slow it down for days, whereas ships powered by steam can provide swift and sure navigation. But that is quite costly, and when it is a question of long or short offshore trade, it's better to use sailcloth than spend for coal.[23]

However, the breeze, weak and intermittent, threatened to reduce the speed of a brig to two or three miles an hour. Yet he had all the equipment, right down to the staysail, the studding sail—every type of sail there was. But if a total calm arrived, without a breath that could wrinkle the surface of the water and where long ground swells rock a ship without moving it on its way, all of its sailing equipment would be of no use. Mr. Gibson could only be helped by currents that generally bear northward in this part of the Pacific.

However, the wind did not fall completely. A full sun seemed to make the sea simmer, as though it had been superheated in its lower layers. The upper sails swelled and the *James Cook* left a slight wake trailing behind.

And during the morning hours, as Mr. Hawkins, Nat Gibson, and the captain were talking about what it is so natural to discuss in the course of navigating—the weather of the moment and the weather to come—Mr. Gibson said:

"I don't think this will last . . ."

"Why's that?" asked the shipowner.

"I see on the horizon certain clouds that will soon bring us a wind . . . or I am sadly mistaken."

"But they are not rising, those clouds," Mr. Hawkins observed, "or if they are rising a bit, they're dissipating."

"No matter, old friend, they'll end up by taking on more substance, and clouds, that means wind."

"Which will be to our advantage," added Nat Gibson.

"Oh!" said the captain, "we don't need a breeze to triple-furl the sails. Just enough to fill the sails and round out the lower ones."

"And what does the barometer say?" asked Mr. Hawkins.

"A slight tendency to sink," replied Nat Gibson after consulting the instrument installed in the deckhouse.

"So let it go down," said the captain, "but slowly, not making leaps like a monkey climbing the coconut palm and then falling out of it . . . If calmness is boring, storms at sea are dreadful, and I believe that all in all . . ."

"I'll tell you what would be preferable, Gibson," interrupted Mr. Hawkins. "That would be having aboard ship a little auxiliary engine, fifteen to twenty horsepower, for instance. That would provide a means to make headway when there's no longer a breath of air at sea, at least to enter the ports and leave them."

"We've gotten along without so far, and we can still do it," replied the captain.

"It's just that you're still a sailor from long ago, the ancient mariner of commerce."

"Indeed, Hawkins, and I'm not in favor of those mixed ships! If they're well made for steam, they're badly constructed for sails, and vice versa."

"In any case, Father," said Nat Gibson, "there's some steam out there that it wouldn't be bad to have right now on this ship."

The young man pointed out a long, dark plume stretching out along the northwest horizon. It could not be confused with a cloud.

It was the smoke from a steamship traveling rapidly toward the brig. Within the hour both ships would be abeam of each other.

The meeting of ships is always an interesting event at sea. One tries to recognize the ship's nationality by the shape of the hull, the mast arrangement, while waiting for it to fly its own colors in a sign of greeting. Harry Gibson brought his spyglass to his eye, and some twenty minutes after the steamer had been seen, he believed he was able to say the ship was French.

He was not mistaken, and when the ship was just two miles from the *James Cook,* the tricolored flag[24] rose to the peak of its mizzenmast.

The brig answered immediately by flying the flag of the United Kingdom.

This steamer of some eight or nine hundred tons was probably a coaler headed for one of the ports of New Holland.

Toward eleven thirty, it was a couple of cable lengths from the brig, and it approached closer as though it were intending to "study" them. Moreover, a very calm sea would favor the maneuver, and presented no risk. Aboard the ship there were no preparations for lowering a tender, and the questions and answers were exchanged by means of a megaphone, which was the usual way.

And this is what was said between the steamer and the brig, in English:

"The name of your ship?"

"The *James Cook* out of Hobart Town."

"Captain?"

"Captain Gibson, and you?"

"The *Assumption,* out of Nantes. Captain Foucault."[25]

"You're heading?"

"To Sydney, Australia."

"Understood."

"And you? . . ."

"To Port Praslin, New Ireland."

"And you're from Auckland? . . ."

"No, Wellington."

"I see."

"Good voyage to you, Captain Foucault!"

"And you?"

"From Ambon in the Moluccas."[26]

"Good sailing? . . ."

"Fine. One piece of information. At Ambon they are very anxious about the schooner *Wilhelmina*,[27] out of Rotterdam, which is a month overdue, coming from Auckland. Have you any news of it?"

"None."

"I've come up from the west, across the Coral Sea," declared Captain Foucault, "and we've not sighted her. Are you expecting to head east for New Ireland?"

"That's where we intend on going."

"It's possible that the *Wilhelmina* has been disabled in some storm."

"Possible, all right."

"We ask you to kindly keep an eye out for her while crossing these seas . . ."

"We'll keep an eye out."

"Very good. Have a good voyage, Captain Gibson."

"And good voyage to you, Captain Foucault!"

An hour later, the *James Cook* had lost sight of the steamer and was sailing up the coast toward the northwest, heading for Norfolk Island.[28]

In Sight of Norfolk Island

A nearly perfect quadrilateral island on three sides, its fourth side features a rounded coastline that rises and modifies its regularity by jutting toward the northwest. At its four corners are Point Howe, Northeast Point, Point Blackbourne, and Rocky Point. More unusual, there is a peak, Mount Pitt, which rises some eleven hundred feet above the sea. Such is the geometrical layout of Norfolk

Island,[1] situated in this area of the Pacific at 29 degrees 02 south latitude and 105 degrees 42 east longitude.[2]

This island has but six leagues of perimeter, and like most of the islands in this vast ocean, it is surrounded by a coral ring that protects it as a wall defends a city. The swells of the deep sea will never gnaw away its base of yellow chalk that a light surf would be enough to destroy, since the waves of the open sea crush each other against the coral reef before reaching it. So ships can reach it only with difficulty, slipping in between narrow and dangerous passes, exposed to all the surprises of currents and eddies. As for a so-called port, none exists in Norfolk. It is only on its southern shore, in the bay of Sydney, that penitentiaries were established. By its isolated location and by the difficulty of landing or leaving, it seems indeed that nature had destined this island to be nothing but a prison.

It is appropriate to mention also that in the south, toward Nepean Island and Philips Island, which complete the small Norfolk group, these coral reefs stretch out as much as six or seven leagues from the shore.

However, despite its restricted dimensions, it is a rich parcel of Great Britain's colonial domain. When Cook discovered it in 1774, he was first struck by its admirable vegetation growing in that climate, both gentle and warm, of the tropics. It might have been considered a basket taken directly from the flora of New Zealand, ornamented as it was with identical plants. A flax of superior quality grew there, the "phormium tenax,"[3] and a species of pine of great beauty belonging to the genus of araucarias. Then, as far as the eye could see, verdant plains stretched out where wild sorrel and fennel grew. Already, at the beginning of the century, the British government had transported a colony of convicts to the island. Thanks to the work of these unfortunates, patches of forest were cleared, agricultural labors were undertaken, and the resulting corn crop became such that bushels were counted by the thousands. It was a sort of granary of abundance there, placed between Australia and New Zealand. But too many reefs and shoals occupied the approaches to the island, preventing one from taking advantage of these harvests in any practical way.

The port of Auckland (from E.-E. Morris, L'Australasie pittoresque*)*

So, the establishment of a penitentiary there, in the presence of these obstacles, had to be abandoned after this first attempt. It is true that this island could very easily hold under an iron yoke the most hardened criminals of Tasmania and New Wales. So the penal colony was later reorganized. It then held as many as five hundred convicts watched over by one hundred and eighty soldiers, and an administration of five hundred employees. A public farm was developed, and the corn harvest assured their food supply in grain.

Moreover, the island of Norfolk was uninhabited at the time when the great navigator Cook established its geographic location. No native, Maori or Malaysian, had been attracted to it despite the richness of the soil. It never had any population other than those condemned by the British government. It was deserted at the time of its discovery, and deserted it became afterward. In 1842, for the second, and no doubt the last, time, England abandoned the penitentiary establishment, which was transported to Port Arthur,[4] on the south coast of Tasmania.

Four days after having glimpsed the last vestiges of New Zealand, the *James Cook* sighted Norfolk Island. With a modest wind, it had gone eighty miles during the second day, a hundred and twenty during day three, as many again on day four, and, the breeze having dropped, only seventy on the fifth day. So toward evening, it had covered the distance of roughly four hundred miles that separates the two islands.

That afternoon, the watch pointed out a mountain that towered in the northeast. It was the peak of Mount Pitt, and by five o'clock the ship was located off the northeast point of Norfolk Island.

In the course of his navigation, Mr. Gibson had had this section of the Pacific carefully surveyed. No wreckage of a ship had been encountered along the route of the *James Cook,* and the mystery of the Dutch ship's disappearance still remained to be solved.

As the sun set behind the peaks of the island, the wind fell and the sea took on a milky appearance, the waves disappearing from its surface, scarcely rolling from the long swell. Surely, the next day the brig would still be in sight of the island. It was but two miles away, and, being cautious, the captain avoided any nearer approach, for the coral banks stretched dangerously out into the sea. Besides, the *James Cook* was practically as motionless as if it had been anchored. No current stirred it; the sails hung from the yardarms in heavy folds. If the breeze came up, all they would have to do was to let them fall to get under way.

So Mr. Gibson and his passengers had only to enjoy this magnificent evening under a cloudless sky.

After dinner, Mr. Hawkins, the captain, and Nat Gibson came aft to sit down.

"Here we are in flat calm," said Mr. Gibson, "and, unfortunately, I can discover nothing that might indicate the breeze returning."

"Well, that won't last long, in my opinion," observed Mr. Hawkins.

"Why not?" the captain asked.

"Because we're not in full warm season, Gibson, and the Pacific does not have the reputation of justifying its name, which was given to it a bit in jest."

"I agree, old friend. Yet, even during this season, ships remain becalmed several days. That could happen to the *James Cook,* and I wouldn't really be surprised."

"Very fortunately," replied the shipowner, "we're not in the days when Norfolk Island contained a population of bandits. Then it would not have been wise to anchor nearby."

"You're right. We would've had to be on guard."

"In my childhood," continued Mr. Hawkins, "I heard about those criminals that no system of correction at any prison had been able to discipline, and so the government decided to transport the whole colony to Norfolk Island."

"They were no doubt well guarded, on the one hand," Nat Gibson said, "and, on the other, how could they escape from an island that no ship dared approach?"

"Well guarded, yes, they certainly were, young man," replied Mr. Hawkins. "A difficult flight, indeed! But, for criminals who don't retreat before anything when it's a question of recovering their freedom, everything is possible, even what seems not to be."

"Were there frequent escapes, Mr. Hawkins?"

"Yes, Nat, and even incredible ones! Either convicts managed to get hold of some government boat, or they secretly made one with strips of bark, and they didn't hesitate to try to escape."

"Having ninety chances out of a hundred of dying," declared Captain Gibson.

"No doubt," Mr. Hawkins replied. "And, when they met some ship like ours in the island's waters, they jumped aboard in no time and rid themselves of the crew. Then they'd go off plundering through the Polynesian archipelagoes, where it wouldn't be easy to track them down."

"Well, there's nothing more to fear now," affirmed Captain Gibson.

One might rightly notice that everything Mr. Hawkins had just said, and which was true, coincided with the plans formed by Flig Balt and Vin Mod. Although they were not locked up in Norfolk Island, they had the criminal instincts of convicts; they only asked to do what convicts would have done in their place, changing the honest brig of the Hawkins firm, in Hobart Town, into a ship of pirates, and then to exercise their brigandage throughout the central regions of the Pacific Ocean, where it would be hard to catch them.

So, if the *James Cook* had nothing to fear at the moment as they approached Norfolk Island since the prison had been transferred to Port Arthur, it was no less threatened by the presence of Dunedin recruits, resolved to carry out the plans of Vin Mod and the bosun.

"Well then," Nat Gibson said, "there's no danger. Father, would you allow me to take out the dinghy?"

"What do you want to do?"

"Go fishing at the foot of the rocks. We've still got two hours of daylight. It's the right time, and I'll keep in sight of the brig."

It was no trouble to grant the young man's request. Two sailors and he would be able to string their lines straight down by the coral banks. These waters were teeming with fish, and they would not return without making a good catch.

Besides, Mr. Gibson thought he should drop anchor there. The current bearing rather to the southeast, he sent down the anchor with thirty-five fathoms of chain to a sandy bottom.

After readying the dinghy, Hobbes and Wickley got ready to accompany Nat Gibson. They were, as we know, two trusted sailors the captain was proud of.

"Hop to it, Nat," he said to his son, "but don't stay out until dark."

"That I can promise, Father."

"And bring us something good to fry up for tomorrow's lunch," added Mr. Hawkins, "and also a bit of wind if there is any left on shore!"

The dinghy was filled, and with the vigorous pull on the oars it had soon crossed the two miles separating the brig from the first coral banks.

Their fishing lines were dropped. Nat Gibson had not needed to toss his grapnel on the reef. No current, not even surf. The dinghy remained motionless once the oars were pulled in.

On the island side, the sandbanks stretched about a half mile. As a consequence, less than in the south toward Philip Island and although the coast was no longer lit by the sun which was hidden by the mass of Mount Pitt, one could still distinguish the details of the island's topography: narrow banks among the rocks of yellowish limestone, closed creeks, rocky points, numerous streams flowing toward the sea, thousands of them crossing through the heavy forests and the verdant plains of the island. This entire coastline was deserted. Not a cabin among the trees, no smoke rising from the foliage, not one canoe beached upside down or pulled up on the sand.

The movement of life was not lacking, however, in the region between the crests of the sandbanks and the land. But it was due uniquely to the presence of aquatic birds, which filled the air with their discordant cries, crows with whitish down, coucals in green plumage, kingfishers whose body is aquamarine, starlings with ruby eyes, the flycatcher, without mentioning the frigate birds that swiftly flew by.

If Nat Gibson had brought along his gun, he could have taken some good shots at them—shots that would've been purely wasted, it's true, for they are inedible. It would be better, in preparing for the next meal, to ask of the sea what the air could not give, and all in all the sea would show itself to be quite generous.

After an hour at the edge of the banks, the dinghy was ready to bring back enough food for the crew for a couple of days. The fish were numerous in this clear water, prickly with marine plants, under which swarmed crustaceans, mollusks, shellfish, lobsters, crabs, shrimp, snails, and barnacles—whose numbers were clearly inexhaustible since the amphibians, seals and the like consumed them in vast quantities.[5]

Among the fish that struck the lines and that represented an enormous variety of species rivaling each other by splendor and color, Nat Gibson and the two sailors brought back several pairs of blennies. The blenny, a bizarre animal, has eyes open on the top of his head, practically no jaw, and is linen gray in color. It lives in the water, runs along the shore, and leaps on the rocks with kangaroo-like movements.

It was seven o'clock. The sun had just gone down, and its last purple gleam was flickering out on the peak of Mount Pitt.

"Mr. Nat," Wickley said, "isn't it time to return on board?"

"That would be wise," added Hobbes. "Sometimes an evening breeze rises, coming off the land, and if the brig can take advantage of it, we mustn't keep it waiting."

"Pull in the lines," said the young man. "Let's go back to the *James Cook*. But I rather doubt we can bring the wind Mr. Hawkins asked me about."

"No," Hobbes declared. "There's not enough wind to fill a beret!"

"Out at sea, there's not a single cloud," added Wickley.

"Let's head back," ordered Nat Gibson.

But before leaving the bank, he stood up in the stern of the dinghy and cast a glance along the edge of all the reefs that circled the northeast point. The disappearance of the schooner that had not been heard from came back to his mind. Would he not perceive some debris of the *Wilhelmina,* some remnant that the currents might have borne toward the island? Wasn't it possible that the hull of the boat, not having been entirely demolished, some part of the carcass would still be visible north or south of the point?

So the two sailors looked up and down the coast for a distance of several miles. It was a vain effort. They saw no remains of the schooner described by the steamer.

Wickley and Hobbes were about to pick up the oars, when, on one of the rocks, separated from the shore, Nat Gibson thought he could make out a human form. As he was a mile or so away, and at a moment when dusk was beginning to obscure the horizon, he wondered if he had made a mistake. Was it a man, attracted to the shore by the arrival of the dinghy? Was the man not waving his arms to call attention for help? It was almost impossible to say.

"Look!" said Nat Gibson to the two sailors.

Wickley and Hobbes looked as directed. At that instant, with darkness invading that part of the shore, the human form, if there had been a human form, disappeared.

"I saw nothing . . . ," Wickley said.

"Nor did I," declared Hobbes.

"Yet," replied Nat Gibson, "I'm quite sure I didn't make a mistake. A man was there a moment ago."

"You think you saw a man?" Wickley asked.

"Yes . . . There . . . on the top of that rock, and he was gesturing . . . Perhaps he called out . . . but his voice wouldn't reach us here."

"Sometimes you can see seals on these shores, at sundown," observed Hobbes, "and when one of them stands up, he can be mistaken for a man."

"I agree," replied Nat Gibson, "and at this distance, it's possible that I didn't see clearly enough . . ."

"Is Norfolk Island inhabited now?" Hobbes asked.

"No," replied the young man. "There are no natives there. However, some shipwrecked men might have been forced to seek shelter here."

"And if there are any shipwrecked people," added Wickley, "do you think they might be from the *Wilhelmina?* . . ."

"Let's go back to the brig," ordered Nat Gibson. "It's likely that the brig will still be in this same place tomorrow, and with our spyglass we'll search all along the shore, which will be in full sun by daybreak."

"Look!" said Nat Gibson to the two sailors.

The two sailors leaned on their oars. In twenty minutes, the dinghy had reached the *James Cook*. Then the captain, still distrusting part of his crew, was careful to have the dinghy replaced in its cradle.

The fish were graciously accepted by Mr. Hawkins, and, as he was interested in natural history, he could study his blennies, which he had never before held in his hands.

Nat Gibson told his father about what he thought he had seen when he was in the dinghy by the coral reefs.

The captain and the shipowner paid strict attention to what the young man had to say. They knew full well that, since the abandonment of the island as a place of detention, it had to be deserted. The natives of the neighboring archipelagoes, Australians, Maoris, or Papouas, never had the thought of settling down there.

"It's possible, nevertheless, that fishermen might be in the neighborhood," Flig Balt remarked, for he was taking part in the conversation.

"Indeed," responded the shipowner, "that would not be surprising at this time of year."

"Did you see any craft inside the reef?" the captain asked his son.

"None, Father."

"Well, I think," said the bosun, "that Mr. Nat might have made a mistake. Dusk had already fallen. So, in my opinion, Captain, if the wind comes up tonight we would be wise to pull anchor."

One can understand that. Flig Balt, already quite vexed by the presence of Mr. Hawkins and Nat Gibson on board the brig, feared nothing as much as taking on new passengers. Under these conditions he would be obliged to give up his plan—which he didn't intend to do. His accomplices and he were formally resolved to take over the ship before arriving at New Ireland.

"However," continued the captain, "if Nat has not made a mistake, if there are shipwrecked men on this side of Norfolk—and why wouldn't they be from the *Wilhelmina?*—we have to help them. I would be wanting in my duties as a man and as a sailor if I set sail without being sure."

"You're right, Gibson," approved Mr. Hawkins. "But I'm thinking, that man that Nat thought he saw, might he not be some convict escaped from the penitentiary and remaining on the island?"

"Well, that man would be very old now," answered the captain, "for the evacuation dates from 1842, and if he were already in prison by then, since we are in 1885, he'd be more than a septuagenarian now!"

"That's true, Gibson, but I'll still prefer the idea that people shipwrecked in the Dutch schooner might have been cast up onto Norfolk, if Nat has not made a mistake."

"No, I don't think so!" the young man confirmed.

"Then," Mr. Hawkins said, "those poor folks would have been there some two weeks, for the shipwreck probably did not occur earlier than that."

"Right, according to what the captain of the *Assumption* told us," answered Mr. Gibson. "So tomorrow, let's do everything we can, all that we have to do. Yes, as Nat believes, if a man is on that side of the coast, he'll stay till daylight to observe the brig, and, despite the distance, we'll make him out with our field glasses."

"But, Captain," insisted the bosun, "I repeat, perhaps a wind, a favorable wind will rise tonight . . ."

"Whether it rises or not, Balt, the *James Cook* will remain at anchor, and we shall not sail without having sent out a reconnaissance boat. I will not leave Norfolk Island until we've inspected the area around Northeast Point, even if we must spend a whole day at it."

"Good, Father, and I'm convinced that it will not be time wasted . . ."

"Isn't that your opinion, Hawkins?" the captain asked, turning toward the shipowner.

"Absolutely," responded Mr. Hawkins.

And, indeed, it would be inappropriate to congratulate Mr. Gibson too much on his resolution. Acting like that, was he not fulfilling a basic humanitarian duty?

When Flig Balt reached the forequarters, he told Vin Mod what had just been said and just been decided. The sailor was no more pleased than the bosun. After all, perhaps Nat Gibson was mistaken

. . . It's even possible none of those shipwrecked on the *Wilhelmina* had sought refuge on that shore . . . The question would be resolved in some twelve hours.

Night arrived, a fairly dark night, a night with a new moon. A curtain of high fog veiled the constellations. Nevertheless, the land was visible, dimly, in the west, a rather somber mass at the edge of the horizon.

Toward nine o'clock a light breeze caused the sea to wash against the *James Cook,* which turned the ninety degrees on its anchor chain. This breeze would have facilitated their navigating north, for it blew from the southwest. But the captain did not change his mind, and the brig remained at its mooring.

Besides, they were only intermittent puffs that skimmed the peak of Mount Pitt. The sea soon fell back to a calm.

Mr. Hawkins, Mr. Gibson, and his son were seated aft. They were not in a hurry to return to their rooms; they breathed deeply of the fresh evening air after the warmth of the day.

Now, it was twenty-five minutes past nine when Nat Gibson, getting to his feet and looking toward land, took a few steps to port.

"A fire! There's a fire!" he said.

"A fire?" repeated the shipowner.

"Yes, Mr. Hawkins."

"And in what direction?"

"Toward the rock where I saw that man . . ."

"That's right," declared the captain.

"You see? I wasn't mistaken," Nat Gibson cried out.

A fire was burning in that direction, a wood fire that sent up good-sized flames in the middle of a thick swirling smoke.

"Gibson," affirmed Mr. Hawkins, "it's surely a signal for us."

"No doubt about it!" responded the captain. "There are shipwrecked people on the island."

Shipwrecked or whatever, human beings were surely asking for help, and how anxious they must have been, what fear they must have felt that the brig had already raised anchor! They had to reassure them, which was done in an instant.

"Nat," he said, "take your gun and answer his signal."

The young man returned to his quarters and came out with a rifle.

Three shots were then heard, and the shore sent their echoes back to the *James Cook*.

At the same time, one of the sailors waved a lantern three times,[6] and it was hoisted to the top of the mizzenmast.

There was nothing further to do but await the return of dawn, and the *James Cook* would set out to make contact with this coast of Norfolk Island.

The Two Brothers

At daybreak, a dense fog covered the western horizon. The rocky shore of Norfolk Island could barely be distinguished. No doubt those mists would soon dissipate. The peak of Mount Pitt rose above the fog and was already bathed in the sun's rays.

Moreover, the shipwrecked men were probably not worried. Although the brig was no doubt invisible to them, had they not heard during the night its signals in response to their own? The boat could not have left its mooring, and in an hour its launch would be sent to shore.

Before lowering the launch, however, Mr. Gibson preferred to wait, and with good reason, for the outcropping of land to emerge from the mist. That was where the fire had been lit, and that is where the abandoned men who called upon the *James Cook* for help would be found. Obviously they did not possess even a dugout canoe, for otherwise they would already have come aboard.

The breeze from the southeast was beginning to stiffen. A few clouds, reclining on the line between sea and sky, indicated that the wind would freshen during the morning. Without the reason that held him to his anchor, Mr. Gibson would have given orders to set sail.

A little before seven o'clock, the foot of the coral reef, along which foamed a whitish surf, stood out under the fog. Curls of vapor rolled by, and the outcropping of land emerged.

Nat Gibson, on top of the officer's quarters, his spyglass to his eye, ran it up and down the shore. He was the first to cry out:

"He's there . . . or rather, they are there!"

"Several men?" asked the shipowner.

"Two, Mr. Hawkins."

The latter took the spyglass in his turn:

"Yes," he said, "and they're signaling to us, shaking a piece of canvas on the end of a stick!"

The spyglass passed into the captain's hands, who confirmed the presence of two individuals standing on the boulders at the very end of the promontory. The fog, dissolved by this time, permitted them to see the men, even with the naked eye. That there were two as Nat Gibson had believed he saw the evening before, there could no longer be any doubt.

"Lower the launch!" commanded the captain.

And at the same time, by his order, Flig Balt hoisted the British flag to the top of the spanker in response to the signals.

If Mr. Gibson had said to prepare the big dinghy for launch, it was in case there was need of taking on more than two people. It was possible, indeed, that other castaways had taken shelter on the island, especially if they belonged to the crew of the *Wilhelmina*. There was even reason to hope that all had reached that shore after having abandoned the schooner.

The craft settled into the water; the captain and his son took their places in it, the former at the helm. Four sailors sat at the oars. Vin Mod was among them, and just as he was slipping over the gunwale he had made a gesture to the bosun that indicated his irritation.

The launch headed for the coral reef. The day before, while fishing along the reef, Nat Gibson had noticed a narrow opening that permitted passage through it. There would only be a distance of seven or eight cable lengths from there to the point.

In less than a half hour the craft reached the opening. They noticed the last puffs of smoke from the remains of the fire that had been kept up all night and beside which the two men were standing.

From the bow of the craft, Vin Mod turned around impatiently to see them, so much so that he interfered with the movement of the oars.

"Watch out you don't go for a swim, Mod!" the captain called out to him. "You'll have time to satisfy your curiosity when we land."

"Yeah, the time!" muttered the sailor, who, out of rage, would have broken his oar.

The channel wound through the coral banks that would have been dangerous to approach. Those sharp ridges, as cutting as steel, would have wreaked havoc on the hull of their craft. So Mr. Gibson ordered the sailors to slow their pace. There was no difficulty, anyway, in reaching the outermost point of the promontory. The water, responding to the breeze from the sea, pushed the craft forward. A fair surf was foaming at the base of the rocks.

The captain and his son watched the two men. Hand in hand, unmoving, silent, they made no gesture, nor did they call out. When the craft turned to round the point, Vin Mod could see them easily.

One was perhaps thirty-five years old, the other a bit younger. Dressed in tatters, head bare, nothing suggested they were mariners. About the same size, they resembled each other enough to be taken for brothers, blond hair, unkempt beards. In any case, they were not Polynesian natives.

And then, even before they could disembark, when the captain and his son were still seated on the rear thwart, the older advanced to the end of the point and in English, but with an accent, cried out: "Thank you for coming to our rescue . . . Thank you!"

"Who are you?" asked Mr. Gibson as soon as they had pulled up on shore.

"Two Hollanders."

"Shipwrecked?"

"Yes, shipwrecked from the schooner *Wilhelmina*."

"Are you the only survivors?"

"The only ones, or at least after the wreck the only ones who reached this coast . . ."

"Thank you for coming to our rescue!"

From the hesitant tones of these last words, it was clear that the man did not know whether he had found refuge on a continent or an island.

The grapnel was tossed ashore and when one of the sailors had set it in a hollow between the rocks, Mr. Gibson and his companions disembarked.

"Where are we?" asked the older man.

"On Norfolk Island," replied the captain.

"Norfolk Island," repeated the younger.

The shipwrecked men then understood where they were, on an isolated island in that section of the western Pacific. They alone were here, moreover, of all those passengers and crew that the Dutch schooner had aboard.

On the question of knowing what had happened to the *Wilhelmina,* if it had gone down with all hands, they could not give a definite answer to what Mr. Gibson was asking. As for the cause of the wreck, this is what they said:

Two weeks before, the schooner had been hit during the night—it must have been four or five miles east of Norfolk Island.

"Leaving our cabin," the older of the two said, "we were dragged into a whirlwind. The night was dark and foggy . . . We caught hold of a chicken coop that was passing within our reach . . . Three hours later the current brought us to the coral reef, and we reached the island by swimming . . ."

"So," asked Mr. Gibson, "you've been on the island for two weeks?"

"Two weeks."

"And you didn't meet anyone here?"

"No one."

"And," added the younger man, "we are fairly sure there is no other human being on this island, or at least this part of the shore is uninhabited."

"It didn't occur to you to search out the interior?" asked Nat Gibson.

"Yes," replied the elder, "but it would have been necessary to venture into deep forests, at the risk of becoming lost, and we might not have found anything to eat there."

"And then," said the other, "what would we have gained, since you just told us we were on a desert island? It was better not to abandon the shore. That would have meant giving up any chance of being seen, or saved, as we have been."

"You were right."

"And your brig . . . What is it?" asked the younger man.

"The English brig, *James Cook*."

"And its captain?"

"Myself," responded Mr. Gibson.

"Well, Captain," the older man said, shaking Mr. Gibson's hand, "you can see that we were right in waiting for you on this promontory!"

Indeed, to go around the base of Mount Pitt, or even reach its peak, the shipwrecked men, experiencing insurmountable difficulties, would have perished from exhaustion and fatigue in the middle of the impassible forests of the interior.

"But how have you managed to survive in these conditions of privation?" asked Mr. Gibson.

"Our food consisted mainly of vegetation," responded the older brother, "some roots here and there, cabbage palms cut from the tops of trees, wild sorrel, milkweed, sea fennel, pine cones of the araucaria. If we had had any line we could have caught fish, for they are numerous among the rocks."

"And fire? . . . ," Nat Gibson asked, "How did you make it?"

"For the first days," replied the younger, "we had to get along without it. No matches, or rather wet matches and quite useless. By good luck, while climbing toward the mountain behind us we found a volcanic fissure, still emitting some flames. Some layers of sulfur were around it, so we managed to cook our roots and vegetables."

"So that's how you've been living for two weeks?"

"That's it, Captain. But I must admit, our strength was ebbing and we were desperate, when coming back yesterday from the fissure I noticed a ship anchored two miles from the coast."

“The wind had given out,” said Mr. Gibson, “and since the current threatened to bear us southeast, I felt obliged to drop anchor.”

“It was already late,” said the elder. “There was scarcely an hour of daylight left and we were still more than half a league in the interior. After running as fast as possible toward the promontory, we noticed a dinghy setting off to join the brig . . . I called . . . With gestures I signaled for help . . .”

“I was in that dinghy,” Nat Gibson said, “and it seemed to me that I saw a man—just one—on that rock, at the moment dusk was moving in.”

“That was me,” said the elder. “I had arrived before my brother . . . and what disappointment I felt when the dinghy moved off without my being noticed! We thought that the last chance of salvation was slipping away! A little breeze came up. Wouldn’t the brig move on during the night? The next day wouldn’t it be far out on the high sea again?”

“Poor fellows!” murmured Mr. Gibson.

“The shore was plunged into darkness. We could see nothing of the ship. The hours slipped by . . . It was then that we thought of lighting a fire on the promontory. Dried grasses, dry wood, we brought it by the armfuls and some hot coals from the fire that we kept alive on this shore. Soon we had a good fire going. If the ship was still at its mooring, the fire would surely be seen by the men on watch . . . Oh! what a joy when about ten o’clock we heard those three shots fired! Then a lantern was burning at the top of the brig’s mast . . . They had seen us! We were sure now that the ship would wait until daybreak before leaving, and we would be rescued after dawn . . . But it was in time, Captain, yes! Your arrival was in time, and, as I said when you first came ashore, thank you . . . thank you . . .”

The shipwrecked men seemed near the end of their tether. Insufficient food, exhaustion, complete misery under the tatters that scarcely covered them . . . One could readily understand that they were anxious to be aboard the *James Cook*.

“Come aboard,” said Mr. Gibson. “You need food and clothing. Then we’ll see what we can do for you.”

The survivors of the *Wilhelmina* had no need to return to shore. Their rescuers would furnish them every need. They would not have to set foot on the island again!

As soon as Mr. Gibson, his son, and the two brothers had seated themselves in the stern, the grapnel was taken in and the craft started back through the channel.

Mr. Gibson had observed, in listening to the way they expressed themselves, that these two men were of a class well above that from which sailors are generally recruited. However, he had wanted to wait until they were in the presence of Mr. Hawkins to learn of their situation.

For his part and to his bitter displeasure, Vin Mod had also recognized that the rescued men did not represent run-of-the-mill seamen like Len Cannon and his comrades from Dunedin, or even those adventurers whom one encounters all too frequently in this part of the Pacific.

The two brothers were not at all part of the schooner's crew. They were passengers, then, and probably the only ones who got out of that sinking ship safe and sound. So Vin Mod returned even more irritated by the thought that his plans would not be carried out.

The craft came alongside. Mr. Gibson, his son, and the shipwreck victims climbed to the bridge. The latter two were presented to Mr. Hawkins, who did not conceal his emotions on seeing what a miserable state they were in.

After shaking hands, he said:

"You're welcome here, my friends."

The two brothers, no less impressed, were about to throw themselves at his knees, but he stopped them.

"No," he said, "no . . . we are most happy . . ."

A good-hearted man, he was at a loss for words, and he could only second the words of Nat Gibson, who called out:

"Let's eat. Let's give them something to eat. They're dying of hunger!"

The two brothers were led to the mess, where their first meal was served, and there they could catch up after two weeks of privation and suffering.

Then Mr. Gibson put at their disposal one of the side cabins, where some clothes, selected from the crew's spare garments, were set out. Then, once cleaned and dressed, they returned aft and in the presence of Mr. Hawkins, of the captain and his son, they recounted their story.

These men were Dutch, originally from Groningen. Their names were Karl and Pieter Kip.[1] The elder brother, an officer in the Netherlands merchant marine, had made a number of crossings as lieutenant, then second in command of commercial ships. Pieter, the younger, was associated with an office in Ambon, on one of the Molucca Islands of Indonesia,[2] an affiliate of the Kip Company of Groningen.

This firm carried out wholesale and semi-wholesale commerce in the archipelago, which belongs to Holland, and more specifically in the trade of nutmegs and cloves, very abundant in this Spice Island colony. If the above-named company did not count among the most important of the city, at least its head enjoyed an excellent reputation in the commercial world.

Mr. Kip Senior, widower for several years, had died five months before. This was a serious loss for the business, and efforts were made to prevent a liquidation that would have been carried out under unfavorable conditions. It was especially necessary for the two brothers to return to Groningen.

Karl Kip was thirty-five years old.[3] A good sailor, about to be appointed captain, he was awaiting his promotion and would not be long in obtaining it. Perhaps of a less acute intelligence than his brother, or less of a businessman, less appropriate for directing a commercial firm, he exceeded him in resolve as well as in strength and physical endurance. His greatest disappointment stemmed from the fact that the Kip Company's financial situation did not permit him to own a ship. Karl Kip would have liked to run his own business of long-distance navigation and trade. But it would have been impossible to divert any funds from the commercial side of the firm, and the elder son's desire had never been fulfilled.

Karl and Pieter were united in a bond of friendship that no discord had ever diminished, even more deeply linked by affection than by blood.[4] Between the siblings, there was no ill feeling, no cloud of jealousy or rivalry. Each remained in his own sphere. The one had his long-range voyages, the emotions and dangers of the sea. The other had his work at the Ambon office and his connection with Groningen. Their family sufficed for them. Neither had ever sought to create a second one, creating new bonds that might have separated them. It was already more than enough that the father was in Holland, Karl navigating at sea, Pieter in the Moluccas. As for the latter, intelligent, having a commercial acumen, he dedicated himself entirely to the business. His associate, also Dutch, applied himself to developing their enterprise. He was confident about increasing the growth of the Kip Company, sparing neither his time nor his zeal.

When Mr. Kip passed away, Karl was in the port of Ambon, aboard a Dutch three-master from Rotterdam, on which he was serving as second in command. The two brothers were grievously stricken by this blow, which deprived them of a father for whom they had a deep affection. And they had not been there to hear his last words, his last sigh!

The two brothers then made this resolution: Pieter would leave the Ambon association and would return to Groningen to direct his father's business.

But at this time the three-master, *Maximus,* on which Karl Kip had come to the Moluccas—already old and in poor repair—was declared unfit for the return home. Severely damaged by foul weather during its crossing from Holland, it could only be demolished. So its captain, its officers, and its sailors were to be repatriated to Europe under the charge of the Hopper firm, of Rotterdam, to which it belonged.

Now this repatriation would require, no doubt, a fairly long stopover in Ambon if the crew had to wait for some ship bound for Europe, and the two brothers were in haste to return to Groningen.

So Karl and Pieter Kip decided to take passage on the first boat leaving, either from Ambon, or from Ceram, or from Ternate, other islands in the Moluccan archipelago.

At that time the three-masted schooner *Wilhelmina* arrived from

Rotterdam, but it had only a short stopover. It was a ship of some five hundred tons, which was going to return to its home post, stopping at Wellington, from where its commander, Captain Roebok,[5] would set sail to reach the Atlantic by rounding Cape Horn.

If the position of the second in command had not been filled, there was no doubt that Karl Kip might have obtained it. But the crew was complete, and not one of the *Maximus* sailors could be hired. Karl Kip, not wishing to miss a chance, reserved a passenger cabin on the *Wilhelmina*.

The three-master put out to sea September 23rd. Its crew included the captain, Mr. Roebok; the second in command, Stourn; two bosuns; and ten sailors, all Dutch by nationality.

The navigation was quite smooth on the stretch across the Arafura Sea,[6] so narrowly squeezed in between the northern coast of Australia, the south coast of New Guinea, and the group of Sula Islands,[7] to the west, which protect it from the heavy swell of the Indian Ocean. To the east, it offers no way out but the Torres Strait, terminated by Cape York.[8]

After entering this strait, the ship encountered headwinds, which stalled it for a few days. It was not until October 6th that it managed to wind its way through the numerous reefs and enter the Coral Sea.[9]

Facing the *Wilhelmina* lay the vast Pacific as far as Cape Horn, which they would pass after a stopover in Wellington, New Zealand. The route was long, but the Kip brothers had no choice.

On the night of the 19th and 20th of October, all was going well on board, with sailors on watch in the forward part of the ship, when a dreadful accident occurred that the most vigilant watch could not have avoided.

Heavy, dark fog enveloped the sea, absolutely calm, as it almost always is during these atmospheric conditions.

The *Wilhelmina* carried the standard lights, green on the starboard, red on the port side. But unfortunately they would not have been seen through that thick fog, even at a distance of half a cable.

Suddenly, without any siren being heard, without any lantern being seen, the three-master was struck on the windward side at the height of the crew's quarters. The frightful shock immediately toppled the mainmast and the mizzenmast.

At the moment when Karl and Pieter Kip rushed from the poop deck, they glimpsed only an enormous mass vomiting smoke and steam, which passed like a bomb after having cut the *Wilhelmina* in half.

For a half a second a white flame had appeared at the mainstay of the ship. It was a steamer, but that was all they were to know about it.

The *Wilhelmina,* bow on one side, stern on the other, sank immediately. The two passengers did not have time to rejoin the crew. They could scarcely see a few sailors tangled among the ropes. To use the lifeboats was impossible, for they were submerged. As for the second in command and the captain, no doubt they had been unable to leave their cabins.

The two brothers, half dressed, were already in the water up to their waists. They felt the remains of the *Wilhelmina* being sucked down into the sea and being dragged into the vortex that swirled about the ship.

"Let's not get separated!" shouted Pieter.

"Count on me!" replied Karl.

Both were good swimmers. But was there any land nearby? What was the three-master's position at the moment of collision in this part of the Pacific between Australia and New Zealand, below New Caledonia, which was observed toward the east forty-eight hours before, in the last ship's log entry of Captain Roebok?

It goes without saying that the colliding steamer was probably far away already, unless it had stopped after the shock. If they had put lifeboats to sea, how, in the middle of a fog, would they find the survivors of this catastrophe?

Karl and Pieter thought they were lost. A profound darkness enveloped the sea. No whistle of machinery or siren indicated the presence of a ship, nor the howl that escaping steam would have emitted if it had remained in the area where the accident occurred. Not a single piece of wreckage was within reach of the two brothers.

For half an hour they tried to support each other, the older brother encouraging the younger, lending him the support of his arm when the younger grew weaker. But the moment approached when both would be at the end of their resources, and after one last clasp, one ultimate good-bye, they would slip down into the abyss . . .

It was around three in the morning when Karl Kip managed to seize an object floating near him. It was one of the chicken cages from the *Wilhelmina*.[10] They both grabbed onto it.

Dawn finally pierced the yellowish banks of fog. The mist was not long in rising and a clapping of little waves began as the breeze blew harder.

Karl Kip turned his eye toward the horizon.

To the east, an empty sea. In the west there was a fairly high slope of land—that is what he was finally able to see.

That shore was less than three miles away. The current and the wind were going in that direction. There was every hope of reaching it, if the swell of the sea did not grow too strong.

Whatever type of land it was, island or continent, this coast assured the shipwrecked men a means of salvation.

The shore, stretching out to the west, was dominated by a peak, which the first rays of sunlight gilded at the very top.

"There! . . . There!" Karl Kip cried out.

There, indeed, for at sea they would have searched in vain for a sail or lanterns of a ship. No vestige of the *Wilhelmina* remained. It had been lost, with all hands and all cargo. Nor was there any sight of the fateful steamer, which, more fortunate no doubt in having survived the collision, was now out of sight.

Lifting himself up a bit, Karl Kip could perceive no debris of the hull or of the masts. The only surviving evidence was the chicken cage that they were clinging to.

Exhausted and stiff, Pieter would have slipped into the deep if his brother had not kept his head above water. Vigorously now, Karl swam on, pushing the cage toward a barely perceptible reef, where the surf whitened its irregular line.

This first fringe of the coral ring stretched out from the coast. It took a full hour to reach it. With the swell that swept them along, it would have been difficult to gain a footing. The shipwrecked men slipped through a narrow channel, and it was a little more than seven o'clock when they managed to pull themselves onto the outcropping of land where the dinghy from the *James Cook* had just rescued them.

It was on that unknown, uninhabited island that the two brothers, barely clad, with no tools, no instruments, no utensils, were going to spend fifteen days of a most miserable existence.

Such was the tale that Pieter Kip recounted, while his brother, listening in silence, confirmed it only with a nod.

It was now known why the *Wilhelmina,* long awaited in Wellington, would never arrive, and why the French ship *Assumption* had not found a wreck along its way. The three-master lay in the depths of the sea, unless the currents had brought some debris further north.

The shipwrecked brothers' story produced an impression that was completely in their favor; naturally no one would have dreamed of doubting its truth. They spoke English with a facility that testified to a formal education and an appropriate upbringing. Their attitude was not at all like those of so many adventurers swarming over this region, and one could feel in Pieter Kip especially an unshakable confidence in God.[11]

So Mr. Hawkins did not hide his positive feelings toward them.

"My friends," he said, "you are on the *James Cook* now, and you will stay here."

"My deepest thanks, sir," replied Pieter Kip.

"But it won't get you back to Europe," added the shipowner.

"No matter," responded Karl Kip. "We have finally left this Norfolk Island where we were without resources, and we can scarcely ask for more."

"Wherever we disembark," added Pieter Kip, "we will find a way to get back to Holland."

"And I will help you reach your goal," Mr. Gibson said.

"What is the destination of the *James Cook?*" Karl Kip asked.

"Port Praslin in New Ireland," replied the captain.

"And it will stay there?"

"About three weeks."

"Then it's coming back to New Zealand?"

"No, to Tasmania . . . Hobart Town, its home port."

"Well, Captain," declared Karl Kip, "it will be just as easy for us to get passage from a ship at Hobart Town, as at Auckland or Wellington."

"Of course," Mr. Hawkins affirmed, "and if you get on a steamer going back to Europe by the Suez Canal, your return will be much more rapid."

"That would be preferable," replied Karl Kip.

"In any case, Mr. Hawkins and you, Captain," said Pieter Kip, "since you are willing to accept us as passengers . . ."

"Not as passengers, but as guests," said Mr. Hawkins, "and we are glad to offer you the hospitality of the *James Cook!*"

Handshakes were once again exchanged. Then the two brothers retired to their cabin to get some rest, for they had been awake all night near their fire on the point.

The slight breeze that had dispelled the fog was beginning to freshen. Calm weather seemed to be at an end, and the seas were turning a greenish hue southeast of the isle. It was advisable to take advantage of it. Mr. Gibson gave the order to hoist anchor. The sails, which had been hanging from their brails, were set for tacking. They hoisted anchor with the capstan, and the brig, setting out to sea, turned toward the north-northwest.

Two hours later, the highest peak of Norfolk Island had disappeared, and the *James Cook* steered toward the northeast, heading for the land of New Caledonia on the edge of the Coral Sea.

8 The Coral Sea

About fourteen hundred miles separate Norfolk Island from New Ireland. After completing five hundred, the first land that the *James Cook* would sight would be the French possession of New

Caledonia, which also includes the little group of Loyalty Islands to the east.[1]

If the wind and the sea favored the progress of the brig, five days would be enough for the first part of the crossing, and about ten days for the second.

Life aboard ship followed its habitual regularity. One watch duty succeeded another, with the monotony of clear-weather navigation, which is not without charm. Sailors or passengers find interest in the slightest incident at sea—a ship en route, a flock of birds flying among the ship's tackle, a group of whales playing in the ship's wake.

Most often the Kip brothers, seated aft in the company of Mr. Hawkins, engaged in long conversations in which the captain and his son mingled quite willingly. They could not hide their concern about the situation of the Groningen firm in Holland. How urgent it was for Pieter Kip to take charge of his business again, a business that might already be compromised! Neither brother hid their apprehensions when they discussed this subject with the shipowner.

Mr. Hawkins continued to answer with words of encouragement. The two brothers would no doubt find some credit. Liquidation, if it had to come to that, would probably take place under better conditions than they could have hoped for. But the worries of Karl and Pieter Kip were only too justified by the delay that the shipwreck of the *Wilhelmina* had imposed upon them.

Not to be forgotten was the impression Karl and Pieter had produced in the mind of Vin Mod. There was no way to count on their assistance to serve his plans—that seemed obvious. The shipwrecked brothers were far from being adventurers without remorse or scruples. Superior to the class from which sailors are generally recruited, they made by their presence on board any plan of revolt quite out of the question.[2]

So one can easily imagine what remarks Flig Balt and Vin Mod exchanged during their next conversation, in which Len Cannon took part.

The bosun's opinion was that, if forced to decide, the Kip brothers would doubtlessly take sides with the shipowner and the captain.

Yet Len Cannon, judging others according to himself, did not appear to be of that mind:

"Do you really know who those Dutchmen are?" he declared. "Have we seen their papers? No, isn't that so, and why should we just take their word for it? And since they lost everything that they possessed in their shipwreck, they would have everything to gain! I've known more than one who looked respectable but who didn't hesitate when it was a question of some bold blow."

"Are you the one who will feel them out?" asked Flig Balt, shrugging his shoulders.

"Me, no, not at all," replied Len Cannon. "Sailors never have the chance of being in contact with the passengers . . . and since they are passengers, those Kips!"

"Len is right," Vin Mod affirmed, "neither he nor I could walk in that direction."

"So, I'd be the one?" demanded the bosun.

"No, not you, Flig Balt."

"Well who, then?"

"The new captain of the *James Cook*."

"How's that, the new captain?" the bosun asked.

"What do you mean by that, Mod?" added Len Cannon.

"I mean," replied Vin Mod, "one has to be at least a captain to be able to talk with those fine Kip gentlemen. And then it would take—insofar as it won't be . . ."

"Well, what then?" Flig Balt exclaimed, impatient with all this reticence.

"It'll take," repeated Vin Mod, "some circumstance, yes, I keep coming back to my idea. A supposition. Suppose that Mr. Gibson falls into the sea, during the night, an accident. Who would take over the ship? Obviously, Master Balt.[3] The shipowner and the kid don't know anything about the sea, and so, rather than taking the brig to Port Praslin, and especially not to Hobart Town . . . well, who knows?"

Then, without otherwise insisting, and not wishing to renounce again the original plan, the sailor added:

"Really, we've had too much bad luck! First, it's that packet that crosses our path, then Mr. Hawkins and Nat Gibson who come aboard at Wellington! Third, those two Dutchmen who are passengers aboard ship! Four extra men. Just as many as we picked up at Dunedin in the tavern of the *Three Magpies!* Good men, those. So that's the way it is now, eight against the six of us, and I wish them eight lengths of rope!"

Flig Balt was listening even more than he talked. No doubt that this perspective of commanding the ship might be of a nature to tempt him. To provoke an accident that would cause Mr. Gibson to disappear—that would be better than starting a fight with the passengers of the *James Cook* and half its crew.

But Len Cannon replied that six resolute men could take over eight who were not on their guard, if they were surprised before they had the time to realize what was happening. It would be enough at first to rid themselves of two, any two, to make the party even . . . and he ended with these words:

"We must take action tomorrow night. Let Balt give the word, I'll warn the others, and tomorrow the brig will be out to sea."

"Well, Balt, what's your answer?" Vin Mod asked.

The bosun remained silent before this formal request.

"So, is it agreed?" Len Cannon went on.

At this moment, Mr. Gibson, who was in the stern, called Flig Balt. The latter went to rejoin him.

"He doesn't want to go along?" Len Cannon asked of Vin Mod.

"Oh, he will," replied the sailor, "if not the next night, at least when the right occasion presents itself."

"And if it doesn't present itself?"

"We'll make it happen, Cannon!"

"Well," declared the sailor, "I hope it happens before we reach New Ireland! My comrades and I, we didn't come aboard this brig to sail under the orders of Captain Gibson. And I warn you, Mod, if it all doesn't happen by then, we'll take off at Port Praslin."

"That's understood, Len."

"You must understand, Mod . . . We're not the ones who'll take the *James Cook* to Hobart Town, where we would have nothing to do but hang around!"

Basically, Vin Mod was worried about Flig Balt's hesitations. He knew his cautious nature led him to be more cunning than daring. And he understood that some day he would have to force him to commit in a way that he could not back out of. But he also understood that all chances of success were on Balt's side, and he invariably returned to the idea of seeing the command of the brig pass into the hands of the bosun. For the present, he promised to hold back Len Cannon, whose impatience could compromise the affair.

The sailing continued under excellent conditions. There were favorable winds rising to quite strong during the day though calming down in the evening. The nights were so beautiful and refreshing after the daily warmth, which kept increasing as the brig approached the Tropic of Capricorn. So Mr. Hawkins, Mr. Gibson and son, Karl and Pieter Kip, chatting and smoking, prolonged their evening gatherings and even remained on the bridge until the first glimmers of dawn. Most of the sailors, even if they were not on watch, preferred the open air to the stifling temperature of their quarters. Under these conditions it would have been impossible to surprise Hobbes, Burnes, and Wickley. In an instant, all three would have been on the defensive.

The Tropic was reached on the afternoon of November 7th. Almost immediately they could glimpse the Isle of Pines and the highlands of New Caledonia.[4]

The great island Balade[5]—such was its native name—is no less than two hundred miles in length from southeast to northwest and twenty-five to thirty in width. Its dependents are made up of the islands of Pines, Beaupré, Botany, and Hohohana, and to its east, the islands of the Loyalty group, of which the southernmost is the island Britannia.[6]

It is known that this neo-Caledonian archipelago belongs to the French colonial empire. It is a place of deportation, where those condemned for crimes of common law reside in great numbers. Although numerous escapes are attempted, it is not easy to leave this penitentiary of the Antipodes. To succeed, one must be aided from the outside by some ship chartered for this purpose, as has been done occasionally for the benefit of political prisoners. But in all

*New Caledonians**

*Facsimile of an illustration published in the *Great Voyages and Great Navigators* by Jules Verne (Hetzel's note).

cases, when the fugitives, lacking other means, must rejoin a ship by swimming, they are exposed to the teeth of huge sharks, which are teeming among the reefs.

Moreover, except for the port of Noumea, the capital of the island, it is almost impossible to approach this archipelago, surrounded by vast coral reefs against which the ocean swells crash with fury.

The *James Cook,* sailing toward the north, followed the coast. At the distance of three or four miles, one could see the whole topography of the island: the hills along the shore were so barren and dry that one might be tempted to conclude that it was infertile. And, in 1774, Captain Cook was at first quite deceived when he discovered these new islands, of which the French admiral, D'Entrecasteaux, later completed a hydrographic survey in 1792 and 1793.[7]

It is of small importance, however. The neo-Caledonian population, estimated at sixty thousand inhabitants, can count on its continued existence just from the products of its soil, which is very rich: yams, sugar cane, taro, hibiscus, pines in abundance, banana trees, orange trees, coconut palms, bread, fig and ginger trees. The interior of the island also has deep forests, with trees that reach prodigious dimensions.

During the ninth day, Mr. Hawkins, Nat Gibson, and the two brothers were able to observe beyond the coast that high chain of mountains which forms the backbone of the island.[8]

Dotted with streams, it is dominated by several peaks: Mount Kogt, Mount Nu, Mount Arago, and the Homedebua, whose height exceeds fifteen hundred meters. When night came, all that could be seen were the fires of the Canaques[9] camped along the creeks, which eventually went out.

Flig Balt, Vin Mod, Len Cannon, and his comrades, they too observed that island, but in a different frame of mind. Could they forget that it enclosed several hundred condemned prisoners, of whom they would have willingly introduced a half dozen more on board?

"There are," repeated Vin Mod, "a lot of worthy people there who could ask for nothing better than getting a good ship for running the Pacific! If only a few had the idea of fleeing tonight, if their ship ran into the brig, if they leaped onto the bridge without asking the permission of either Mr. Hawkins or the captain, we would have gotten along well with them."

"No doubt," replied Len Cannon, "but that won't happen."

And it didn't happen, either. Moreover, should the occasion arise, unless they were taken by surprise, fugitives from Noumea would not have been as welcome as shipwrecked men of the *Wilhelmina*. An honest ship does not aid in the escape of criminals!

The following day, the eighth, the northern part of New Caledonia was still visible. The last reefs that extend for some hundred leagues toward the north were left behind that afternoon. And the *James Cook* cruised across the Coral Sea with all sails set.

In ten days with a fine wind, the brig would cross the distance of nine hundred miles that separates New Caledonia from New Ireland.

This Coral Sea is perhaps, according to navigators, one of the most dangerous on the globe. On a stretch of two degrees latitude, above and under the surface, it is bristling with madreporite reefs, studded with banks of coral, crisscrossed with irregular and ill-known currents. Numerous are the ships that were lost there, with all hands and cargo. It would be appropriate to have it marked with beacons as found in certain bays in America or Europe. During the night of June 10, 1770, despite the advantage of a good wind and a bright moon, even the illustrious Captain Cook almost shipwrecked there.

One had to hope that Mr. Gibson would not put them in peril. The hull of his brig would not be opened on any of those coral snags, and, as the English navigator had done, he would not be reduced to passing a sail under the keel to clog a leak. To avoid this fate, night and day, the crew had to pay the closest attention in order to avoid the reefs. Luckily, during this era, thanks to several hydrographic studies that had been conducted with precision, one could now rely on ship's maps. What's more, Mr. Henry Gibson was not on his first voyage across the Coral Sea, and he understood its dangers.

Karl Kip himself had already frequented these difficult regions, whether on his ship that had been searching in the east the entry to the straits of Torrès, or while leaving the seas of Alfouras during his cruises in the extreme west. Close surveillance would clearly be the order of the day aboard the brig.

All in all, the weather favored the crossing of the *James Cook,* and it sailed rapidly under the constant breeze of the Pacific without obliging the men to maneuver.

These regions are, in general, seldom visited. To rejoin the seas of Europe, the merchant marine greatly diminished its distance returning from the Philippines, from the Moluccas, from the Sunda Islands, and from Indochina by going through the Indian Ocean, the Suez Canal, and the Mediterranean. Unless their destination is the ports of western America, the steamers do not venture at all on the Coral Sea. It is scarcely frequented except by sailing ships, which prefer the route around Cape Horn to that of the Cape of Good Hope, or by those which, like the *James Cook,* carry on offshore coastal trade between Australia, New Zealand, and the northern archipelagoes. It is therefore quite rare to see a sail on the horizon. As a result, it often becomes a quite monotonous navigation to which, if not the crews who are not interested in distraction, then at least the passengers must resign themselves, and for whom these crossings can seem interminable.

In the afternoon of November 9th, Nat Gibson on the forward rail called the captain, who had just come out of his quarters, and pointed out to him a sort of blackish mass, two miles to port.

"Father," he said, "could that be a reef?"

"I don't think so," replied Mr. Gibson. "I took our position at noon, I'm sure it's right."

"No reef is indicated on the map?"

"Not a one, Nat."

"But something is there . . ."

After having examined the mass with his spyglass, the captain responded:

"I'm not sure about it . . ."

The two brothers had just joined them as well as Mr. Hawkins.

They looked attentively at that irregular mass, which it would have been impossible to mistake for a coral bank.

"No," Karl Kip said after peering through the telescope, "it's definitely not a reef."

"It seems to be floating, for it rises with the waves," said Mr. Hawkins.

And, indeed, the object in question was not immobile on the surface of the sea; it was rising and falling with the swell.

"And besides," said Karl Kip, " you can't see any surf at its edge . . ."

"You might even say it was adrift," remarked Nat Gibson.

The captain cried out to Hobbes who was at the helm:

"Come into the wind a bit, so we get closer . . ."

"Aye, Captain," answered the sailor, giving the helm a turn.

Ten minutes later the brig had approached enough for Karl Kip to say:

"That's a wreck!"

"Yes . . . a wreck," affirmed Mr. Gibson.

No doubt, it was the hull of a ship floating across the *James Cook*'s course.

Mr. Hawkins asked, "Might that be the remains of the *Wilhelmina?*"

Nothing was impossible, indeed. Twenty days after the collision, there was no reason to be astonished that the debris of the three-master might have floated into this area.

"Captain," said Pieter Kip, "please allow us to investigate that wreck. If it comes from the *Wilhelmina,* we might find some objects . . ."

"And," added Mr. Hawkins, "who knows, if there are any victims, there might yet be time to save them!"

There was no need to insist further. An order was given to come into the wind a little more, so they could heave to about three cable lengths from the wreck.

The sails trimmed, its royal flapping already, the brig moved forward for a few minutes.

And then Karl Kip cried out:

"Yes . . . It's the *Wilhelmina!* The debris of her after-quarters and her poop deck . . ."

Flig Balt and Vin Mod, close to each other, were speaking in low tones.

"That's all we need . . . to take aboard one or two more!"

The bosun simply replied with a shrug of his shoulders. That there were shipwrecked people under that hull was highly unlikely.

And in fact, no one appeared. If there had been one or more men, short of being half dead or suffering, they would have showed themselves, they would have signaled to the brig a long while ago . . . and . . . no one.

"Drop the launch!" ordered Mr. Gibson, turning to Flig Balt.

The boat was immediately lowered from the davits. Three sailors on their thwarts took up their oars. Vin Mod, Wickley, Hobbes. Nat Gibson embarked with the two brothers, and Karl Kip took over the helm.

It was certainly the after-quarters of the *Wilhelmina,* of which the poop deck had almost entirely survived following the collision. The foresection was missing, having likely sunk under the weight of its cargo, unless the current had borne it elsewhere. The cabin boy, Jim, sent to the top of the mainmast, shouted down that he could see no other wreckage on the sea's surface.

On the rear nameplate, still intact, could be read these two names: *Wilhelmina—Rotterdam.*

The launch came alongside. The poop deck, leaning sharply to its port side, was floating above that part of the hold reserved for the food storage, which was totally immersed. Of the mizzenmast, which crossed the wardroom, there remained only a section two or three feet high, broken off at the height of the cleats, from which the tatters of a few halyards were still hanging. The boom was completely pulled off in the collision.

Moreover, it would be easy to penetrate into the poop deck. Its door had been staved in, and the swell of the waves was rolling about inside.

The sea did not wash completely across the wreck.

All they needed to do was to set foot on the wreck and to check out the cabins of the wardroom, among others that of the two brothers.

As for the quarters of the captain and the first mate, who occupied the forward part of the poop deck, they were entirely demolished.

Karl Kip brought the launch alongside the wreck, to make it possible to disembark, and Vin Mod wound a line around one of the uprights of the starboard rail.

The sea, rather calm at this time, did not wash completely across the wreck, but flowed back and forth at the end of the bridge. At times, the pitching uncovered the hold, emptied of all it once contained.

Karl and Pieter Kip, Nat Gibson and Vin Mod, leaving the launch in the care of the sailors, stepped into the wardroom.

The first thing they wanted to be sure of was whether there were any survivors of the *Wilhelmina*. Wasn't it possible for some men on the crew to have found refuge on the poop deck, just as the other part of the ship was engulfed?

But no one, dead or alive, could be found on the wreck. The captain and the first mate, were they able to get out of their cabins? No doubt they would never find out whether the forepart of the ship had remained on the surface of the sea with parts of the crew quarters. It was quite probable that the *James Cook* had encountered all that was left of the *Wilhelmina*.

It was easy to imagine what the violence of the shock had been when the two ships had crashed into each other. The steamer, going at full speed in the fog, had sliced through the hull of the three-master like a bullet, perhaps without having experienced any grave injury that would have prevented it from continuing on its way. Had it been able to stop, put its lifeboats to sea, pick up a few castaways?

The two brothers, Nat Gibson and Vin Mod, with water up to their knees, inspected the wardroom.

In their cabin Karl and Pieter Kip found a few, mostly damaged items: clothes, linens, some toilet articles, and two pairs of shoes. The bunks still contained their bedding, which was removed and brought to the lifeboat.

It would have been fortunate if the two brothers could have put their hands on their papers, especially those dealing with the Ambon office and the firm in Groningen. The disappearance of the papers was something that could hamper the settling of their affairs. But there was no trace, and the sea, entering the cabin, had carried out its work of destruction. That was likewise the case of some thousand piastres belonging to Pieter Kip, which had also disappeared—the little chest where they were located, under the lower berth, having been crushed in the collision.

"Nothing . . . nothing . . ." Pieter Kip said.

While they were checking the wardroom, it is not surprising that Vin Mod, urged on by his pillaging instincts, continued to rummage in all corners of the wreck. Without being noticed, he entered the Kip brothers' cabin.

There, under the cabin's lower berth where the drawer was still open, he found an object that had escaped the searching eyes of Karl and Pieter Kip.

It was a dagger of Malaysian make, one of those saw-toothed krisses,[10] which had slipped down in the interstice between two planks in the deck that had been separated. This weapon, fairly common among the natives of the Pacific, was of no great worth, but might have served to fill out the trophy case of an amateur collector.

Had Vin Mod been thinking about appropriating that weapon for himself? In any case, he grabbed the kriss and secretly stuffed it under his jacket, with the intention of hiding it in his bag as soon as he returned on board.

One can rest assured that if, instead of that discovered weapon, he had found Pieter Kip's thousand piastres, he would have had no scruples about taking them as well.

There was nothing more to remove from the shipwreck. The brothers' belongings, clothing, linens, bedding, were moved to the dinghy. Besides, it wouldn't be long before the wreckage would break completely apart. The deck of the mess room, waterlogged, was giving way beneath their feet. With the first bad weather, only shapeless debris would be floating on the surface of the sea.

The *James Cook* had been brought abeam of the wreck, and the current was beginning to carry the latter off. The breeze was freshening, the swells were growing, and it was best to return to the brig. Every now and then the megaphone sounded, hailing those who were on the launch.

"They're commanding us to return on board," said Nat Gibson, "and since we have taken all that is salvageable . . ."

"Yes, let's go," replied Karl Kip.

"Poor *Wilhelmina!*" murmured Pieter Kip.

Neither of the two tried to hide the emotion they were feeling. If they had hoped to find any more of their possessions, they would now have to abandon that hope!

The launch loosed its mooring. It was Nat Gibson who took the helm while Karl and Pieter, facing astern, continued to look at the remains of the *Wilhelmina*.

As soon as the launch had been hoisted back into its cradle, the brig set its sails, and, served by a strong breeze, it rapidly sailed off toward the northwest.

For five days, they navigated without incident, and on the morning of the 14th, the watch shouted out the appearance of the first peaks of New Guinea.

Crossing the Louisiade

The next day, November 15th, some thirty miles toward the northwest was all that the *James Cook* had managed since the day before. The breeze had fallen at dusk, and the night was calm and hot. Passengers and crew spent it on deck. Sleeping in the cabins in this suffocating heat was impossible, even for an hour.

Besides, at that time, the ship was cruising in dangerous areas, and the watch could not be allowed to slacken.

Mr. Gibson had had a tent set up forward of the bridge, tied to the posts of the railing. It was in this tent that meals were eaten, it being more agreeable than inside the wardroom.

That morning, during breakfast, conversation bore on the Louisiade Islands, near which the brig would undergo the most dangerous part of its crossing. Its position placed it about four hundred and fifty miles from the New Ireland group. In four days, provided they were not becalmed too long, which happens frequently during the warm spells between the Tropics and the Equator, they'd be dropping anchor at the mooring of Port Praslin.

"You've gone through the Louisiade archipelago several times?" Peter Kip asked, addressing the captain.

"Yes, several times, when I was taking on cargo in New Ireland," replied Mr. Gibson.

"Isn't it hard to navigate?" added Karl Kip.

"Hard, all right, Mr. Kip. You've never had a chance to visit this part of the Pacific?"

"Never, Mr. Gibson, and I've never gone beyond the latitude of New Guinea."

"Well," Mr. Gibson affirmed, "a captain who was imprudent or inattentive would risk running his ship onto the innumerable reefs of the area. Just imagine madreporic reefs some two hundred miles long and a hundred wide. Unless one had experience with them, one might leave one's sheathing there, even one's hull."

"Have you ever put into port on the principal islands?" Pieter Kip asked.

"No," replied Mr. Gibson. "Besides, what sort of commerce could you have with Rossel, St. Aignan, Trobriant, D'Entrecasteaux?[1] Unless you wanted to fill your hold with coconuts . . . these islands have the most beautiful coconut palms on Earth . . ."

"Anyway," observed Mr. Hawkins, "if ships don't take on cargo in the Louisiade, it's not because the archipelago is uninhabited."

"True enough, my friend," declared Mr. Gibson. "The population here is vicious and cruel . . . maybe even cannibalistic despite the efforts of the missionaries."

"Have there been recent instances of cannibalism?" Pieter Kip asked.

"That's only too true," affirmed the captain, "horrible episodes. So a ship that wasn't always on guard would no doubt risk attack from these natives."

"And not just those in the Louisiade, but also in New Guinea as well," declared Karl Kip. "I believe the Papuans are just as fearsome."

"All these savages are alike," replied the captain, "just as perfidious and bloodthirsty! It's been over three hundred years since these islands were discovered by the Portuguese Serrano, then visited in 1610 by the Dutchman Shouten[2] and in 1770 by James Cook, who was welcomed here with spears. And finally the Frenchman Dumont d'Urville, at the time of the voyage of the *Astrolabe,* in 1827, had to respond with gunshot to the hostile attacks of those Polynesians. Well, since that era, civilization has made little progress among these tribes."

"And it's still just the same," added Nat Gibson, "in the whole area of the Pacific between New Guinea and the Solomon Islands. Just remember the voyages of Carteret, Hunter, and the American Morrell,[3] who almost lost his ship, the *Australia!* One of these islands is even called Massacre Island, and a number of others would merit bearing the same name."

"Indeed," concluded Mr. Hawkins, "it's up to you Dutch gentlemen to civilize these natives. Your flag flies over the neighboring lands, protecting the Mollucan archipelago. People would thank you for having assured the safety of commercial navigation."

"And in fact," replied Karl Kip, "the Batavian government never ceases to be concerned about it. Not one year goes by without a ship being sent to Triton Bay, on the north side of New Guinea, where we've founded a colony."

"And we'll try to establish others as well," added Pieter Kip. "Isn't that in our obvious interest since Germany has laid its hands on the northern archipelagoes?"

"As a matter of fact, all the maritime powers would take an interest in helping you," Nat Gibson observed. "Don't they have, most of them, colonies in that part of the Pacific? Just look at the names written on the maps: New Caledonia, New Zealand, New Hebrides,

New Hanover, New Britain, New Ireland, not to mention Australia, which once called itself New Holland and which England now has exclusive possession of!"

Quite correct, that observation. National flags of all colors float over this colonial domain, and the spread of civilization should make rapid progress there.[4]

What is no less true is that this region is insufficiently policed. Mainly between the Solomons, the Hebrides, New Guinea, and northern groups, navigation is conducted only with great risk.

It is not surprising, for example, that the *James Cook,* in preparing to sail in that direction, was armed with a small copper cannon, that could fire a fifteen-pound shot some six hundred meters, and that the rack in the deck house contained a half-dozen guns and revolvers. If some suspicious dugout came along, it could be kept at a distance.

These Papuans, or Papous, or Negritos originally, constitute an intermediate race between the Malayans and the Negroes. They are divided into Alfakis, which are the highlanders, and the so-called Papuans, who live along the shore. These indigenous people, neither farmers nor shepherds, form distinct tribes under the command of elder chiefs to whom is given the designation of "capitans." They live in wretched huts. They are barely dressed in animal pelts or loincloths of bark. But life is easy in these territories of New Guinea and the Louisiade. Food is abundant: turtles, fish, taros, yams, many shellfish, sugar cane, bananas, ignames, coconuts, sago, and cabbage. In the magnificent forests of the interior, rich in nutmeg, latanier palms, and ebony trees, various edible species of ringdove, pigs, kangaroos, and pigeons are abundant. Also found there is an excellent habitat for the ornithological species: cockatoos, parrots, coucals, lories, parakeets, turtledoves, gouras, green pigeons, kookaburras, and lyrebirds. Especially noteworthy are those most remarkable specimens of birds of paradise, eight admirable species from the great emerald to the royal *manucode,* all highly prized by the merchants of East Asia. Hence a traveler could call this region the El Dorado of Oceania, where neither precious woods, nor gold, nor pearls of great value were lacking.[5]

*Native hut in Dori, New Guinea**

*Facsimile of an illustration published in the *Great Voyages and Great Navigators* by Jules Verne (Hetzel's note).

There was no question, however, of the *James Cook* visiting the principal points of New Guinea: the Dori harbor, the MacCluer Gulf, the bays of Geelwink, Humboldt, and Triton, where the Dutch have several establishments.[6] It would be satisfied just to go past Rodney Cape, at the far eastern end of the great island, taking the high sea to avoid its innumerable reefs.

Which is exactly what occurred during the 15th of November. From that distance they could make out the Astrolabe mountain chain, at some three to four thousand feet, and the mountain peaks that dominate it, both the Simpson and the Sucking. Then, under reduced sail, so as to be quickly maneuverable and always ready to be more closed or opened, the brig faced that sea bristling with reefs that lay between the Solomon archipelago and the long point of land that Papua New Guinea extends toward the southeast.

There was no other ship in sight; no native boat could be seen in that direction.

During the night, however, everyone on board was extremely vigilant. The topsails had been taken in despite the breeze being gentle, and the *James Cook* navigated only under its storm jib and its brigantine.

Beyond Cape Rodney,[7] some fires, fairly numerous, were seen along the coast, on the backside of the Papouasian point and on D'Entrecasteaux Island, which a few narrow miles separated from the cape. The darkness was profound, and the weather was becoming overcast. Not a star shone in the sky. An hour after sunset, the moon's crescent had disappeared behind the clouds upon the horizon.

Perhaps between eleven o'clock and midnight, the men on watch caught sight of a few dugouts near the *James Cook,* but they were not sure. In any case, there was no reason to go on the defensive, and the night passed without incident.

The next day, the wind, which had freshened at daybreak, suddenly fell. The sea took on an oily appearance. Since the clouds thinned out at about ten o'clock, they readied themselves for high temperatures since this latitude was only ten degrees from the

Equator and the month of November corresponded to the month of May in the northern hemisphere.

A little before noon, while passing D'Entrecasteaux Island, which they soon left behind on the port side, the watch signaled the approach of a canoe. This craft was probably coming from the mainland, after skirting the south end of the isle, and now approached the *James Cook,* immobilized by the calm.

As soon as Karl Kip noticed the canoe, he said to Mr. Hawkins:

"Either I'm very mistaken, or that craft is trying to come alongside."

"I think so as well," replied the shipowner.

Mr. Gibson, his son, and Pieter Kip, leaving the wardroom, walked toward the bow.

The canoe, made of bark and equipped with a side-pontoon, was of small size. It was being paddled, leisurely, between the many rocks that jutted out of the water and stretched out to the southeast of D'Entrecasteaux Island.

When he had observed it with his telescope, Mr. Gibson declared:

"It contains only two men."

Mr. Hawkins said, "Two men? Well, if their intention is to come aboard, I do not believe there is much danger in receiving them."

"And I'm curious to examine a bit closer these Papuan natives," added Nat Gibson.

"Let it come closer," the captain said. "In ten minutes the canoe will be right beside us, and we'll find out what these natives want."

Mr. Hawkins suggested, "Some kind of trade, no doubt."

"There's no other boat in sight?" asked Pieter Kip.

"None," replied Mr. Gibson, who had just examined the open sea, then to the north and south of D'Entrecasteaux Island.

The canoe drew closer to the brig, propelled by the double blades, paddles that rose and sank with a mechanical regularity.

When it was only some fifty feet away from the *James Cook,* one of the natives stood up and cried out this word:

"Ebourra . . . ebourra!"

The captain, leaning over the rail, turned to his friends and said:

"That's a word that means 'bird' in the language of the natives of New Ireland, and I suppose that the Papuans of New Guinea give it the same meaning."

Mr. Gibson was not mistaken. The savage held in his right hand a bird that was well worth adding to any ornithological collection.

It was, in fact, a bird of paradise of the *manucode* species, as they soon saw, its plumage velvety and brownish red, its head partially orange in color with a blackish spot at the corner of his eye, a bronze-like throat, crossed by a brown stripe and a metallic-green stripe, the rest of the body being a perfect whiteness, with its side garnished with feathers that were tipped with emerald green, some red, others yellow, and with wispy, hornlike feathers fringed with fine barbules, rolled up at the ends. This bird, some six inches in length, is one of those, it is claimed, that never perch and whose nest natives have never discovered. It is one of the most curious, most interesting species in all this Papuan land, where they are found in great abundance.

"My word," said Mr. Hawkins, "I would not be sorry to have one of those birds of paradise, which Gibson has mentioned to me so often."

Pieter Kip replied, "It would be easy to obtain one, for this native is certainly coming to trade it."

"Have him come aboard," ordered the captain.

One of the sailors lowered the rope ladder. The canoe came alongside and the native, bird in hand, quickly climbed to the bridge, repeating:

"Ebourra! . . . ebourra!"

His companion had remained in the canoe, the line wound about the cleat, and he continued to examine the brig without responding to the gestures the sailors were making to him.

The native who had just come aboard belonged to that distinctive type of Malayo-Papuan race that occupies the shores of New Guinea: medium size, strong, vigorous constitution, nose exceedingly flat, wide mouth with thick lips, angular traits, hair unkempt but straight, skin of a dusky yellow and not too dark, harsh face, but not devoid of intelligence, even astuteness.

This man, in the opinion of Mr. Gibson, was some captain or tribal leader. About fifty years old, almost naked, his sole clothing was a kangaroo pelt about his loins, a bark-like cape about his shoulders.

Since Mr. Hawkins could not refrain from making an admiring gesture at the sight of the bird, it was to him that the native addressed himself at first. After raising the bird of paradise to the height of his eyes, he shook it and turned it around to show all sides of it.

Mr. Hawkins, with his mind made up to purchase this magnificent *manucode,* wondered what he could give in exchange. Very likely the Papuan would not be intrigued by the offer of a piastre, whose worth he would not be able to assess.

The latter soon drew him out of his perplexity by repeating, his mouth wide open:

"Wobba . . . wobba!"

This word Mr. Gibson translated as "A drink! . . . a drink!" and he had a bottle of whiskey brought up from the storeroom.

The "capitan" took it, assured himself it was full of the amber liquid that he was familiar with, and, without uncorking it, he put it under his arm. Then he was off, striding up and down the deck from stem to stern, looking less at the ship's equipment and rigging than at the sailors, the passengers, and the captain. One would have said that he was seeking to find out the number of people on board. That's what Karl Kip thought he noticed, and he whispered a word about it to his brother.

Nat Gibson then had the idea of photographing this fellow. Not at all with the thought of giving him the portrait, for there was no time to develop the negative, but he wanted to enhance his collection by introducing an authentic Papuan.

"It's a good idea," Mr. Hawkins said, "but how could we prevent that devil from moving?"

"Let's try," Nat Gibson responded.

He took the native by the arm in order to lead him toward the stern. But the latter, not understanding what was expected of him, was putting up some resistance.

"Assai," Mr. Gibson told him.

This word is the vocative form of the verb "to come" in the Papuan language, and the man responded by heading for the deckhouse.

Nat Gibson brought his camera to the stern and set it up on the tripod. Then, before focusing on the savage, he tried to place the latter in a suitable pose so that he would get a good picture.

But the "capitan," quite agitated and demonstrative, started shaking his head, his arms, and how could one make him be still for the two seconds needed for the photograph? Fortunately, when he saw Nat Gibson disappear under the black veil of the camera, his surprise stopped him cold.

That instant was enough for the photo, and the operation over, the "capitan," his bottle in hand, returned to the ladder on the starboard side.

But, passing in front of the deckhouse, whose door was open, he entered as though to assure himself that there was nobody inside. And it was the same curiosity that led him to the door of the crew's quarters, whose hatch was pushed back. Finally his eyes stopped at the small copper instrument, trained forward, and of whose power he was not unaware, for he cried out:

"Mera . . . mera!"

Another word of the native vocabulary, which means "thunder," as "oura" means lightning or bright light.

At that moment the capitan's eye gleamed with a flame that disappeared just as suddenly, and his face returned to the vacuousness that distinguishes these representatives of the aborigine race.

Finally back at the ladder, the Papuan straddled the railing, went down to the canoe, swept his eyes for the last time from one end to the other of the brig, and seized one of the paddles while his companion took the other. The craft, maneuvered rapidly, was not long in disappearing around the curve of D'Entrecasteaux Island to reach a point of the mainland beyond.

"Did you notice," Karl Kip then asked, "how attentively that man looked over the *James Cook,* and especially its crew?"

"That struck me too," replied Mr. Hawkins.

For his part, Captain Gibson had noted it as well. In any case, it was not certain that the Papuan had come aboard to estimate the strength of the brig. He had a bird to sell, he sold it, they had paid for it with a bottle of whiskey, he had been happy with that, and the canoe had taken him back from whence he had come. An hour from now he would be dead drunk, and they would not see him again.

But it was nevertheless regrettable the *James Cook* was becalmed where they were off D'Entrecasteaux Island. The breeze was felt only as momentary puffs. The last waves on the sea disappeared, and its surface barely rolled from the long swells. Mr. Gibson wondered if they could not just anchor with fifty fathoms of chain. By getting closer to the isle, he would find a good mooring place and he could wait for the winds to pick up from the southeast.

He talked this over with the bosun, who saw no problem in lowering the anchor.

Flig Balt had his reasons for agreeing with the captain, or rather Vin Mod, who had said to him:

"The sky is clouded over, the night will be rainy, one of those rains without wind, that falls from evening to daybreak. It is probable that Mr. Hawkins, the Gibson son, and the two Dutchmen will go to sleep in their quarters. On the bridge there will only be the captain and the men on watch. When Len Cannon, Sexton, Kyle, and Bryce come on duty, the others will be in their quarters. This might be the chance we've been waiting for, to surprise Mr. Gibson, to get rid of him, and if we don't succeed in taking over the brig, at least we'd have Flig Balt as our captain."

That's how the conversation had also played itself out between Vin Mod and Len Cannon. Yes, first and foremost, get rid of the captain; then they'd see.

Well, the circumstances would indeed be more favorable if the brig remained at anchor instead of being under sail all night. Mr. Gibson would be the only one on watch, no doubt, and by some accident, he would soon disappear . . .

But what thwarted Vin Mod's plans is that the captain wanted to hear Karl Kip's opinion about staying there all night.

And Karl Kip replied without hesitation:

"If I were you, Mr. Gibson, I wouldn't do anything like that. This area is not a safe one. An attack by the natives is always to be feared. If that happens, it's best not to be moored, and no matter how little the wind may blow, to be ready to move on without hoisting the anchor and raising the sails."

The captain, understanding the wisdom of his reasoning, yielded to it. So, to the extreme discontent of the bosun and his accomplices, the *James Cook* kept its night sails when the sun set, and they remained in sight of D'Entrecasteaux Island, some three miles distant.

Moreover, the rain, which had begun around five o'clock in the evening, did not last. The storm revealed itself to be mostly heat lightning and the distant rolling of thunder. The temperature was quite high, the Fahrenheit thermometer registered 90 degrees.* Thus, neither Mr. Hawkins, nor Nat Gibson, nor Karl and Pieter Kip went to their quarters. All, including the sailors who were not on duty, stretched out on the deck.

Decidedly, ill luck had once again befallen Flig Balt, Vin Mod, and their partisans.

It goes without saying that Mr. Gibson had given orders and taken measures so that anything approaching the brig would be carefully watched. The men had to remain on watch in bow and stern. Whatever Mr. Hawkins might say, Karl Kip's observation remained uppermost in his mind. Had the native come aboard simply with the intent to exchange his bird of paradise for any object offered, or was it to reconnoiter the brig and its strength?

In front of the crew quarters, they talked about the incident at first, then of other things. The tent had been opened so as to provide more air. A profound silence prevailed around the ship. On the sea, not a single light could be seen, nor toward D'Entrecasteaux Island, which was surely uninhabited.

Then the conversation diminished little by little. Eyelids grew heavier, and no doubt sleep was about to conquer even the most

*Thirty-two degrees centigrade (Author's note).

resistant of the men, when a voice was heard, Jim's voice, as he was walking along the gangway.

"Canoes . . . canoes!" shouted the cabin boy.

Everyone—captain, passengers, and crew—leaped immediately to their feet and made their way to the port side.

It was in this direction that Jim had glimpsed, or believed that he had glimpsed, some crafts headed for the brig.

In the middle of that dark night, had he been mistaken?

They thought so at first. But a swirl of water, such as a paddle might make, had soon proved that Jim had not erred, and Nat Gibson himself cried out in turn:

"There . . . there . . . some boats!"

A sailor shone the light from a lamp in that direction, which revealed several canoes only thirty feet away. Without Jim's vigilance, the brig would have been surprised by a sudden attack, and they would not have had time to defend themselves.

"Rifles! . . . revolvers!" Mr. Gibson quickly ordered.

The sailors raced to the deckhouse, and arms were distributed. Each man received a rifle or revolver with spare cartridges, and they posted themselves along the port railing, so as to repel any assailants who might try to reach the deck.

At sea, moreover, in the opposite direction from D'Entrecasteaux Island, they could see nothing suspicious, no sound of paddles could be heard. Not the slightest movement of the sea's surface, and it was unlikely that other canoes should come from the east.

The natives, however, seeing the light from the lantern trained on them, understood that they were discovered. No surprise assault was possible. So the attack began at once. A flight of arrows and a host of stones, launched from slings, came crashing against the side of the brig, or passed above the bridge through the rigging.

No one was hit, but from the quantity of projectiles, they realized that the enemy was numerous. And in fact they were no less than sixty, embarked in some ten canoes. Now the captain had at his disposal only fifteen men, including Jim the cabin boy.

"Fire!" he ordered.

And multiple shots rang out as a welcome to the attacking Papuans in their canoes. No doubt several had struck a target. Wails from those injured rose up; at the same time a second shower of arrows and stones fell upon the ship.

"Just wait now," ordered the captain. "Don't fire except at point blank range at the first devils who try to climb to the railing."

That was not long in happening. An instant later the canoes crashed into the side of the brig. Then the Papuans grasped the mounting of the anchor as they struggled to hoist themselves up to the rail to invade the deck and engage in a hand-to-hand combat.

Evidently, under these conditions, once aboard, the natives would no longer be able to use either bow or lance. But they would not be unarmed. They brandished a sort of iron cleaver, called a "parang" in island idiom, that they knew how to handle with as much vigor as skill.

Hence the need to repel the assault with rifle fire, revolver shots, cutlass blows, and drive the horde back into the sea before they had the chance to set foot on deck.

But the Papuans arrived at the railing, bracing themselves against the shrouds of the mainmast and the mizzenmast. Immediately repelled, they fell back among the canoes.

By the light of the shots fired, they recognized one of the attackers. It was the capitan, leader of the whole band, who had come on board with a view to carry out this attack.

However, the number of assailants was so great, the forces so disproportionate, that the situation could not but be of the gravest nature. If the capitan and the Papuans overran the bridge, the personnel of the *James Cook,* despite the superiority of their arms, would end up being overwhelmed. Reduced to seeking refuge in the stern crew quarters or in the forward post, they would in either case ultimately be overrun. A massacre would follow in which all of the ship's crew would be slaughtered. Impossible to use the small artillery pieces. Excellent when firing long distance at a canoe, they were useless when the canoes were against the side of the brig.

The passengers and sailors of the *James Cook* were defending themselves with as much vigor as courage. In the beginning, five or six natives hoisted themselves up along the hull. Their feet braced on the listel, they tried to straddle the railing, but against revolvers and cutlasses, they were forced to fall back, some into the canoes, others into the sea.

It is true that, on the side of the beleaguered, a few men were soon wounded—among others Pieter Kip and the sailor Burnes, struck with a blow of the parang, the former on the arm, the latter on the shoulder. These wounds, fortunately slight, did not require them to abandon their post. All in all, the firearms were causing more serious damage among the natives.

The combat lasted just ten minutes, and the Papuans did not succeed in taking possession of the brig. For an instant, the capitan and two natives, their cleavers in hand, had succeeded in hoisting themselves up to the shrouds and were about to climb the rail while two or three canoes headed for the stern. Then Karl Kip, seconded by Nat Gibson, chased down the braggart warrior, piercing his chest with two bullets. The young man then fired on the canoes.

When the Papuans saw their leader fall and his body sink into the water, they slowed their attack and seemed ready to abandon it altogether. Having failed to surprise the brig, they knew they would not succeed despite their advantage of four against one. Those who still were trying to leap onto the bridge by the prow or the coping were soon retreating. Obliged now to defend themselves, they tried to reembark in their canoes. A few, grievously wounded, drowned. And if two or three more of the ships' seamen ended up wounded with parang gashes, at least there was no fatality on their side.

It was quarter past ten when the canoes finally began to draw away from the brig. A final few shots were leveled at them, for as long as they could be seen. At that moment, no doubt by someone's clumsiness—and the profound darkness would have been his excuse—a bullet grazed the captain's head so close that his hat sailed off astern.

The captain did not worry particularly about it, although the bullet did come very near to penetrating his skull. He raced forward, followed by his son, whom he had just called, and both rapidly swung the little copper artillery piece into position.

The canoes, at one cable length away from the *James Cook,* still

A few, grievously wounded, drowned.

presented a muddled mass toward which Hobbes directed the lantern glow.

The artillery piece, loaded, charged, was ready to fire to port.

The shot was discharged, and savage howls answered its detonation.

Even though they had not seen it happen, one of the canoes must have been struck by the projectile and sunk with the Papuans who were in it.

The cannon was immediately recharged, not for a second shot, but in case of a possible offensive attack, which did not occur.

The luminous beam of the lantern, playing over the western waters, lit up nothing but an absolutely deserted sea, for already the canoes had taken shelter behind D'Entrecasteaux Island.

Now the *James Cook* had nothing more to fear; at least it would not be surprised again. Precautions would be taken, and the crew would be vigilant, all arms at the ready, until the break of day.

Pieter Kip's wounds, and those of Burnes, along with those of the three other sailors, were then inspected. Mr. Hawkins, who knew about such injuries, could assure everyone that they presented no danger. The pharmacy on board sufficed to apply a first bandaging, and none of the wounded even thought to return to his cabin, or even the crew's quarters.

When Flig Balt and Vin Mod found themselves alone together at the bow of the ship, the sailor said in a low voice:

"Missed . . . We missed him!"

And if Flig Balt, as was his habit, did not reply, Vin Mod knew full well what that silence meant.

"But what do you expect, Bosun Balt, in the middle of such a dark night, one's aim is poor! . . . After all, he didn't even seem to have noticed! . . . Next time . . . we'll be luckier!"

Then, bending over his companion's ear, he whispered:

"Unfortunate, even so! By this time Flig Balt would've been the captain of the brig, and Vin Mod his bosun!"

Heading North

When the last shades of night had dissipated, all eyes searched the sea around the brig. The *James Cook* was still in the same place as the day before, at three miles to the east of D'Entrecasteaux Island, as if it had been anchored there. No current could be felt, and no breath of wind wrinkled the surface of the sea, barely raised by a long, soft swell that did not move the ship.

No canoes were in sight; floating here and there was the debris of one that the cannon's shot had shattered. As for those who had been in it, either they had managed to be brought aboard the other boats, or the abyss[1] had swallowed them up.

Mr. Gibson scanned the island shore with his telescope, then across the scattering of coral reefs circling the southern point. Thousands of birds were flying above with a great flapping of wings. But neither canoe nor man could be seen. No one doubted that, beyond the narrows, the natives had returned to some riverside village of New Guinea.

Nevertheless, it was important to leave these parts and to make their departure as soon as possible. From certain weather signs, Mr. Gibson knew that the breeze would not be long in picking up.

That was Karl Kip's opinion as well, when the sun rose amid purplish vapors on the horizon. The sea "was brewing something" in that direction, and a stronger lapping of the waves could already be heard.

"I'd be surprised," said the captain, "if we didn't have a good wind in an hour or so."

"And, if it holds up for just four days," agreed Mr. Hawkins, "we'll reach our destination."

"Indeed," replied Mr. Gibson, "there are barely three hundred miles separating us from New Ireland."

The James Cook *was still in the same place.*

Assuming the calm would end during the morning, the continuation of the *James Cook*'s voyage would be assured. The brig would then be right in the zone of the trade winds from the southeast that blow from May through November, followed by the monsoon in the other months of the year.

Mr. Gibson was quite ready to hoist the topsails as soon as the breeze could fill them. They could not leave this dangerous region of Papua and the Louisiade too soon. Aided by a good wind, high and strong, no canoes with paddles would ever catch the *James Cook* if the natives chose to renew their attack.

However, they did not appear again. So the arms, rifles, and revolvers were returned to quarters and the small artillery piece was withdrawn from the port bow. The brig would no longer need to stay on the defensive.

And, in this regard, Mr. Gibson then alluded to the stray bullet that had grazed him the evening before, when Karl Kip repelled the Papuan capitan and threw him into the sea.

"What's that?" cried out Mr. Hawkins in utter astonishment, "You were almost . . ."

"Hit, my friend; a half an inch closer and that bullet would've struck me in the head."

"We didn't know," Pieter Kip declared. "But are you sure it was a bullet? Was it not perhaps a javelin or spear that one of the natives had thrown?"

"No," replied Nat Gibson. "Here's my father's hat, and you can see that it was pierced by a bullet."

There remained no doubt after examining the hat. But, all in all, it was not surprising that in the midst of the struggle, in the profound darkness, one of the revolvers had been badly aimed. And no one thought of it again.

Around seven-thirty, the breeze had picked up enough strength and regularity so that the brig could set its sights on the northwest. Topgallant and royal sail, studding sails and staysails, which carry well the high wind, were raised. Then, getting under way, the *James Cook* resumed its navigation, which had been interrupted for some twenty hours.

Before noon they passed the extreme northern tip of D'Entrecasteaux Island. Beyond it, and for the last time, there appeared the mainland where the outline of the highest mountains dominating the eastern coast of New Guinea could be seen.

As far as one could see, the sea was empty. Any fear of a second attack disappeared. To the east stretched the immense liquid plain, limited only by the perimeter of the sea and the sky.

However, instead of the natives whom they no longer had to fear, they now had to be careful of the sudden gales that ravage this portion of the Pacific between the Papouasie, the Solomon Islands, and the archipelagoes of the north. These storms do not last, however, and are only dangerous for the negligent or inexperienced captain, whom they take by surprise. They call them the "black squalls." A ship that is not on guard risks capsizing under sail.[2]

During the day and the night that followed, they did not encounter any such squalls. The direction of the wind did not change at all. When the *James Cook* had left behind Monyon Isle[3] to port, arid and uninhabited, rising in the middle of its coral ring, it ventured into a sea that was somewhat less encumbered by reef-building coral and managed to maintain a speed of ten knots an hour.

Under these conditions, it was understandable that the opportunity still awaited by Flig Balt, Vin Mod, and others was not forthcoming. Mr. Gibson, his son, the shipowner, and the Kip brothers did not spend their nights in their cabins, nor did the sailors Hobbes, Wickley, Burnes, or Jim, the ship's boy, who were all at their posts. Hence, the impossibility of getting rid of the captain—by accident—since he was never alone.

Although they were in the period of the year when sea-going navigation was carried out with some degree of safety across the Melanesian seas, the brig did not encounter another ship on its route. That was because trading posts were not very numerous or very important in these archipelagoes situated between the Equator and the northern coast of the Papouasie. They do not yet receive the constant traffic that in the future will no doubt develop. Mr. Gibson, once at Port Praslin, would probably not find there any other ship, and he would leave without making contact with any English or German sailors.

That is, moreover, how the archipelagoes are configured, from both a political and geographical point of view.

For a number of years, as it often did, England, more or less legally, extended its protectorate over these island neighbors of New Guinea, when in 1884, an agreement was reached between Germany and the United Kingdom.

As a consequence of this agreement, all islands located in the regions to the northeast of Papouasie, as far as the hundred and forty-first degree of longitude to the east of the Greenwich meridian, were declared German possessions.[4]

It was a population judged to be some hundred thousand souls, increasing the colonial domain of Germany, which was trying to attract emigrants there.

And it is especially useful to draw the reader's attention to the principal group, as far as this story is concerned.

The two most important islands of this group are Tombara, or New Ireland, and Birara, or New Britain. They both take the shape of a narrow curve. The latter is separated from New Guinea by the Dampier Strait.[5] The Saint George's Channel[6] stands between the southern point of the former and the northeast point of the latter, in the midst of numerous coral reefs.

The maps next indicate New Hanover Isle, York Isle, and several others, inhabited or deserted, with a total area of fifteen hundred and eighty square kilometers.

One should not be surprised to learn that, after the treaty of separation between the two powers, the English or Melanesian names were replaced with German ones. Thus Tombara or New Ireland became New Mecklenburg, Birara or New Britain became Neu-Pommern or New Pomerania, and York became New Lauenburg. Only New Hanover kept its name, and for good reason, because it was already Germanized.

All that remained was to rebaptize these islands, which constitute a rather important colony in that part of the Pacific. Today, this group figures on the maps under the name of the Bismarck Archipelago.

When Pieter Kip asked Mr. Hawkins in what circumstances and under what conditions he had trade relations with the archipelago, and more especially with New Ireland:

"I was," replied the shipowner, "the intermediary with a firm in Wellington, New Zealand, which did business with Tombara."

"Before the partition treaty, Mr. Hawkins?"

"Ten years before that, Mr. Kip; and when that firm was liquidated, I picked up the remainder of its business. Then, after the agreement of 1884 between England and Germany, I established a relationship with the new businesses founded by the German settlers. It was the *James Cook* in particular that was earmarked for these trips, and whose profits have been growing."

"Has business expanded since the treaty?"

"Yes, indeed, Mr. Kip, and I think it will keep on developing. The Teutonic race is happy to emigrate in the hopes of making a fortune."

"And what does the archipelago export?"

"Mostly mother of pearl, which is abundant. And since the most beautiful coconut palms in the world are found in abundance on these islands, as you can well imagine, they furnish shiploads of copra,* of which we're about to take on three hundred tons at Port Praslin."[7]

"And how," asked Karl Kip, "did Germany establish dominion over this archipelago?"

"Quite simply," responded Mr. Hawkins, "by parceling out the different islands to a commercial company, which also holds political power. But, in reality, its power is not very broad, and its activity with regard to the natives is minimal. It's limited to assuring the safety of emigrants and the security of its transactions."

"Besides, as Mr. Hawkins says," added Nat Gibson, "everything

*Copra is the almond of the coconut which, once it is crushed and sun-dried on sand, is ready to be sent to the mill to extract its oil for making soap (Author's note).[8]

leads one to believe that the prosperity of the archipelago will grow. We've been able to make great progress, especially in Tombara, whose discovery was made in 1616 by the Dutch Shouten. He's one of your compatriots, Mr. Kip, and was the first to venture across these dangerous seas."

"I know, monsieur Nat," replied Karl Kip. "Moreover, Holland has left its imprint in the Melanesian regions, and its sailors have become famous for it several times over."

"That's true," declared Mr. Gibson.

"Yet it has not kept ownership over all its discoveries," observed Mr. Hawkins.

"No, without a doubt, but by keeping the Moluccas they've kept a big part, and willingly gave up the Bismarck Archipelago to Germany."

It was the navigator Shouten who, in the beginning of the seventeenth century, had explored the eastern part of New Ireland. The first encounters with the natives were hostile, attacks of pirogues filled with natives and their slings, replies with muskets, and this early contact was marked by the death of about a dozen savages.

After Shouten, there was another Hollander, Tasman, the one who was to give his name to Tasmania, also called Van Diemen's Land, from the name of another Hollander, Van Diemen, who sailed along that shore in 1643.

After them come the English, and among them Dampier, whose name has been given to the narrows that separates New Guinea from Birara. Dampier took over the shore from north to south, landed in several places, and had to push back an attack of the islanders in a bay he called Rebellion Bay.

In 1767, Carteret, a British navigator, visited the southwest part of the island, put in at Port Praslin, and then continued on to the port that bears his name in the English cove.

In 1768, during the course of his navigation around the world, Bougainville[9] also dropped anchor at Port Praslin, and called it thus in honor of the minister of the navy, the promoter of the first voyage of the French around the world.

In 1792, D'Entrecasteaux headed for the eastern part of the island, unknown until then, mapped its contours, and spent a week in Carteret Bay.

Finally, in 1823, Duperrey[10] sailed his ship to Port Praslin, whose hydrographic map he worked out with great care. He dealt frequently with the Indians who came by canoe from the village of Like-Like, located on the eastern shore of New Ireland.

During the morning of the 18th, the direction of the ship had to be modified for several hours. The wind, which blew with the usual constancy of trade winds, quite suddenly dropped and did not pick up again. The sails sagged, batted against the masts, and the *James Cook* responded no more to the helm.

Given such sudden changes in meteorological conditions, a prudent captain had to always be ready for them and take them into account, and that is just what Mr. Gibson did, for he would not allow himself to be taken by surprise.

Now, at this very moment, Karl Kip, scanning the horizon, pointed out a western cloud to the captain, a sort of vaporous balloon with rounded flanks, whose speed must have been rapid, for one could see it grow.

"A black squall is coming our way," Mr. Gibson said.

"It certainly will not be of long duration," replied Karl Kip.

"No, but it could be of great violence," added the captain.

And, on his command, the crew immediately set to maneuver. The royal sail, the topgallant, the studding sail, and the staysail were hoisted immediately. They clewed up the foresail, the grand sail, and the brigantine. The *James Cook* rested beneath its reefed topsail, its storm-jib and its second main jib. It was just in time. Scarcely had the brig secured itself under those reduced sails than the gale struck them with an extraordinary rage.

While the sailors held to their posts, the captain stood in front of the deckhouse, and Mr. Hawkins, Nat Gibson, and Pieter Kip moved to the stern. Karl Kip was at the helm, and in his hands the *James Cook* would be well cared for.

It is understandable that when the squall hit the ship, it shook as though being rammed. It heeled over so much toward the starboard

"A black squall is coming our way," Mr. Gibson said.

that the extremity of its main yard dipped into the white, foaming sea. A strong turn of the helm righted it, and maintained it. Rather than heave to and defy the squall, Mr. Gibson preferred to flee in front of it, knowing by experience that these squalls pass like a sudden shower and do not last long.

However, one might wonder if the brig would be carried away as far as the Solomons, if it wouldn't run into Bougainville Island, the first of that group, which extends into the northeast of the Louisiade. At that time, it would be no more than thirty miles away.

In fact, it is possible that that island might have been visible for an instant. It presents a great mass on the northeast side and if that were the case, it's because the *James Cook* would have been driven off course to a heading of some hundred and fifty-three degrees of longitude.

It's likely Flig Balt and Vin Mod felt no regrets seeing it thrown off course. They enjoyed anything that contributed to slowing down their arrival at New Ireland. This archipelago of the Solomons is a propitious place for outlaws. Adventurers abound, and it was frequently the scene of criminal acts. The bosun could run into—on Rossel Island or others—several old acquaintances who would not refuse to support his projects. And, in what regions of the Pacific had not Vin Mod dragged his kitbag, and would he not find former comrades, ready for anything?

Moreover, what provoked the bosun and his cursed co-conspirator is that Len Cannon and his companions were constantly badgering them. They weren't about to continue sailing under these conditions, and they stubbornly repeated:

"If the attack doesn't come before our arriving in Port Praslin, we won't re-embark when you leave . . . That's a sure thing."

"But what will happen to you on New Ireland?" observed Vin Mod.

"They'll hire us as colonists," replied Len Cannon. "The Germans need workmen. We'll wait for some good opportunity, which won't happen in Tasmania, and we'll never go back to Hobart Town."

This resolution was enough to set Flig Balt and his accomplice into a rage. Without the four recruits, they would have to renounce their plans. And they certainly wouldn't be taking away from the *James Cook* campaign all they had hoped for . . .

It is true that if Len Cannon, Kyle, Sexton, and Bryce all deserted ship in Port Praslin, the captain would be very hard put to return to sea. They could scarcely hope to recruit other sailors from the Isle of Tombara. Port Praslin was neither Dunedin nor Wellington nor Auckland, cities that were usually swarming with sailors in search of a job.

Here, nothing but colonists settled for their own good, or employees in business firms. As a result, there was no possibility of completing a crew.

But Mr. Gibson was unaware of the threat against him, just as he was ignorant of the plot hatched against his ship. The recruits gave no cause for complaint. As for Flig Balt, always flattering, he did not arouse suspicion. If he had fooled Mr. Hawkins as well, at least the Kip brothers, in whom he inspired no confidence, had always been cautious toward him, which he had noticed. Really, it was playing with misfortune to have saved the shipwrecked brothers of Norfolk Island! And if the *James Cook* would have at least disembarked them at Port Praslin! No, it had to carry them on to Hobart Town!

To come back to Len Cannon and his companions, the hopes that they had had of being blown off course to the archipelago of the Solomons was of short duration. After three hours during which the squall unleashed its violence, it came to a sudden end, and the weathercock, at the top of the main mast, obeyed only the rolling of the swell. Under the hand of Karl Kip, the ship behaved admirably and had never been battered by any of the fearsome waves of the storm as they fled with the wind from behind. A boat does not control itself, or controls itself badly, and nothing is so difficult as controlling the yaws that cast it to one side or the other. At the helm, Karl Kip had had the chance to demonstrate both his talent and his sangfroid. Not a single man in the crew could have held the tiller better during this gale.

If the wind fell suddenly, such was not the case with the dreadful raging sea. The waves beat against each other so much that one would think that the brig was navigating in the midst of breakers or at the edge of a madreporic reef. Yet the air was calm, and after the torrential rain that had accompanied the squall and emptied the western clouds, the trade winds almost at once picked up their normal direction.

Mr. Gibson then had the topsail reefs cast off, set up the foresail, the main sail, the brigantine, the topgallant, and the royals. He did not raise the studding sails, for the breeze was fresh and they mustn't overload the masts. The brig, with its tacking to starboard, made such good headway that on the 19th, after covering some hundred fifty miles from Bougainville Island, it found itself near Saint George's Channel, a narrow waterway flowing between the two islands of Tombara, or New Ireland, and Birara, or New Britain.

The channel only measures a few miles in breadth. Navigating it is not easy, and dangerous reefs are encountered all along it, but it shortens the distance by a good half. It is true that, for any ship wishing to reach the extreme west of Tombara in this way rather than continuing along the southern shore of Birara and passing through the Dampier Strait, it would require someone with as excellent experience as Captain Gibson.

Nevertheless, there was no need to attempt it since Port Praslin, toward which the *James Cook* was now heading, is situated in the southern part of New Ireland, on the shore facing the Pacific, near Cape Saint George, almost at the entrance of the channel.

Since the *James Cook* was practically becalmed on its approach toward land, Mr. Hawkins, Nat Gibson, and the Kip brothers were able to observe leisurely this part of the coast.

The backbone of the island is formed by a double chain of mountains of an average altitude of six thousand feet, which begins on this point of the coastline. Forests cover them up to their summits. Impenetrable to solar rays, there arises a constant humidity, and the temperature is more bearable than in those other neighboring countries of the Equator, where the air is as dry as it is scorching. This circumstance fortunately reduces the heat that ordinarily pre-

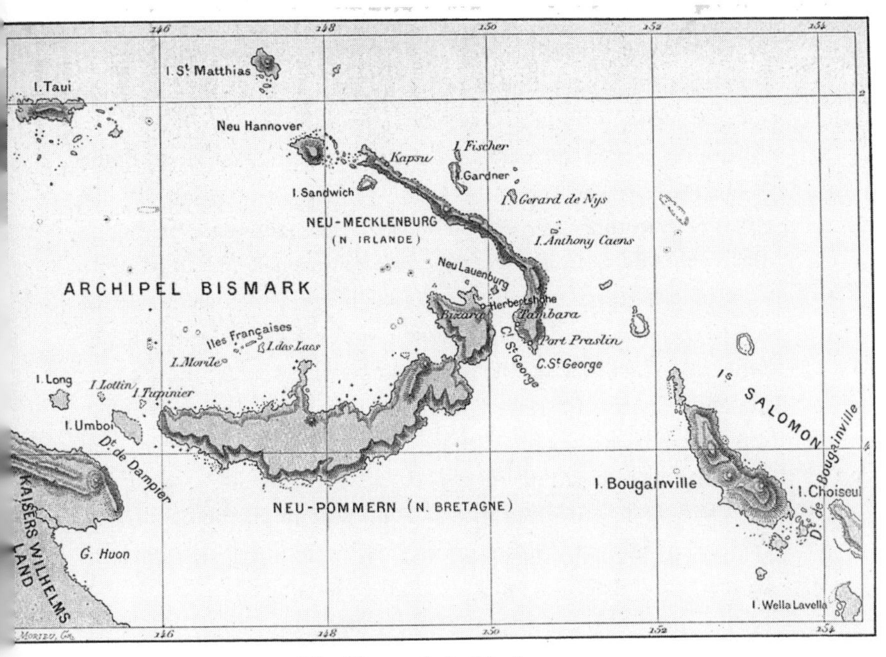

The Bismarck Archipelago

vails in the Bismarck islands, and it is rare that the thermometer's mercury rises above eighty-eight degrees Fahrenheit.*

During that day, the brig passed only a few canoes without side-pontoons, which were square-rigged. They glided along the shore and never tried to approach the ship. Moreover, there is nothing to fear from these natives of New Ireland or rather of New Mecklenburg, since the archipelago was now under the German flag.

No sea-related incident—or any other—troubled their night. When the breeze picked up after twenty-four hours of calm, they had to maneuver under a small sail between the madreporic banks and the coral reefs, more numerous as one approached Port Praslin.

A ship had to be careful to avoid damage, which would not be easily repaired. So the whole crew remained on deck, and it was often necessary to brace the yardarms. Needless to say, these coasts are not yet lit up between nightfall and sunrise, and it is difficult to see the landmarks in the darkness. But Mr. Gibson knew full well the environs of Port Praslin.

When daylight arrived, the lookout announced the opening to the harbor of Port Praslin, overlooked by the high mountains of Lanut. The *James Cook* entered into the channel, navigable at high tide. Around nine o'clock in the morning, it moored with two anchors in the middle of the harbor.

11

Port Praslin

The first visitor to present himself on board the brig was Mr. Zieger, a New Ireland businessman in commercial relations with the Hawkins firm.[1] Middle-aged and vigorous, having lived for some twelve years in Port Praslin, Mr. Zieger[2] had founded this company warehouse even before the treaty of partition had imposed on the

*Thirty degrees centigrade (Author's note).

island the name of New Mecklenburg and on the group of islands that of the Bismarck Archipelago.

The relationship between Mr. Hawkins and Mr. Zieger never ceased being excellent. They did not limit themselves simply to exchanging merchandise between Hobart Town and Port Praslin. Several times already, Mr. Zieger had traveled to the Tasmanian capital, where the shipowner took great pleasure in receiving him. These two businessmen held each other in great esteem. Nat Gibson was no stranger to Mr. Zieger, or to Mrs. Zieger, who accompanied him on his travels. All were going to be very happy to spend this relaxing time together in New Ireland.

As for the captain and Mr. Zieger, they were old acquaintances, friends who shook each other's hand warmly, as if they had parted company only the day before.

Mr. Zieger, who spoke English fluently, said to the shipowner:

"I am hoping, Mr. Hawkins, that you will accept the hospitality that Mrs. Zieger and I plan to offer you in our home in Wilhelmstaf."

"You want us to abandon our *James Cook?*" replied the shipowner.

"Of course, Mr. Hawkins."

"On condition, Mr. Zieger, that we will not be any trouble . . ."

"In no way, I assure you. Your room is already prepared, and may I add, there is one also for Gibson and his son."

The offer was made so warmly that they could not refuse. Besides, Mr. Hawkins, unused to living in the close quarters of a ship, could hope for nothing better than exchanging his cabin for a comfortable room in the Wilhelmstaf villa.

This proposition was also accepted by Nat Gibson. However, the captain declined, as he had always done before.

"We will see each other every day, my dear Zieger," he said. "However, my presence is needed on board, and my rule is to never leave my ship throughout my stopovers."

Mr. Zieger replied, "As you like, Gibson, but it's understood that we'll meet at my table morning and evening."

"That's agreed," said Mr. Gibson. "From today on, I'll go to visit

German trade bureau in the Bismarck Archipelago (from M. Hess Wartegg, Samoa, Nouvelle Guinée, et archipel Bismark*)*

Mrs. Zieger with Hawkins and Nat, and I'll take my share of your family meals."

When the two shipwrecked men were then introduced, their story was told briefly by the shipowner. Mr. Zieger welcomed the Kip brothers with great feeling and expressed the desire to receive them as often as possible at Wilhelmstaf. If he did not have a room available, they would find a comfortable inn in Port Praslin where they could stay, if they chose, until the *James Cook* departed.

Pieter Kip said, "Our resources are limited, or rather nonexistent . . . We lost everything we had in our shipwreck, and since Mr. Hawkins was so obliging as to accept us as passengers, it is our preference to remain on board."

"You can do as you like, my friends," declared the shipowner. "The brig is still at your service. I would even add that if you need to buy any clothes or linens, I am at your beck and call."

"And I as well," Mr. Zieger said.

"We thank you both," replied Karl Kip, "and as soon as we get to Holland we will send you . . ."

Mr. Hawkins continued, "There's no question of that, now. We'll work it out later on; you mustn't worry about it."

Mr. Gibson asked the businessman how long, in his opinion, the brig would need to remain in Port Praslin to unload its cargo and pick up a new one.

"Approximately three weeks," affirmed Mr. Zieger. "If one is enough to unload your merchandise, which I will see to selling profitably in the colony . . ."

"Certainly . . . one week will be enough," Mr. Gibson said, "on condition that our three hundred tons of copra are ready . . ."

"I have a hundred and fifty here in the warehouse," Mr. Zieger declared. "As for the other hundred and fifty, they'll put them on in Kerawara . . ."

The captain replied, "That's fine. The crossing is short. We'll go to Kerawara; then the *James Cook* will come back to Port Praslin to complete its cargo."

"The boxes of mother of pearl are ready, my dear Gibson," Mr. Zieger said, "and so you will have no delay to contend with."

Mr. Hawkins added, "It's a pleasure doing business with your firm, Mr. Zieger, and I see that our stopover will not last more than three weeks."

"This is November 20th," concluded Mr. Gibson, "the brig has no damage to repair, and on December 14th it will be ready to set sail."

"And during that time, Mr. Hawkins, you will be able to visit the environs of Port Praslin. It's worth your trouble. Besides, Mrs. Zieger and I will do all we can so the time you spend here will not be unpleasant."

Mr. Hawkins, the Kip brothers, and Nat Gibson disembarked, leaving the captain to his concerns, though he would join the group again at Wilhelmstaf for dinner.

Just as Mr. Gibson had thought, no ship was anchored at the moment in Port Praslin, nor was one expected there before the new year. All that could be seen were ships belonging to the trading posts and some native canoes. The ships under German flag docked by preference in the principal port of the German archipelago on Kerawara Island, which is located south of York Island, now known as New Lauenburg.

Yet Port Praslin is very sheltered at the back of its bay. It offers excellent anchorage to ships of heavy tonnage. The depth of the water there is everywhere the same. Also, between Birara and Tombara, the sounding lines show up to fourteen hundred meters. The brig had been able to moor in thirty fathoms. The anchor hold was good, one of those coral bottoms, sown with the debris of shells, where anchors bite solidly.

Port Praslin held only a hundred or so colonists, the vast majority of German descent, and several immigrants of English descent. They occupied houses scattered both east and west of the port, under the magnificent shade trees along the shores.

Mr. Zieger's house was built about a mile to the west further up the coast. The businesses and shopkeepers were found on a small, irregular square at the back of the port, where other companies had also set up their trade bureaus and offices.

The natives of New Ireland live apart from the colonial population. Their villages are simple agglomerations of huts raised for the most part on pilings. They frequent Port Praslin and often meet the agents who represent authority in the German Melanesia. So, while disembarking, Mr. Hawkins and his companions met several of them.

Although these natives are not workers by nature, and most of them spend their day doing nothing, occasionally they are eager to earn a few piastres. So it is not a rare thing that they are employed to help load or unload the ships. The shipping companies hire them, and, provided that they watch them somewhat closely, for they tend to steal, they have no reason to regret doing so.

The New Ireland native is not tall in stature, averaging only five feet two. He has a yellowish brown skin, and not dark like the Negro. His stomach is protuberant, his limbs somewhat frail. His hair is woolly, and he lets it fall on his shoulders in a curly mat, a hairdo that in civilized countries is the attribute of the female sex. It is noteworthy that the typical native's forehead is narrow, the nose flat, the mouth wide, and the teeth gnawed by the abuse of the betel nut.[3] On the septum and the sides of the nose, as well as from the ear lobes, both pierced with holes, hang rods to which are attached the teeth of animals, tufts of plumes, along with other articles of adornment. These natives are skimpily clad in fabric loincloths, which, in recent years, they have substituted for bark loincloths. In order to complete their dress, they turn to painting diverse parts of the body. Using ochre thinned with coconut oil, they tint their cheeks, their forehead, the tip of their nose, chin, shoulders, chest, and stomach. There is little that is not tattooed, and this tattoo is obtained not by pricking but by cuts made by means of stones and shells. All this ornamentation does not succeed in hiding leprosy, which affects their skin, despite the oily massages to which they subject themselves, nor the scars from wounds received in frequent battles, especially with their cousins from Birara.

There is no doubt that the natives of this archipelago have, in the past, been cannibalistic. That they still are occasionally might also be the case. In any event, the practice of cannibalism has diminished a great deal, thanks to the missionaries who settled on Roon Island, in the southwest of New Pomerania.

Native fishermen in the Bismarck Archipelago
(from M. Hess Wartegg, Samoa, Nouvelle Guinée, et archipel Bismark*)*

The natives, grouped on the pier, belonged to the stronger sex. No women accompanied them, and no child. It's in the villages and the countryside where the New Ireland women are working in the fields that one can encounter them, for they rarely come close to the trading posts.

"We'll make a few excursions to the interior," Mr. Zieger said, "and you'll have the time to study these people at leisure."

"That will be with pleasure," agreed Mr. Hawkins.

"In the meantime," added Mr. Zieger, "I'm eager to introduce you to Mrs. Zieger, who is probably a bit impatient."

"We're right behind you," replied the shipowner.

The road winding along the shore in the direction of Wilhelmstaf was very shaded. The plantations, arranged in tiers upward toward the interior, only stopped when reaching the very edge of the surf, on the furthermost rocks of the cove. On the right, thick forests spread up to the summits of the central chain, dominated by the two or three peaks of the Lanut. When any obstacle, stream or swamp, forced one to leave the riverbank, one could take off under the trees, along paths that were barely discernible. There, one could see cashews, screw pines, and prickly pears. A network of vines, a few of a striking yellow, like gold, circled the trunks of these trees, twisted among their branches, and climbed to their tops. One needed to watch out for the tearing thorns, and Mr. Zieger repeated to his guests:

"I recommend that you be careful; if not, you'll arrive home half-naked, which is not acceptable, even in New Mecklenburg."[4]

There was really reason to admire, both for their diversity and for their magnificent growth, the many plant species of these New Ireland forests. As far as the eye could see, there were hibiscus, whose leaves recalled those of the linden tree, palm trees garlanded with festoons of convolvulus, callophyllums whose trunks measured up to thirty feet in circumference, rotins, peppers, cycas palms with straight trunks, from which the natives collect the marrow for bread-making, lobelias half-submerged in water, pancratiums with stems embellished with white corollas and among whose leaves scarabs nest, which is not a bird but a beetle.

This whole forest reached colossal proportions: the coconut palms, sago palms, bread trees, nutmeg trees, bourbon palms, areca palms, whose terminal bud is cut like a palm cabbage and is readily edible; then innumerable arborescent plants, ferns with light foliage, parasitic epidendrons, inocarpe trees of a stature greater than similar trees on other islands of the Pacific and whose roots, emerging from the soil, form natural hutches, where there is room for five or six people.

Sometimes there were clearings, bordered with enormous shrubs, watered by the rios' clear waters, which are used for farming; fields of sugar cane, sweet potatoes, and taros, carefully kept up, where several native women were working.

There was nothing, moreover, to worry about concerning the fauna, neither wild beasts nor any other dangerous animals, not even poisonous snakes. Animal life was less varied than the flora. Nothing but wild pigs, less fearsome than the wild boar, and for the most part domesticated; some dogs called "poulls" in the Tombarian language; cuscus, opossums, lizards and also a multitude of rats of a small size. Lastly were the termites or white ants, which hang their spongy nests on the tree branches; among them are sometimes hung, like a thread, webs woven by legions of spiders of purple and azure colors.

"Don't I hear some dogs?" Nat Gibson asked, when his ears were struck by what seemed to be distant barking.

"No," replied Mr. Zieger, "they aren't barking dogs, but rather the cry of birds."

"Birds?" asked Mr. Hawkins, quite surprised.

Mr. Zieger affirmed, "Yes, a species of crow that is unique to the Bismarck Archipelago."

Nat Gibson and Mr. Hawkins had been mistaken, as had been Bougainville the first time that he walked through the New Ireland forests. Indeed, this crow imitates the barking of a dog so well as to completely deceive anyone hearing it.

Moreover, on these islands, ornithology has both numerous and sometimes curious representatives, or "mains," to use the native word.

On all sides can be seen flying loris, a sort of scarlet parrot, papous, with a voice as hoarse as that of the Papuans, parakeets of various species, nicobar pigeons, crows with a white down and a black plumage that the natives call "cocos," parrots tinted in a glossy green, and pinon doves with a pinkish-gray head and neck, their wings and back a golden green with tints of copper below and whose flesh is extremely savory.

When Mr. Zieger and his companions approached the river, there were flocks of starlings and swallows, kingfishers of several varieties, among others "alcyon" to which the natives gave the name of "kiou-kiou," whose head and back were a greenish-brown, wings of an aquamarine, and tail of the same color, six inches in length; then came the souimange, or sunbird, olive in color with a yellow tail, the cuckoo shrike, the gray-rumped sandpiper, the flycatcher, "conice, tenouri, kine, and roukine" according to the Melanesian denomination. And all the while the tortoises climbed on the sand, the crocodiles basked, sharks moved through the channels, and the oceanic eagles glided through the air, their broad wings almost immobile.

As for the seashore, covered or not covered according to the time of the tides, whose height is of little note, they would have provided the conchologist with unlimited riches in crustaceans or mollusks, crabs, pagures, shrimp, ocypods, sponges, urchins, organ-pipe coral, porcelain shells, top shells, giant clams, ovoles, abalone, sting winkles, limpets, oysters, mussels, and as for zoophytes, slugs, sea anemones, molls, medusas, and jellyfish of a remarkable species.[5]

But the shellfish worthy of attracting the special attention of Mr. Hawkins and Nat Gibson were the scarabs, which by preference hide between the wet leaves of the pancratium on the edge of creeks; the bulimus and pond snail, who both seek the shelter of branches; and a nerita fluviatile, or river mollusk, which can sometimes be found at a great distance from water courses, attached to the highest branches of the screw pine.

And as Nat Gibson responded to Mr. Zieger about one of his traveling shellfish:

"But, it seems to me that there's a fish who could follow the nerita in his terrestrial promenades, and that the Messrs. Kip saw on Norfolk Island, if I am not mistaken."

"You mean the jumping blenny," replied Mr. Zieger.

"Precisely," confirmed Mr. Hawkins.

"Well," Mr. Zieger declared, "there are a lot of them around. And you'll also find in the bay of Port Praslin some amphibians that live in fresh water or salt water, that run on the beaches, leaping like opossums, and that climb the shrubbery like insects!"

Mr. Zieger's house appeared at the bend where some trees clustered. It was a sort of villa, built of wood in the middle of a vast enclosure of live hedges, in which there were rows of orange trees, coconut palms, banana trees, and a large number of others. Shaded under their high-rising fronds, Wilhelmstaf was composed of one story, surmounted by a roof structure of tarred canvas, necessary due to the frequent rains, which render quite tolerable the climate of an archipelago situated almost at the Equator.

Mrs. Zieger was a woman of some forty years, German, as was her husband. As soon as the gateway had been opened, she hurried to greet her guests:

"Ah, Mr. Hawkins," she exclaimed, offering her hand to the shipowner, "how happy I am to see you!"

"And I as well, dear lady," replied Mr. Hawkins, kissing her on both cheeks. "Your last trip to Hobart Town must've been four years ago now."

"Four years and a half, Mr. Hawkins!"

"Well," declared the shipowner, smiling, "despite those extra six months, I find you just as you were."

Mrs. Zieger resumed, "I won't say that about Nat Gibson. He has changed, he has! He's no longer a child, he's a young man."

"Who will ask your permission to imitate Mr. Hawkins," replied Nat Gibson, giving her a hug in his turn.

"And your father?" asked Mrs. Zieger.

"He stayed aboard," replied Mr. Hawkins, "but he won't miss his chance to be here at dinner time."

Mr. and Mrs. Zieger had no children. They lived alone in this villa named Wilhelmstaf with their servants, a German couple like themselves, and a family of colonists lodged in an annex. These farmers, along with some native women, cultivated a variety of crops on the property. Fields of sugar cane, potatoes, taros, and yams stretched out for a square mile.

In front of the house the ground was covered with a green lawn sown with casuarinas and bouquets of latania, watered by a brook of fresh water, which came from a stream in the neighborhood. Behind the outbuildings, equally shaded, a poultry yard and an aviary, the former enclosing the most handsome birds on the archipelago and populated with pigeons, doves, and some domestic birds to whom the natives bestowed the name of "cock" by onomatopoeia, for their guttural cry.

It goes without saying that Mr. Hawkins and his companions found refreshment awaiting them in the living room of the villa.

Karl and Pieter Kip had been introduced to Mrs. Zieger, and she was very moved in learning under what conditions the two brothers had been picked up aboard the *James Cook*. The excellent woman placed herself at their disposition in every way that might be helpful to them, and they thanked her for the sympathetic welcome.

Mr. Hawkins and Nat Gibson went to visit the chambers that were prepared for them, attractively decorated with large furnishings made in Germany, as comfortable as the living room and the dining room. Mrs. Zieger excused herself for not being able to offer hospitality to the two Dutchmen. But, as we know, it was agreed at their request that they would not leave their cabin in the brig.

A bit before noon, Mr. Gibson arrived, accompanied by sailor Burnes. The latter was carrying diverse objects offered as gifts by Mr. Hawkins to Mrs. Zieger, fabrics, linens, and a pretty bracelet, which gave her great pleasure. Needless to say, the captain was also received with open arms.

They sat down at the table, and the meal, well served, was particularly appreciated by guests endowed with hearty appetites. The main dishes were furnished by the barnyard and the bay of Port Praslin. As for the vegetables, cabbage palms, yams, sweet potatoes, and for fruits, bananas, oranges, coconuts, they all came from their own fields. For the fermented drinks, one only had to bring them up from a fine cellar, stocked with wines from France and Germany that ships arriving at New Mecklenburg regularly brought in.

They complimented Mrs. Zieger on the excellence of her table, which could rival the best of Hobart Town, and the amiable hostess seemed quite appreciative of those compliments.

"There is but one dish that I can no longer offer you, dear friends," said Mr. Zieger, "because it is no longer made in this country."

Mr. Hawkins asked, "And what is that?"

"A pâté made of sago, coconuts, and human brain."

"Was it good?" cried out Nat Gibson.

"The king of pâtés!"

"Have you ever eaten any?" asked Mr. Hawkins, laughing.

"Never. And I'll never again have the chance to do so."

"That's the way it is," exclaimed the captain, "for having destroyed cannibalism in the archipelago!"

"As you say, my dear Gibson!" replied Mr. Zieger.

The captain was to return on board the *James Cook* as soon as lunch was over. He did not like to remain away very long, despite his trust in his bosun. His great fear was always about being hampered by new desertions, and he had little confidence in those hired on at Dunedin.

As a matter of fact, the question was posed again that very day by Len Cannon in a conversation that he and his comrades had with Flig Balt and Vin Mod. They kept returning to their decision to disembark. In vain did Vin Mod employ his eloquence by bringing up the gallows, as was his wont. He could not persuade them in the least bit. Those stubborn sailors persisted in their desire to leave the ship.

"Well," he said, running out of arguments, "it's not the ship that displeases you?"

"Yes, it is," replied Len Cannon, "from the moment that we came under command of its captain."

"And if this captain happened to disappear? . . ."

"That's the twentieth time you've sung that refrain, Mod," retorted the sailor Kyle, "and here we are in Port Praslin, and in three weeks we'll take off for Hobart Town."

"Where we don't want to go," said Bryce.

"And," declared Sexton, "we've made up our minds to take off this evening."

"At least wait a few days," said Flig Balt, "until the brig leaves! We don't know what will happen . . ."

"And then," observed Vin Mod, "deserting is fine . . . but what do you hope to do here?"

At this moment, the cabin boy, Jim, who was suspicious about these discussions between the bosun and the recruits, approached the group. Flig Balt, who saw him, immediately shouted:

"What are you doing, cabin boy?"

"I was coming down for lunch."

"You can eat later!"

"And I'm sure," added Vin Mod, "that the cabin of the Kip brothers has not yet been picked up. You'll end up on the gallows, you wretched ship's boy!"

"Go take care of the wardroom," ordered the bosun, "and don't make a sloppy job of it!"

Vin Mod watched the young boy, and made a sign to Flig Balt that the latter understood, no doubt. Then the conversation went on.

As for Jim, without answering back, he went aft, and since he was in fact in charge of the cabins, he entered the Kips' room.

The first object that struck his view was a Malaysian dagger, laid out on a packing case, and which he had never seen before.

It was the one Vin Mod had stolen from the hull of the *Wilhelmina* and that the two brothers did not know was in his possession.

Was it by chance that the kriss had been placed there, in such a way that the cabin boy could not help but see it?

Jim took the dagger, examined its saw-like teeth, the ornate handle with copper nails, and replaced it on the shelf. What occurred to him was that one of the brothers had brought the dagger back with the few objects picked up from the wreck, and without giving any further attention to it, he carried on with his duties.

Jim took the dagger, examined its saw-like teeth . . .

However, Flig Balt, Vin Mod, and the others continued their discussion, but in a way not to be overheard by Wickley or Hobbes, whom the bosun had sent up into the rigging. Burnes, as we know, had accompanied Mr. Gibson to the Wilhelmstaf villa.

Len Cannon was obstinate, Vin Mod tried to convince him . . . at least during the brig's stopover, he and his companions would not be lacking in anything . . . There would still be time to disembark . . . During the trip of the *James Cook* from Port Praslin to Kerawara to load up the hold, perhaps some opportunity would present itself? It was possible that neither Mr. Hawkins nor Nat Gibson would be making that trip. Who knows, even the Kip brothers . . . And then . . .

In short, Len Cannon, Kyle, Sexton, and Bryce agreed to stay until the day the brig should set sail for Hobart Town.

And, when Flig Balt and Vin Mod were alone:

"That wasn't easy!" the latter said.

"We're not any further along!" replied the other.

"Patience," concluded Vin Mod with the tone of a man whose mind was made up, "And when Captain Balt chooses his bosun, I'm fully counting on his not forgetting Vin Mod!"

Three Weeks in the Archipelago

The following days were employed in unloading the cargo from the brig. Len Cannon and his companions did not refuse to give a hand. Mr. Gibson had no suspicion of their plans.

A few natives joined the crew—a half-dozen—robust and not unskilled men. So the work was carried out under excellent conditions.

Jim had not spoken to the Kip brothers about the Malaysian kriss. So they did not know that this weapon had been laying on one of the shelves in their cabin.

Indeed, Vin Mod had been careful to take back the dagger before their return on board, and the kriss was now hidden in his sack, where no one could have found it. It was enough, no doubt, that it had been seen by the cabin boy. As to what he planned to do with it, perhaps even Flig Balt did not know.

While the captain remained to watch over the unloading, Mr. Hawkins, Nat Gibson, Karl and Pieter Kip, accompanied by Mr. and Mrs. Zieger, spent time on interesting walks around Port Praslin. They visited the principal factories established on that part of the coast. Some belonged to the German colonists; the others were still in the hands of English firms, founded before the treaty of partition.

All of them had fairly good businesses. Imports and exports in the former Tombara as in the former Birara generated much profit for the Germanic Melanesia.

Everywhere the guests of Mr. Zieger received an excellent welcome. This honest trader occupied a leading position in the commercial company, which also exercised some political authority. He was, by that fact, invested with a certain judiciary power that the natives did not refuse to recognize. Besides, not a single year rolled by without a warship coming to put into port at one of the islands of the Bismarck Archipelago and responding with regulation honors when Mr. Zieger had the German colors hoisted on the Port Praslin flagpole.

Besides, the imperial government had left to the natives their almost complete independence. The tribes have no real chief. If some authority falls to the elderly, at least all members of the tribe are on equal footing. No slaves exist, even in villages in the interior; all workers are free. So it is as free men, earning a salary paid in manufactured goods or food products, that they work in the factory or in the field. Moreover, before the suppression of slavery, slaves were treated quite well by their masters.

This beginning of civilization is certainly due to the zeal and devotion of missionaries who settled at different points on the archipelago. They travel continually, with Gospel in hand. In Port Praslin there is a Protestant chapel where two such pastors serve and which satisfies the need for religious worship.

It was during an excursion to the central section of the isle, some three miles from the port, that Mr. Hawkins, Nat Gibson, and the Kip brothers, guided by Mr. Zieger, visited a Tombarian village.

This village was but the agglomeration of some fifty wooden huts and, although the soil was not swampy, they were set on piles.

The natives were without doubt of the Papouasian race, only slightly different from those of New Guinea. This village contained about one hundred sixty men, women, oldsters, children, divided up into families. It goes without saying that they knew Mr. Zieger, and would submit to his authority if need be, although he rarely had to exercise it among the tribes of the interior.

His companions and he were welcomed by two aged natives, who assumed a look of dignity by remaining impassive and indifferent. The women and children stayed in their huts, and it was difficult to approach them. True, it was still unclear as to the exact nature of the family structure as well as the social state of the diverse Melanesian peoples.

Natives no longer went around almost nude, or simply dressed in a loincloth of filaments held together by sewing fibers. Thanks to the cotton goods, both English and German, that were now widespread throughout the country, both men and women dressed in striped fabrics. This decency must be considered a beginning of civilized reform.

Mr. Zieger was able to provide both precise and valuable information on the customs of these natives, whose sense of vision, smell, and hearing are extraordinarily developed. Thus they bring an incomparable skill and dexterity to all physical activities. But to commit themselves to any kind of work, they must be moved by the basic need of nourishing themselves. Of an indolent character, they love repose above all. In this village, most of the inhabitants were resting outside their huts. Abandoning themselves to a complete nonchalance, legs crossed one over the other, hands on the chest, watching but scarcely speaking, they chewed betel nuts the way Orientals smoke opium or Occidentals smoke tobacco.

This betel is composed of chalk, obtained by the calcination of madrepores, and of a fruit with a red peel, the name of which is “kamban.” It is a powerful sialagogue,[1] whose very acrid ingredients possess an intoxicating savor with a taste that has nothing unpleasant. Its disadvantage is the darkening of the teeth, corroding them, making them bleed into the mucous of the mouth. By a custom that is never broken, the young people have no right to this sought-after pleasure, and it is only mature natives who are permitted to chew betel.

As to the industry of the natives of New Ireland, it is limited to the weaving of straw into the needles of the screw pine and making diverse objects, crude pottery. And yet it is to the women, less lazy than the men, that this work has been left, not to mention the agricultural labor or the daily preparation of food.

Eating calls for little culinary science. The natives do not eat at fixed hours, or rather they eat at any hour. As one traveler has said of them:

“Whatever animal falls under the hand of a savage, it is immediately thrown over the burning coals, roasted, devoured, without even making the effort of skinning it, if it’s a quadruped, or to pluck it if it’s a bird.”

Fish, marine tortoises, octopuses, shellfish of all sorts, crayfish, enormous crabs called koukiavars, reptiles, lizards, insects of little appeal, they eat them with an appetite of gluttons. With fruits, there are the “mape” and the “laka,” a sort of abundant chestnut “inocarpe,” coconuts or lamacs, sugar cane, bananas, yams or ignames, and wild bread fruits. As for quadrupeds, the natives raise only pigs and hunt only cuscus,[2] animals which belong to the subgenus of phalangers.

The New Ireland natives, however, do not show themselves to be rebellious toward efforts to civilize them. Missionaries try to convert them to the Christian religion.[3] But, in their culture, their attachment to paganism is very tenacious and mixes with certain Moslem beliefs, which come to them from relations with the Malays. It is even to be presumed that these savages are polygamous. In each village they construct the “tambou” or public house with its idols, of which the elderly have the upkeep and protection.

Mr. Hawkins and his companions did not experience any difficulty in visiting this "tambou," the doors of which are less often closed than those of private homes, and which Mr. Zieger was readily able to open. They found on the inside of this large building several clay statues, crudely done, daubed with white, black, red, whose eyes of mother of pearl sparkled like glowing embers. Bakoui, such is the name these idols bear. Among other objects placed around them, one could make out two tom-toms that a native struck on the order of an old man with a long beard, who was covered with ochre dust. There was also an ornament attached to these statues, a prapraghan of wood, finely sculpted, which ordinarily decorates the prow of the native canoes.

Nat Gibson had brought along his photographic apparatus. He obtained, from the interior and the exterior of this "tambou," some very successful photos to enrich Mr. Hawkins's collection.

During this visit to the Tombarian village, the afternoon passed by quickly. Evening was already approaching when Mr. Zieger and his guests took to the Wilhelmstaf road through the forest. If the celestial stars were gleaming by the thousands above the top of the great trees, it was by the millions that certain earthbound stars were projecting their phosphorescent light into the middle of this hanging foliage and through the blades of grass below. Such were the abundance of those glow worms, which are called "kallottes" in the Melanesian language, and which lit up the undergrowth. It seemed that one's feet walked through a luminous turf, while a cloud of brilliant stars gleamed down between the branches.

In this way days were spent on interesting excursions, along the shore and in the interior of the island. One day, Karl Kip, Nat Gibson, and Mr. Hawkins, guided by one of the men from the trading post, even climbed the mountain behind the villa. It required a few hours of fatigue, although the hike took place under the thick shade of the forests.

This mountain does not rank among the highest in the central chain—roughly five thousand feet. But this altitude permits one's gaze to reach the Saint George's Channel between New Britain and

New Ireland. Beyond, there appeared other heights. To the south is visible the island of New Pomerania, whose contours stretch out as far as the eye can see.

It goes without saying that Mr. and Mrs. Zieger, like landowners who do not wish to overlook any part of their domain, took care not to forget one of the most picturesque sites that can solicit the admiration of tourists in the east of Port Praslin. It was a marvelous waterfall to which the Frenchman Duperrey gave the name of Bougainville.

The springs that the mountain sends off to the sea fall some fifty feet in this place. They gush from the mountain's flanks and foam along the surface in five tiers among the mountain's green crests. The waters, containing a heavy proportion of salt, create calcareous stalactite borders along the many strata of carbonated chalk, over which they flow. One cannot help but note the accuracy of the account of Captain Duperrey when he speaks of those "stone outcroppings whose steps, almost regular, rush and diversify the fall of that cascade and the varied levels which form a hundred scattered pools where the crystal water falls, colored by immense trees, a few of which plunge their foot into the very basin."[4] This excursion provided some new photographs for Mr. Hawkins's collection, and the most beautiful that had been taken so far of the Bougainville Falls.

The unloading of the *James Cook* was completed on the afternoon of November 25th. All the inexpensive goods consigned to the Zieger firm had found immediate placement in the stores, being composed of everyday household items manufactured in Germany or England.

The brig was now ready to take on its cargo for the return trip, consisting, as has been said, of tons of copra and cases of mother of pearl destined for Hobart Town. Of the three hundred tons of copra, a hundred and fifty were to be delivered to Port Praslin by the Zieger firm and a hundred and fifty to Kerawara, one of the small islands situated to the south of York Island (or New Lauenburg).

The captain, in agreement with Mr. Hawkins and Mr. Zieger, decided that the load from Kerawara would be the first on board. The

*The Bougainville Falls**

*Facsimile of an illustration published in the *Great Voyages and Great Navigators* by Jules Verne (Hetzel's note).

James Cook would go take delivery and then return to Port Praslin to complete its cargo.

Moreover, even if the brig had no damage to repair, it was necessary for its hull to have a thorough cleaning and that it be repainted from bow to stern above the waterline. This work would require three or four days. The crew set to work immediately. It was completed according to schedule, and departure was set for the morning of November 29th.

It has not been forgotten that Flig Balt and Vin Mod had hoped the passengers of the brig would stay in Port Praslin during this trip to Kerawara, that the captain would be on board alone, and that they could profit from this circumstance to accomplish their nefarious plan. Once they had taken over the ship, they would head northeast and Mr. Hawkins would wait in vain for the *James Cook* to reappear in the waters of New Ireland.

The bosun and his accomplices were to be disappointed. Not only would Mr. Hawkins, Nat Gibson, and the Kip brothers be on this short trip, but Mr. Zieger also proposed accompanying them, and his proposal was met with enthusiasm.

Flig Balt and Vin Mod were hard put to hide their fury. The possibility of taking over the *James Cook,* or at least the eventuality of it that they were counting on, slipped away from them once again.

"The devil himself is protecting that wretched captain!" exclaimed Vin Mod when he heard of this decision.

"You'll see, Mod, that he'll come back to Hobart Town!" added the bosun.

"No, Bosun Balt," declared Vin Mod. "If we can't get rid of him on his boat, perhaps we could . . ."

"How about the others, what'll they do?" replied Flig Balt.

The others were Len Cannon, Sexton, Kyle, and Bryce. Were they going to quit the ship right away, or would they make the trip to Kerawara before leaving with their bags? If they were not to get anything in the course of this trip, why should they continue their service?

It is true, during this stopover in Port Praslin, they became convinced that it would not be easy to make a living on the island, and that had given them cause for reflection. That's what Vin Mod pointed out, and he got them to agree that they would continue on to Kerawara, free to disembark on the return trip.

The brig left on the morning of the twenty-ninth. One day to clear York Island, two days to load on the hundred and fifty tons of copra, one more day to return to Port Praslin; the whole trip should not take more than four or five days.

The political and commercial capital of the Bismarck Archipelago had first been the little island of Mioko, to the south of York Island. It occupied an intermediary point between the two large islands of the archipelago of Bismarck. Then, because of unhealthy conditions, the capital was changed to Matupi Island, located in the middle of a crater of Blanche Bay, which is situated at the extreme northern end of Birara. Earthquakes there having compromised its security, the government then established definitively the capital city on Kerawara Island.

They navigated through Saint George's Channel, though not without some delay due to contrary winds on the surface of that vast bay, where the sounding line showed up to four thousand feet of depth. The channel is formed by the islands of Tombara and Birara, which approach each other at their southeast and northeast points. However, it was not possible for Mr. Hawkins or Nat Gibson to go ashore, to their keen regret, for Birara deserves to be visited. Surrounded by an amphitheater of volcanic cones—such as the Mother, Daughter of the North, and the Daughter of the South—they are the largest of the archipelago, the most mountainous, the most forested, as well as the richest in coconut palms. And certain ethnological particularities also make it a quite special island. Where in the world would you find an island where a son-in-law never dares address his mother-in-law, and even hides when he finds her, an island whose residents are said to have their toes connected by a membrane, an island even where legend has it that there exist an indigenous people who have a caudal appendage, in other words, men with a tail![5]

But, if the brig was not to put into port here, it would at least travel along its length in crossing Saint George's Channel to reach York Island.[6]

It was Carteret, in 1707, who gave it the name of York in place of its Melanesian name of Amakata. Mentioned in 1791 by Hunter, in 1792 by D'Entrecasteaux, in 1823 by Duperrey, its exact geographic position is known to be between 150°2' and 150°7' of longitude and 4°5' and 4°10' of south latitude. Its length is eight miles from the northeast to the southwest by five miles in width, and its average altitude above sea level is rather considerable.

However, as populated as it is and as safe as its available moorings are, it does not contain the capital city of the archipelago. A number of small islands surround it: Makada, Burnan, Ulu, Utuan, Kabokon, Muarlin, Mioko, and Kerawara. And it is this last island, situated more to the south, that the German government definitively selected.

The next day, the 30th, very early in the morning, the watch signaled Cape Brown of Makada Isle. The *James Cook,* turning south, skirted Cape Makukar of the large island, steered toward the opening of the northwest passage between it and the island of Uln, sighted the small island of Kabokon, and reached its mooring off Kerawara.

This island, which has the shape of a sickle, measures no more than three miles from west to east. Endowed with a very safe harbor, it offers ships all the advantages of an excellent port.

The principal German agent, Mr. Hamburg, had frequent contacts with Mr. Zieger. He was the head of one of the most important manufacturers of the group, and his company was to deliver to the *James Cook* the hundred and fifty tons of copra. This amount would be placed on board in forty-eight hours. The stay at Kerawara would only be a short one.

While the crew, under the surveillance of the captain, was busy at this operation, Mr. Hawkins, Nat Gibson, and the Kip brothers had the leisure time to visit the island.

It is, to tell the truth, a vast forest where the diverse aspects of

New Ireland meet. A few hills, of which the largest measures some eight hundred feet, dominate it. This capital city of the archipelago at that time counted a thousand inhabitants, of whom a quarter were European and the rest of Melanesian descent. These natives were not absolutely sedentary. For the most part, settled on York Island or the neighboring islets, they came to Kerawara to carry out their business. The channels of this small group of islets, continually traversed by their remarkably constructed canoes, showed much activity.

Mr. Hamburg could give interesting details about this island group. The choice of Kerawara Island as the political capital seemed to him quite justified. Relations between New Britain and New Ireland were cordial.

There were at this moment in the port two merchant ships—one carrying the flag of Germany, the other carrying the British flag—that were busy unloading their cargo. Before continuing on to their destinations, the first to Sidney, Australia, the second to Auckland, New Zealand, their stopover in Kerawara was to last three more weeks. Messrs. Hawkins and Gibson knew the English captain, whom they had seen sometimes in Hobart Town, and they were happy to shake his hand.

Mr. Hamburg's home was situated halfway up the slope, in the middle of the forest, which was traversed by a wide path. A half mile separated it from his portside office.

The governor had invited Mr. Hawkins, Mr. Gibson, and his son to have dinner with him the next day. The loading of a hundred and fifty tons of copra would be finished that afternoon, December 2nd, and the *James Cook,* the following day, would take to the sea to return to Port Praslin.

The Kip brothers were included in the invitation offered by Mr. Hamburg, but they had declined with the modest reserve of people who do not wish to impose. They would profit from this evening to take one last walk about the port. As for the crew of the brig, since desertion was not to be feared, they had permission to go ashore and would not fail to fraternize with the crews of other ships. The evening would end no doubt with drunkenness in the main tavern of Kerawara. That was difficult to prevent, and Mr. Gibson only recommended they not let things go too far.

Flig Balt assured the captain that he could be counted on. But, while talking with his usual obsequiousness, why could he not conceal the worry that seemed to bother him? Noticing it, Mr. Gibson said to him:

"What's wrong, Balt?"

"Nothing, Mr. Gibson, nothing . . ." replied the bosun. "I am a bit tired, that's all."

And his eyes, turning from the captain, fastened on Vin Mod, who was watching him.

Toward five o'clock, Mr. Hawkins, Nat Gibson, and Mr. Zieger found themselves at Mr. Hamburg's home, where dinner was to be served at six-thirty. The captain, delayed on board ship to complete the final paperwork, would not arrive before that time. He was to bring a sum of two thousand piastres in gold, payment for the cargo now stored in the hold of the *James Cook*.

While waiting for him, the guests of the governor explored the property, carefully maintained, and one of the most beautiful on Kerawara. Nat Gibson took several photos of the house and area around the terrace. The view, passing over the towering trees, extended to the open sea. Toward the northwest, they could see the distant promontory of the great Isle of Ulu, westward, the headland of the little islet Kabokon, beyond which the sun set under a horizon magnificently purpled with clouds to the very edge of the sky and sea.

When the clock indicated six-thirty, the captain still had not appeared.

Mr. Hamburg and his guests remained in the garden awaiting his arrival. The evening was splendid; the air was slightly cooled by the wind, which rose as night approached. They breathed deeply the fragrant scent of orange blossoms.

Meanwhile, time passed. At seven o'clock, Mr. Gibson had still not been seen.

"My father must have been held up at the last moment," Nat Gibson said. "Otherwise I cannot explain this delay . . ."

"Was he to go to your office, Mr. Hamburg?" asked the shipowner.

"Yes, but only to pick up his papers."

"That must have taken some time . . ."

"Patience," the governor said. "We've only waited half an hour."

When another half hour had passed, Mr. Hawkins, Mr. Zieger, and Nat Gibson began to be concerned.

"Could Gibson," Mr. Zieger said, "have gotten lost on the way?"

"Unlikely," replied Mr. Hamburg. "The road is straight, and he knows it, for he has come several times to our home."

"Suppose we go to meet him . . . ," proposed Nat Gibson, getting to his feet.

"Let's go," Mr. Hawkins said.

Mr. Hamburg called one of his servants, who provided him with a lantern, and, accompanied by his guests, he left the enclosure to enter the forest.

The darkness was already profound under the thick foliage, which formed a vault of branches above the path.

They listened for footsteps in the direction of the port . . .

No sound.

They called.

No reply.

This part of the forest seemed absolutely deserted.

Finally, after a half mile, they emerged on Kerawara square.

From the main tavern, well lighted and animated, one could hear the confused noise of men drinking. Although part of the brig's crew had already returned on board, some sailors were still seated at their tables in the tavern, among them Len Cannon and his comrades.

As for Pieter and Karl Kip, who had just returned to the ship, they were seated in the stern of the *James Cook*.

A bit before, Flig Balt and Vin Mod had also returned to the ship after an absence of about half an hour.

They called. No reply.

Arriving at the dock, Nat Gibson called out in a worried voice:

"And the captain?"

"The captain, Mr. Gibson?" replied Vin Mod. "Isn't he at Mr. Hamburg's home?"

"No," the governor responded.

"But he left the brig to go there," the sailor Burnes declared.

"And I saw him take the path," added Hobbes.

"When did he leave?" asked Mr. Zieger.

"About an hour ago," responded Vin Mod.

"I fear some misfortune has occurred . . . ," observed Mr. Hawkins.

So he and his companions spread out through the streets of the port, from office to office, and also checking all the taverns.

It became clear that the captain had not been seen anywhere.

They were obliged to search a larger area in the forest.

Perhaps Mr. Gibson had reached the house by some detour?

It was to no avail. After several hours Mr. Hamburg, Mr. Hawkins, Nat Gibson, and the Kip brothers, who had joined them, had to return home.

The night passed in great apprehension. The captain did not reappear. They walked back and forth, with lanterns and torches, along the path between the port and Mr. Hamburg's house. Harry Gibson was not to be seen anywhere.

Nat Gibson gave way to despair. Mr. Hawkins, no less despairing, could not succeed in calming the young man, who was profoundly troubled at the thought that he might never see his father again.

This sense of foreboding was not misplaced.

At daybreak the news quickly spread that the body of Captain Gibson had been discovered in the forest, half a mile from the port.[7]

The Murder

This is what had happened:

As soon as he had given his last instructions so that the *James Cook* would be ready for sailing the next morning at daybreak, the captain disembarked and went first to the office.

A small pouch that he was carrying contained the sum of two thousand piastres in gold, which he was to put into the hands of Mr. Hamburg.

Part of the crew had left the brig after him, and the Kip brothers were already taking a stroll around the port.

When Mr. Gibson arrived at the office, one of Mr. Hamburg's employees handed him various papers, his bill of lading and so forth.

The sun, for another two hours, would continue to light up the peaks of the little island of Kabokon. The captain knew the route leading to the villa, and he had no fear of going astray.

Once in the forest at the far end of the port, Mr. Gibson walked half a mile and was ready to turn left when he was violently thrown to the earth!

Two men leapt upon him, and one of them was strangling him!

Dazed by the blow that had struck him in the chest, he did not recognize them, having lost almost immediately the use of his senses.

His attackers took him by the shoulders and feet and carried him five hundred feet through the forest.

After stopping at the edge of a clearing, the criminals dropped their victim on the ground, and one said:

"We have to finish him off . . ."

At that moment Mr. Gibson's eyes reopened.

"Flig Balt! . . . Vin Mod!" he exclaimed.

It was indeed the bosun and Vin Mod who had committed this

"Flig Balt! . . . Vin Mod!" he exclaimed.

crime. Vin Mod would at last be free of Harry Gibson and finally realize his hope that Flig Balt would obtain command of the ship. So, under the direction of the new captain, instead of sailing for Hobart Town, the brig would alter its direction and, without Mr. Hawkins's noticing, would take an easterly course toward the area of the Solomon Islands. Once there, they would see to ridding themselves of the shipowner, Nat Gibson, the Kip brothers, and those men who would not agree to join them in piracy. What had not been done from New Zealand to the Bismarck Archipelago would be done after leaving Port Praslin.

After Mr. Gibson had shouted out the names of the two assassins, these words escaped from his lips:

"Scoundrels . . . scoundrels!"

He tried to rise up, to defend himself, but what could he do, without weapons, against two men who were both powerful and armed?

"Help!" he shouted again.

Vin Mod threw himself on the unfortunate man, and with one hand he closed the doomed man's mouth while Flig Balt, with the dagger that had been stolen from the *Wilhelmina* wreck by his accomplice, stabbed him full in the chest.

Harry Gibson uttered a final groan. Then, with his eyes wide open and filled with horror, he stared at his murderers one last time.[1] The blade of the dagger had struck his heart, and, after one final moment of agony, he fell back dead.

"Captain Balt . . . I salute you!" said Vin Mod, raising his hand to his beret.

The bosun, terrified, shrank back before the eyes of his victim, which, brightly lit by a ray of sunlight, were still staring at him.

Vin Mod, having kept all his wits about him, searched the captain's pockets, where he found the boarding papers and the pouch, from which he withdrew the two thousand piastres.

"A pleasant surprise!" he exclaimed.

Then, tapping the bosun on the shoulder, who was still standing as if transfixed under the dead man's gaze:

"Let's take off!" he said.

Leaving the body in its place, where it would probably not be discovered before the brig was at sea, they both regained the path and turned toward the port.

A quarter of an hour later, they strode onto the deck of the *James Cook*.

Flig Balt returned to his cabin. Vin Mod went down to the crew quarters, empty at the moment, and hid the captain's papers, the stolen piastres, and the dagger that had served as the murder weapon at the bottom of his bag.[2]

A half hour had passed since Karl and Pieter Kip returned aboard ship, and, while waiting for the return of those invited to Mr. Hamburg's home, they sat on deck behind the crew quarters.

As for Vin Mod, the scoundrel went up on the forward bridge. Pretending an extreme gaiety, he began talking to Hobbes and Wickley, who had not gone ashore.

Thus had the crime been committed.

It was the employee of a warehouse who the following day, while walking through the clearing, discovered Captain Gibson's body. He returned with all possible speed to the factory, and a report of the murder spread immediately.

At this news, Nat Gibson fainted as though thunderstruck. It was clear what bonds of affection united the father and son. Mr. Hawkins, just as terribly smitten as the poor young man, was unable to care for him. The Kip brothers had to transport the son to his cabin, where he finally regained consciousness. Both, moreover, expressed their most heartfelt grief and deepest indignation.

The crew was devastated. Jim wept heavy tears. Hobbes, Wickley, and Burnes could not believe the death of their captain. Flig Balt and Vin Mod overflowed with violent threats against the murderer.

Only the Dunedin recruits showed a complete indifference. It must be remembered that Len Cannon and the others had decided to disembark that very day—which would have compromised and even prevented the brig's departure. But, with Mr. Gibson now out of the picture, their plans were no doubt going to be modified. On several occasions, Len Cannon shot a questioning look at Vin Mod. The latter simply turned his head as though not understanding.

However, Nat Gibson, after regaining his senses, dashed out of his cabin, shouting:

"My father, I want to see my father again!"

Karl Kip tried to hold him back. Nat pushed him aside and rushed out onto the bridge.

Mr. Hamburg, who had not returned to his home, had hastened from his office as soon as he was told of the murder. He arrived on board at the moment Nat was seeking to leave the brig, and told him:

"I'll go with you."

It was eight o'clock when Mr. Hamburg, Mr. Zieger, Mr. Hawkins and Nat Gibson, the Kip brothers, and a few employees from the warehouse headed through the forest to reach the clearing, which required but ten minutes at the most.

The corpse was as the murderers had left it, stretched out on the ground, his eyes still open very wide, as though life had not yet fled the body.

Nat Gibson kneeled down beside his father. He embraced him, called out his name, and also the name of his mother . . . When Mrs. Gibson learned of this dreadful misdeed, would she survive it, the poor woman?

Meantime, Mr. Hamburg, whose responsibility it was to make an inquest, examined the traces left on the grass, and he believed he could see recent footsteps that led him to think the murder had been perpetrated by two men. Then, after opening up Mr. Gibson's clothing, he determined that the chest had a wound produced by a saw-toothed blade, a wound that had bled little. As for the money and papers that the captain had been carrying, they had disappeared.

So it was certain that theft was the motive of the crime. But who committed it? Some colonist from Kerawara? . . . That seemed rather doubtful . . . Wasn't it perhaps natives? . . . And, in truth, they seemed rather suspicious . . . But how and where would you track down the assassins? . . . Once having done the murder, wouldn't they have simply left Kerawara in their canoe to return to York Island? . . . In a few hours they could have placed themselves beyond any pursuit . . .

It was probable, therefore, that this crime would go unpunished, like so many others for which this region, from New Guinea to as far as the Solomon Islands, had been the theater.

At present, it was necessary to transport the body to the local mortuary. Mr. Hamburg had a litter brought, on which they placed the body. Then all, Nat Gibson on Mr. Hawkins's arm, took the road back to the port.

The body was placed in a room at the local mortuary until Mr. Hamburg had completed his inquest. As for the burial, this sad ceremony was to be carried out the next day, for decomposition occurs rapidly in this searing climate of the tropics.

The missionary who was then stationed in Kerawara came to kneel and pray beside the victim.

Mr. Zieger brought back on board Nat Gibson, who, in an alarming state of unresponsiveness, remained on the bunk in his cabin.

Meanwhile, Mr. Hamburg worked incessantly, searching for information that could lead to tracking down the murderers. After he had brought Mr. Hawkins and Mr. Zieger to the local administration office, he discussed the subject with them, and when they asked what sort of people he believed were the authors of the crime, he replied:

"Natives, most assuredly."

"To rob poor Mr. Gibson?" asked Mr. Hawkins.

"Yes. They probably heard he was carrying a sum of money. So they kept an eye on him, followed him into the forest, attacked him, robbed him . . ."

"But how can they be found?" asked Mr. Zieger.

"That will be practically impossible," declared Mr. Hamburg. "What evidence is there to base a search on?"

"There is one thing to do," observed Mr. Zieger, "and that is to photograph the wound made by the murderer's weapon and if that weapon could be located, perhaps we could learn to whom it belonged."

"You are right," Mr. Hamburg answered, "and I request that Mr. Hawkins proceed with that undertaking immediately."

"Yes . . . of course," approved Mr. Hawkins, whose voice trembled with emotion, "and may this frightful crime not go unpunished."

Mr. Zieger went aboard to find the camera and returned a few minutes later. The chest of Mr. Gibson being stripped bare, a new examination of the wound was done, in very minute detail. The wound measured only a half inch in width and its sides presented a tooth-like pattern as though the skin had been sawed.

And then Mr. Hamburg said:

"As you can see, he was stabbed by some native weapon, one of those kriss-type knives with a toothed blade that the natives use."

Two photographs were taken with extreme precision. One reproduced Harry Gibson's chest, and the other his head. His eyes were still wide open, and Mr. Hawkins closed them afterward.[3] It was agreed that these photographs would be left in the hands of Mr. Hamburg for his inquest. As for the negatives, which Mr. Hawkins would keep, they would serve to make other prints. The photo of his unfortunate friend, deceased in Kerawara, would be brought back to his native city.

In the afternoon, it was necessary to commit his body to the coffin. The burial service would be the next day. A plot was chosen in the little cemetery of Kerawara. It would have been too long a delay to wait for his return to Port Praslin for his burial.

That sad day ended amid general desolation. When night came, Nat Gibson, with muffled sobs, was unable to find a moment of sleep.

The next day, the funeral was attended by the entire population of Kerawara, English and German. The flag of the *James Cook* hung at half-mast, and the other ships dropped theirs to mid-mast as a sign of sympathy.

The coffin, draped in the national flag, was carried by four men from the brig. Nat Gibson, the governor, Mr. Hawkins, and Mr. Zieger walked along behind, followed by Flig Balt and the rest of the crew, whom sailors from other crews had joined.

The Anglican missionary, preceding the coffin, recited liturgical prayers.[4]

The funeral procession reached the cemetery, and there, before the grave, Mr. Hamburg pronounced several words in memory of Captain Gibson.

Nat's extreme grief aroused much pity. Mr. Hawkins could scarcely hold him up. One last time, the young man tried to throw himself on his father's coffin. Then the bier was lowered into the grave, on which Mr. Hamburg had placed a wooden cross with this inscription:

To Captain Harry Gibson
of Hobart Town
Murdered on December 2, 1885
His son, his friends, his crew
and the people of Kerawara
MAY GOD RECEIVE HIS SOUL!

Mr. Hamburg's investigation had yielded no result. The crime accomplished, the murderers had no doubt left Kerawara in haste to seek refuge among the tribes of New Lauenburg. Under these conditions, how could one ever hope to discover them, for there was a large traffic of native canoes, day and night, between the little islet and the island? Would they find the weapon that had been used in the assassination and the person it belonged to? Chance alone could be the decisive factor in this affair, but would it work in their favor?

The brig did not prolong its stay in Kerawara. That very morning when the news of the murder spread, it was ready to go to sea to return to Port Praslin.

So, in agreement with Mr. Zieger, Mr. Hawkins summoned the bosun to the officer's wardroom and said to him:

"Flig Balt, the *James Cook* has lost its captain . . ."

"And that is a great misfortune," replied Flig Balt, whose voice was trembling with an emotion that was far from grief.

"I know," Mr. Hawkins continued, "how much my unfortunate friend had confidence in you . . . and this trust I am prepared to continue to offer to you."

The bosun, his eyes lowered, bowed without pronouncing a single word.

"Tomorrow, Flig Balt," the shipowner went on, "the *James Cook* will set sail, and you will take her to Port Praslin. There, we will finish loading, and as soon as that is completed, she will sail to Hobart Town."

As he withdrew, Flig Balt replied, "At your service, Mr. Hawkins."

Mr. Hawkins had explicitly stated that the bosun would replace Mr. Gibson in handling the ship, but not that he would be its captain. Perhaps he didn't even think of officially conferring this title and found it sufficient that Balt fulfill the functions during the trip from the Bismarck Archipelago to Tasmania. The bosun had clearly noticed it. So he explained it to Vin Mod moments later:

"Oh, what's the difference!" retorted the sailor. "Let's take the brig to Port Praslin. Whether you're the captain or the bosun, it's all the same, Bosun Balt! When we take over the ship, we're the ones who'll name you its captain, and may I be strung up if that nomination is not worth just as much as the one Mr. Hawkins could make!"

Moreover, as for Len Cannon and his companions, even if they did not know that Flig Balt and Vin Mod were the assassins of Mr. Gibson, they were sure that the brig would not return to Hobart Town, and they did not say anything more about disembarking.

The next day, December 5th, Mr. Hawkins took leave of the governor. Mr. Hamburg hugged Nat Gibson and promised he would faithfully pursue the murderers of his father. If he succeeded, German justice would show no pity for them! . . . They would pay with their heads for this abominable crime.

Then Mr. Hawkins, Mr. Zieger, and Karl and Pieter Kip said their good-byes—and such sad ones!—to the governor and the other agents of the Kerawara warehouses.

Weighing anchor was carried out under Flig Balt's orders.

An hour later, the brig, leaving behind the madreporic reefs, sailed southeast, passed by Cape Barard, the furthermost point of land of York Island, and headed for the entrance to the Saint George's Channel.

The crossing was going to be rapid and not require more than twenty-four hours. Flig Balt had no complaints about the crew, who performed their duties according to regulations. No maneuvers to execute, moreover, with this favorable wind that required no tacking. Whether Flig Balt was or was not a good sailor, this short trip would not permit one to judge. One could only wait until the ship was brought to Hobart Town. Furthermore, he was not occupying the captain's cabin but kept his own at the entrance of the crew's quarters.

During the night, Vin Mod answered Len Cannon's question when they were both on watch, in a way that satisfied him and his companions. The *James Cook* would not return to Tasmania . . . Captain or not, Flig Balt would know how to deviate its course . . . Once among the Solomon Islands it would not be difficult to get rid of the passengers on board . . . Are there not always honest sailors around in quest of adventure who, in case of need, would be eager to lend them a hand? . . . Len Cannon and the others, therefore, had no reason to leave the *James Cook,* for they would not be long in becoming its masters.

The heights of Lanut were sighted on the morning of December 6. Before noon, the ship would be at its anchorage in front of Mr. Zieger's trading post.

Since it arrived with its flag at half-mast, the populace of Port Praslin realized that some misfortune had occurred.

And what general mourning there was when they discovered how Captain Gibson had met his death! Mrs. Zieger, who had hastened to the dock, caught Nat Gibson in her arms the moment he was leaving the ship. She too was choked up with sobbing, and as soon as she could gather her words:

"Poor dear Nat . . . my poor child . . . and your mother . . . your mother," she repeated, while her eyes drowned in tears.

Nat Gibson had to accept staying in Wilhelmstaf during the last days of his stopover, as did Mr. Hawkins as well. Thus both returned to their rooms and sat at the table of this hospitable home where Mr. Gibson would never again return!

Mr. Zieger did not wish to let anyone else take on the responsibility of watching over the loading of the hundred and fifty tons of copra as the remainder of the brig's cargo. In this task he was helped by Karl and Pieter Kip, who did not leave the ship, even for an hour. The older of the brothers knew perfectly well how to handle this stowage, and, in the end, Flig Balt managed it without difficulty, so zealously did the crew pitch in.

Once the copra was in the hold, they divided, forward and aft, the cases of mother of pearl bound for Hobart Town. In addition, because before his voyage to Kerawara the captain had already made arrangements for the ship's cleaning and painting, the departure was not delayed for this reason.

Everything was finished on the afternoon of the ninth.

That evening, Mr. Hawkins and Nat Gibson, accompanied by Mr. and Mrs. Zieger, returned on board so the *James Cook* could set sail in the morning.

When they arrived, they were met by Flig Balt, who was at the ladder. Mr. Hawkins then said to him:

"Everything set?"

"Yes, Mr. Hawkins."

"That's fine, Flig Balt. Tomorrow we'll take to sea. You brought the ship from Kerawara to Port Praslin, now take it from Port Praslin to Hobart Town. You are henceforth in command . . ."

"Thank you, Mr. Hawkins," replied Flig Balt, while the crew murmured sounds of approval.

The shipowner shook hands with the new captain, but did not notice that it was trembling within his.

Mr. and Mrs. Zieger said their good-byes to Nat Gibson, to Mr. Hawkins, and did not forget the Kip brothers, for whom they had developed a strong liking. Then, with the promise of dropping by when they could and spending a few weeks in Tasmania visiting the two families, they returned to their home.

The next day, at five in the morning, Captain Balt made his preparations to rig out the sails.

An hour later, after leaving the channels of Port Praslin, the *James Cook* was at sea off New Ireland, heading southeast.

14

Incidents

The distance between the Bismarck Archipelago and Tasmania is approximately two thousand four hundred miles. With a favorable wind and an average of a hundred miles per twenty-four hours, the *James Cook* would take no more than three weeks to traverse it.

The season of the trade winds was reaching its end, and the tropical monsoon weather would soon follow it. In fact, the regular breeze was not long in establishing itself in the west, after a calm of short duration.

The brig would be in fine shape for crossing the difficult regions of the Louisiade and the Coral Sea.

This time, the passengers of the *James Cook* were different from those before who, in the course of an pleasant voyage, had been interested in the navigation itself. They no longer were able to feel those joyous impressions of a return trip that they might have experienced if their stay in Kerawara had not ended in a frightful calamity.

When Nat Gibson left his cabin, he came to sit in the stern, Mr. Hawkins nearby. Nothing could distract them from their grief. They thought of their next arrival in port, about Mrs. Gibson who was awaiting the *James Cook* so impatiently, and how the unfortunate woman would learn that it was not bringing back its captain . . .

The Kip brothers, wishing to respect their mourning that the passage of time had not as yet softened, kept for the most part to themselves. However, without seeming to, Karl kept his eye on the progress of the ship. The bosun had never inspired confidence in him. In various circumstances, those qualities that made up a true sailor had seemed to him rather lacking in Flig Balt's case. Two or three times, when Mr. Gibson was in his cabin, several ill-directed maneuvers caused him to doubt that Balt was a true man of the sea.

But, all in all, that not being his concern, he had not spoken about it. Though what did not seem to be serious concerns under Captain Gibson's command, did seem so now when Flig Balt was in command of the *James Cook*.

This particular day, Karl Kip spoke to his brother about these misgivings.

"So you think Flig Balt is not up to what his functions require?"

"I think it's fair to believe so, Pieter. During the squall that caught us in the Coral Sea, I became certain that he didn't know his trade."

"Well, Karl, it is your duty to keep alert, and if some maneuver seems dangerous to you, don't hesitate to speak up."

"Which Flig Balt will respond to, Pieter, by asking me not to interfere with his directing the ship."

"That's not important, Karl. You owe it to yourself, and in case your advice is not heeded, address yourself directly to Mr. Hawkins. He is a man of good sense; he'll listen to you and explain it all to the ex-bosun, and certainly he will take your side against his."

"We'll see, Pieter. Unfortunately I don't have the charts at my disposal, and it is hard for me to monitor our course without them."

"Do the best you can, my dear Karl. The *James Cook* has been through enough and ought to be spared further tribulations!"

As one can see, Karl Kip, while not believing there was maliciousness on the part of Flig Balt, still considered him a mediocre sailor. So, without the latter being able to notice, he wanted to keep an eye on him as best he could. Moreover, the presence of Karl Kip did not fail to cause the new captain a certain anxiety, and he planned to act with prudence, despite the impatience of Vin Mod, when trying to change their course in such a way as to head for the archipelago of the Solomon Islands.

After having passed through Saint George's Channel, the brig simultaneously lost sight of the furthermost lands of New Ireland and of New Britain. Crossing that part of the sea, Balt was right to head south, for he did not want to approach New Guinea. Better to lengthen the course by fifty miles and remain off D'Entrecasteaux.

He could not expose the ship to a second attack of the Papuans, which they might not repel as fortunately as the first time.

It was on the fifteenth that the *James Cook* reached the outer edge of the Louisiade. The crossing had been accomplished without incidents. After having left Rossel Isle to the west, the major one of the group, the Coral Sea opened wide before him on the twelfth degree of south latitude.

From this parallel on, the direction would be due south in order to reach the eastern coast of Australia at the height of Brisbane. With a wind blowing regularly from the west, the *James Cook* could reach its maximum speed.

Now, it was exactly at that limit of the Coral Sea that Flig Balt should modify his direction by running toward the east if he wanted to come in sight of Mangara Isle,[1] located at the end of the Solomons. But since that would have involved a noticeable change in the brig's course, Flig Balt simply cut toward the south-southeast.

Nonetheless, this change was observed by Karl Kip, who, after checking the compass, said to the captain:

"You're letting the wind carry us, Mr. Balt . . ."

"Yes . . . by two quarters . . ."

"Yet you'd find the sea calm in the shelter of the Australian coast."

"Possibly . . ." replied Flig Balt, who was starting to look askance at the Dutchman.

"Then," asked the latter, "why don't you hold your course?"

"Because storms from the northeast are always to be feared, and I don't want to be driven against the shore."

"Oh! there's room enough," interrupted Karl Kip, "and you'd have the time . . ."

"That's not my opinion," declared Flig Balt curtly.

And when he reported this exchange of words to Vin Mod, the latter said:

"What's this Hollander from Groningen butting in for? And when will we be rid of these people?"

Besides, the original plan, which consisted of throwing overboard the troublesome crew members, was still to be carried out, if the occasion presented itself. And, doing so in proximity of the Solomons, perhaps even with the help of some of the criminals who are numerous in this region, would definitely increase their chances of success.

All in all, this modification of their course noticed by Karl Kip was not important, and, without being justified in any absolute way, it was acceptable to a certain degree. Indeed, supposing that a tempest rose up at sea, a ship is less exposed when it is not too close to the coast, when it has sufficient "escape room," to use the maritime expression.

So Karl Kip did not believe he had to warn Mr. Hawkins. Yet, despite Flig Balt, who took notice of it, he continued to check the directions given to the helmsman.

In any case, Flig Balt and his accomplices were soon served by circumstance.

On the evening of the seventeenth, the weather changed. The sun had just set on a horizon charged with heavy clouds. The sea, responding to something, rolled with a heavy swell. All day long the heat had been oppressive. On several occasions, the breeze having disappeared, the sails beat against the masts.

Around three o'clock in the afternoon, the Fahrenheit thermometer had registered a hundred and three degrees in the shade,* and by five o'clock the barometer had fallen to twenty-seven inches.** This rapid fall in the column of mercury indicated a severe atmospheric disturbance.

In addition, the swell was becoming choppy; some waves were breaking already, indicating that the wind was raging somewhere in the west.

This atmospheric disturbance was soon followed by a violent storm. Toward nine o'clock, after a distant rolling of thunder, the horizon began to light up with bolts of lightning so bright, so frequent, that the sea in reflecting them seemed to be rolling in

*39.44 degrees centigrade (Author's note).

**730 millimeters (Author's note).

waves of fire. When they did not strike the surface, they leapt from cloud to cloud endlessly. The bursts of thunder became so loud that they were deafening; everyone's eyes were nearly blinded by these flashing discharges of electricity.

Around eleven o'clock, the storm reached its highest intensity. Several times the lightning struck the top of the masts, without causing any damage, disappearing down the lightning rods.

One could be sure now that this storm would be followed by a terribly violent wind, and they had to be ready for it.

Now they could not risk getting blown in toward the shore, as Flig Balt had said. Quite the contrary, and, short of sailing toward the Solomon archipelago, the brig would not find any obstacle in the east.

Mr. Hawkins, Flig Balt, and Karl Kip, together in front of the crew quarters, well understood the imminence of the tempest, and the shipowner said:

"This typhoon will soon be on top of us."

"That's for certain," replied Flig Balt, "and this time it's no little squall lasting for only a few hours!"

"That's what I'm afraid of," replied Mr. Hawkins.

"We'll have to run further out to sea," observed Flig Balt.

"And why not hold head-on into the storm?" Karl Kip asked, "and furl some sails?"

"Could we even do it?" interrupted Flig Balt. "A ship loaded as heavy as is the *James Cook,* barely holding to its waterline, will it rise to the wave? . . . Won't it simply be totally swept under?"

"A sailor should always try to keep on his course," replied Karl Kip, "and only flee if he has no other choice."

"That's what I believe," declared Mr. Hawkins, "for otherwise we could be dragged way off to the east."

"And even to the northeast!" added Karl Kip. "You can see the clouds, pushing up from the southwest, and with the wind at our tail we'd end up among the Solomon Islands."

Assuredly, and that was how Flig Balt and Vin Mod intended it.

It would have been difficult for the ex-bosun not to recognize that the Dutchman was speaking like a sailor. But, to lose this opportunity to change the course of the *James Cook,* that he just could not accept. So he said:

"I have the responsibility of being captain. Mr. Hawkins will understand that. And I do not have to accept any orders from Mr. Kip."

"Those aren't orders, I'm just giving you some advice," replied Karl Kip, who could not help but be surprised by his stubbornness.

"Orders that I do not need," responded Flig Balt, very irritated by the opposition facing him.

"Gentlemen," intervened Mr. Hawkins, "I want this discussion to come to an end. I thank Mr. Kip for having offered his advice. But since Captain Flig Balt does not judge it wise to follow it, then let him act as he will. I gave him command of the ship, and it is his right to claim the responsibility of his decisions."

Karl Kip bowed and went to join his brother, to whom he said:

"To me this Flig fellow seems incompetent, and I'm afraid he might put the ship in great danger! . . . But after all, he is the captain!"

In any case, there was not an instant to lose. The force of the wind was increasing minute by minute, and the frightful gusts that battered the ship risked carrying off its sails.

By order of Flig Balt, the helm was put hard over; the brig began to turn, not without experiencing some pummeling hits. The masts throbbed, the shrouds threatened to snap. Twice the maneuver almost failed. Finally they pulled around, and the *James Cook,* with its jib aback, its topsail furled, fled the storm, heading northeast.

For a half hour or thereabouts, the navigation continued under near normal conditions. The only difficulty was preventing the brig from yawing to starboard or port. The helm would not respond when the waves were moving as fast as the ship. Every moment they threatened to get ahead of it and to turn the ship. If this occurred, its situation would be quite desperate, for it would be exposed to the full force of the waves on its flanks.

And yet to increase the sails was absolutely impossible. One of the jibs that Flig Balt had hoisted in order to render the helm more sensitive, more effective, was instantly torn to shreds. The topsail was flapping so hard that it was ripping. There was reason to wonder if it would not be better to flee with dry sails. Which is almost the same as saying that the ship is disabled, incapable of taking any direction, that it has become the plaything of the waves.

A bit after midnight even the most ignorant sailor would have realized that the *James Cook* could not continue in that way. Its veering from side to side was constant. It was literally being swallowed by the sea. With the waves having twice the speed of the ship, the helm no longer responded.

Mr. Hawkins did not hide the worry that was gnawing at him. It was not a question of the ship and its cargo—that they could have thrown overboard in case of necessity—but of the life of the passengers and the crew. Flig Balt had full responsibility of command, but he, the shipowner, had the responsibility of having named him captain of the *James Cook*. Suppose the ex-bosun was not up to his new responsibilities? Suppose, by his incompetence, the safety of the ship was becoming compromised? And suppose Karl Kip, a seasoned sailor after all, had been right?

All these thoughts, these uncertainties, whirled about in Mr. Hawkins's mind. He spoke of them to Nat Gibson, who shared his apprehensions and showed little confidence in Flig Balt.

From time to time, when the latter approached, Mr. Hawkins asked him, pressed him with questions that he responded to with only unintelligible, incoherent answers, denoting a profound uncertainty and an obvious inability to face the perils of this situation.

And in the glare of the last lightning bolts, when Mr. Hawkins returned to Karl Kip; he saw him standing beside his brother, speaking to him in low tones. He appeared to be in the grip of the most violent feelings, and only containing them with difficulty. Yes! it seemed that he, Karl, was about to fling himself upon the helm, to turn the brig in the opposite direction!

Besides, to obstinately hold to that course—even supposing that the ship was never hit by a debilitating wave, was not rolled over on its side, which would require of them to take the extreme measure of cutting down the masts—where would they end up? . . . In the heart of the Solomons, among islands that swarmed with reefs and against any one of which they would surely be lost, with all hands!

Flig Balt understood this. Vin Mod and the men understood this also. It was certain that the brig would be lost if the storm continued for another forty-eight hours. The most elementary procedure called for a change, at no matter what cost, in a westerly direction, as long as a shred of sail was aloft.

Flig Balt decided to try it. It was a most perilous maneuver on a sea gone wild, and perhaps it would be impossible to change direction, to reverse course.

The helm was put hard over and they unfurled the spanker to help the rudder.

At that moment the brig laid over to port, and the end of its main yard disappeared under the foam of the waves.

At that moment a man rushed to Mr. Hawkins and shouted these words:

"Let me take over!"

"Do so!" replied the shipowner.

And then he witnessed what a true seaman, with all his sangfroid, was capable of doing and being, compared to the ex-bosun.[2]

By Karl Kip's command, by his imperious voice, by the clarity of the orders he gave, the crew maneuvered as one and decisively. The *James Cook* straightened up little by little, maintaining its masts, and, taking advantage of relative moments of calm, Karl Kip succeeded in setting the ship upright, atop the wave. The storm, although extraordinarily fierce, was less dangerous, since it now attacked the ship by the bow, and no longer by the stern. The crew managed to set up, not without great difficulty, a heavy-weather jib, capable of resisting the wind's blasts. Under its storm jib and its small topsail whose reef Karl Kip had unfurled, both of which were trimmed tightly, the brig held close to shore, while Seaman Burnes, an excellent helmsman, imperturbably maintained the *James Cook* on its proper course.

At one moment, Vin Mod, approaching Flig Balt, said in a furious voice:

And he witnessed what a true seaman was capable of . . .

"Everything is undone, with Captain Kip in command instead of Captain Balt!"

The next day, December 21st, contrary to what seemed probable, the violence of this tempest began to diminish substantially. That was due to the wind having shifted, which was now haling from the west-northwest.

A very fortunate circumstance: it was important for the brig not to continue toward land but continue toward the south.

That is what Karl Kip managed to do, as soon as the wind permitted, at the same time he let out the main topsail, the main jib, and the spanker. Under this sail set and with a fresh breeze, the *James Cook* would rapidly regain what it had lost toward the east.

It is true, the sea would probably not calm down as fast as the wind. It would remain high and choppy for a few hours more. And the brig would continue to be terribly shaken by the rolling and the pitching.

Around ten o'clock, the sun having reappeared, Karl Kip took the elevation. His position, which was completed by the noon sighting, gave him the exact location of the ship: 150°, 17' of west longitude and 13°, 27' of south latitude.[3]

At that moment Mr. Hawkins rejoined him and said:

"I thank you, Mr. Kip."

Karl Kip bowed without answering.

"Yes . . . I thank you," continued the shipowner, "on behalf of myself and the whole crew."

"I did only what every sailor would have done in my place," replied Karl Kip. "I deserve no thanks for that. And I am going to give the ship's command back to the captain."

"No," Mr. Hawkins declared in a firm voice that all could hear. "In agreement with Nat Gibson, I beg you to keep the command of our ship."

Karl Kip wished to decline with a gesture, but Mr. Hawkins continued:

"To the one who saved the ship goes the command! It is up to you, Captain Kip, to bring us back to Hobart Town!"

Meanwhile Flig Balt, in the most intense anger, advanced toward Mr. Hawkins and protested in these words:

"You named me to be captain of the *James Cook,* and I claim to remain captain until arriving at our destination!"

"Balt," responded Mr. Hawkins, whose decision was now irrevocable, "there is no captain except the one I choose, as owner and manager of this ship. I have judged that you were not up to your functions. From now on, it is Captain Kip who is the master on board, master after God!"

"I will claim my rights before the maritime authorities in Hobart Town," replied Flig Balt.

"As you please," replied the shipowner.

"I have been officially named, and . . ."

"That's enough, Flig Balt," said Karl Kip. "Not one word more! Back to your post! As for you sailors, I count on your devotion and obedience!"

Thus did the command of the ex-bosun end; thus did he lose his last chance to take over the ship. From that instant, the sailors understood that they were dealing with an energetic, resolute captain who was a sailor in his soul and who would accept no resistance to his orders. Mr. Hawkins could only applaud the resolution that he had just taken in the interest of the *James Cook.*

And now, would Vin Mod and Len Cannon and his comrades abandon their mutinous plans? . . . Would they not try one last assault before arriving in Tasmania? . . .

In any case, they would be carefully watched. Karl Kip, alert to trouble, would maintain strict discipline on board his ship.

Their navigation offered nothing of note for the week of December 20th to the 27th. The brig had approached the Australian shore. Under the shelter of the highlands, its course was favored by a manageable wind. On this date the observation was made that they were now located near Sydney, a bit above the 34th parallel south. The ship had easily made up its hundred miles in twenty-four hours. So on the afternoon of the 30th it found itself at the opening of the Bass Strait, which separates Tasmania from the Australian continent.

*The bay of Sydney**

*Facsimile of an illustration published in the *Great Voyages and Great Navigators* by Jules Verne (Hetzel's note).

If circumstances remained good, the *James Cook* would, in three or four days' time, be in sight of Hobart Town—to the great displeasure of Flig Balt, of Vin Mod, and especially of Len Cannon and the other recruits from Dunedin.

One can understand that the anger of the bosun and his accomplices was at its height. An irresistible spirit of revolt dominated them, not a muffled revolt that wants to proceed by surprise and in the shadows. No! an open revolt, before arriving in port, and in which they would make their final play, for all or nothing.

Karl Kip was quite aware that a mutiny was fomenting among some of the crew; but he would know how to deal with them in the same way he had won out over the tempest in the Solomon Sea.

Besides, without counting Mr. Hawkins, Nat Gibson, or his brother, Karl Kip could put his entire trust in the three sailors Hobbes, Wickley, and Burnes, who were honest and devoted. As for Vin Mod, thanks to his habit of inciting others and then backing off in time, perhaps the new captain felt a certain indecision. On the other hand, his opinion was set in regard to Len Cannon, Kyle, Sexton, Bryce, and Koa the cook.

Karl Kip was therefore not surprised when, on the evening of December 30th, rebellion broke out aboard the *James Cook*. Flig Balt, bringing along his accomplices, tried to force an entry into the wardroom to seize the arms. They would then attack the Kip brothers, and after getting rid of them, they would force Mr. Hawkins, Nat Gibson, and the three sailors to give up. They would make it impossible for them to resist. They would become masters of the ship . . .

The attitude and decisiveness of Karl Kip promptly thwarted this attempt. He rushed into the midst of the rebels, seized by the throat Len Cannon who tried to attack him, threatening him with his revolver. One more twist of his arm, and the wretch was thrown down onto the deck.

At the same instant, Nat Gibson, Mr. Hawkins, Hobbes, Wickley, and Burnes seized the other recruits, while Pieter Kip, having thrown back Flig Balt, snatched the cutlass Balt had armed himself with.

The struggle scarcely lasted a minute. How could six men—Vin Mod having prudently held himself back—ever get the best of seven whom they had been unable to surprise?

Karl Kip found himself in a state of legitimate self-defense. Putting a bullet into the brain of the bosun was fully within his right, and perhaps he would have done it without the intervention of Mr. Hawkins. The latter stopped him, preferring to deliver Flig Balt to maritime justice as soon as the brig entered the port of Hobart Town.

Flig Balt was sent down into the hold and placed in irons with two of the rebels who had shown themselves to be the most violent, Len Cannon and Kyle. The security of the brig was now assured until the end of the voyage.

Moreover, the crossing would be over in less than sixty hours, and Karl Kip would seemingly no longer need these three men. Besides, this area was populated. Many coastal vessels navigated along this eastern side of Tasmania, and flotillas of ships could be encountered near the Bass Strait. So, if necessary, by paying a daily wage, one could easily hire a few sailors to fill in the crew if Karl Kip were forced to use harsh measures against Len Cannon's other mates, highly suspected of the part they had played in the rebellion.

Karl Kip forbade all communication between the crew and the prisoners. The latter would only leave the hold of the *James Cook* for the maritime prison of Hobart Town. They were only allowed two hours on the bridge, during the afternoon, and it was forbidden to address a word to them. As for food, it was Jim who brought it to them, and there was no reason to mistrust the ship's boy, so affectionate was he toward Mr. Hawkins and Nat Gibson.

As a consequence, Vin Mod was unable to communicate with Flig Balt, although he had a great desire to do so—either because he had some recommendation to make, or a plan to explain to him before the latter's appearance before the Maritime Council. But he was under a particularly close watch. For the slightest dubious action, he too would be imprisoned, and, without doubt, his plan required that he have the liberty to act as soon as they disembarked in Hobart Town.

The voyage continued under excellent conditions, with favorable wind and sea. Karl Kip was not even obliged to take any additional sailors to pilot his ship into port.

All in all, Mr. Hawkins could only applaud himself for having replaced the unworthy bosun with a captain such as Karl Kip.

When the brig approached Cape Pillar at the southernmost extremity of Tasmania, it had to sail close to the wind, in order to round the point first, and then, further to the west, Cape Raoul. It took twenty-four hours to reach Storm Bay, which indents so deeply this part of the Tasmanian coast.

The configuration of the highlands often modifies the atmospheric currents. So the *James Cook* found at the opening of Storm Bay a fairly fresh breeze from the southeast. With full sails, it crossed the bay from south to north, reaching the mouth of the Derwent River, and, on the second of January, at about three o'clock in the afternoon, the *James Cook* dropped anchor in the port of Hobart Town.[4]

END OF PART ONE

LES FRÈRES KIP

SECONDE PARTIE

Hobart Town

Hobart Town

Tasmania, discovered in 1642 by the Hollander Abel Tasman, drenched in the blood of the Frenchman Manon[1] in 1772, visited by Cook in 1784 and by D'Entrecasteaux in 1793, was finally recognized to be an island by Mr. Bass, surgeon of the Australian colony. It first bore the name of Van Diemen's Land, in honor of the governor of Batavia, principal town of the colonial domain of the Netherlands in this section of the Far East.

It was in 1804 that Tasmania passed into the control of Great Britain and during this era when the English emigrants founded Hobart Town,[2] its capital.

After having first belonged to the political territory of New South Wales, one of the provinces of southern Australia located a hundred and fifty miles distant on the other side of the Bass Strait,[3] Van Diemen's Land subsequently separated from it. Since that time, it has preserved its autonomy while remaining dependent on the crown, like the majority of British possessions overseas.

It's a nearly triangular island, crossed by the forty-third parallel south and the hundred and forty-seventh meridian east of Greenwich.[4] It is vast—about one hundred seventy-five miles by one hundred fifty—and fertile, and all produce of the temperate zone can be harvested in abundance here. Divided into nine districts, it possesses two principal cities, Hobart Town and Lanweeston,[5] formerly Port Dalrympe.[6] One is on the northern coast, the other on the southern coast, and they are joined by a fine highway, which the Australian convicts constructed.

Indeed, it was these deported criminals who became the first inhabitants of Tasmania, where important penitentiary establishments were founded, such as the one in Port Arthur. Nowadays, thanks to the colonizing genius of England, it is a country of free men where a deeply rooted civilization now prevails, where formerly there had been the most complete savagery.

Moreover, the indigenous population has entirely disappeared. In 1884 could be seen, as an ethnological curiosity, the last Tasmanian, an old woman. Of those Negroes, stupid and warlike, belonging to the lowest rung of humanity, there now remains not a single representative. No doubt, this same fate awaits their Australian brothers under the powerful hand of Great Britain.

Hobart Town is built nine miles from the mouth of the Derwent River, on the little bay of Sullivan Cove. Regularly developed—too regularly perhaps—following the example of American cities, all its streets cross at right angles. But its setting is extremely picturesque, with its deep valleys and thick forests, overlooked by high mountains. The extraordinary jagged coastline around Storm Bay, the multiple fringe-like outcrops of Cookville Island, and the ragged indentations of the Tasman Peninsula indicate the violence of the telluric forces that were at work during their plutonic formation.

The port of Hobart Town is nicely sheltered from the sea winds. The waters of its harbor are deep, and anchorage is very good. It is protected by a long jetty that breaks up the swell as would a breakwater, and the *James Cook* found its usual mooring there in front of the office of the Hawkins firm.

Hobart Town has only about twenty-five to twenty-six thousand inhabitants. Everyone knows each other in this society of shipowners, businessmen, and maritime agents, which comprises the largest part of the essentially commercial city. And, although the taste of scientific, artistic, and literary study is well developed in this very vibrant city, how could commerce not fail to be in the first rank? The Tasmanian territory is of a remarkable fertility; its forests, which contain numerous species, are, one might say, inexhaustible. As for products from the soil, it is located on a latitude which is that of Spain in the northern hemisphere and produces grains, coffee, tea, sugar, tobacco, thread, wool, cotton, wine, and beer. Cattle raising is successful in every part of the island. And such is the unbelievable abundance of its fruit that it has been said that Tasmania alone could supply preserves for the rest of the world.

As mentioned, Mr. Hawkins occupied a very honorable position in the high commerce of Hobart Town. His firm, to which Mr. Gibson was attached in the capacity of associate and sea captain, enjoyed the esteem and respect of the public. As a result, the misfortune which had just struck him was to be the cause of much chagrin. And, even before the *James Cook* had attached its mooring lines, the city knew for certain that a catastrophe had occurred aboard ship.

As soon as the brig was sighted at the entrance to Sullivan Cove, one of the employees from the office had gone to forewarn Mrs. Hawkins. This woman, accompanied by her friend Mrs. Gibson, hurried to the port. Both wanted to be there when the *James Cook* arrived at the dock.

Already a few people were mourning. Indeed, there was no mistake about it, the British flag, instead of being hoisted to the tip of the stern mast, was floating at mid-halyard, half-mast.

Several sailors, standing on the wharf, exchanged the following remarks:

"Some misfortune has happened!"

"A sailor has died during the voyage."

"Surely there's been a death at sea."

"Let's hope it was not the captain!"

"Did the *James Cook* have passengers?"

"Yes, word has it they were to take on board Mr. Hawkins and Nat Gibson at Wellington."

"Would they put a flag at half-mast for a member of the crew?"

"Even so!"

Mrs. Hawkins and Mrs. Gibson were not familiar enough with maritime customs to have noticed what seemed striking to the men in the port. These men were careful, moreover, not to call the women's attention to such a detail. It would have been upsetting to them, and for no good reason, perhaps.

But when the brig was at the dock, when Mrs. Gibson did not recognize her husband in the captain who was commanding the maneuver, when she did not see her son rush down to embrace her, when she saw him seated in the stern, his features drawn, barely daring to turn in her direction, and, nearby, Mr. Hawkins looking grief-stricken, she cried out:

"Harry! . . . Where is Harry?"

An instant later, Nat Gibson was at her side and pressing her to his heart, smothering her with kisses amid his own sobs. And then, finally, she understood the frightful tragedy that had befallen her; she murmured a few words in a suffocated voice; she would have fallen if Mr. Hawkins had not held her up!

"Dead . . . ," he said.

"Dead? . . . ," repeated Mrs. Hawkins, terrified.

"Dead! . . . murdered!"

A carriage was brought and Mrs. Gibson, who had fainted, was placed in it, next to Mrs. Hawkins. Mr. Hawkins and Nat Gibson took their places facing the women. Then the carriage, bypassing the port, headed toward the home that the son was returning to, and where the father was never again to return. The poor wife was transported to her room, without having recovered consciousness. More than an hour was to pass before she could respond with tears to the sobs of her son.

This tragic news immediately spread through the city. The consternation was profound, and everyone felt immense sympathy for the honorable Gibson family. And, then, is anything more saddening than a ship returning to home port without its captain?

Before parting, the shipowner had asked Karl Kip to continue in his duties during the unloading and laying up of the *James Cook*. That would only take a few days, and the two brothers could remain on board. That would not prevent them from seeking a ship destined for Europe, and Mr. Hawkins would keep them apprised of maritime departures.

Karl and Pieter willingly accepted the proposal of the shipowner, who, the very next day, would put them in contact with his business firm.

The first concern of Karl Kip was to ask the port authority what measures should be taken in the case of Flig Balt and his accomplices.

The port authority officer was quick to present himself, and learned that there had been a shipboard mutiny under the conditions previously described:

"The bosun is in irons?" he asked.

"With two of the sailors who had been recruited in Dunedin," replied Karl Kip.

"And the rest of the men?"

"Except three or four that I will set ashore, they can be counted on."

"Very well, sir," said the officer, "I am going to send you a squad of constables, and the rebellious ones will be confined in the port prison."

A quarter of an hour later several police arrived; they placed themselves in the bow, near the main hatch.

Flig Balt, Len Cannon, and Kyle were then brought out of the hold and led onto the bridge.

The bosun, his teeth clenched and without pronouncing a word, simply glared at Karl Kip with hatred and vengeance. Len Cannon, more demonstrative, threatened him with his fist and with such a torrent of curses that one of the constables had to gag him.

During this time, Vin Mod, crouched behind the capstan, stood up and leaned over to Flig Balt's ear, whispering in such a way that no one overheard:

"All is not over. Do what we've agreed on. We'll get the papers and the money."

Evidently, Vin Mod, despite the precautions taken during the bosun's incarceration, had been able to communicate with him. They had set up a plan together, to which Flig Balt had only to conform. So, to the several words uttered by his accomplice, he responded with an affirmative gesture.

When the constables had made preparations to take away the three prisoners, murmurs arose in the group that included Sexton, Bryce, and the cook Koa. But these were immediately silenced, and Karl Kip nearly sent the two recruits off to rejoin their companions.

A moment later, Flig Balt, Len Cannon, and Kyle disembarked

"Do what we've agreed on."

onto the dock, and, followed by a noisy crowd, they were led to the port prison, where they would be held until the day of their appearance before the maritime court.

In addition, almost immediately after their departure, Karl Kip summoned Vin Mod, Sexton, Bryce, and the cook. Then, with no further explanation, he excused them with the admonition that, once ashore, they were forbidden to return on board, for any reason whatsoever. They could report to the office of the Hawkins's firm, where money due them would be settled.

Vin Mod was expecting this step, and, no doubt, it satisfied him. He went down to his quarters and returned to the bridge with his sack. As for Sexton and Bryce, the reader may remember under what conditions they had embarked in Dunedin to escape the police after the incidents at the tavern of the *Three Magpies,* and the only gear they owned was already on their backs.

"Come," Vin Mod said to them.

And they followed the sailor, who led them first to the office of the shipowner, then to an innkeeper he knew, where the three took a room.

Now, with Hobbes, Wickley, Burnes, and Jim, Karl Kip had nothing further to fear. These fine men would suffice as the on-duty crew. Then, with the cargo placed ashore, the *James Cook* would be laid up.

The night that Nat Gibson spent with his mother cannot be described. Mrs. Hawkins had not wanted to leave the unhappy woman, and what care could be more devoted than hers, what friendship more consoling! It was necessary to tell her the long, grievous story. She had to be told under what circumstances the unfortunate captain had been killed, and that the authorities still had no leads on the murderer. It was necessary to show her in what corner of the little cemetery in Kerawara her husband was lying. And then they had to show her the photograph that Mr. Hawkins had taken. She insisted on seeing it, and how could they refuse her wish! But when she saw the faithful image of the captain, his chest torn by the knife blade that had plunged into his heart and his eyes opened inordinately wide and seemingly fixed on her, she immediately broke down and had to be watched all throughout that interminable night!

The next day a doctor was called. His care brought some calm to Mrs. Gibson. But what an existence awaited her in the sadness of that house!

A few days passed by. Under the direction of Karl Kip, they had finished the removal of the cargo from the brig. The three hundred tons of copra and the cases of mother of pearl were deposited in the storeroom of the trading post. Now the sailors were busy removing the navigational equipment, taking down the yardarms, the halyards, and other common procedures, then cleaning the hold, the crew quarters, the cabins, and the bridge. The *James Cook* was not to take to the seas for several months. Then, after the crew had received its pay, they moved the brig to the far end of the port where it remained under the eye of a watchman.

The Kip brothers would have to take up living on terra firma. Needless to say, they had daily meetings with the shipowner. More than once they had dinner together. Mrs. Hawkins, who shared her husband's feelings about them, never ceased giving them evidence of her friendship.

Mrs. Gibson received no one. Once or twice, however, she made an exception for the two brothers, who, respecting her grief, showed an extreme discretion toward her. As for Nat Gibson, he often came aboard, and could only join his thanks to those of Mrs. Hawkins.

On January 7th, before Karl and Pieter Kip left the brig, the shipowner came to talk with them about their situation, and it will come as no surprise that he made the following proposals:

"Mr. Karl Kip," he said, "I have had only cause to congratulate myself over your devotion and your zeal in the sad circumstances in which our ship found itself. Without you, it might well have gone down with all hands, during that tempest on the Coral Sea."

"I am pleased, Mr. Hawkins, to have been useful to you."

"And I am very grateful for it," replied the shipowner. "And if the *James Cook* had had to leave soon, I would have offered you the continuing command of it."

"You are too kind, Mr. Hawkins, and I am very honored by your proposal. Nor would I have hesitated to accept it if pressing and grave matters were not obliging us, my brother and me, to return home as soon as possible."

"Indeed, Mr. Hawkins," added Pieter Kip, "and we are going to inquire about a ship leaving for Europe."

"I understand, gentlemen," declared Mr. Hawkins, "and it is not without a true sense of sadness that we will be separated, perhaps never to see each other again."

"Who knows, Mr. Hawkins?" Karl Kip said. "When the affairs at Groningen—where our presence is crucial—are settled, perhaps business relations might be established between our two firms?"

"I do indeed hope so," agreed the shipowner, "and I would be happy if it were to work out that way."

"We would be as well," Karl Kip answered. "As for me, I plan on looking for a ship, as soon as our liquidation is done in Groningen, and it's possible that I will come back to Hobart Town."

"Where you will be welcomed as a friend," assured Mr. Hawkins in a most cordial tone. "It's well understood, gentlemen, that my coffers will be open to you. You have lost what you possessed in the wreckage of the *Wilhelmina,* and everything that you may need in Hobart Town . . . We'll do an accounting later, all right?"

"We thank you for your kindness, Mr. Hawkins," replied Karl Kip, "And I hope that we will not have to take advantage of it. Perhaps I'll find the opportunity to take a job as second in command on the ship that will take us back to Europe, and my wages will serve to pay my brother's passage."

"So be it, Mr. Karl Kip. But, if this opportunity doesn't present itself, just remember that I am at your disposal."

The two brothers only replied with a firm handshake.

"In any case," continued the shipowner, "you have earned a captain's honorarium, Mr. Karl Kip, for that last part of our trip on the *James Cook,* and I could not accept a refusal in that regard."

"As you like, Mr. Hawkins," replied Karl Kip, "but we cannot forget the way you welcomed us on board your brig. You acted like men of heart when faced with two shipwrecked Dutchmen, and whatever happens we'll always be in your debt."

Then Mr. Hawkins promised that he would help the two brothers find a ship. He would keep them up to date on departures, and would do his best to procure a position as second in command for Karl Kip, which would enable them to return to Europe without asking for financial help from anyone, since that was their wish.[7]

Then the shipowner and the Kip brothers separated after once more exchanging the warmest declarations of friendship.

Karl and Pieter Kip soon found a modest hotel, where they would live until leaving Hobart Town. It was a pretext for them to visit this city, which the older brother, during his many long sea voyages, had never chanced upon previously.

There is no doubt that the capital of Tasmania merits the admiration of tourists. It is one of the most beautiful cities of British Australia. Its streets are broad, airy, well maintained, and agreeably laid out. Public gardens are everywhere, and it possesses a magnificent park of four hundred hectares dominated by Mount Wellington in the west, with its snowy peaks lost among the clouds.

During their walks, Karl and Pieter Kip occasionally met some sailors from the *James Cook,* among others Vin Mod and Bryce. Were these seamen in search of a ship or were they proposing to remain a while on land? In any case, it seemed likely that the two men would probably not separate, for they were often seen walking together about the city. But what Karl and Pieter Kip had not noticed was that Vin Mod and Bryce had been ceaselessly following them while they were looking for a room.

There would have been no doubt in the Kip brothers' minds that the two sailors were taking an unusual interest in this question, if the Kip brothers had only overheard them as one repeated several times to the other:

"They're never going to get done! They're real demanding when it comes to choosing a hotel!"

"Their pockets are empty though, or almost," observed Bryce.

"Unless that idiot of a shipowner—may the devil strangle him—has managed to fill them up!"

"And provided that he does not offer them lodging!" continued Bryce.

"No, let's hope not, no! . . ." exclaimed Vin Mod. "For a nice room anywhere else, I'd pay them ten shillings a day!"

This exchange between Vin Mod and Bryce proved two things: first, they were worried about knowing where the Kip brothers would live after laying up the brig, and, second, if Mr. Hawkins offered them hospitality in his house that would somehow thwart their plans.

Which plans? Assuredly some evil deed that they were preparing against Karl and Pieter Kip since it seemed important to these two wretches that they be able to find a way into their room.

Indeed, what might be possible if they were to lodge in a hotel, would not be possible if they were to stay at Mr. Hawkins's home until their departure.

So that was the reason for this espionage on the two brothers, during which they did not worry overly much about being seen or not. Moreover, as of January 8th, they had reason to be satisfied.

In the morning the sailor Burnes, carrying the case that had been salvaged from the *Wilhelmina,* which contained all that the brothers possessed, accompanied Karl and Pieter Kip into one of the streets neighboring the port.

It was there, not in a hotel but in a small inn of modest appearance yet nicely kept, that they had made a choice of a single room on the second floor.

Vin Mod was able to assure himself of this fact a few minutes later, and when he had returned to Bryce, who was waiting for him on the dock, he said:

"Fleet Street," he said, "an inn called the *Great Old Man.* We've got them now!"

Future Projects

The catastrophe that had just struck so cruelly the Gibson family would result in a modification of Mr. Hawkins's plans.

It has not been forgotten that, wishing to extend his business, the shipowner had gone to New Zealand in order to found a bank with Mr. Balfour, one of the honorable merchants of Wellington. Nat Gibson, who accompanied him in this voyage, was to be the associate of Mr. Balfour later on. Commercial relations would subsequently be established especially with the Bismarck Archipelago. Mr. Zieger, who had been consulted when the *James Cook* had put in at Tombara, asked to enter into correspondence with the new bank, to which he could direct a large flow of business. One of the ships of the Hawkins line would make the long trip between Wellington and Port Praslin.

It will also be remembered that it was in Wellington that Captain Gibson rejoined his son and Mr. Hawkins to take them to Hobart Town, after having delivered some cargo to the islands of the Bismarck Archipelago. It would only be after his return to Tasmania that Nat Gibson would then go to settle permanently in the capital of New Zealand.

Mr. Gibson having died in the aforesaid circumstances, there was no question of continuing these projects. Mrs. Gibson would not accept the idea of being separated from her son. Nat Gibson would in no way have consented to abandon his mother, alone in that house where widowhood had just created so much emptiness. All the friendship, all the devotion of Mr. and Mrs. Hawkins would not have been sufficient—Mrs. Gibson had to have her son nearby so that she could give herself over to his care, his tenderness. The shipowner was the first to understand this. He would work things

Scenes from Hobart Town
(from E.-E. Morris, L'Australasie pittoresque*)*

out with Mr. Balfour; he would find him another associate, and Nat Gibson would assist him at the Hobart Town bank.

"Nat," she said, drawing her son close, "I have always looked upon you as my dear child, and now I want you to be it all the more. No, I shall never forget my unfortunate husband."

"My father, my dear father!" murmured the young man. "And not knowing who killed him."

In his grief, through his sobs, there dominated that thirst for vengeance that he had been unable to quench.

"The wretches!" he added. "We may never know who they are, and that abominable murder will not be avenged!"

"Let's just wait for the next mail from Port Praslin," replied Mr. Hawkins. "Perhaps the inquest of Messrs. Hamburg and Zieger will have some substantive result! Maybe they have found some new clues! No, I cannot believe that this crime will remain unpunished!"

"And if the murderers are not found," cried Nat Gibson, "I will go! Yes! I will go . . . and I . . ."

He could not finish, so much was his voice trembling.

Yet, before this crime could be taken to trial, if it was to be, another trial would take place before the Maritime Council—the trial of the mutineers of the *James Cook*.

Karl Kip, as captain of the brig, had given his report to the authorities. Flig Balt as leader and Len Cannon as accomplice risked extremely serious penalties, for English laws are very hard in cases of this sort, which affect discipline aboard commercial ships.

From the day of their incarceration, those who were held had not had any contact with their companions. Sexton, Kyle, and Bryce would appear only as witnesses at the trial.[1] The report did not involve them in this attempt at mutiny, so quickly put down, thanks to the energy of the new captain. It was even possible that they would no longer be in Hobart Town when the affair came before the Council, if they found berth aboard another ship, and no doubt that would have suited them.

As for Vin Mod, who was really the driving force of the revolt and whose detestable influence the bosun was under, this cunning person was another case entirely. He did not seek to avoid the consequences of his actions by flight, the investigation of which would establish proof. Who knows even, if Flig Balt might not speak or, if pressed by questions and seeing himself lost, might not disclose Vin Mod's complicity? . . . And besides, weren't they tied together, like two prisoners, by the blood that they spilled, the blood of the unfortunate Harry Gibson?

So, distrusting the bosun's weakness, Vin Mod had every reason to pull him out of his difficulty, and perhaps he had the means to do so. Very intelligent, very resourceful, he knew that Flig Balt counted on him. If he could just manage to twist the arm of justice in the *James Cook* affair, neither one of them would have anything further to fear! Who would have suspected that they were the perpetrators of this murder committed in the distant regions of New Ireland? For the present, Vin Mod could linger safe and sound in Hobart Town and, what's more, with the money stolen from the captain, he didn't need to worry about daily necessities.

So this scoundrel must have concocted a plan that Flig Balt agreed to—a plan that he would try to put into action since he enjoyed complete freedom. But with no possibility of communicating it to the bosun, he spoke to himself, ruminating on his ideas and studying his plan, in such a way as to leave nothing unforeseen:

"Could he have really understood me? Yet it's so simple . . . That would explain the mutiny, even excuse it! . . . Ah! if I were in his place! . . . It is true, I would not be where I am, and I need to be here! . . . Unfortunately, he is not a man to grasp something unless it's spelled out for him. You must pound things into his head! . . . Let's see . . . Is there any way I can get close to him? . . . Me . . . or someone else? . . . Kyle, Sexton . . . and tell him: 'It's done! . . .' But it has to be done . . . and just on the eve of the trial . . . The brothers would have noticed it too soon . . . Well, I'll think about it . . . Above all, it's essential to get him out of there . . . and we'll get our revenge on that damn hand-me-down captain! Curse me if I don't see that fellow doing a two-step, with his brother, on the end of a rope!"

And while Vin Mod was reasoning in this way, his face grew pale, his eyes grew dark red with rage, his entire physiognomy bespoke a ruthless hatred.

It is obvious that Vin Mod was weaving some dark machination against the Kip brothers. Now, by bringing together certain facts, there would be no doubt that the crime of Kerawara had been committed in such a way as to implicate them. Also, since the arrival of the brig, and their disembarking, Vin Mod had been especially preoccupied with what Karl and Pieter Kip were going to do. They were eager to leave Hobart Town as soon as possible to return to Europe, and he understood this situation all too well. But they had to find a ship that was ready to put out to the sea, and, short of an unusual piece of luck, such departures are not encountered every day.

Moreover, Vin Mod was fully aware that Karl Kip was seeking a position as a second officer on a ship, with the help of Mr. Hawkins. Now that was another reason for delay, and it seemed certain that the two brothers would not depart before the Maritime Council judged the rebels of the *James Cook,* which would have compromised the plans of Vin Mod.

And besides, wasn't the presence of Karl Kip necessary as a witness in this trial? The prosecution could get along without his brother—that was quite evident since Mr. Hawkins, Nat Gibson, and the sailors on the brig would be summoned to give evidence. But the deposition of the captain would be the most important, and how could he avoid appearing before Council as a principal witness?

Vin Mod intended not to lose the two brothers from sight during their stay in Hobart Town. As soon as he had noted that they were lodging in the *Great Old Man* on Fleet Street, and after making himself unrecognizable by means of a false beard, he rented a room for himself there and paid a fortnight in advance after registering under the alias of Ned Pat.[2] Then it was his real name of Vin Mod that he gave to the innkeeper at the *Fresh Fish Inn* where Sexton, Kyle, and Bryce were staying in another part of the city. At the former hotel, he left early, returned late, and did not take his meals there. All this was to keep Karl and Pieter Kip ignorant of what he was doing. In reality, these measures were such as to never bring them together, and, besides, the two brothers would never have recognized him.

Vin Mod had taken great care to choose a room that adjoined the one they occupied at the *Great Old Man*. Their windows opened onto a common balcony, and it would be easy to get into their room or simply listen to the conversations between Karl and Pieter Kip when he slipped out onto the balcony after dark. These two, not realizing they were being spied upon and only speaking of personal matters in no way compromising, did not take the precaution of talking in low tones. Most often, due to the excessive heat, the window was ajar behind the shutters on the balcony.

And, on the evening of the 13th, this is what he managed to hear, taking great care not to be noticed. The darkness was profound, the room lit only by the feeble light of an oil lamp. Vin Mod was able not just to hear but also to glimpse inside the room. It contained only modest furniture, two iron beds placed in the corners, a large bureau, a table in the middle, a three-legged washstand, three bentwood chairs. In the fireplace was a grate filled with old ashes.

The valise brought in from the wreck of the *Wilhelmina* was propped on a stool. It contained everything the two brothers owned: what survived the wreck, what they had bought in Hobart Town, and linens and other objects bought with money from the office of Mr. Hawkins. Some clothes, acquired in the same way, were hung up in an armoire to the right of the doorway, which opened onto a hall that was shared by several rooms—among others, the one occupied by Vin Mod.

Pieter Kip, seated before a table, was consulting several different papers about the Ambon office, when his brother entered the room and said in a satisfied voice:

"I have succeeded, Pieter . . . I have succeeded! . . . Our return home is now assured!"

Pieter Kip understood that these words concerned certain steps, begun a few days before, aimed at obtaining the position of second officer on one of the Dutch ships that was preparing to leave Hobart Town shortly for a European port.

He seized his brother's hands and said:

Vin Mod slipped out onto the balcony after dark.

"So the firm of Arnemniden accepts you as second in command aboard the *Skydnam?*"[3]

"Yes, Pieter, and thanks to the strong recommendation of Mr. Hawkins . . ."

"That excellent man to whom we already owe so much!"

"Who, in so doing, gave me a very valuable helping hand!" declared Karl Kip.

"Yes! We can count on him in every circumstance, my dear Karl. If he owes you some gratitude for your conduct aboard the *James Cook,* we certainly owe him for all that he has done up till now! You see how we have been welcomed into his family, and into the Gibson family, too, despite the dreadful misfortune that has befallen them."

"The poor captain!" exclaimed Karl Kip, "and why did I have to replace him! Mr. Hawkins is inconsolable about the death of his unfortunate friend. Ah! may those wretched murderers be discovered and punished!"

"They will be . . . they will be," answered Pieter Kip.

And at that declaration, which no doubt seemed to him much too affirmative, Vin Mod simply shrugged his shoulders and murmured:

"Yes . . . they will be punished . . . and sooner than you think, Karl Kip!"

Pieter Kip continued:

"Have you been introduced to the captain of the *Skydnam?*"

"This very evening, Pieter. And I have only praise for him. He's a Hollander, from Amsterdam. He seemed to be a man I would get along with easily. Aware of events aboard the *James Cook,* he knows how I filled the function of captain when Flig Balt was removed from his command."

"Which is not enough, Karl. The ex-bosun must be severely punished! After almost losing the brig by his incompetence, and then wanting to hand it over to the rebels, putting himself at the head of the revolt . . ."

"And because of this, Pieter, the Maritime Council will not treat him gently, you can be sure of that."

"I wonder, Karl, if you weren't wrong, arresting only Flig Balt and Len Cannon . . . The latter's comrades, recruited in Dunedin, are no better, and you know that Captain Gibson had no confidence in them."

"That's true, Pieter."

"And I must add, Karl, that for my part I've always been suspicious of this Vin Mod, who seems to me a master in the art of deceitfulness. His attitude has always been very suspect, in a number of circumstances. Although he has known how to avoid being implicated, he's probably behind Flig Balt. If the revolt had not been put down, I'm sure he would have become the new captain's mate."

"That's possible," replied Karl Kip. "Indeed, the last word has not been said about this affair, and it is probable that the proceedings will have some surprises for us! For example, the sailors of the *James Cook* will be asked to testify, and who knows what their testimony will reveal? Vin Mod will be interrogated, they will pressure him with questions . . . If he has been plotting with the bosun, perhaps the latter will let the truth slip out! And then again, perhaps those honest sailors, Hobbes, Wickley, Burnes, will speak, and if they accuse Vin Mod . . ."

"We'll see about that," murmured Vin Mod, who was not missing a single word of this conversation, "and things will turn out differently than you expect, you damned Dutchman!"

At this moment, Karl Kip approached the window, and Vin Mod had to withdraw quickly so as to not be seen there, but after a few moments he returned to his post. In truth, the conversation interested him enough to make him want to hear it out, in order to find some way to profit from it.

Meanwhile, the two brothers had returned to the table and sat across from each other. While Pieter Kip gathered together the papers he was consulting, his brother said:

"So, Pieter, I am now hired as a second in command on the *Skydnam,* and that is already a happy circumstance. But there is another no less fortunate."

"Is it possible, brother, that good fortune is beginning to return to us? After all the misfortunes that have overwhelmed us? Are we finally finished with these ordeals?"

"Perhaps, and here's what we can expect in the future. I know that Captain Fork, who is in command of the *Skydnam,* is on his last voyage. He is already an old man, whose fortune is made, and he is to retire upon his return to Holland. Now if, during the return, I have given satisfaction to the Arnemniden firm, it is not impossible that I'll be appointed to replace Mr. Fork as captain when the *Skydnam* returns to sea. In that case, I would have nothing further to hope for!"

"And what would be fortunate for you, dear brother," replied Pieter Kip, "would also be fortunate for our business."

"I think so," affirmed Karl Kip. "I have not yet lost all hope, and why shouldn't things work out better than we might have thought? We have good friends in Groningen; our father left the reputation of a good man there."

"And, moreover," added Pieter Kip, "we have formed several personal relationships here. The support of Mr. Hawkins will not fail us. Who knows if, thanks to him, we might not be able to establish commercial relations with Hobart Town, and with Wellington through Mr. Hamburg, and with the Bismarck Archipelago through Mr. Zieger?"

"Ah, dear brother!" exclaimed Karl Kip, "there you go, flying high toward the future . . ."

"Yes, oh yes, Karl, and I fully hope to avoid a harsh fall in the present! I don't think that I'm just dreaming. There's a chain of good luck here that we must take advantage of. And, really, the best beginning is that you will be second in command on the *Skydnam.* Then, when I get back to Holland, I'll work hard. Our reputation will be reestablished, and we'll make the Kip Company of Groningen more flourishing than ever!"

"May God hear you, Pieter!"

"And He will hear me, for I have always put my hope in Him!"

Then, after a moment of silence:

"One question, Karl. Will the departure of the *Skydnam* be soon?"

“I have every reason to believe that it will take place about the 15th of this month.”

“In less than two weeks?”

“Yes, Pieter, for according to what I have observed, it will be loaded up by that date.”

“And how long will the voyage take?”

“If things go right, the *Skydnam* will take no more than six weeks to travel from Hobart Town to Hamburg.”

Indeed, such a length of time would probably suffice for a steamer of excellent speed, following the western route across the Indian Ocean, the Red Sea, the Suez Canal, the Mediterranean, and the Atlantic. It would not have to pass by the Cape of Good Hope, nor negotiate Cape Horn, after having crossed the Pacific Ocean.

Pieter Kip then asked his brother if he was going to start immediately his post as second in command aboard the *Skydnam.*

“Tomorrow morning,” replied Karl Kip. “I have a meeting with Captain Fork, who will introduce me to the crew.”

“Is it your intention, my dear Karl, to live on board right away?”

This question was of great interest to Vin Mod, considering his projects. Would it still be possible to execute his plans if the two were to leave the *Great Old Man* inn?

“No,” replied Karl Kip. “The repairs will take another dozen days or so. I will not embark before the 23rd, and, at that time, Pieter, you will be able to move into your cabin, too. I’m holding one of the best of them for you, right next to mine.”

“Gladly, brother, for I must admit I am somewhat in a hurry to leave this inn.”

And he added, laughing:

“It’s no longer worthy of an officer who is second in command on the *Skydnam!*”

“And even less,” replied Karl Kip on the same tone, “of the head of the Kip Brothers’ Co. in Groningen!”

How they were happy, those two brave hearts! Confidence returned to them, and, in truth, was it not their first piece of good luck that Karl Kip had found a way for them to return home under such advantageous conditions? That night, for the first time in a long while, their sleep would not be troubled by concerns for the future.

Ten o'clock had just rung, and they got up to begin preparations for bed.

With the conversation over, Vin Mod was about to return to his room, slipping along the balcony, when one last question brought him back to the window.

"So, Karl, the *Skydnam* will be leaving around the 25th."

"Yes, brother. Everything will be ready by that date . . . within one or two days, of course."

"But isn't Flig Balt to be put on trial a few days before?"

"It's on the 21st that Len Cannon and he will be brought before the Maritime Council, and we will testify as witnesses along with Mr. Hawkins, Nat Gibson, and the crew."

"That's perfect," answered Pieter Kip, "It all works out for the best, for your presence at the trial is really indispensable."

"Very true, and my testimony will, I think, permit the Council to have no mercy for this bosun, who did not hesitate to push his men to mutiny."

"Oh!" Peter Kip said, "in such a case, English laws are unforgiving. It's a question of guaranteeing security of navigation in commerce, and I would be very surprised if Flig Balt got away with less than ten years in the penitentiary at Port Arthur."

And Vin Mod, grinding his teeth in anger, murmured:

"It's not ten years of hard labor that's awaiting you, Kips! And before being sent to Port Arthur, if he ends up going there, Flig Balt will have seen you strung up to the highest gibbet in Hobart Town!"

Pieter Kip asked one more question of his brother:

"Did Mr. Hawkins know that you were named second officer on the *Skydnam?*"

"I tried to let him know this good news," replied Karl Kip, "but it was already too late, and he wasn't in his office."

"We'll go tomorrow, Karl."

"Yes, at the earliest hour."

"And now good night to you."

"Good night."

A few moments later, the room was plunged in darkness, and Vin Mod had only to withdraw quietly.

As soon as he had returned to his room, before leaving the inn of the *Great Old Man,* as was his habit, to return to the inn of the *Fresh Fish,* he carefully closed the armoire, which contained his papers and a number of other objects—among them, the dagger that had been found on the hull of the *Wilhelmina*. Then he left and headed toward the port.

And, along the way, he said to himself:

"It is not before the 22nd that they are planning to move on board the *Skydnam*. Fine! It's the 21st that Flig Balt is to be called before the Council. Good! Let's not mix up the dates! On the evening of the 20th the whole deal will be set up. But Flig Balt must be forewarned. How can I get word to him?"

Last Maneuver

The satisfaction of Mr. Hawkins was complete when he received a visit the next day by Karl and Pieter Kip. He was happy that his intervention with the Arnemniden firm had been successful, but he didn't feel that this favor deserved their thanks. All his credit, all his influence, he would gladly offer to the brothers. Was he not greatly obliged to them? The excellent man congratulated Karl Kip for having been hired as second officer aboard the *Skydnam,* and he did so as warmly as if he had not had a part himself in this nomination.

Nat Gibson, who was at Mr. Hawkins's house at that moment, could only join his congratulations to those of the shipowner. He already had the position of associate in the business firm. But his preoccupation with the business and his constant work could not turn his mind away from the sad memories of the past. The image of his father was always before his eyes,[1] and whenever he returned home it was to mix his own tears with those of his mother. To this chagrin was added the continuing horror of the unknown identity of the murderers who probably would never be caught or punished.

That very day, Karl Kip, accompanied by his brother, came to assume the duties of second in command aboard the *Skydnam,* where Captain Fork offered them a most warm welcome.

The *Skydnam,* a steamer of twelve hundred tons and six hundred horsepower, made regular voyages between Hamburg and various ports along the Australian shore. It would bring coal and return with wheat. For several days, its cargo had been waiting dockside. Workmen were making several repairs and adjustments to the hold and the poop deck, cleaning the boilers and machinery, as well as checking for damage to the masts.

"Certainly," affirmed Captain Fork, "everything will be completed by the end of this week, and then all that will remain to do will be loading the hold. That'll be partly your responsibility, Mr. Kip."

"I will not lose a day, or even an hour, Captain," answered the new second, "and my only regret is to be unable to occupy my quarters as of today."

"No doubt," replied Mr. Fork, "but you can see we are in the hands of the workers, the carpenters, the painters. It will require at least ten days or so for them to finish their work. Neither your cabin nor my own is in a condition to receive us at present."

"No matter, Captain," Karl Kip declared. "I'll be on board at sunup and stay until evening. I will do everything I can to assure that the *Skydnam* will be ready on the 24th."

"Agreed, Mr. Kip," replied Captain Fork. "Then I will leave the ship in your care, and if you need me, you will most often find me in the office of the Arnemniden firm."

Because of this arrangement, Karl Kip spent all his days aboard the steamer. For his part, Pieter Kip would seek to develop business contacts in Hobart Town. He decided to visit the principal merchants, with Mr. Hawkins's reference. Sowing so many seeds would assure future harvests.

Meanwhile the affair of the mutiny on the *James Cook* was following its course. The pretrial investigation, entrusted to the court prosecutor, was carried out according to the special regulations of the maritime code.

Locked up in the port prison with Len Cannon, Flig Balt had not been isolated from the others. Besides, this prison only served to confine sailors who were arrested either for insubordination or for common law cases. Brought in for the night were sailors in an advanced state of intoxication, disturbers of the peace picked up on the streets or in the taverns no less boisterous, no less rowdy than the one in Dunedin where Vin Mod recruited Len Cannon and his comrades. However much Sexton, Kyle, and Bryce may have wished to, they had not as yet left Hobart Town. They disliked leaving Len Cannon in the hands of the court and accused with such a grave crime. Now, if they were called as witnesses in the *James Cook* affair, Vin Mod planned to provide them with a fine piece of witnessing right at the last moment. He met them each day, for they had a room at the *Fresh Fish,* a horrid "flophouse" where Vin Mod had also taken a room under his real name. When the three sailors had eaten and especially drunk up their paycheck—which they cashed upon reaching shore—Vin Mod would intervene and pull them out of trouble, and had already covered for them with the owner of the inn. Obviously, Sexton, Kyle, and Bryce were not concerning themselves with trying to find jobs as crewmen aboard another ship.

"Wait . . . just wait!" Vin Mod kept repeating to them. "No hurry . . . what the devil! . . . Our friend Balt will have you come as witnesses and we'll close the yap of all who want to charge him, him and his comrade Len Cannon! Was it not our right to send that damned Hollander to his cabin as a passenger . . . to return the brig to the worthy Englishman who was its captain? It's true . . . right? Well . . . that's just what Flig Balt wanted to do, and they condemned him for that! . . . That's what Len Cannon wanted to do . . . that's what we all wanted to do! Believe me, friends, our former bosun will be acquitted, and Len Cannon will leave prison at the same time as he!"

"But," observed Bryce, "isn't there a danger they'll arrest us, implicate us in the same way they did Len Cannon?"

"No," Vin Mod declared, "you're witnesses . . . just witnesses . . . and when Len Cannon ships out of here for New Zealand or wherever, you'll go together. I'm the one who'll find you a boat . . . a good one . . . along with our friend Balt . . . and we'll do better maybe than the *James Cook!*

It was in this manner that Vin Mod managed to keep the comrades of Len Cannon in Hobart Town, with the idea that they would have a role to play in the trial where he was hoping for an acquittal in favor of the bosun.

While he was preparing these secret intrigues, which, if successful, would destroy the Kip brothers, the latter remained unsuspecting and busy with their own affairs.

Loading the *Skydnam* was moving along methodically under the direction of the second officer, the repairs were proceeding well with the help of the port workers, and departure would take place on the date set.

The Arnemniden firm could only appreciate the zeal and intelligence of the officer whom it had chosen. Captain Fork did not stint in his praise, after seeing that Karl Kip had a complete understanding of those very complicated shipboard duties of the second in command. So what congratulations, what thanks Mr. Hawkins received in this regard!

"And provided that your protégé is just as skillful at sea," Captain Fork told him one day, "I would call him an expert seaman."

"Have no fear, Captain," replied the shipowner, "have no doubts! Did we not have the opportunity to judge him aboard the *James Cook?* Did he not prove himself when, instinctively and on his own initiative, he took command of our ship? Have I ever repented one instant for having named him, rather than reverting to that miserable Flig Balt, who had placed us at risk? Yes, Karl Kip is a true seaman!"

"We'll see him at work, Mr. Hawkins," continued Captain Fork, "and I am quite certain that if Karl Kip justifies during this crossing the good opinion we have of him, the firm of Arnemniden will keep that in mind, and his future will be assured."

"Yes, he will justify that good opinion," Mr. Hawkins declared with a tone of conviction in his voice, "he will justify it!"

Obviously the shipowner was, not without reason, quite taken with the two brothers. What he thought of the older one, he thought equally of the younger, having recognized in Pieter Kip a remarkable understanding of commercial affairs. He felt sure that this young man could return the Groningen company to a solid footing thanks to the business relationships that would be established with Tasmania and New Zealand.

One can understand what feelings of gratitude the two brothers held toward Mr. Hawkins, who had helped them so often. They saw him as often as possible, and sometimes when the day was over, they sat at his table. Mrs. Hawkins shared the warm sentiments of her husband for these men of intelligence and of heart. She loved to be together with them, talking over future projects. From time to time, Nat Gibson would come to spend the evening in that hospitable home. He took a keen interest in Pieter Kip's canvassing. In a few days the *Skydnam* would take to sea. The year would not pass by without his returning to Hobart Town. It would be a pleasure for him if they could see each other again.

"And," said Mr. Hawkins, "it will be Captain Kip, commander of the *Skydnam,* whom we will receive then, and with such pleasure! Yes! The worthy Fork has a right to his retirement upon his arrival in Europe. You will replace him, Karl Kip, and in your hands the *Skydnam* will be what was . . . what might be the *James Cook!*"

Unfortunately, this name always evoked the saddest memories. Mr. Hawkins, Nat Gibson, and the two brothers remembered being in New Ireland, in Port Praslin, in Kerawara, in the midst of that forest where the unfortunate Gibson had fallen, in front of that modest cemetery where the captain reposed.

And when this name was pronounced, Nat suddenly paled. All his blood flowed to his heart, his voice trembled with rage, and he cried out:

"My father, my poor father, will you not be avenged?"

Mr. Hawkins tried to calm the young man. They had to await the news that would arrive from the Bismarck Archipelago by the first courier. Mr. Hamburg and Mr. Zieger would have perhaps discovered the identity of the guilty ones. It is true, communications are not frequent between Tasmania and New Ireland. Who knows if months might not pass before discovering the results of the inquest?

The date was January 19th. Within forty-eight hours the trial of the *James Cook* mutineers would come before the Council, and, no doubt, unless something unexpected happened, the proceedings would be terminated that very day.

Three days later the *Skydnam* would head out to sea, and the Kip brothers would have left Hobart Town on their way to Hamburg.

The next day, during the afternoon, Vin Mod could be seen prowling around the port prison. Rather agitated, although normally quite sure of himself, he was walking with rapid steps, avoiding the looks of others, muttering snatches of words interrupted with restless gestures that no doubt would have been interesting to overhear.

What did he hope to achieve as he passed several times before the prison door? . . . Was he trying to get in to talk to Flig Balt? . . . No! he did not have that in mind, and in any event it would have been impossible for him to get through the door . . .

Might it be, on the other hand, that he was attempting to spot the bosun through some window from the building whose top floor looked out over the surrounding wall? It was quite improbable, unless, on his side, Flig Balt, knowing that the trial was to come the next day, had suddenly had the thought that Vin Mod would try to communicate with him, no matter how. And, even then, was it not already agreed upon in advance, through a plan that they had worked out?

In these conditions, one outside, the other inside, both would have been reduced to using simple signs to communicate, a head movement, a gesture of the hand . . . Would they manage to understand each other?

In any case, Vin Mod did not catch sight of Flig Balt, and Flig Balt did not catch sight of Vin Mod. The latter, when evening arrived, after one last look at the somber edifice, slowly returned to his tavern.

Still engrossed in his thoughts, he then said to himself:

"Yes . . . that's the only way to warn him, and if it fails . . . Well, anyway, I am to be called as a witness . . . and I'll talk . . . and about things Flig Balt may not mention, perhaps . . . I'll say it, myself . . . yes! . . . I'll say it . . . and they'll get caught, those Kip brothers!"

It was not to the tavern of the *Fresh Fish* that Vin Mod went that evening, but to the inn of the *Great Old Man*.

It was seven o'clock. A fine, penetrating rain had been falling since noon. The quarter was drowning in a profound darkness, which the gas lamps scarcely dispelled.

Vin Mod, without being seen, took the alley leading to his room, went up the stairs, slipped out onto the balcony, and looked into the window whose shutters had not been closed.

After listening and hearing nothing inside, he was certain that the room was empty for the while.

In fact, that evening Karl and Pieter Kip were dining at Mr. Hawkins's house, and they were not to return to their room before ten or eleven o'clock.

Thus Vin Mod was served by circumstance: time would not be lacking for what he needed to do, and he was running no risk of being discovered.

So he returned to his room and, opening an armoire, withdrew several papers, to which he added a certain number of piastres, worth about three or four Malaysian pounds, then the kriss that Flig Balt had used to stab Captain Gibson.

A few moments later, Vin Mod entered the brothers' room from the balcony, without having had to break a pane in the window, for it remained partly open.

He was quite familiar with their lodging and the layout of the room because of the many times he had eavesdropped on the conversations between Karl and Pieter Kip. He did not even have to light up the room, which might have betrayed his presence there. He knew how the furniture was arranged, that the valise that had been rescued from the *Wilhelmina* was now on a stool.

Vin Mod needed only to undo the straps of this valise. After lifting up the clothing that it contained, he slipped in the papers, the coins, and the dagger. And then he closed it back up.

A fine, penetrating rain had been falling since noon.

"It's done!" he murmured.

He left by the window, pulling it shut behind him, crossed the balcony, and reentered his own room.

A moment later Vin Mod came back down the stairs, reached the street, and went toward the *Fresh Fish* tavern, where Sexton, Kyle, and Bryce would be awaiting him.

It was seven thirty when he entered the common room, where he rejoined his drinking companions.

Sexton and Bryce had already emptied a number of glasses, whiskey and gin. They were intoxicated—not to the point of noisy, aggressive drunkenness, just to a melancholic, half-witted stupor. They would have been unable to understand what Vin Mod said if he had needed to tell them anything important.

Only Kyle, forewarned no doubt, and with whom Vin Mod generally got along better, had scarcely touched the bottles set on the table.

So when Vin Mod appeared in the room, Kyle got to his feet, ready to approach him.

Vin Mod made a gesture to remain where he was, and they both sat down together.

There were some twenty drinkers in the tavern—almost all sailors on a shore-leave binge—seated at tables under the lamps in the stifling atmosphere.

Intoxicated patrons continually drifted in or drifted out. The noise made it possible to talk low without the risk of being overheard. Besides, Kyle's table was in the darkest corner of the room.

After sitting down, this is what Vin Mod said to his comrade:

"You've been here an hour already?"

"Yes . . . waiting for you, as arranged."

"And the others just couldn't resist tossing a few down?"

"No . . . just think . . . a whole hour! . . ."

"And you? . . ."

"Me . . . I just filled up my glass, and it's still full . . ."

"You won't be sorry for that, Kyle, for I need you to have a clear head."

"I have it, Mod."

"Fine . . . if you haven't had anything before, you can drink now . . ."

"To your health!" replied Kyle, raising his glass to his mouth.

Vin Mod took his arm and forced him to set his glass back down on the table without even wetting his lips.

"You don't want me to drink?" asked Kyle.

"No . . . but I want you to pretend to be drinking, and look as though you had too much."

"What for, Mod?"

"Because, pretending to be drunk, you're going to get up, walk around the room, look for a quarrel with somebody, threaten to break stuff, anything, to get the tavern keeper to call the police so they'll take you off and stick you in prison."

"In prison?"

And, in truth, Kyle did not know what Vin Mod was getting at. Pretending to drink, that was only halfway appealing; getting jailed for a nighttime ruckus, that was definitely not to his liking.

"Listen," said Vin Mod to him. "I need you to do a job . . . which will bring you a nice reward if you carry it out . . . if you play your role carefully."

"And no risk?"

"Maybe you get banged up a little, but there will be five or six pounds to earn."

"Five or six pounds?" repeated Kyle, warming to this proposition.

Then, pointing to his friends:

"What about the others?" he asked.

"Nothing for them," replied Vin Mod. "Look at them, they're not in a state to understand, much less act!"

It was true—none of them had even recognized Vin Mod when the latter had come in to sit down. They couldn't hear, let alone see. Their arms lifted their glasses mechanically and fell back to the table. Sexton was murmuring some incoherent words of a drunkard or humming some shipboard tune, accompanying it with wild stabs of his fists into the air. Bryce, with his head lowered, shoulders sagging, and his eyes half closed, would not be long in falling into a brutish sleep.

Meanwhile, the crowd noise grew louder, shouts, calling from one group to another, and sometimes provocations about nothing.

The tavern keeper, quite used to such behavior, was coming and going, pouring out yet another round of those abominable drinks.

"Well," Kyle said, approaching more closely his interlocutor, "what's up?"

"What's up," said Vin Mod, "is that I have a few words to tell Flig Balt . . . and so, since Flig Balt is in prison, you have to get in to join him there."

"This evening?"

"This evening . . . because tomorrow the Council is meeting and it will be too late. So, there's no time to lose—I'm counting on you to play the drunk."

"Without drinking . . ."

"Without drinking, Kyle. Won't be so hard . . . Just stagger around . . . shout . . . howl . . . pick a fight with other drinkers . . . hit them if need be."

"What if I catch a few hard blows myself? . . . in the middle of a brawl."

"Then I'll double the reward," replied Vin Mod.

This response seemed to remove the last of Kyle's hesitations, though he was not up to a beating quite yet. He had but one observation:

"If it's necessary to communicate with Flig Balt, why should it be me rather than you trying to get close to him?"

"Enough small talk, Kyle!" replied Vin Mod, beginning to get a bit impatient. "I need to be free . . . to be there when they judge Flig Balt. Once in prison, it's for twenty-four hours at least, and I repeat, it's important for me to be at the trial."

And, for his last argument, Vin Mod, searching his jacket pocket, pulled out a pound and slipped it into the sailor's hand.

"Down payment," he said. "The rest as soon as you get out . . ."

"And . . . when I've been released, I'll find you . . ."

"I'll be right here . . . every evening."

"Agreed," responded Kyle. "Right now a glass of gin to get me started . . . It'll just make me more convincing as a drunk."

He raised his glass, filled with the burning, corrosive liquor, and swilled it down.

"It's time," Vin Mod began again, "and listen well . . . What I have to tell Flig Balt, I could have written down, a scrap of paper that you would have handed to him from me . . . But if they found it on you, the whole deal would blow up . . . Besides, a few words will suffice and you will remember them . . . As soon as the police stick you in jail, try to find Flig Balt. If you can't find him tonight, then tomorrow, but before they come take him to the trial."

"I understand, Mod," replied Kyle, "and what do I tell him?"

"You'll tell him . . . that the deed is done . . . and that he can go ahead and accuse."

"Who?"

"He knows!"

"Good . . . Anything else?"

"Nothing else."

"Fine, Mod," said Kyle. "Now here I go, this time as drunk as the drunkest of the Queen's subjects."

Kyle stood up, staggering, falling, grabbing a table. He threatened the drinkers, who answered him back with a powerful shove. He cursed the tavern keeper for refusing him a drink, and charged into him, head first, sending him rolling into the street through the half open door.

The tavern keeper, losing his temper as he had lost his footing,[2] immediately called for help. Two or three policemen ran up and grabbed Kyle, who only put up a slight resistance and then only to avoid their blows. In the end, he was apprehended, tied up, led down the noisy street, and shut up in the port prison.

Vin Mod had followed him, and after personally verifying that the prison door had indeed been shut on Kyle, he returned to the tavern of the *Fresh Fish*.

Before the Maritime Court

Given the sad events that had taken place on the *James Cook* during the course of its last voyage, it is not surprising that they had created a considerable stir in Hobart Town. When, on the one hand, there was the murder of Captain Gibson, committed under mysterious circumstances and, on the other, the attempted mutiny by Flig Balt that was subdued by Karl Kip, it did not take much to raise the emotions of the whole town.

About the murder, little else was known from the day when the brig had reentered the port, its flag at half-mast.

As for the mutiny, the maritime authorities were about to judge the guilt or innocence of Flig Balt and his accomplice. Public opinion felt that the bosun, given his conduct on board, which constituted an aggravation to the crime, would be severely condemned and sentenced to at least ten or fifteen years of hard labor.

The principal witnesses—Mr. Hawkins, Nat Gibson, Karl and Pieter Kip, the sailors Hobbes, Wickley, and Burnes, and the cabin boy, Jim—had already been heard at the inquest. The others, cited by the accused—Vin Mod, Sexton, Kyle, and Bryce, and the cook Koa—were to be summoned as witnesses for the defense.

In short, unless unforeseen circumstances were to arise, the entire affair would be rapidly concluded and would occupy only a single hearing.

There was a large crowd that day in the courtroom of the Maritime Council. At nine o'clock in the morning people began to stream into the visitors' area made available to the town's businessmen, shipowners, officers of the merchant marine, and journalists. In the back, there were a number of sailors arriving from the nearby taverns and probably very favorable toward the accused.

Mr. Hawkins and Nat Gibson, arriving at the beginning of the hearing, sat down on the seats reserved for witnesses.

The Kip brothers entered the room several moments later and exchanged friendly handshakes with them.

That day, the presence of Karl Kip was not required aboard the *Skydnam*. The loading on board of the merchandise had just been finished the day before. As for the repairs, there remained only a few touch-up jobs to complete. Coal filled the bunkers, the engine was in excellent condition, and the crew was well trained. In three days, at sunrise, the steamer would make preparations to get under way.

Accordingly, Karl and Pieter Kip, planning to come aboard to occupy their cabins that very evening, were going to leave their room at the *Great Old Man*.

On a bench behind them, the sailors Hobbes, Wickley, and Burnes had taken seats, along with Jim, the cabin boy, to whom Mr. Hawkins and Nat Gibson gave an amiable greeting.

Then, on another bench, were sitting Vin Mod, Sexton, Bryce, and the cook Koa, whose enormous black face grimaced, and who was no doubt astonished not to be among the accused.

Only Kyle was missing, not yet having been released, and he would remain in prison until forty-eight hours had gone by, having overplayed his role of a false drunkard when fighting with the policemen.

Moreover, his testimony would not be very important; but what worried Vin Mod was not knowing whether Kyle had been able to communicate in the prison with Flig Balt—if he had passed along the message to him. Perhaps, that anxiety would disappear as soon as he and the bosun were in the presence of each other. If Flig Balt had been forewarned, a practically imperceptible sign or even one glance would suffice. When that moment came, Flig Balt would change from being the accused to being the accuser.

While awaiting the entry of the Council members, Mr. Hawkins talked with the Kip brothers and told them about the morning news arriving from New Ireland.

"A letter from Mr. Zieger?" asked Pieter Kip.

"No, a telegram sent to me by my correspondent, Mr. Balfour. A ship put in yesterday at Wellington, coming from Kerawara, an English ship that left the Bismarck Archipelago ten days after the *James Cook,* bearing a letter from Mr. Zieger. Mr. Balfour immediately cabled me the contents of the letter, and I received his telegram this morning."

"And," Karl Kip asked, "what did Mr. Zieger say relative to the inquest?"

"Nothing," replied Nat Gibson, "nothing . . . The murderers have not yet been discovered."

"That's only too true!" added Mr. Hawkins. "Mr. Zieger and Mr. Hamburg have done everything in their power, but with no result."

"They haven't uncovered the slightest clue to provide their investigation with even the smallest chance of success?" Pieter Kip asked.

"No," replied Mr. Hawkins, "and there are no suspects. It's only too certain the crime was committed by natives who had the time to flee over to York Island, where it will be very difficult to find them."

"There is no need, however, for Mr. Gibson to lose all hope," declared Karl Kip. "If the stolen papers were destroyed, there remains that sum in piastres which has not been recovered, and if the murderers try to dispose of it they'll certainly get caught."

"I'll return to Kerawara," said Nat Gibson. "Yes, I must return there!"

And who knows if Nat would not follow through on this plan!

This conversation ended upon the entry of the members of the Maritime Council, who came to take their seats on the platform: a commodore, a captain, and a lieutenant, assisted by a court prosecutor who had written up the act of accusation.

The hearing opened, and the presiding official gave the order to introduce the accused.

Flig Balt and Len Cannon, led by the police, took their places side by side on the bench to the left of the tribunal.

The bosun seemed quite sure of himself, his face calm, cold, his look indifferent. But if he was successful in reining in the feelings that no doubt stirred within him, his entire person nevertheless projected a profound shrewdness.

And it was like a revelation to Mr. Hawkins.[1] It seemed to him that he was seeing Flig Balt the way he really was. Yes! . . . how could Captain Gibson and he have been so blind as to have placed all their confidence in this wretch, to have allowed themselves to be taken in by the obsequious manners of such a treacherous man! . . .

But what astonished Mr. Hawkins did not astonish the Kip brothers. The bosun had always inspired in them a great antipathy, a reaction that had not gone unnoticed by him.

As for Len Cannon, his attitude scarcely played in his favor. He was throwing shifty glances to the right and left, some at Vin Mod, some at Sexton or Bryce, wondering perhaps why they were not seated on that bench since they had done just as much as he.

Now if—as Vin Mod surmised—Len Cannon seemed less assured than Flig Balt, it's because Flig had not told him about the communication that Kyle was supposed to have given to him. But this communication, had it been delivered, or did Flig Balt know nothing about it yet? That is what Vin Mod was anxious to find out.

In reality, Kyle had succeeded in his task. Flig Balt and he had met that very morning. The bosun could make his accusation. To one questioning look that Vin Mod sent him, he responded by a gesture that left no doubt in the latter's mind.

"And now," Vin Mod said to himself, "the fuse has been lit . . . watch out for the bomb!"

The magistrate gave the floor to the court prosecutor. The prosecutor offered a brief summary of the whole affair. He indicated under what circumstances Flig Balt had received command of the *James Cook;* under what conditions this command had to be withdrawn from him; how, for reasons of gross incompetence, Flig Balt was replaced by the Dutch seaman Karl Kip, a passenger on board; how Flig Balt had incited the crew to mutiny against the new captain and had placed himself at the head of the rebels, assuredly with the goal of taking over the ship.

As far as Len Cannon was concerned, it was impossible not to see in him an accomplice of Flig Balt. He was the one, thanks to his influence over his comrades recruited in Dunedin, who had brought them along. Moreover, he had made himself conspicuous from the beginning of the mutiny by his exhortations and his violence. After attacking Karl Kip at knife point, he had not backed off until the latter's revolver was pushed firmly against his chest. There was no question of his complicity and his culpability.

When the prosecutor had finished his reading, he requested the maximum penalty against the accused.

At this moment the witnesses left the hearing and withdrew into a neighboring room.

The magistrate, interrogating Flig Balt, asked him what he had to say about the accusation brought against him.

"Nothing," declared the bosun, simply.

"You recognize the facts mentioned in the report?"

"I recognize them."

These few words were pronounced in a very sharp voice that surprised the listeners.

"And you have nothing to add to your defense?" continued the magistrate.

"Not one word," replied Flig Balt, and, considering his interrogation at an end, he sat back down.

Vin Mod, who was watching, began to feel apprehensive. Had not Flig Balt missed the best moment to let it all out? Had he, Vin Mod, not mistaken the gesture that the bosun had made to him? Was it possible that the former did not understand, or perhaps did not even receive Kyle's communication?

Ah, what difference did it make, after all! If Flig Balt wasn't talking, Vin Mod would talk when he was called upon to testify.

Len Cannon, interrogated in his turn, made only some evasive remarks, feigning not to understand the questions asked by the magistrate, and, no doubt, Flig Balt had asked him to say as little as possible.

Vin Mod then had the thought that the bosun did not wish to allow the debate to go on or the testimony to be heard—among others that of Karl Kip. Foreseeing the accusations that he was ready to let loose against them, it would be best for the two brothers to have already explained their side to the Council.

Vin Mod, said to himself:

"Oh, that's shrewd . . . Flig Balt is right . . . He'll tell his story at the right moment!"

The interrogation of the principal accused and of his accomplice being terminated, the first witness was asked to make his deposition.

It was Karl Kip, and a light murmur ran through the audience when he presented himself at the bar.

Karl Kip gave his surname and forename, his nationality: native of Holland, born in Groningen; his profession: officer of the merchant marine—after having served for several weeks as captain aboard the *James Cook,* now second officer on board the steamer *Skydnam,* soon to depart for Hamburg.

These preliminaries finished, Karl Kip expressed himself in the following terms, with such a tone of sincerity that his honesty could not be the object of any doubt:

"My brother and I," he said, "passengers on the *Wilhelmina,* were picked up on Norfolk Island, where we had found refuge after a shipwreck, by Mr. Hawkins and Captain Gibson. I insist on giving public acknowledgment to these humane and generous men who have done everything for us and who deserve our deepest gratitude.

"During the trip of the *James Cook* from Norfolk to Port Praslin, I had many occasions to observe the conduct of the bosun. He inspired in me a strong distrust, a feeling all too justified by the events that ensued. I was astonished that even the shipowner and the captain had allowed themselves to be taken in by him. On the other hand, that was not my business, and I never made my observations known. But what I also noticed is that Flig Balt was not competent in the post that he was filling. When Captain Gibson relied on him for certain maneuvers that should be within the capability of a bosun, they were often so badly commanded that I was on the point of intervening. However, since these maneuvers did not compromise the security of the ship, I abstained from speaking to the captain.

"On November 20, the *James Cook* arrived at Port Praslin to unload its cargo and make some repairs. This putting in lasted nine days; then the ship went to Kerawara, the capital of the Bismarck Archipelago.

"It was there, on the evening of December 2, that the unfortunate Captain Gibson fell beneath the blows of murderers who have continued to remain unknown up to this very day."

These words were expressed with such grief that the audience could not contain its own emotions.

At that moment, Flig Balt, who was listening with head bowed, straightened up on his bench, stood up even, with the look of a man who could no longer contain himself.

The president then asked him if he had something to say to the Council.

"Nothing!" responded the bosun.

And he sat down again after having glanced rapidly at Vin Mod who, rather unnerved, was beginning to feel extremely impatient.

At that instant also, Karl Kip cast such a penetrating look at Flig Balt that the latter lowered his eyes.

Karl Kip resumed his deposition. With Harry Gibson dead, it was necessary to place the ship under new command. No English captain could be found in Port Praslin or Kerawara to replace him. It was clear that these functions needed to be turned over to the bosun. But, in Karl Kip's mind, that would be placing the *James Cook* in the hands of an incapable and dishonest man.

"However," he added, "Mr. Hawkins could not have done without him, and Flig Balt was first charged with bringing the brig to Port Praslin. Its lading completed at Kerawara, the *James Cook* returned to sea."

"It was then that the functions of the captain were granted to the bosun. On the tenth of December, the brig weighed anchor and left the archipelago. During the first few days of crossing through the region of the Louisiade Archipelago, the navigation presented no difficulties to speak of. The wind was favorable, and no maneuvering was called for. Only I noticed that the *James Cook* was drifting off course slightly to the east instead of following the direct route toward the south.

"That could not help but appear strange to me. I showed my brother what was happening. Pieter urged me to warn Mr. Hawkins and Nat Gibson, for he shared also my distrust of this new captain. I couldn't make up my mind about it, however, mostly because I find denunciations of this sort to be repugnant. But I did not cease to monitor carefully the direction of the brig as much as I could. No doubt Flig Balt noticed this, and perhaps it annoyed him to a certain extent."

And, since Karl Kip seemed to hesitate completing his thought, the presiding judge felt he needed to tell him:

"You have testified, Mr. Kip, that Flig Balt seemed to be trying to alter his route. With what intent would he be doing so?"

"I couldn't tell you exactly," responded Karl Kip, "but as far as I am concerned, the intention was clear. Flig Balt was trying to bring the ship eastward, toward those ill-famed archipelagoes that offer so much danger to the security of a ship. So, since Flig Balt tried to provoke a mutiny on the ship, I wonder if his intention was not to take over the *James Cook*."

Facing direct attack, the accused seemed indifferent, and simply gave a light shrug.

"Whatever the case may be," continued Karl Kip, "a storm that hit us on the edge of the Coral Sea might have assisted in this plan by pushing the ship out east. In my opinion as a sailor, I thought we had to face up to the fierce westerly winds and hold firm. That was not the opinion of the new captain. He fled in the direction of those dangerous latitudes of the Solomon Islands, and with sails trimmed in such a way as to compromise the safety of the brig. At one moment, I saw that he was going to be overwhelmed by the sea—the waves submerged him completely, and he was no longer at the wheel. I felt that the ship would be lost if I did not intervene. I rushed toward the helm. The crew was panic-stricken. Flig Balt was shouting incoherent orders. 'Let me take over!' I cried out. Mr. Hawkins had understood me, and without hesitating he shouted back to me: 'Do so!' So I took over command . . . the sailors obeyed . . . and I succeeded in changing the course of the brig. The next day, the storm having diminished, we only had to seek the shelter of the shore.

"That's when Mr. Hawkins gave me the command of the *James Cook,* after removing it from Flig Balt. The latter protested; I made him obey. Wasn't this my chance to pay back Mr. Hawkins's kindness by my devotion and my zeal?

"Soon after, the *James Cook* returned to its route heading due south, and we were close to Sydney when, on the evening of December 30, mutiny broke out on board ship. The rebels were led by the outraged bosun, who directed his accomplices toward the deckhouse to take over the arms. Len Cannon rushed toward me to stab me with a knife. I grabbed a revolver and threatened to blow his brains out. My strong reaction gave these men pause. As the worthy sailors lined up on our side, the others returned toward the bow. I had Flig Balt and Len Cannon seized and placed in irons.[2]

"We had no fear of a second attempt, and our voyage continued under more favorable circumstances. On December 31 the *James Cook* sailed past Cape Pillar and the next day arrived at the mooring in Hobart Town.

"That's all I have to say," added Karl Kip, "and I said nothing that is not true."

His statement completed, he returned to the witness bench with the certainty that all present granted his testimony full credence. When he seated himself near Mr. Hawkins and Nat Gibson, both shook his hand warmly.

"Accused, what have you to say?"

"Nothing," repeated Flig Balt.

The remaining witnesses were called one after the other to the bar, and their statements all confirmed what Karl Kip had said.

Mr. Hawkins acknowledged his misjudgments about the bosun, misjudgments entirely shared by Harry Gibson, who had absolute trust in Flig Balt. So, after the murder committed in Kerawara, he didn't hesitate to turn over to him the command of the brig for the return trip. The crew on the whole seemed to have approved. But when the storm assailed the ship north of the Coral Sea, it quickly became evident that the new captain was incapable of fulfilling his functions. He lost all calm, and the *James Cook* would certainly have foundered without the intervention of Karl Kip, to whom Mr. Hawkins wished to express publicly his gratitude.

Nat Gibson, who was summoned to the bar after the shipowner, could only confirm this testimony. But, when he had to talk about his father, the burning anger he felt for the murderers was obvious!

Pieter Kip retold in shorter form the account that his brother had just given before the Council. He underscored the feelings of antipathy that the bosun had always inspired in them, and the suspicions that they felt when Karl Kip noticed the ship's change of course. He had no doubt but that it had been done with criminal intent, as was made clear by the attempted mutiny.

As for the depositions of the sailors Wickley, Hobbes, Burnes and the ship's boy, Jim, they were in total agreement. It was determined that they had been forced into this rebellion. If they had been surprised by the scene of December 30—before being able to forewarn Captain Kip—at least they all stood by his side.

So the presiding judge praised them for their conduct under the circumstances.

The statements of the witnesses for the prosecution being completed, the case now proceeded to testimony by the defense witnesses, who seemed more or less compromised in the affair and who were no doubt feeling a bit anxious about the way this would turn out for them.

Vin Mod was the first to be interrogated about what he knew.

There was no frankness to be expected from such a cunning man. He spoke in such a way as to clear himself of all responsibility. He did not think that Flig Balt had ever had the intention of modifying the brig's route, as Karl Kip supposed it was. Flig Balt was a good sailor, he had proven as much . . . one could only approve of his handling of the ship during the tempest . . . and it was an injustice to have him removed from his command.

"That's enough!" said the magistrate, who was revolted by the tone and attitude of Vin Mod.

The latter returned to his seat, not without having cast a meaningful glance at Flig Balt, who responded with an almost imperceptible gesture. And this glance meant:

"Speak! . . . Now's the time!"

The statements of Sexton and Bryce were unimportant. Still hung over and unsteady from the libations of the preceding day, they barely understood what was asked of them.

The magistrate then ordered Flig Balt to stand. The depositions were going to end, and before the Council withdrew for deliberation, the bosun could for one last time take the floor:

"You know what crime you are accused of, Flig Balt," he said to him. "You have heard the charges brought against you. Do you have anything to say?"

"Yes!" declared the bosun, in a very different tone from the one with which he had uttered the word "nothing" in his previous response.

There was the most profound silence in the room. The public felt that some incident was about to occur—perhaps a revelation that would change the course of the trial.

Flig Balt, standing, facing the judges, his eyes still lowered, his mouth slightly contracted, was waiting for the magistrate to ask him a specific question.

And he did so in the following terms:

"Flig Balt, how do you defend yourself with regard to the testimony made against you by your accusers?"

"By accusing in my turn," replied the bosun.

Mr. Hawkins, Nat Gibson, and the Kip brothers looked at each other, not quite ill at ease, but surprised. None of them could imagine what Flig Balt was planning, or against whom he would level an accusation.

Then Flig Balt spoke:

"I was the captain of the *James Cook,* having received my regular commission from Mr. Hawkins. I was to take the brig to Hobart

Town, and, whatever anyone might think, I would have brought it to Hobart Town, when a new captain was named in my place. And who? . . . a foreigner . . . a Dutchman! Now, Englishmen . . . on board an English ship . . . cannot consent to navigate under the orders of a foreigner. That is what pushed us to revolt against Karl Kip."

"Against your captain," affirmed the magistrate, "and despite any right, for he occupied this post legally, and you owed him your obedience."

"Fine," replied Flig Balt in a decisive voice. "I admit that we are guilty on that point, but this is what I have to say: if Karl Kip accuses me of revolting against him, and if he accuses me, without proof, of having tried to shift the *James Cook* off its course in order to seize control of it . . . I myself, I accuse him of a crime that he cannot exonerate himself of!"

In the face of this serious accusation, although not yet knowing on what basis it rested, Karl and Pieter Kip had quickly risen to their feet as though to go toward the bench where Flig Balt regarded them brazenly.

Mr. Hawkins and Nat Gibson held them back as their anger was about boil over.

Pieter Kip was first to regain his calm; he seized his brother's hand, continued to hold it tightly, and in a voice mastered with great difficulty:

"What does that man accuse us of?" he asked.

"Of the crime of murder!" replied Flig Balt.

"Murder!" exclaimed Karl Kip. "Us?"

"Yes, you, the murderers of Captain Gibson!"

It would be impossible to depict the emotional response of the audience. A feeling of horror spread across the room, but a horror toward the bosun who had dared formulate such an accusation against the Kip brothers.

However, by an irresistible instinct, Nat Gibson—it can be understood, given his state of his mind—had immediately drawn back from them in repugnance; Mr. Hawkins had tried in vain to restrain him.

"Yes, you, the murderers of Captain Gibson!"

Pieter and Karl Kip, paralyzed for an instant by such an abominable accusation, were about to respond in righteous indignation, when the magistrate cut them off saying:

"Flig Balt, your audacity exceeds all limits! And you're imposing on the court . . ."

"I'm telling the truth."

"And why, if it is the truth, did you not say so, right off?"

"Because I did not learn about it until the return voyage. Then I was arrested when the *James Cook* docked, and I had to wait for this trial to accuse, publicly, those who were accusing me!"

Karl Kip was in an absolute rage, and in a thundering voice, like the voice of a captain in mid-storm, he cried out:

"Miserable . . . miserable liar! . . . Such accusations must be supported with proof!"

"I have it. The court can have it anytime it wishes!" responded Flig Balt.

"And what is your evidence?"

"Just go look in the valise that the Kip brothers retrieved from the *Wilhelmina*. There you will discover the papers and money of Captain Gibson!"

The Follow-Up

The effect of this last declaration by the bosun on all those present in the courtroom is difficult to describe.[1] In the audience a long and painful murmuring grew so loud that the magistrate had difficulty suppressing it. All eyes were fixed on the two brothers, now accused of a capital crime. Karl and Pieter Kip, motionless, gave the appearance of men whose surprise was equal to their horror. The older brother, impetuous by temperament, threatened with his fist the odious Flig Balt. The younger, his face pale, eyes moist, arms crossed, contented himself with shrugging his shoulders, as a sign of profound scorn for his accuser.

Then, both of them, by order of the magistrate, left the witness bench and advanced to the foot of the platform, accompanied by policemen charged with keeping them under watch.

Mr. Hawkins, Hobbes, Wickley, Burnes, and the cabin boy, Jim, after a first gasp of protestation that they had been unable to restrain, remained silent, whereas Sexton, Bryce, and Koa exchanged words in low tones.

Nat Gibson, his head bowed, his hands feverish, his face convulsed, was gripping his seat. And when his eyes rose toward the Kip brothers, they contained a look of hatred. Had he already become absolutely convinced of their guilt?

As for Vin Mod, he impassively awaited the result of this allegation by the bosun against Karl and Pieter Kip.

When the deeply troubled audience had recovered a bit of its calm, the magistrate gave the floor to Flig Balt so that he could complete his declaration.

Flig Balt did so very succinctly and in terms that did not fail to produce a favorable impression.[2]

On December 25th, toward evening, when he was no longer in command of the brig, he found himself in the crew quarters. The door of the cabin occupied by the Kip brothers was not closed. At that moment a violent rolling shook the ship, and a valise was thrown out into the middle of the wardroom. It was the one that had been brought back from the hull of the *Wilhelmina*. As it slid along the deck, this valise had opened and papers fell from it, as well as a handful of piastres that were strewn about on the floor.

The noise of the gold pieces attracted the attention of Flig Balt as well as provoking his astonishment. It was well known that Pieter and Karl had lost everything they possessed in the shipwreck. Be that as it may, after picking up those gold pieces, Flig Balt was going to replace them in the valise with the papers, when he recognized a few papers from the *James Cook*—the bill of lading and the ship's contract that Captain Gibson was carrying on himself the day of his murder and which had never been seen since.

Flig Balt, dumbfounded by this discovery, left the quarters. He could no longer doubt that the Kip brothers were indeed guilty. His first move was to run to Mr. Hawkins to tell him: "Here's what I've discovered! " and to find Nat Gibson and cry out to him: "Here are the murderers of your father!"

Yes, that's what the bosun ought to have done. He did nothing of the sort. He did not even speak to anyone about the secret he had just uncovered. But to then remain under the orders of a criminal, of the murderer of his captain, this he was unable to bring himself to do. He wanted to wrest the command from him, the command of which he, Flig Balt, had been so unjustly relieved, and so he led the sailors to revolt.

His attempt did not succeed. Disarmed and powerless, he was thrown into the hold by order of the wretch who betrayed the confidence of Mr. Hawkins. However, he resolved to be silent about what he knew until the arrival of the ship at Hobart Town, and to await the legal proceedings that would be brought against him. So it would be in public, facing the Maritime Council, that he would denounce the authors of the Kerawara crime.

After this formal deposition, which was followed by a great tumult among the people in the courtroom audience, the magistrate did not believe he should continue the proceedings. The hearing was recessed, and the police brought Flig Balt and Len Cannon back to the port prison. The judges would decide if there was need to follow up on this affair. As for Karl and Pieter, arrested forthwith, they were brought to the city prison.

Before leaving the Council chamber, Karl Kip, being unable to contain his indignation, protested violently against the man who was accusing them. Pieter tried to calm him by saying:

"Let it be, my poor brother. Leave to justice the responsibility of proclaiming our innocence!"

As they left, not one hand—not even Mr. Hawkins's—was stretched out toward them in friendship.

No doubt, Karl and Pieter Kip must have believed that nothing at the inquest would serve to establish their guilt. They had not, of course, committed that abominable crime. Those piastres, the papers that Flig Balt declared he had seen in their valise, they simply would not be found there when it was searched. They could wait without fear for the results of a police examination that was going to be carried out in their room at the inn of the *Great Old Man*. The bosun's declaration alone would not suffice to convict them of theft and murder.

So imagine their stupefaction, and also the feeling of horror that ran through the entire city when, that very day, it became known that the police search confirmed Flig Balt's accusation!

The police had gone to the inn of the *Great Old Man*. The valise designated by the bosun had been opened and searched. Under the clothing, they had found a sum of sixty pounds in piastres, along with the papers of the *James Cook* stolen from Captain Gibson!

And then—perhaps an even more telling proof—in the valise was hidden a weapon, a Malaysian dagger . . . a kriss with a saw-toothed blade! From the evidence obtained in Kerawara, the photograph taken by Mr. Hawkins, it had been demonstrated without a doubt that the captain's wound had been inflicted by a weapon of exactly this sort.

It was no longer a simple accusation that implicated the Kip brothers, but formal proof—material proof—just as Flig Balt had announced in full court. And, what made the bosun's veracity even less open to question was that he had not said anything about this Malaysian kriss, for he did not know it was in the valise, or he would have spoken of it just as he had done with regard to the papers and the piastres of Harry Gibson.

But the reader will recall that Jim had seen this dagger, placed on a counter in the cabin by Vin Mod, and that the latter had withdrawn it immediately after the cabin boy left. And who knows whether the young lad should not give evidence of this fact in the Kip trial, adding this damning testimony to that of the bosun's?

By now it was quite clear that the plot hatched by this miserable Vin Mod was both strong and well thought out. All the tactics used to compromise and to destroy these two brothers had been successful. Would they ever be able to explain this mysterious set of circumstances and counter the terrible accusation that was brought against them?

In any case, this serious incident—Vin Mod was counting on it—led the prosecution to drop its charges against Flig Balt and Len Cannon. Of what importance was the attempted mutiny aboard the *James Cook* compared to the revelation that had just been produced? The bosun would no longer appear as an accused, but as a witness in the name of justice.

There is no need to describe the violence—that's the word—with which Nat Gibson pursued this investigation. They were known at last, and they would be punished, the murderers of Kerawara! It would come as no surprise if, in his state of mind, the unfortunate young man had forgotten everything that could have been called upon to defend the Kip brothers: their attitude since the day when the *James Cook* had picked them up on Norfolk Island, their conduct during the attack of the Papuans from New Guinea, the pain they showed upon learning of the death of Captain Gibson; then during the crossing on the way back, Karl Kip's intervention during the height of the storm, which saved the brig from imminent destruction, or even his energetic suppressing of the mutiny led by the bosun! . . . Nat Gibson no longer remembered the warm sympathy that, until then, those shipwrecked on the *Wilhelmina* had inspired in him! All such feelings were erased, when faced with his hatred of the murderers—whom all evidence seemed to condemn—and the imperious need to avenge his father!

Moreover, it must be acknowledged that in Hobart Town the public's change of opinion was virtually complete. Just as it had earlier taken an interest in the Kip brothers by helping them—in procuring them a return to Holland, in preparing for commercial relations with Tasmania for the Groningen firm—so were they now doomed to universal loathing. In contrast, Flig Balt became a sort of hero. What strength of character! To keep his secret until the day of appearing before the Maritime Council! And was there not good reason to excuse this attempt at revolt since its goal was to remove the *James Cook* from the command of a murderer—a revolt in which the bosun risked his very life? And even those honest sailors, Hobbes, Wickley and Burnes, dragged into this general upheaval, no longer could remember the esteem they had felt for their new captain, the devotion that they had offered him in every circumstance.

And, of course, what no longer seemed to be in doubt in Hobart Town would not cause the slightest doubt in Port Praslin and in Kerawara. Neither Mr. Zieger nor Mr. Hamburg would have anything to do with an inquest that had now become pointless.

Mrs. Gibson, herself, was more grief-stricken at having lost her husband than from regretting that his death had not been avenged. But what could she have said to her son that would have raised a suspicion in his mind? For her, as for so many others, and for everyone who believed Flig Balt's declaration because it seemed supported by material proof, were not the two brothers the true murderers of Harry Gibson?

For everyone? Perhaps not. Mr. Hawkins wasn't fully decided on the matter.[3] Although his confidence in Karl and Pieter Kip was shaken, he did not feel entirely convinced of their guilt. To accept that idea, that those men for whom he professed so much esteem were the authors of such a misdeed, was repugnant to him. Moreover the motives for this murder escaped him. Was it to appropriate a few thousand piastres from Captain Hawkins, or to clear the way so that Karl Kip could become his successor as commander of the brig? Those reasons did not satisfy Mr. Hawkins's sense of logic, and when Mrs. Hawkins, influenced by his objections, repeated to him:

"The proofs are there, the material proofs . . . that money . . . the ship's papers . . . and finally the dagger! Can anyone claim that our unfortunate Gibson was not struck by that weapon?"

"I know," answered Mr. Hawkins, "I know. There are these proofs, and they seem overwhelming. But I have such positive memories of these men! I continue to have my doubts, and unless these unfortunate men confess their crime . . ."

"My dear," went on Mrs. Hawkins, "would you use this language in front of Nat?"

"No . . . he wouldn't understand. What's the use of trying to discuss it with him when he is so agitated? Let's wait for the trial . . . Who knows, Karl and Pieter Kip might succeed in proving themselves innocent! And, even if they are found guilty, I still say: 'Let's wait to see what the future holds.'"

After the police search of their room at the *Great Old Man,* the affair followed its normal course through the criminal justice system and would soon be adjudicated. The only witnesses that could be called were living in Hobart Town. As for gathering information in Holland about the family of the two brothers, about their personal situation and their past history, the telegraph could bring it within twenty-four hours. The inquest would require neither foreign research nor extensive documentation.

Three days went by. On the 25th, as scheduled, the *Skydnam* went to sea, after Captain Fork had chosen another second in command. Neither Karl nor Pieter Kip were aboard, and Mr. Hawkins was heartbroken in watching its departure!

One can easily imagine that Flig Balt and Vin Mod now thought they had nothing more to fear with regard to the crime in Kerawara. Who could have seen through the frightful machination into which the two innocent brothers had been drawn, that had so thoroughly trapped them in its snare, from which they would find it impossible to disentangle themselves?

Indeed, the bosun and his accomplice alone had devised this odious stratagem. Neither Sexton, nor Bryce, nor the cook Koa had the slightest inkling of it, and they were among the most astonished by this surprise revelation that had exploded before the audience of the Maritime Council. As for Kyle—the one who had been released after forty-eight hours—although he had served as intermediary between Vin Mod and Flig Balt, there was nothing to make him suspect that these two had committed the murder and that the Kip brothers had fallen into a trap. For his part, Len Cannon knew no more than the others. But these contemptible sailors no doubt appreciated the turn that the affair was taking. Flig Balt, now out of prison, was free to seek with them a vessel on which they could all ship out. And even if they had the ability to do so, they would do nothing to help the two brothers. In the evening of the 25th, after the departure of the *Skydnam,* Flig Balt and Vin Mod were conversing on the dock that bordered the west side of the port. At that time of day it was quite vacant, and they could talk without running the risk of being overheard.

"Bon voyage to the *Skydnam!*" said Vin Mod, "A good voyage, indeed, since it is not taking those two Dutchmen along to Holland! Ha! Karl Kip once took your place aboard the *James Cook,* Master Balt . . . Well, now he's taking it a second time, but in a prison cell where he's locked up tight!"

"Our little caper worked out," replied the bosun, "and perhaps more easily, more completely, than I was hoping."

"Oh! our plans were prepared long beforehand! There's no way that the two Kip brothers will get out of this."

"Let's wait until it's all settled, Mod."

"It's all known in advance, Master Balt! Ha! The face they'll make when they realize somebody stole their valise! Ha! Lucky for us we found the wreck of the *Wilhelmina,* and their valise was still in it! And what do you know but they had in their possession the captain's papers and his money! How careless of them! You know, I had to sacrifice a hundred piastres, but we can't regret it."

"Do we have any left?" asked Flig Balt.

"Close to two thousand still. So, no problem if we leave, any time we like!"

"After the trial."

"Fair enough! Just don't forget that Flig Balt, ex-commander of the *James Cook,* is the principal witness, and I just hope he doesn't cut his own throat by . . ."

"Nothing to be afraid of, Mod."

"By the way, Master Balt, it's a good thing that in the hearing when you made your declaration, you just talked about papers and piastres! So that when they got their hands on that Malay dagger, you saw their reaction to that discovery! No doubt about it! And, you'll see, the Kip brothers will have a hard time saying they didn't know the dagger had been picked up off the shipwreck—nobody'll believe them, and besides, they'll have to admit it belongs to them! Let's not forget, either, that these are honest guys, incapable of lying!

Flig Balt and Vin Mod, conversing on the dock

True! I'm looking forward to seeing what sort of grimace honest guys make at the end of a gallows rope!"

And the wretch laughed about his little joke, yet was unable to amuse the bosun. The latter, always preoccupied, was still in the grip of a number of worries. Assuredly, the affair had been well managed, but one never knows if certain complications might arise!

"Yes, Vin Mod, I'll believe that it is all finished and well finished only after the Kips are sentenced—when we've left Hobart Town to seek our fortune far from here, on the other side of the world!"

"There you go, Master Balt! You just can't get your mind at ease. It's part of your nature."

"I'm not saying you're wrong, Mod."

"Because you just don't see things the way they are! I repeat, there's nothing to be afraid of as far as we're concerned! Were we to admit, just now, that we really did it, I'm sure people wouldn't believe us!"

"Tell me, Mod," the bosun continued, "no one ever noticed you at the *Great Old Man* inn?"

"No one . . . known or unknown! It's not Vin Mod who lodged there, it was a certain Ned Pat, who does not look anything like me."

"It was risky . . . yet what you did there . . ."

"Not at all. And you can't imagine how it changes my looks when I wear a beard . . . a beautiful russet beard which went right up to my eyes . . . Besides, I only came in the evening, at bedtime, and I left before daybreak."

"And you haven't yet checked out of that inn?" asked Flig Balt.

"Not yet. I figured it's best to stay on there a few more days. If I had left as soon as the Kips were arrested, such a move might've seemed suspicious. Someone might've put two and two together. Also, to be on the safe side, I won't leave until after the sentencing of the murderers of our poor Captain Gibson."

"Well, Mod, the important thing is that you not be recognized later on . . ."

Don't worry, Master Balt. You know, three or four times when I was going to the inn, I passed Sexton, Kyle, and Bryce in the street . . . and they never suspected their buddy was walking right by them . . . Even yourself, you wouldn't have said, 'My . . . that's Vin Mod!'"

Indeed, all precautions had been taken, and nothing would allow anyone to discover that Vin Mod, under the name of Ned Pat, had occupied at the *Great Old Man* the room next to that of the Kip brothers.

Meanwhile the inquest was proceeding, entrusted to the magistrate responsible for the investigation. Nobody had the slightest doubt about the guilt of those two Hollanders, so clearly accused, among whose belongings they had seized the papers and money of the captain. It was quite clear that those items could not have been stolen by anyone except the murderers of Harry Gibson, who, at the moment of his death, was still carrying them on his person.

Besides, under the clothing in their valise, the police had seized a dagger.

One question remained: was this the weapon that had struck down Captain Gibson?

But, to this question, how could one fail to answer in the affirmative? The wound, cut with a saw-toothed blade, could only have been made by a kriss of Malaysian manufacture. It would be a simple matter to determine this in the photograph that Mr. Hawkins possessed.

It is true, in Melanesia, these daggers are quite common. The natives of Kerawara and of York Island, those of New Zealand and New Britain, use them habitually as weapons of combat along with assegais and spears. Was it certain that the kriss belonging to Karl Kip was used as the instrument of the crime?

Yes, and the material proof of this fact was not long in becoming evident.

On the morning of February 15th, a three-masted English ship, the *Gordon*, from Sydney, had dropped anchor in the port of Hobart Town.

Three weeks before, this same ship had left the Bismarck Archipelago, after several layovers at Kerawara and Port Praslin.

The mail on the *Gordon* contained one letter, accompanied by a small package addressed to Mr. Hawkins by his correspondent, Mr. Balfour.

This letter came from Hobart Town. It was Mr. Zieger who had written it subsequent to the news that had already reached Wellington and forwarded to Mr. Hawkins by his correspondent, Mr. Balfour—news that revealed no new incident related to the inquest. This letter read as follows:

Port Praslin, January 22nd

My dear friend,

I am taking advantage of the departure of the *Gordon* to send this letter to you, asking you first to express my sorrow to Mrs. Hawkins and to tell Mrs. Gibson and her son how deeply Mrs. Zieger and I share your grief.

Mr. Hamburg in Kerawara and myself in New Mecklenburg have made constant inquiries relative to the murder, with no results. Investigations among the native tribes of York Island have not led to finding any of the papers that belonged to Captain Gibson, nor the money that he was carrying. It is quite possible that the crime was not committed by the natives on York Island, for we would have surely discovered such an important sum of piastres somewhere on the island.

But there is one more thing. Yesterday, by chance, in the forest of Kerawara to the right of the path leading to the Hamburg home, in the precise location where the murder had been committed, one of the employees from the factory picked up a copper ring which must have fallen off the dagger at the very moment the murderer was wielding it to strike down our friend.

By sending along this ring to you, I am not assuming that it will be a conclusive piece of evidence since the weapon used in the crime has not been found. However, I thought I should send it along, and may this heinous crime not continue to go unpunished!

Please accept, dear friend, all our warmest wishes for Mrs. Gibson and Nat, and for Mrs. Hawkins and yourself. If I learn anything new, I will let you know right away. And I beg you to keep us informed as well.

Affectionately yours,

R. Zieger

Now, what Mr. Zieger did not know was that the magistrates of Hobart Town held in their possession the weapon that was ostensibly used by the murderers of the captain. And this particular kriss, found in the two brothers' room, happened to be missing the ring in its handle.

And when this ring was placed on it, the magistrates discovered that it fit perfectly.

Given this new piece of evidence, the next time Nat Gibson was at the shipowner's home, he said to him:

"Now, Mr. Hawkins, can you still doubt the guilt of those wretches?"

For his only answer, Mr. Hawkins lowered his head.

The Verdict

The inquest was drawing to an end. The Kip brothers had been interrogated and confronted by the bosun who was their adversary—or, rather, who was their only accuser to date and the only one who had discovered the condemnatory items in the Kips' cabin aboard the *James Cook*. They had answered with formal denials. But how could they have hoped that a ruling of lack of evidence could be pronounced in their favor when so many charges were leveled against them and when so many proofs of the crime pointed toward them, proofs that were impossible to ignore?

Further, they had had no opportunity to prepare their means of defense together, to comfort or sustain each other. They could only communicate through the lawyer chosen to defend them. When the magistrate proceeded to interrogate them, they were not together even in his presence, and they were not to see each other until the day when the case appeared before the criminal court.

Mr. Zieger's letter and the package accompanying it were now known to the public. The newspapers in Hobart Town had reported on this incident. It was no longer debatable—the dagger seized in the valise was indeed the weapon used by the murderers, and from that fact emerged the well-founded accusation brought against the Kip brothers. The jury's verdict could then only be the death penalty, given the aggravating circumstances of the crime.

And yet, as the day of the hearing approached, Mr. Hawkins felt his incertitudes growing stronger. Numerous memories came back to his mind. What? Those two men who had inspired in him so much sympathy could have committed this dreadful crime! . . . His conscience refused to believe it; his heart revolted at the thought! He noticed that there were some mysterious points in this case, unexplained, inexplicable perhaps! . . . But, all in all, his uncertainty was based on purely moral grounds, whereas the material nature of facts acquired during the inquest arose before him like an unassailable wall.

In addition, Mr. Hawkins avoided discussing this matter with Nat Gibson, whose convictions on the matter could not be shaken. Once or twice, visiting Mrs. Gibson, he had been led to offer a few ideas relating to the innocence of the Kip brothers, and also the hope that they would be able to demonstrate their innocence. Mrs. Gibson, without replying, took refuge in a stubborn silence—it was all too clear that she shared her son's opinions. Moreover, she had never been able, like Mr. Hawkins, to appreciate the character of the shipwrecked passengers of the *Wilhelmina,* to understand their past, to take an interest in their future . . . The widow was only to see in them the criminals, the living murderers of the captain.

As for Mrs. Hawkins, how could she not have had confidence in her husband's perspicacity and in his sureness of judgment? Since he was not convinced, she also was unable to be so. Thus she had come to share his doubts—for it was only a question of doubts. But in all likelihood, in the entirety of Hobart Town, they were the only ones to think that way. In the depths of their prison, the accused could not have imagined to what degree public opinion had risen against them, and the newspapers continued to inflame this bias in articles of an inconceivable violence.

The trial was to convene on February 17th. Now, since twenty-five days had elapsed since the hearing of the Maritime Council where Flig Balt had made his accusation against Karl and Pieter Kip, Vin Mod did not believe it necessary to further prolong his stay at the inn of the *Great Old Man*. So he gave up the room that he was occupying under the name of Ned Pat and settled his bill. Then, having no further need of a disguise, he came to share the lodging of the bosun at the tavern of *Fresh Fish*. From there, these scoundrels intended to follow the results of this stratagem so cleverly prepared and whose final outcome would assure their personal security.

As for the other sailors, they had found shelter at the home of lodgers in the neighborhood, awaiting the chance to ship out.

Proceedings on the case opened on the morning of February 17th, before the Criminal Court of Hobart Town. This court was composed of a presiding judge and assisted by two magistrates and a counsel for the prosecution. The jury was comprised of twelve jurors who were not to part company until they arrived at a common verdict.

There was a crowd inside the room, and a crowd in the nearby streets. Shouts of vengeance greeted the accused upon their exit from the prison. At that moment they were scarcely able to shake each other's hand. The police separated them immediately and had to protect them until they arrived at the Court House. They understood quite well that they had nothing to expect from public opinion.

The various witnesses who had figured in the trial of the Maritime Council were seated before the court: Mr. Hawkins, Nat Gibson, the sailors of the *James Cook*. But it was on Flig Balt, on his words, that the prosecution's entire case was built. How would the two brothers respond to it? That's where the public's interest was focused. Karl and Pieter Kip were provided with a defense attorney,

Shouts of vengeance greeted the accused.

whose task would be difficult since, given the bosun's allegations, which were supported by material proofs, his only possible defense was simple denials.

According to English law, the presiding judge limited himself to asking them if they pleaded guilty or not guilty.[1]

"Not guilty!" they responded together with strong voices.

And then all they could do was to reiterate the sworn statement they had made at the first trial, to repeat what their conduct had been during the voyage, from the embarkation on Norfolk Island to the disembarkation in the port of Hobart Town.

They affirmed that the valise they brought on board the brig contained only a little underwear and a few clothes. As for the Malaysian dagger, they had not found it on the shipwrecked hull and could not explain how it came to be in their possession. To Flig Balt's accusation that the said valise contained the papers and money of Captain Gibson, they offered the clearest denial. Either the bosun was mistaken or he knowingly altered the truth.

"For what purpose?" asked the presiding judge.

"In order to condemn us," declared Karl Kip, "and to seek vengeance!"

These words were greeted by an unsympathetic murmur from the audience.

It was now up to the attorney for the prosecution, a simple lawyer who was filling the functions of voluntary counsel for the Queen, to interrogate the witnesses. Then it would be up to the defense to proceed with a cross-examination.

Then Flig Balt, who had been called to the stand, responded:

"Yes, during the return trip I had just entered the officers' dining quarters . . . at that moment a violent wave pitched the valise out of the Kip brothers' cabin, where the door was open. Pieces of gold rolled about on the floor, some piastres along with some papers slid out of the valise. Those papers were ship's papers, which had disappeared since the murder of the captain."

As for the dagger, if Flig Balt had not mentioned it, that was because he had not seen it. He did not even know that this weapon belonged to the accused. But, at present he was no longer surprised that the police had seized it at the inn of the *Great Old Man* since that was the one that had stabbed Harry Gibson. Besides, if the Kip brothers had no hesitation about saying they had bought it on the Molucca Islands, at Ambon, they also had no doubt that it had disappeared in the shipwreck of the *Wilhelmina*. What they affirmed was that neither one of them brought it aboard the *James Cook,* and they could not understand how it had been rediscovered in their valise.

Pieter Kip simply observed:

"You find a great number of these kinds of krisses in the Melanesian archipelagoes. There are few natives who do not own one. It's a weapon they are quite familiar with. So it is possible that the one you say was the instrument of the crime was not ours, for all the krisses look alike, being of Malaysian manufacture."

This response provoked murmurs that the presiding judge had to suppress. Then the attorney pointed out that this dagger was certainly the one that served as the murder weapon, since the ring that was missing from it, sent on by Mr. Zieger, fit it perfectly.

"I must add," Pieter Kip responded, "that no one on board has ever seen that weapon in our hands, and if we had found it on the wreckage of the *Wilhelmina,* it is likely that we would have shown it to either Mr. Hawkins or Nat Gibson."

But his brother and he felt certain that this argumentation was not very convincing. There was no doubt that this dagger belonged to them, and there was no doubt that its ring was the one that had been picked up at the scene of the crime in the forest of Kerawara.

So Pieter Kip simply declared:

"My brother and I are victims of truly inexplicable circumstances. For us, to have struck down Captain Gibson, the man to whom we owe our rescue . . . our lives! This accusation is as odious as it is unjust, and we refuse to answer to these charges!"

This last sentence, pronounced in a voice that betrayed no anxiety, seemed to produce a certain emotion among the public. But the people's minds were already made up, and they did not choose to see in this declaration anything but a defense tactic. If the Kip brothers refused to respond to any further questions that might be asked, was it not because they had no good answers to give?

Other witnesses were heard, first Nat Gibson, who, unable to contain himself, condemned Karl and Pieter Kip, who cast a look of pity toward him. And if they had spoken, it would have been to say:

"We understand your grief, young man, and we do not have the strength to think ill of you."

When Mr. Hawkins presented himself at the bar, his attitude was that of a man troubled by his memories. Could he admit that the two brothers shipwrecked on the *Wilhelmina* and guests aboard the *James Cook* could have repaid the kindness of its captain with the most abominable of crimes? They owed him their life. Could they have murdered him in order to steal from him, when they knew that both Harry Gibson and he himself were ready to do anything to help them? True . . . no doubt, overwhelming charges had been brought against them! Mr. Hawkins simply did not understand . . . and choked by emotion, he could speak no further.

There was nothing special revealed in the depositions of the sailors from the *James Cook,* Hobbes, Wickley, and Burnes, nor in those of Len Cannon, Sexton, Kyle, Bryce, and Koa.

As for Vin Mod, his responses to the attorney were very affirmative in all that concerned Flig Balt. A few days before the attempted revolt broke out on the brig, the bosun had seemed to him to be prey to a kind of muted anger. Was it only because Karl Kip had replaced him as commander of the brig? Vin Mod had always thought that Flig Balt must have had some other motive . . .

"Well, he did not confide anything to you?" asked the attorney.

"Nothing," replied Vin Mod.

There remained one consideration quite in favor of the two accused: it is that the dagger was never seen in their hands during the crossing. That was clear even from Flig Balt's declaration, and Pieter Kip could declare again, with certain reason:

"If this kriss had been found by us on the hull, if we had brought it back to the brig, we wouldn't have hidden it any more than we hid other things contained in our valise. Is there any witness who saw this dagger in our possession? No, not a single one! It is true that during the police search at the inn of the *Great Old Man,* the agents seized it along with the money and the papers of the captain . . . Well, we contend that, since it was there, someone had put it there in our absence and unbeknownst to us!"

At that moment the proceedings were marked by a most decisive incident, an incident of a nature to destroy all uncertainty in the minds of the jurors, if there still existed any, in favor of the accused.

The cabin boy, Jim, was called back to make his statement.

"Jim," said the presiding judge, "you must say everything you know, and nothing that you are unsure of."

"Yes . . . sir," replied Jim.

And it seemed as though his restless look sought out Mr. Hawkins.

The shipowner immediately noticed it, and he felt that a revelation of great importance was about to be made by the young lad, something that Jim had not dared to speak of so far. And when the attorney interrogated him:

"It's about this dagger . . . that no one seems to have seen on board . . . ," he replied, ". . . of this kriss that belonged to the Kips . . ."

After having pronounced these words, Jim, troubled, stopped speaking. He seemed to be hesitant about making his statement. But the president urged him on, and he ended up by declaring:

"This dagger . . . well . . . I saw it."

The Kip brothers raised their heads. Was this last hope they were clinging to about to slip away from them?

The kriss was presented to Jim.

"Is this the dagger you saw?" the attorney asked.

"Yes, I recognize it."

"And you confirm having seen it on board the brig?"

"Yes."

"Where?"

"In the Kips' cabin."

"When?"

"While the *James Cook* was at its first stopover in Port Praslin!"

And Jim related under what circumstances he had seen the

weapon, how it had attracted his attention, how he had handled it, then replaced it where it had been.

The reader will remember that the dagger had been placed in the cabin by Vin Mod a few moments before Flig Balt had sent the cabin boy there, just so it would be seen by Jim; then Vin Mod had taken it back and hid it in his own sack.

The effect of this declaration from the young lad was profound, and it created an emotional response that neither the judges, nor the jurors, nor the audience could escape feeling. Was there any doubt remaining in their minds? The Kip brothers affirmed that the kriss had never been brought on board, yet it had been seen there, and it had just been discovered in their valise at the inn of the *Great Old Man*.

"Did the dagger have its ring, when you held it in your hands?" asked the attorney of the cabin boy.

"Yes," replied Jim, "and nothing was missing from it."

So it was established with absolute certainty that that ring must have fallen off during the struggle with the murderers of Captain Gibson, since it had been picked up some time later in the Kerawara forest.

To this statement of Jim's there was nothing to reply, and the accused did not respond.

Even Mr. Hawkins at that moment could not help but feel very shaken. And how could he have imagined that the Kip brothers were truly the victims of an elaborate plot prepared by Vin Mod, that this wretched man had secretly brought the dagger aboard, that he had let the ship's cabin boy see it for an instant in the accused's cabin before using it in the killing, that the murderers of Captain Gibson were his accomplice Flig Balt and himself, working together in this dreadful plot to destroy two innocent men!

At that instant, Nat Gibson asked to speak. He wanted to call the attention of the jury to one fact that had not as yet been mentioned, a fact that it was important to bring up.

And, with the authorization of the presiding judge, he expressed himself in these words:

"Judges, gentlemen of the jury, you are well aware that during the crossing from New Zealand to the Bismarck Archipelago, the *James Cook* had to undergo and repel the attack of the Papuans near the twelfth parallel and the Louisiade. Officers, passengers, crew, all contributed to the defense of the brig. My father was at the forefront of the fighting. Now, at the height of this battle, a rifle was fired, we don't know by whom, and a bullet grazed the head of Captain Gibson! Well, gentlemen, up till now I thought it was a work of misfortune, which could be explained by the profound darkness and the intensity of the defense. But I don't think that way anymore . . . I now have reason to believe, and do believe, that this was a premeditated attempt, directed against my father, whose death had already been decided on, by none other than those who were to murder him later on!"

Under the violence of this new accusation, Karl Kip rose to his feet, his eyes ablaze, his voice trembling with rage.

"Us . . . us?" he cried out. "Nat Gibson . . . you dare say! . . ."

Karl was beside himself. But his brother, taking his hand, calmed him, and he sat down, his chest heaving with sobs.

There was no one in the room that was not deeply struck by this scene, and a few tears flowed from the eyes of Mr. Hawkins.

As for Vin Mod, he squeezed the bosun's knee and looked at him with lowered eyes that seemed to say:

"My word . . . I had never thought of that! . . . The captain's son . . . he has never forgotten it!"

Henceforth, the prosecutor's task was only too easy. The previous history of the Kip brothers was brought to the attention of the jurors, their awkward situation, the bankruptcy that threatened the Groningen firm. They had lost everything they possessed in the wreck of the *Wilhelmina*. The money they brought from Ambon. No doubt they might have found it on the wreck, without saying a word about it, just like the dagger that they used a few weeks later! Then they had stolen from the unfortunate captain those few thousand piastres, of which only a portion had been seized in their valise. And lastly, who knows if Karl Kip had not already thought of succeeding him as commander of the *James Cook*—which subsequently occurred?

Under what conditions had the crime been committed? The jurors were no longer in ignorance. When Harry Gibson left to go to Mr. Hamburg's home, the two brothers were no longer aboard ship. They waited for him, they caught sight of him, followed him through the Kerawara forest, attacked him there, dragged him off the path, stripped him of his belongings, and after their return to the *James Cook,* no one could suspect them . . . And the next day they did not hesitate to join the procession accompanying the captain to his last resting place, and to mix their tears with those of his son!

So, what the prosecutor demanded of the jury was to be without pity for such criminals . . . to offer a verdict that was affirmative on every count . . . a verdict that would recommend capital punishment for Karl and Pieter Kip.

The defense attorney then spoke, and he did not fail in his task. But how could he dream that his efforts would be successful? Did he not feel that the decision of the judges and the people had already been made? To the material proofs brought against the accused, what did he have to offer? Nothing but moral presumptions that would weigh little in the balance. He spoke of the past of his clients, of the honorableness of their life, recognized by all those who were close to them. That the Groningen firm was not in a prosperous situation, that they had lost their last resources in the shipwreck of the *Wilhelmina,* all too true! But that, in order to procure a relatively small sum, two or three thousand piastres, they would have planned to murder Captain Gibson? That they would have killed their benefactor? No, that was not admissible! The Kip brothers were the victims of an inexplicable twist of fate. The many doubts remaining in this case should work in their favor and . . . lead to an acquittal.

The proceedings closed, the jury withdrew into its room for deliberation.

Nat Gibson remained on the witness bench, his head in his hands. But don't imagine for a moment that the lawyer for the defense had succeeded in changing his mind the least bit! No! For him Karl and Pieter were certainly the murderers of his father.

Mr. Hawkins stood apart from the others, his heart broken, looking at the empty space where the two accused would return and hear the verdict pronounced.

At that instant, the cabin boy, Jim, approached and in a trembling voice: "Mr. Hawkins . . ." he said, "I couldn't have made a different statement . . . could I? . . ."

"No, you couldn't, my child!" replied Mr. Hawkins.

Yet the jury's deliberation dragged on. Perhaps their guilt did not seem to be demonstrated clearly enough? Perhaps the jury would grant them the concession of attenuating circumstances, due to the very worthy attitude of the two brothers, who had not failed to conduct themselves impressively during the course of the debate?

Meanwhile, there were two men who were scarcely able to hide their impatience. They were the bosun and Vin Mod, seated side by side, not even daring to utter a few words to each other in low tones . . . But they did not need to talk to each other in order to understand each other, to share the same thoughts . . . What they hoped for, what they needed to assure their own safety, was capital punishment—the execution of the Kip brothers! . . . Once they were dead, the affair was over. But alive, even in the depths of some prison, they would protest their innocence. And who knows if some fluke of chance might not someday put the police on the track of the real guilty parties?

After thirty-five minutes of deliberation, the bell rang and the jury immediately returned to their seats in the jury box. Their verdict was unanimous.

The public then refilled the room, stifling, crushing each other, amid great noise and agitation.

At almost the same time, the magistrate returned, and the presiding judge proclaimed the reopening of the trial.

The chairman of the jury was invited to announce the verdict.

Affirmative on all counts—it did not grant the accused attenuating circumstances.

Karl and Pieter then returned, approached the bench, and remained standing.

The presiding judge and his colleagues deliberated a few moments about the penalty to be applied: the crime was premeditated murder, that is to say, murder in the first degree.

Karl and Pieter Kip were condemned to death.[2] And, when the sentence was announced, some applause could be heard.

The two brothers, after sharing a look of deep sorrow, took each other's hand. And then, with arms spread wide and without a word, they embraced . . . heart against heart.

Awaiting Execution

The Kip brothers had nothing further to expect from the justice system: it had condemned them, without even admitting the extenuating circumstances for the crime attributed to them. None of the arguments presented by the defense had swayed the jury—neither the firm and dignified demeanor of the accused during the course of the trial, nor the anger of Karl Kip whose indignation broke out on occasion, nor the calmer explanations of Pieter Kip. Nothing could mitigate the negative effects of the alleged facts in the case, of the charges so treacherously made against them, and of the declarations of that miserable Flig Balt and supported by the final deposition of the ship's cabin boy, Jim.

And indeed, as long as Karl and Pieter Kip had been able to maintain that the instrument of murder had not been found in their hands and to argue, not without apparent justification, that the kriss was the weapon most in use among the Melanesians and that the one with the missing ring must have belonged to a native of Kerawara, York Island, or the neighboring islets, some uncertainty seemed admissible. But this dagger was surely the one that they had taken from the shipwreck and brought on board the *James Cook* without showing it to anyone. And how could one doubt the declaration of the cabin boy, who had seen it in their own cabin?

This condemnation had at first given satisfaction to the population of Hobart Town. In the general hatred felt for the murderers of Captain Harry Gibson, there entered a great measure of that egotism so visible among the Saxon races, the proof of which no longer needs to be shown. It was an Englishman who had been killed; they were foreigners, Dutch, who had been condemned.[1] And when facing such a crime, who would have felt the slightest pity for the authors of it? So no one, publicly, not even a single one of the numerous newspapers of Tasmania, spoke out to ask that the sentence be commuted.

The son of the victim should not be reproached for the horror that the Kip brothers inspired in him. He believed in their guilt as firmly he believed in God—a guilt based, not on presumption, but on material proofs. Denials and protestations were all that the accused had to oppose the witnesses' statements, which were both precise and in agreement with each other. After having long despaired about finding the murderers of his father, he finally had them, those two monsters who owed their lives to the captain and who repaid him by the most cowardly of murders! Of those few reasons, whether more or less convincing, that might have pointed toward their innocence, he did not want to take into account at all; he couldn't see anything through that thick veil of indignation and pain.

So, the day when the sentence was handed down by the criminal court, when he reentered Mrs. Gibson's house:

"Mother," he said in a voice that emotion made tremble, "they'll pay for this crime with their heads, and my father will be avenged!"

"God have mercy!" murmured Mrs. Gibson.

"Mercy on those wretches?" cried Nat Gibson, who understood in this sense the response of his mother.

"No, pity on us, my child!" replied Mrs. Gibson, drawing her son toward her and clasping him to her heart.

These were the first words that Nat Gibson had spoken since he had crossed the threshold of the family home.

Now here is what the shipowner said when he found himself in the presence of Mrs. Hawkins when the hearing was over:

"Condemned."

"Condemned?"

"To death, the poor men! May the heavens not let human justice be mistaken."

"You're still in doubt?"

"Still!"

Evidently, perhaps by prescience rather than by logic, Mr. Hawkins still could not bring himself to recognize the guilt of the Kip brothers.[2] He could not believe them capable of a crime so odious toward their benefactor, toward whom they had always shown gratitude! A motive, an indisputable motive, escaped him. All in all, what would they have gained from Mr. Gibson's death? A few thousand piastres. And as to the hope of replacing him as commander of the brig, how would that have been feasible, since the bosun, in carrying out the duties of the second in command, would obviously become captain upon the former's death?

In all truth, Mr. Hawkins's faith in them had not been shaken by the deposition of the ship's boy, Jim. He was certain that the dagger, found in the room of the two brothers at the inn of the *Great Old Man,* had been seen by Jim in their cabin aboard the *James Cook.* Karl or Pieter Kip had brought it from the wreck of the *Wilhelmina,* and if they had not shown it to anyone, it's just that it didn't suit them to do it. So the prosecution thereby concluded that the idea of the crime had already germinated in their minds.

But no! Despite so many overwhelming proofs, despite the guilty verdict rendered by honest jurymen who were completely independent, no! Mr. Hawkins refused to give in. This conviction outraged him. This entire Kip affair troubled him deeply, and, if he never mentioned it to Nat Gibson, given the latter's feelings, he didn't suffer any less knowing him so stubborn in his belief. But he did not lose hope that the justice system would prove him right some day.

However, if in similar cases opinions would often have been divided—some claiming the innocence of the accused, others his guilt—such was not what happened in Hobart Town and the other cities in Tasmania. Who could ever foresee a sudden change of opinion occurring in favor of the Kip brothers? Mr. Hawkins was aware that everyone would be against him. But that did not discourage him in the least. He had faith. And he also hoped that time would be his ally, since time is often the great reformer of human errors.

It is true, perhaps time would run out. The appeal that the Kip brothers had made against their condemnation would not take long to be rejected. There was no reason for annulment, and it was predicted that the execution of the sentence would take place in the second half of March, a month after the verdict was pronounced.

And, it must be acknowledged, this execution was being awaited with a truly ferocious impatience by that sector of the population that is always given to brutal actions and always ready for the worst excesses, the one that asks only to take the place of the agents of justice and to lynch immediately the guilty, or those it believes are guilty. And this perhaps would have happened in Hobart Town if the jury had not given satisfaction to those deplorable instincts of the crowd, if a death sentence had not been pronounced by the criminal court. On the day of the brothers' death, that crowd would swarm around the prison.

They would be there too, in the front row, those abominable wretches, Flig Balt and Vin Mod! They would want, with their own eyes, to assure themselves that Karl and Pieter Kip had paid with their lives for that crime of which they themselves had been the perpetrators!

And then they could leave in complete safety and pursue other adventures, without having anything to fear from the future!

After the hearing, the two brothers were brought to prison. Not surprisingly, their passage through town provoked those crude insults of which the cowardly mob is so prodigal, and against which it was necessary to protect them. To these outrages they responded only with a most dignified attitude and disdainful silence.

When the doors of the prison were closed behind them, the head warden did not lead them back to the chambers that they had occupied separately ever since their incarceration, but to a cell reserved for those condemned to die. At least, amid so much misery they had the consolation of being reunited. During these last days of their existence, they would call up memories of their common past and keep each other company all the way to the gallows.

In truth, it was not this shared solitude in this little cell that they so strongly wished for. The guards did not leave them alone night or day, watching and listening to them constantly. Even during their most intimate outpourings of emotion to each other, there would always be the presence of these unsociable third parties, who no doubt felt no pity for them.

If, more than once, Karl Kip gave full course to his outrage about this abominable injustice of two innocent men being put to death, his brother tried in vain to hold back Karl's anger, and was more resigned to his fate.

Besides, Pieter Kip had no illusions about the plea for clemency that, deferring to the advice of their lawyer, both had signed. Although Karl, at the bottom of his soul, had kept alive the hope that the conviction would be overturned, that a new judgment would be made and that the time gained would allow the truth to appear in all its glory, he, Pieter, held no such hope. Thinking about the enormous weight of the charges against them, where would such a rescue come from? What intervention would be strong enough to save them, unless it were providential?

And then, their spirits flagged, and they pondered all the blows of ill fortune that had overwhelmed them, beginning with the shipwreck of the *Wilhelmina,* which was the cause of so many vicissitudes, and which had led them to the impasse they were now at. Oh! It would have been better for the *James Cook* never to have ventured by Norfolk Island! That their signals had not been observed! No doubt they would not now be faced with this ignominious death on the gallows, a death reserved for murderers!

"Pieter! . . . Pieter!" Karl Kip cried out. "What would our poor father think if he were alive today . . . if he saw his name dishonored! . . . The shame would surely kill him!"

"Can you imagine that our father would have believed us guilty?"

"No . . . brother, never . . . never!"

And then they began talking about those individuals whom they

"Can you imagine . . . ?"

had come to know during the past several weeks, and to those whom they owed so much gratitude! About how, in the excess of his grief, Nat Gibson had taken such an accusing attitude toward them, and how they understood him and shared his despair over the loss of his father! . . . But how could they pardon him for choosing them as the murderers! . . .

As for Mr. Hawkins, just by the reserved manner of his statement, they felt sure that a shadow of doubt still remained in his mind. They said to each other that the heart of this excellent man was perhaps not entirely closed to them. In response to the incriminating testimony given by the bosun and the cabin boy, Jim, though he had been able only to vouch for their character, at least he had presented these approbations to the jury in all good conscience.

As for the different witnesses, could they have testified other than they had done? For Flig Balt, the two brothers saw in the conduct of this miserable man only the satisfaction of his hatred, an act of vengeance against the new commander of the *James Cook,* against the captain whose energy had suppressed the mutiny and sent its leader to the brig. As for the Harry Gibson papers and the dagger that belonged to them, if they were found in their valise, it's because they had been placed there by the person who had stolen them with the aim of destroying the two brothers. And how could they have known that one of the murderers of Kerawara was the bosun?

Even though Mr. Hawkins sought new leads, he was unable to find any. To his mind, moreover, the crime must have been carried out by the natives of York Island, and who knew if the German authorities might some day identify them?

Be that as it may, the day and the hour were rapidly approaching when these men, two brothers, would pay the final price for a crime that they had not committed, that they were incapable of committing . . .

Mr. Hawkins, more and more obsessed by the idea that Karl and Pieter Kip were innocent, although he was unable to prove it, had undertaken certain procedures in their favor.

The governor of Tasmania was particularly well known to Mr. Hawkins. The latter considered His Excellency Sir Edward Carrigan[3] to be a man of great sense and of sound judgment. So he resolved to ask him for a hearing as soon as possible. And on the morning of February 25th, he arrived at the governor's mansion and was received immediately.

The governor had little doubt about the reason that brought Mr. Hawkins into his presence. Along with everyone else, he had followed with great interest the testimony in the Kip case, and he did not doubt the guilt of the condemned.

So His Excellency was profoundly surprised when Mr. Hawkins explained his opinion in the matter.

Since Carrigan gave him his full attention, Mr. Hawkins opened up to him without reserve. He spoke with so much warmth about these two victims of judicial error, he highlighted with simple logic all the points in the case that were obscure, unclear, or at least unexplained in their cause, that the governor felt somewhat shaken in his certitude.

"I see, my dear Hawkins," he declared, "that during this trip aboard the *James Cook,* you developed a great liking for Karl and Pieter Kip . . . and that they have always shown themselves worthy of it."

"I considered them honest people, Mr. Governor, and I still do," affirmed Mr. Hawkins with a voice of conviction. "I cannot provide you with material proofs to justify my feelings, because they have escaped me so far, and perhaps they will always escape me . . . But nothing that was said in the course of the trial, not one of the depositions that were given, could weaken the certainty that I feel about the innocence of these two unfortunate men. And, Your Excellency will note, all the testimony can be reduced to a single one, that of the bosun, whom I have reason to regard as suspicious. He acts out of hatred; it is through a thirst for vengeance that he accuses the Kip brothers of a murder they are not guilty of, and which I attribute to some natives from Kerawara."

"But there's other testimony besides that of Flig Balt, my dear Hawkins . . ."

"Yes, what the cabin boy, Jim, witnessed, Mr. Governor. And I accept it just as he gave it, for this young man is incapable of lying.

Yes, Jim saw in the cabin of Karl and Pieter Kip that dagger that they did not know was in their possession. But is this really the weapon that was used in the murder, and this matter of the ring, is it not due to a coincidence, quite fortuitous?"

"Nonetheless it was relevant to the case, and wasn't it important to consider, my dear Hawkins?"

"Assuredly, Mr. Governor, and it probably decided the jury's verdict of guilty. However, and I repeat, the entire past of the Kip brothers pleads in their favor. In order to speak to you this way, I must forget the grief caused by the death of my friend Gibson, which could have blinded me, as has happened to his son whom I pity and forgive! Myself . . . I can see the truth amid the obscurities of this affair, and I am entirely convinced that it will shine forth some day!"

It was obvious that the governor felt very impressed by Mr. Hawkins's declaration, whose honest and upright nature he knew so well. No doubt his argument rested only on a moral basis, but after all, in causes of this sort, material proof is not everything and it is appropriate to take other kinds into consideration.

Sir Edward Carrigan, after a few moments of silence, replied in these terms:

"I understand. My dear Hawkins, I appreciate and value your opinion. And now I will ask you . . . what do you expect of me?"

"That you be willing to intervene . . . at least to save the life of these unfortunates."

"Intervene?" responded the governor. "Are you not aware that the only intervention possible is by appealing the verdict that was pronounced? Now, this appeal, you know that it was introduced within the proper time limit . . . and there remains hope only in its being accepted . . . in the very near future . . ."

While His Excellency was talking, Mr. Hawkins had been unable to restrain his gestures of denial, and he said in his turn:

"Mr. Governor, I have no illusions about the appeal. The legal procedures have all been correctly followed in this affair. There is no reason that would justify overturning the verdict, and the appeal will be thrown out."

The governor was silent, knowing full well that Mr. Hawkins was right.

"I repeat, it will be thrown out," continued the latter, "and then, Mr. Governor, you alone could make one last effort to save the heads of the condemned . . ."

"Are you asking me to make a plea for pardon?"

"Yes . . . a plea for pardon from the Queen. A dispatch can be sent by you to the Lord Chief Justice in order for the sentence to be commuted, which would give us time, or at least defer execution of the sentence. And then . . . I will take new measures . . . I will return to Port Praslin, if necessary to Kerawara . . . I will assist Mr. Hamburg and Mr. Zieger . . . and we will discover the real guilty parties, sparing no time or expense! If I am pursuing this matter with such passion, Mr. Governor, it's because I feel pushed by an irresistible force—because once the truth is discovered, the justice system will not have to reproach itself later for the death of two innocent men!"

Mr. Hawkins then left the governor, not without the latter inviting him to return to see him about this case. And that is what this devoted man did every day. Thus, thanks to his dedication, the cause of the two brothers gained favor in the mind of His Excellency, who wanted to be associated with the righting of this wrong.

Meanwhile, the governor and Mr. Hawkins kept between them the secret of these proceedings. No one knew that, without awaiting the decision relative to the appeal, Edward Carrigan had sent an official telegram to England proposing a plea for pardon to Her Majesty.

On March 7th, a rumor circulated about the city that the appeal requested by the Kip brothers had been rejected. The news was true; and it provoked no feeling of surprise. Since the beginning of the case, people were expecting a guilty verdict, and even the death sentence, and no one doubted that it would be followed by an execution.

Moreover, no one thought that the governor of Tasmania would intervene with the Queen, or that Mr. Hawkins would have taken urgent steps toward that end.

The people of Hobart Town counted on the execution to follow, and it is well known how, among the Saxon races as among the Latin, these punishments stimulate irresistible and unhealthy curiosities.[4]

If, according to English law, the hanging of the condemned is not carried out in a public place but only in the presence of designated people, that is at least some progress. Nonetheless, the crowd still persists in gathering outside the prison walls.

So, on March 7th, before sunrise, even in the early hours after midnight, numerous curiosity seekers began to flood into the area to see the black flag hoisted, which marks the time of execution.

And it would come as no surprise that, among them, Flig Balt and Vin Mod were there, as well as Len Cannon and his other comrades who had not left Hobart Town. Yes! It was with their own eyes that the bosun and his accomplice wanted to see the flag come down after the execution of the sentence! They could then be certain that others had paid the debt of their crime for them! There would be no further reason to return to this matter, and those two wretches would return with their companions to the bar of the *Fresh Fish,* where the stolen piastres would flow into whiskey and gin.

As for Mrs. Gibson, neither she nor her son were to be in Hobart Town that day, and they would return only after justice had been done. When Nat explained this plan to Mr. Hawkins, the latter simply replied:

"You are right, Nat, that would be better!"

Since the end of the trial, the shipowner had often encountered the sailors Hobbes, Wickley, and Burnes and also the ship's boy, Jim. These worthy men had not yet begun to look for another ship, and perhaps their intention was to wait until the *James Cook* was refitted under another captain.

They knew, moreover, that they could count on Mr. Hawkins when he reassembled the brig's crew, or even another ship of his fleet. They had, of course, broken all relations with Flig Balt, Vin Mod, and their comrades of the former crew of the brig.

The date was now March 19th, and the city began to wonder why the order of execution had not yet arrived—which caused Flig Balt and Vin Mod some worry about their personal futures. Moreover, they were quite resolved that, if there were to be a reprieve, they were leaving Hobart Town, and with that in mind, they were seeking some ship that was ready to leave.

Now, on the 25th, a telegram arrived from London, sent by the Lord Chief Justice to His Excellency, the Governor of Tasmania.

The plea for pardon had been accepted by Her Majesty, the Queen of England, Empress of the Indies, and the death penalty imposed on the Kip brothers was commuted to hard labor for life.

Port Arthur

One month after the day when these death-row prisoners had been granted a commutation of their sentence, two men were working under the whip of the guards in the penitentiary of Port Arthur.[1]

These two convicts did not work in the same squad. Separated one from the other, unable to exchange a word or glance, they had in common neither a mess hall nor lodging. Each went his own way, clad in the ignoble tunic of the galley slave, pummeled by the curses and blows of the guards, amid the gang of convicts that Great Britain sent to its overseas colonies. In the morning they left the labor camp and returned only in the evening, exhausted with fatigue, inadequately nourished with bad food. There they took to their cot, side by side with a chained companion, vainly seeking relief in a few hours of sleep. Then, at daybreak, in the stifling heat of summer or in the frightful cold of winter, they would begin again—and continue on in this way until the moment when a hoped-for death would deliver them from this abominable existence.

The two were the Kip brothers, who three weeks before had been transported to the Port Arthur penitentiary.

It is known that, until the middle of the seventeenth century, Tasmania was inhabited by the poorest people on the globe—natives who were located, one might say, on that borderline which separates animality from humanity. Now, the first Europeans who were to settle on that large island were scarcely any better, no doubt, than those savages. But, after them came the emigrants, who, by their continual labor and the weather helping, made it a most flourishing colony.

At that time, Great Britain had already founded a similar colony on Botany Bay,[2] on the eastern side of Australia, then called New South Wales. As Great Britain might assume that the French intended to create a similar convict prison on Tasmanian land, it hastened to beat them to it, just as they did later on in New Zealand.

Toward the middle of the year 1803, John Bowin,[3] leaving Sydney with a detachment of colonial troops, disembarked on the left bank of the river Derwent, some twenty miles above its mouth, in a place called Ridens.[4] He brought along a certain number of convicts, whose numbers reached four hundred the following year, under Lieutenant-Colonel Collins.

This officer, abandoning Ridens, set up the foundations of Hobart Town on the other bank of the Derwent, in a place where a little river furnished fresh water, at the rear of Sullivan Cove in which ships, even of large tonnage, could find excellent moorings. The new city soon grew, and, among the various civil buildings created, one of the first constructed was the prison, enclosed in four high walls of stone as hard as granite.

Three types of people made up the population in Tasmania: the free men—the emigrants or colonists, who voluntarily came here from the United Kingdom; the emancipated men—the prisoners, to whom was granted a pardon by reason of their good conduct or whose sentence was completed; and the convicts—the deportees who, upon landing, pass under surveillance of the overseer or superintendent of prisoners.

These convicts made up three categories: (1) those given the most serious punishment, who spend their lives in penal servitude and who, under the watchful eye of the constables, are used to perform hard labor, especially the building of roads; (2) those condemned for slighter crimes—English magistrates sometimes have a heavy hand—who can obtain permission to enter into the service of the colonists without pay, but on condition of being appropriately lodged, fed according to regulation rations, and allowed to attend religious services every Sunday; and (3) those who, thanks to their good conduct, have the freedom to work for their own account—and, of those, a few who have achieved a fortune and independence. It is true, despite the efforts made by the governors, not one of them can regain his rank in the society of free men.

Such then were the first measures adopted in the beginning of the colony for penal organization, and such were the different categories of convicts, both men and women. According to what Dumont d'Urville notes at the time of his arrival in Tasmania around 1840, the following increasingly severe punishments were inflicted according to the misdeed: reprimand, condemnation to turning the mill wheel for a specified time, hard labor on the roads, hard labor on the chain gangs, and, finally, being sent to the penal establishment of Port Arthur.[5]

About this last establishment, it is fitting to recall that in 1768 a prison had been founded on Norfolk Island—that island where the *James Cook* rescued Karl and Pieter Kip, the shipwrecked men of the *Wilhelmina*. But, beginning in 1805, the government had it evacuated because, for lack of a port, it was very difficult to land there. The isle, however, later once again became the base of a penal colony, and it is to there that the British administration deported the most hardened criminals from Tasmania and from New South Wales. Later, in 1842, it was abandoned definitively and replaced by the one in Port Arthur.[6]

Thus, without counting the prison in Hobart Town, Tasmania possessed a second one, whose history and situation should be described in some detail.

The great island, deeply indented in its southern portion by Storm Bay, is bordered on the west by a very broken coastline, which the Derwent crosses and where Hobart Town occupies the right bank. To the east, it is bordered by the Tasman Peninsula, which, on its other coast, is battered by the long swells of the Pacific. To the north this peninsula attaches itself by a very narrow isthmus to the Fores-

Port Arthur (from E.-E. Morris, L'Australasie pittoresque*)*

tier Peninsula, which itself joins the district of Panbroke[7] only by a narrow tongue of land. To the south, Southwest Cape and Cape Pillar project their sharp points toward the open sea.

From the isthmus that ties together Forestier Peninsula and Tasman Peninsula to Cape Pillar is approximately six miles, and it was in a small bay on the south end that the British administration founded the town of Port Arthur.

The Tasman Peninsula is covered with thick forests and is very rich in materials appropriate for maritime construction—among other things, a hardwood that has the appearance and qualities of teakwood. A number of these trees, already a century old, can be recognized by their gigantic trunks without any lateral growth and whose foliation spreads out only at the peak.

The little town of Port Arthur developed in the shape of an amphitheater on the hill at the back of the bay. Its port, well designed with a pier for disembarking and sheltered by the surrounding hills, offers full security for ships, which are sometimes prevented from sailing into Storm Bay because of the dreadful squalls coming out of the northwest. Actually, except for the needs of the prison, ships seldom enter there unless storm-bound. The reason is that there is scarcely any commerce in this port, to which the future reserves a certain prosperity if its destiny happens to change.

Indeed, the population of Port Arthur is of a quite unique composition: government employees, constables, and soldiers of two infantry companies. This personnel, under the authority of a captain, is assigned to maintain the security of the penal establishment. The commander, Captain Skirtle,[8] in residence at Port Arthur, was occupying at the time a comfortable home, built on an elevated point of the coastline, and whose view extended well out to sea.

During this period, the penitentiary included two divisions, assigned to two quite distinct categories of convicts.

The first appeared on the left as one entered the grounds. Its name of Point Puer[9] indicated that it was destined for the young detainees, comprised of several hundred youngsters from twelve to eighteen years of age. Too often deported for misdemeanors of slight importance, they occupied wooden barracks containing workshops and sleeping quarters. There, the attempt was made to reform them by having them work, by moral instruction that the rules called for, and by lessons they received from a minister charged with developing their religious practices. Finally, it was from there that they emerged sometimes as good workers in shoemaking, woodwork, carpentry, and other manual careers that could assure them an honest existence. But it also made for a hard life for these young inmates, who were always under threat of punishments—internment in a cell, being put on bread and water, and the whip constantly brandished by the constables against any recalcitrants.

In all, of those who leave the penitentiary at the end of their punishment, some remain in the colony as workers, and the others return to Europe. In the first case, they retain most of the good lessons they received; but in the second, they rapidly forget them. Falling back into a life of crime, they are again condemned to deportation—when they don't end up on the gallows—and it is to the men's penitentiary that they are sent this time, sometimes for life, and are subjected to all the rigors of an iron discipline.

This other division of Port Arthur contained about eight hundred convicts. They have been aptly called the "dregs of English criminals," those who had fallen to the last rung of human degradation. Such were, in days gone by, the deportees from Norfolk Island before they were evacuated to Tasmania. There was not a soul among them who did not have a judicial record filled with murders or robberies. For most—at the limit of the ultimate punishment—they had but one penalty to pay, which was death.

It is not surprising that many precautions were taken in Port Arthur to prevent escapes. It is by sea that the best chance of success lies, on condition that the fugitives are able to take over some boat that would drop them off along the coastline beyond the Tasman Peninsula. In any event, these instances are rare. The convicts have no access to the port, or if they are employed there at some type of work, they are held under rigorous surveillance.

But as difficult as it is to escape by sea, would it not be possible to escape by land since, in reality, the deported men are no longer enclosed on an island as they were in Norfolk? Yes, fugitives are sometimes able to escape from the penitentiary, take refuge in the surrounding woods, and escape all pursuit by condemning themselves to a more dreadful life than that of the labor camp, and most die of sickness or starvation. Besides, they would constantly run the chance of being recaptured in the middle of these forests where the number of posts has been multiplied, and guards relieved at two-hour intervals, with patrols both day and night!

It would be necessary for the fugitives to be able to escape from Tasman Peninsula, but that in itself was impossible.

Indeed, the isthmus that attaches it to the Forestier Peninsula, called the Eaglehawk Neck, measures at best a hundred paces in width at its narrowest point. On this piece of land, which contains no shelter, the prison authorities had implanted a series of guard posts, fairly close to each other. To these posts are attached dogs with chains long enough to overlap each other—some fifty mastiffs as ferocious as wild animals. Whoever would try to force his way through this line would be devoured in an instant. Finally, if an escapee managed to get through these, other dogs, enclosed in kennels raised on pilings, would indicate his presence along the beach, where alert sentinels are always stationed. In such conditions, the prisoners could have no hope of escape.

Such was the penitentiary of Port Arthur, reserved for the most difficult criminals, the most hardened. That is where Karl and Pieter Kip were transported some two weeks after the commutation of their sentence. During the night, a boat taking them to the far end of the port put them aboard the little sloop that serves as a launch to the penal establishment. That sloop crossed Storm Bay, rounded Southwest Cape, entered the harbor and came alongside the pier. The two brothers were immediately incarcerated, waiting for the moment to appear before the warden of Port Arthur.

Captain Skirtle, aged fifty, possessed the energy that his difficult functions required. He was pitiless when necessary, but just and kind toward the wretches that deserved his justice and his kindness. If he punished with great harshness the serious lapses of discipline, he did not tolerate the abuse of force among the staff that were under his authority. The severity of the law that he applied to the prisoners, he applied equally to the guards charged with their oversight.

Captain Skirtle had resided at Port Arthur for some ten years already, with Mrs. Skirtle, his wife, aged forty, his son William and his daughter Belle, in their fourteenth and twelfth years respectively. Living in their villa, Mrs. Skirtle and her children had never had any contact with the personnel of the penitentiaries. The captain arrived alone there each morning for the longest part of the day, and only returned to his villa in the evening. Every month he made several inspection trips to the interior of the peninsula as far as the isthmus of Eaglehawk Neck, inspecting different posts, passing in review the squads at work along the roads. As for his family, besides taking walks around Port Arthur, across the admirable forests that surrounded them, they were transported by the launch to Hobart Town whenever they desired, so their relations were maintained with the Tasmanian capital.

As soon as he arrived at the penitentiary in Port Puer, the commander had the children who had misbehaved the previous day brought before him, and he admonished them and then applied the regulation punishment. What a degree of perversion those little monsters sometimes reached! One of them who had a grudge against a police guard, when they gave him a glimpse of the gallows in the near future if he did not mend his ways, replied: "Well! My father and mother have shown me the way, and, before being hanged, I will kill that constable!"

After his visit to Point Puer, Mr. Skirtle went to the penitentiary for men where, on the morning of April 5, Karl and Pieter Kip appeared before him.

The captain was familiar with the Kip trial, whose repercussions had been considerable, ending as it did with the death penalty for the accused. Although the Queen had spared their lives, the crime of murder—and under conditions that made it even more odious—weighed no less upon their name. They were therefore to be treated with extreme severity, and no softening of their punishment would be considered.

And yet the captain could not help being struck by the attitude that the two had in his presence. After having responded to the questions that they were asked, Karl Kip added in a firm voice:

"Man's justice has condemned us, sir, but we are innocent of the murder that ended the life of Captain Gibson."

They took each other's hand, as they had done before the Criminal Court, and it was the last time that they could exchange a brotherly embrace.

The guards led them off separately, the order having been given not to allow them to be together. Each assigned in a different squad, with the impossibility of ever talking to each other, they would scarcely have the chance even to glimpse one another.

Thus began and continued for them the dreadful existence of a prisoner, dressed in yellow, the special color of the Port Arthur penitentiary.[10] They were not teamed up, as is done in other countries, to a partner with whom they shared a chain. To the honor of Great Britain, this torture, more mental than physical, was never imposed on the English colonies. But a three-foot chain hinders the movement of each prisoner's legs, and in order to walk he must pull it up to his waist. However, if this permanent chaining together of inmates does not exist at Port Arthur, occasionally, as a disciplinary measure, the prisoners of one squad are attached together and work that way in the transport of heavy objects.

The Kip brothers were not subjected to that terrible punishment of the "chain gang."[11] During long months without having been able, even once, to speak to each other, they worked in separate squads in building roads that the government was opening across the Tasman Peninsula.

Most of the time, once the day's work was done, they returned to the sleeping quarters in the penitentiary, where the convicts were locked up in groups of forty. Ah! how comforting it would have been at that moment after so much misery, if they had been permitted to be together, to take their rest near one another, or even when they were on the job when they spent the whole night out in the open air!

One single day each week, Sunday, Karl and Pieter Kip had the

The convicts worked on building roads.

joy of seeing each other when the prisoners assembled in the chapel run by a Methodist minister. And what must they think of the justice of men, these innocent brothers, in those crowds of criminals whose chains rattled mournfully between the songs and the prayers?

What broke Karl Kip's heart, what provoked in him feelings of revolt, the consequences of which could have been quite serious, was that his brother was subjected to such fatiguing hard labor. He, with his iron constitution and his exceptional vigor, would have the strength to survive that, despite the fact that the pitiful rations barely sufficed to nourish him: three-quarters of a pound of fresh meat or eight ounces of salted meat, a half pound of bread or four ounces of flour, a half pound of potatoes. But Pieter with his weaker constitution, would he not succumb to such conditions? From the recent heat of an almost tropical intensity, clad only in the wretched yellow tunics of the penal colony, they were also going to suffer from the intense north wind, the cold, glacial storms, and thick snowfalls. They would have to continue their work under the threats of the constables, under the whip of the brutal guards. No rest except for the moments given over to the noonday meal, while waiting for their return to the penitentiary. Then, at the slightest sign of resistance, severe punishments would fall on these wretches: solitary confinement in the cells, the torture of the "chain gang," and finally, the most terrible of all save death—and yet which sometimes brought it on—the flaying of the guilty whose flesh would be torn by the lashes of the cat-o'-nine-tails![12]

Certainly, such an existence must have produced in those convicts the violent, irresistible desire to escape. Some did try, although, with so many dangers to surmount, they had so little chance of success. And when the fugitives were recaptured in the forests of the peninsula, it was this "cat" that punished them in front of all the personnel of the penitentiary. The cat-o'-nine-tails, in the hand of a vigorous guard, would lash the back of the prisoner who was stripped to the waist, streaking his flesh and transforming it into a bloody pulp.

However, if Karl Kip was sometimes at the point of rebelling against the rigors of prison discipline, his brother Pieter submitted to it, hoping that the truth would some day become known—that some fact, an incident, a discovery would proclaim their innocence. He just accepted it, as painful, as dishonoring as it might be, this life of the penal colony. And even if he did not possess the physical endurance of his brother, at least his moral energy allowed him to tolerate it, along with the strength of his faith in God. What tormented him especially was the fear that Karl would not be able to control himself, that he might resort to some violent act. Of course, Karl would not try to escape; he would not want to leave him alone in the penitentiary, from which they would emerge only together! . . . But in some hour of despair, would Karl get carried away, when he, Pieter, would not be there to calm him down, to hold him back? . . .

So, perturbed by these worries, Pieter thought that he should try do something, and one day during the warden's inspection he attempted to address a word to him. And what he requested in a respectful tone was not to be reunited with his brother, or to work in his squad, but the favor of spending a few moments with him.

Captain Skirtle allowed Pieter Kip to talk, observing him with close attention and, perhaps, with a certain amount of interest. Was it that Karl and Pieter Kip belonged to a social class whose members were not often found as inmates at a penal colony? . . . Had Mr. Hawkins with the support of the governor made additional efforts on their behalf? . . . Could it be that, after the commutation of the sentence arranged by him, this fine man was continuing his struggle in order to obtain for them some softening in the penal colony regime? . . .

Whatever the case may have been, Mr. Skirtle did not reveal anything he was thinking. The Kip brothers were not and could not be, in his eyes, more than two men condemned for a crime of murder. It was already a great deal that the pity of the Queen had spared them the ultimate punishment. Later he might be able to honor Pieter Kip's request, but there was no way of agreeing to it as yet.

Pieter Kip, his heart heavy and choking back sobs, would not have had the strength to insist. He understood that it would be pointless, and he returned to his place in line.

Nearly six months had gone by since the arrival of the two brothers in the penitentiary of Port Arthur. The end of the winter was approaching. It had been hard on these poor men, and how could they have foreseen the possibility that any change whatsoever could modify their situation? . . . Yet that is what happened, and under the following circumstances.

September the 15th, on a beautiful morning, Mr. Skirtle, his wife, his son, and his daughter had just made a long trip through the forest. Arriving at the isthmus of Eaglehawk Neck, they had just stepped down from their carriage.

In this place, some convicts were busy digging out an irrigation canal, and the captain had wanted to inspect what they had done.

Now the squads that Karl and Pieter Kip belonged to were working there, but at a certain distance from each other, for the trees formed a thick hedge at the very beginning of Eaglehawk Neck.

The inspection completed, Mr. Skirtle and his family were getting ready to climb back into their carriage when some shouting broke out in the direction of the fence that closed off the isthmus. Almost immediately furious barking could also be heard.

This barking was from the guard dogs attached to the posts that were set into the beach at less than three hundred paces from the edge of the woods.

One of these animals, having broken his chain, was running toward the forest amid the shouts from the guards and the howls of remaining dogs. It almost seemed as if the dog wanted to leap upon the convicts, whose costume was quite familiar to him. But, frightened by their vociferations, he bounded toward the woods before the guards could catch him.

What the captain had to do was get back into the carriage and leave the place before the animal frightened the horses. Unfortunately, the latter took fright and, despite the efforts of the coachman, galloped away in the direction of Port Arthur.

"Come! . . . come!" shouted Captain Skirtle to his wife and children, whom he hurried off to a thicket where they hoped to take refuge.

Suddenly the guard dog appeared, frothing at the mouth, his

The man held a pickax in his hand . . .

eyes flaming. He was howling like a savage beast, and, in a single bound, he pounced upon the young Skirtle boy, knocking him over and seizing him by the throat.

One could hear the shouts of the guards rushing in from the forest's edge.

Mr. Skirtle, seeing the danger his son was in, was about to throw himself on the animal, when he felt two strong arms push him back.

An instant later, the young boy was saved, and the dog was fighting with the boy's savior, having seized the man's left arm in his bloodied fangs and tearing at it in a rage.

This man held a pickax in his hand, and he plunged it into the dog's body, who fell back, panting, upon the ground.

Mrs. Skirtle held her son in her arms and was showering him with caresses, while the captain turned toward the man who had rescued the boy—a convict in his yellow clothes.

It was Karl Kip. He had been working some hundred yards away. He had heard the cries of the guards, and he had noticed the dog running through the forest. And then, without thinking of his own danger, he rushed after the animal.

The captain recognized this man, who was bleeding from a dreadful wound. He was about to walk up to him in order to thank him and to get him some medical attention, when Pieter Kip got there ahead of him. When the shouts were heard within the woods, the squads had rushed in that direction at the same time as the guards.

Emerging through the trees, Pieter Kip saw his brother stretched out on the body of the beast, and raced toward him shouting:

"Karl . . . Karl!"

In vain would the guards have tried to hold him back. Besides, with a sign from the captain toward whom Mrs. Skirtle was stretching out her hands and whose son implored pity for his savior, he signaled the guards to keep back. And for the first time after seven long months of separation, misery, and despair, Karl and Pieter Kip wept in each other's arms.

Together

Karl Kip, after having been transported in the captain's carriage to the penitentiary in Port Arthur, was brought to one of the rooms in the infirmary where his brother, authorized to stay at his side, was not long in rejoining him.

What feelings of thankfulness Mr. and Mrs. Skirtle must have felt toward that man! Thanks to his courage, their son had been spared the most horrible of deaths. Right after the incident, in an irresistible and heartfelt impulse, the boy had thrown himself at his father's knees, repeating in a voice broken with sobs:

"Have mercy on him . . . Father . . . have mercy on him!"

Mrs. Skirtle had joined her son, and both begged the captain, as if he could grant their wish, or had the authority to give Karl Kip his freedom!

After all, could their crime be forgotten, the crime for which the two brothers, after their death sentence, were locked up forever in the penal colony of Port Arthur? Knowing nothing about the maneuvers of Flig Balt and Vin Mod, how could Mr. Skirtle have doubted the guilt of these two prisoners? From the fact that one of them had, by risking his life, just saved the young boy, were they any less the murderers of Harry Gibson and needed any less to be punished as such? That act of selflessness, as impressive as it may have been, could it redeem such a frightful crime?

"My dear," said Mrs. Skirtle, as soon as her husband had returned to the villa after leaving the wounded man in the hands of a doctor. "What can be done for that poor man?"

"Nothing," replied the captain, "nothing except recommending him to the consideration of the administration, so that in the future he will benefit from a less severe regime . . . that he be exempted from hard labor . . ."

"Well then, we must inform the governor, today, of what has happened."

"He will know before this evening," answered Mr. Skirtle. "But it will be limited to softening, and not to shortening the sentence. Karl Kip and his brother have already been the object of a favor—and what a favor!—since their life was spared . . ."

"And I thank heavens for that, as I thank this poor man, since he saved our poor child."

"My dear," responded the captain, "I will do everything possible out of gratitude to Karl Kip. Moreover, since these two brothers arrived in Port Arthur, their conduct has been irreproachable, and they have never broken the rules. I repeat, I may perhaps be able to obtain permission from the higher administration that they no longer be compelled to work outdoors, even more difficult for men of their condition, and to occupy their time in the offices of the penitentiary. That would be a great improvement in their situation as convicts. But you know for what crime they have been brought before the Court, and on what indisputable proofs the jury has based its conviction."

"My dear," exclaimed Mrs. Skirtle, "how could someone capable of such an act be deemed a murderer?"

"And yet . . . there is no doubt on that score . . . Never have the Kip brothers been able to establish their innocence."

"You certainly know," insisted Mrs. Skirtle, "what Mr. Hawkins's opinion is."

"I know. That fine man does not believe they are guilty, but he is influenced by his fond memories of them. And he has been unable to achieve anything for them, except of course the commutation of the sentence by the intercession of the governor."

"And think," continued Mrs. Skirtle, "how all the more unjust that condemnation will seem to him when he learns how Karl Kip saved our son."

The captain did not reply, for he had been very impressed already by what Mr. Hawkins had told him relative to the two brothers. But, upon reflection, in the presence of the material proofs—Harry Gibson's papers in the possession of Karl and Pieter Kip, the kriss, instrument of the crime that was discovered in their valise—how could he doubt it?

"In any case, my dear," continued Mrs. Skirtle, "I have a favor to ask of you . . . a favor that depends only on you, and that you couldn't refuse me."

"That favor is that the two brothers not be separated any more."

"Yes . . . you understood me! . . . As of today kindly authorize Pieter Kip to remain near his brother . . . To care for him."

"I will do it, of course," Mr. Skirtle promised.

"And I too, I want to visit him," continued Mrs. Skirtle, "I shall make sure that this unfortunate man lacks for nothing. And who knows . . . later on?"

Thus the wish of the two brothers—that which they had desired most ardently—was about to be fulfilled: they would no longer be separated.[1]

So, from this moment on, Karl and Pieter Kip saw each other throughout the day. Then, three weeks later when, his wound almost scarred over, Karl Kip had been able to leave the infirmary, both walked about in the courtyard of the penitentiary. Now they occupied the same room, they slept in the same sleeping quarters, they worked in the same squad. And they were employed at work on the inside, with the hope of soon being assigned to the offices of Port Arthur.

One can easily imagine all that the two brothers had to say to each other, what subject of conversation they constantly returned to, and how they envisaged the future.

And when the younger saw his older brother abandon himself to the fear that the truth might never be known, he repeated:

"Not to hope, brother, would be failing in our duty to God! Since our life has been spared, it's because Providence wishes the murderers to be identified some day . . . and that our redemption be publicly proclaimed!"

"May Heaven hear you, Pieter," replied Karl Kip, "and I envy you for having such confidence. But, really, who can the killers of Captain Gibson be? Obviously some natives from Kerawara or York Island, perhaps even some other island in the Bismarck Archipelago!

But how could they possibly be discovered in the middle of this Melanesian population, dispersed throughout the territory?"

It would be difficult; Pieter Kip was in agreement. No matter, he had faith. Something unexpected would no doubt occur. Mr. Zieger and Mr. Hawkins would obtain new information.

"And besides," he said one day, seeing his brother in the depths of despair, "is it certain that the murderers are necessarily natives?"

Karl Kip had seized his hands and cried out, looking deep into his eyes:

"What do you mean? Explain! Do you think that some colonist . . . or factory worker committed the crime?"

"No . . . brother . . . no!"

"Well . . . who then? Some sailors? Yes, there were several ships in the port of Kerawara . . ."

"And there was also our brig, the *James Cook,*" replied Pieter.

"The *James Cook!*"

And Karl Kip, repeating this name, sought an answer from his brother. So Pieter shared with him the suspicions that haunted his mind. Did the crew of the brig not include some very dubious characters, among others those sailors recruited in Dunedin and who took part in the revolt stirred up by Flig Balt? And among these men—Len Cannon, for example—could not they have known that Captain Gibson was carrying out not only ship's papers but also a sum of several thousand piastres to Mr. Hamburg's firm? That very afternoon Len Cannon and his comrades had gone ashore . . . Would they not have been able to spy on Captain Gibson, follow him through the Kerawara woods, attack him, murder him, and rob him?

Karl listened to his brother with an anxious and intense attention. It seemed that a revelation had suddenly taken shape in his mind. It had never occurred to him to explain the murder other than by the intervention of some natives . . . And here was Pieter pointing out to him how others might be guilty, such as Len Cannon or the other recruits on board ship! . . .

After a few moments of reflection, he continued:

"But, admitting that the murderers must be sought among those men, it is no less certain that Captain Gibson was struck by a Malaysian dagger."

"Yes . . . Karl . . . and may I add with our own . . ."

"Ours?"

"That is only too certain," Pieter Kip affirmed, "and it is certainly ours whose ring they found in the Kerawara forest."

"And how could this dagger have been in the possession of murderers?"

"Because it was stolen, Karl!"

"Stolen?"

"Yes . . . on the *Wilhelmina* shipwreck . . . while we were searching it."

"But stolen by whom?"

"By one of the sailors who was in the dinghy and who, like ourselves, went onto the floating hull."

"But who were those sailors? . . . Do you remember, Pieter? . . . Their names? . . ."

"Somewhat vaguely, brother . . . First, there was Nat Gibson, who wanted to go along. As to the men designated by the captain, I no longer remember . . ."

"Wasn't the bosun with them?" asked Karl Kip.

"No, brother . . . I think I can assure you that Flig Balt stayed on the ship."

"And Len Cannon?"

"Yes . . . I believe so . . . I think I can remember him on the hull, maybe . . . But I am not sure . . . Anyway, he or someone else could have entered our room, and even after us, discovered the kriss there, that we had not noticed in some corner . . . And then later on when those wretches dreamed up this plan of murder, they used this weapon to commit it; then they replaced it in our valise."

"But we would have found it, Pieter!"

"No, not if they had put it there at the last moment."

How close Pieter Kip was coming to the truth! Only he was mistaken about the true murderers. Although his suspicions focused on Len Cannon or some other recruit, quite capable of being suspected, they did not turn toward either Flig Balt or Vin Mod. What was certain was that the bosun had not gotten into the dinghy to go to the wreck, but it was uncertain whether Vin Mod had been there—neither Karl nor Pieter Kip could remember. The reader may recall how this deceitful rogue had operated, with enough cleverness and cunning to avoid raising any suspicion.

So this is the conversation these two brothers would probably have had earlier if they had not always been separated, first in the prison of Hobart Town, then in the penitentiary at Port Arthur.

It is true, what was a certitude for them, because they were not the perpetrators of the crime, would only be presumption for another person. How could they succeed in establishing clear proof that the kriss had been taken from the shipwreck by one of the sailors of the *James Cook* and that this sailor had used it to strike down Captain Gibson? It was obvious—and they understood it fully—that appearances were against them. Pieter Kip's hypotheses were perfectly logical; but they could only be put forth by themselves, who knew they were innocent. And that's really what made them lose hope, and most especially Karl Kip, whose deep despair Pieter, strengthened by his own unbreakable faith in divine justice, had such trouble counteracting at times!

Meanwhile, after the steps taken by Captain Skirtle, the governor and penal administration of the United Kingdom had authorized the admission of the Kip brothers into the offices of Port Arthur. It constituted a great easing of the regimen that had been imposed on them until then. They no longer had to join the squads assigned to the construction of roads or the digging out of canals. They were occupied in bookkeeping, or even, under the surveillance of guards, in the planning of work at diverse points on the peninsula. However—a very painful necessity—when night came, they had to return to their common dormitories, without being able to escape the horrible crowding of the prison.

Now, it happened that this new situation stirred up wild jealousies. Murderers, condemned to death, whose sentence had been commuted and who now enjoyed such favors! . . . Was the good deed rendered by Karl Kip to the family of Captain Skirtle really worth that much? . . . To have thrown oneself on a dog at the risk of a few bites, who would not have done that? . . . The Kip brothers often had to defend themselves against these brutes, and it took no less than Karl's considerable might to bring them to reason.

However, in the middle of this horde of convicts with whom they lived in common rooms, two convicts had sided with them and defended them against their companions.

They were two men of between thirty-five and forty years old, two Irish fellows, one named O'Brien, the other Macarthy. For what crime they had been condemned had never been explained. As much as possible they remained by themselves, and, endowed with exceptional strength, they had managed to impose respect for themselves among the prisoners. Assuredly they were no run-of-the-mill convicts, and they had received an education well above that of the ordinary inmates of a penal colony. So, revolted no doubt by seeing their fellow prisoners join together in a band of twenty against the two Kip brothers, the Irishmen had helped the latter protect themselves against the convicts' odious brutality.

It was foreseeable, then, although these Irishmen were very somber, very unsociable, and of a character that was not very communicative, that a certain closeness would grow between them and the Kip brothers, when a new administrative decision gave them only rare occasions to meet each other in the daily life of Port Arthur.

Indeed, Mr. Skirtle had not been long in learning about the conduct of several convicts, the most incorrigible of the lot. He came to realize that Karl and Pieter Kip had been the object of personal attacks, and that they were exposed to the worst treatment at night when they had to share their sleeping quarters with their penal companions.

And also, Mrs. Skirtle, who had never ceased being interested in the two brothers, did everything she was able to do in order to make their life more bearable. After having spoken of them a number of times when she visited Mr. and Mrs. Hawkins in Hobart Town, she began to harbor certain doubts, and, without going so far as to admit they might be innocent of the Kerawara crime, she thought at least the proof of their guilt did not seem absolutely conclusive. And besides, how could she forget what she owed to the courage of Karl

Kip? . . . That's why this grateful woman, pursuing her urgent requests as far as the governor of Tasmania, ended up by obtaining the privilege for the two brothers to occupy a private room at night.

Before moving into that room, Karl and Pieter Kip tried one last time to thank O'Brien and Macarthy for their kind assistance.

The two Irishmen responded rather coldly to this gesture. They had only done their duty, after all, in defending the two brothers against those criminals. And when the brothers offered their hand at the moment of separation, they did not take it.

And later, when they were alone, Karl Kip exclaimed:

"I do not know what crime these two men were condemned for, but it cannot be for murder, since they refused to touch the hand of the two murderers that we are."

And overcome with anger, he added, "We . . . so-called murderers! . . . And nothing . . . nothing . . . to prove that we are not!"

"Hope, dear brother Karl . . ." replied Pieter. "Justice will be granted us some day."

In the month of March 1887, a year had gone by since the two brothers had been deported to Port Arthur. What more could they have obtained than a softening of the penitentiary regimen in their favor? So, whatever confidence Pieter Kip had in the future, the fear still remained that they would be forever victims of this judicial error. And yet, they were not as abandoned as they probably believed. Outside the prison, if not friends, at least there were advocates who had not stopped taking the most serious interest in their situation. Though Nat Gibson, blinded by his sorrow, refused to admit there were presumptions in their favor, Mr. Hawkins continued his inquiries into this unfortunate affair. He maintained a frequent correspondence with Mr. Zieger in Port Praslin and with Mr. Hamburg in Kerawara. He urged them to pursue the investigation, to extend their inquiry to New Ireland as well as New Britain. If they did not succeed in establishing that the crime had been committed by the natives, could he not identify some foreigners as perpetrators—some factory workers, some sailors from the ships which were at that moment in the ports of the archipelago?

The two Irishmen responded rather coldly . . .

Following this line of inquiry, Mr. Hawkins came to wonder if he should not seek the murderers even among the crew of the *James Cook,* as Karl and Pieter were doing. Were there not grounds for suspecting Len Cannon and his comrades . . . others perhaps? And sometimes the name of Flig Balt crossed his mind. But, of course, they were all pure hypotheses not supported by the statements of the witnesses heard during the trial, or by the material proofs produced in the proceedings.

Mr. Hawkins then had the thought of going to Port Arthur. He felt an irresistible need to see his protégés again; it was a sort of instinctive presentiment that led him to the penitentiary.

One can easily imagine the extreme surprise and also the unspeakable emotion that the Kip brothers experienced when, on the morning of March 19th, they were summoned to the warden's office and found themselves in the presence of the shipowner.

The latter was no less moved on seeing again the survivors of the *Wilhelmina* in their convict uniforms. Instinctively, Karl Kip was going to rush toward his benefactor. His brother restrained him. And as Mr. Hawkins—who imposed on himself a certain reserve, which is understandable—made no advance toward them, they remained still and quiet, waiting for him to say the first word.

Mr. Skirtle remained in the background, appearing indifferent. He wanted to leave Mr. Hawkins free to conduct this interview in the way that he judged appropriate and to decide the course it should follow.

"Gentlemen," said the shipowner.

And this word was like a moral lift for these two unfortunate men who were two prisoners from the penal colony!

"My dear Kips . . . I have come to Port Arthur to bring you up to date on things that are of interest to you and on which I have spent much time."

The two brothers first had the thought that this declaration was related to the Kerawara affair . . . They were wrong—it was not proof of their innocence that Mr. Hawkins had brought. And he continued in these words:

"It's about your business in Groningen. I tried to enter into correspondence with various businessmen of that city, where, I must tell you, it seems that public opinion has remained favorable to you."

"We are innocent!" cried out Karl Kip, unable to suppress the revolt in his heart.

"But," continued Mr. Hawkins, who had some difficulty in maintaining his own calm, "you have not been in a position where you could see to your business. It has suffered from your absence. It was important for the liquidation to be carried out, and I have taken your interests in hand."

"Mr. Hawkins," responded Pieter Kip, "we thank you! It is one good deed added to so many others!"

"I wanted to let you know," the shipowner continued, "that this liquidation has been carried out under the most advantageous conditions that we could hope for. The market was high, and the merchandise found buyers at high prices. As a result, the balance sheet is in your favor."

The most profound satisfaction showed on the pale face of Pieter Kip. Amid the many torments that assailed him in this abominable existence in the penal colony, so many times he thought of his business suffering, of his commercial holdings being reduced to bankruptcy, of this new shame that would stain the name of his father. And then Mr. Hawkins came to tell him that a liquidation had taken care of their interests, and favorably!

Karl Kip then spoke:

"Mr. Hawkins, we do not know how to express our gratitude! After all that you have already done for us, after the friendship that you have shown us—which we were worthy of and are still worthy of, I swear it!—thanks to you, the honor of our business has been saved! . . . and it was not doomed to disgrace after all! No . . . we are innocent of the crime for which they have condemned us. We are not the murderers of Captain Gibson!"

And as they had done before the Court, the two brothers, hand in hand, called to Heaven as their witness.

Mr. Skirtle watched them with emotion, and he felt touched by the sincerity that filled their voices.

And then, Mr. Hawkins gave way to his emotions, incapable of holding in all that he held in his heart . . . And he did it by expressing the warmest of words. No! He did not believe in the guilt of the Kip brothers. He had never believed in it! Unfortunately, the investigation that took place in Port Praslin, at Kerawara, and on the other islands of the Bismarck Archipelago, never reached its goal. So far, they had sought the track of the murderers among the native tribes in vain. Nevertheless, he did not despair of success and of arriving at a retrial of the whole affair.

Retrial![2] That word was pronounced for the first time in front of the two condemned men, who had little hope of ever hearing it. A retrial, which would send them before new judges, who would accept the introduction of new evidence!

But for these new judges, for this new evidence, it would be necessary to have one new, indisputable fact or some judicial error, so that another accused could be substituted for the Kips, who had been condemned in his place! The real perpetrator of the crime, would they succeed in finding him and bringing him to face the two brothers in front of the jury in Hobart Town?

Then Mr. Hawkins and the others went over the principal points of the prosecution's case. Yes! Captain Gibson was surprised by the evidence of the dagger seized in the room of the two brothers, which did belong to them. They had not found it on the wreck of the *Wilhelmina* . . . and they had not brought it aboard the brig. If it had been seen by Jim in their cabin, it is because someone else had placed it there, and if their valise contained the captain's papers, that is because someone else had put them there. Now this "someone" could only be the one who had stolen them along with the money from Harry Gibson, after murdering him in the Kerawara forest! Yes! That had to be the very truth, even though the proof was still lacking.

Under these conditions, suspicion would bear exclusively on the sailors of the *James Cook*. One of them had been able to take the kriss from the cabin of the *Wilhelmina*, one of those sailors brought there by the dinghy. Immediately Karl Kip cried out: "Was Flig Balt among them?"

"No," replied Pieter, "no! . . . my memory is not mistaken . . . Flig Balt did not put his foot on the wrecked ship."

"Now I remember . . . he did not leave the brig," declared the shipowner.

"Then who were the men who went in the dinghy?" asked Karl Kip.

Mr. Hawkins answered, "Hobbes and Wickley. I had occasion to ask them about this, and they are sure they got on with Nat Gibson and you."

"Len Cannon wasn't there?" continued Pieter Kip.

"They told me no."

"That's what I thought . . ."

"But," continued Karl Kip, "Hobbes and Wickley cannot be suspects . . ."

"No. Certainly not," replied Mr. Hawkins. "They are honest sailors. But there was a third one with them."

"And who was that, Mr. Hawkins?"

"Vin Mod."

"Vin Mod!" exclaimed Karl Kip. "Vin Mod, that treacherous rogue . . . that wretch!"

"Vin Mod," Pieter added, "whom I always considered to be the evil twin of Flig Balt!"

By this time, neither the bosun nor Vin Mod was in Hobart Town. Could their trail be picked up at this late date?

The Fenians

It was in 1867 and with the goal of freeing Ireland from the intolerable domination of Great Britain that the political association of Fenianism was formed.[1]

Already, two centuries before, the Catholic subjects of Green Erin had endured widespread persecution when the soldiers of Cromwell, as intolerant as they were vicious, tried to impose on the Irish populations the yoke of reform. The persecuted resisted nobly, loyal to their religious faith as they were to their political allegiance. The years rolled by, the situation did not improve, and England's brutal hand of subjugation was felt even more harshly. So, at the end of the eighteenth century, in 1798, a revolt broke out; it was quickly repressed and resulted in the abolition of the Irish parliament, the national defender of Irish freedoms.

In 1829, a protector appeared, whose name echoed through the entire world. O'Connell came to sit in the House of Commons.[2] There, his powerful voice protested against the British violence, and in favor of the seven million Catholics out of eight million inhabitants that Ireland then numbered.

To what degree of impoverishment and distress the unfortunate country had arrived can be judged by this single fact: that out of five million arable hectares, fifteen hundred thousand had been abandoned by their poverty-stricken farmers and remained fallow.

There's no point in going into detail about that troubled period which was to incite the reprisals of the Fenians, and it is only necessary to discuss it in its relationship to this story.*

O'Connell died in 1847, before being able to finish his work and even to glimpse the possibility of success in a future that was still more or less distant. However, individual efforts continued to manifest themselves, and in 1867 the government of the United Kingdom found itself in the presence of a new revolt, which broke out not in a city of Ireland but in an English city. Manchester witnessed for the first time the raising of the Fenian flag—whose name, no doubt, comes from the Celts of olden days—and it flew high for the cause of independence.

This revolt was put down as the first had been, and with the same implacable force. The police seized the principal leaders, Al-

*This period in Irish history has already been discussed in the *Voyages extraordinaires* in the novel *Lit'l Fellow* (Hetzel's note).[3]

len, Kelly, Deary, Lasken, and Gorld. Imprisoned and then brought before the criminal court, the first three were executed on the 23rd of November in Manchester.

During this period there was another incident due to the unrelenting tenacity of Burke and Casey, who, arrested in London, were shut up in the Clerckenwell prison. Their friends and accomplices were not to abandon them. Resolved to free them, on December 13th they blew up the walls of the prison, an explosion that resulted in some forty victims, killed or wounded. Burke, having been unable to escape, was condemned to fifteen years of hard labor for the crime of high treason.

Seven Fenians were arrested: William and Timothy Desmond, English, O'Keefe, Michael Barrett, and a woman, Anna Justice.

Before the court, these rebels had the celebrated attorney John Bright to defend them, as he had already defended, before Parliament, the rights of Ireland.[4]

The efforts of this great orator failed in part. The accused were brought in April 1868 before the central criminal court. One of them, Michael Barrett, twenty-seven years old, received the death penalty, and Bright was unable to save him.

However, if, since the explosion at Clerckenwell, Fenianism had lost favor in public opinion, the government's crackdown was not enough to curb the Fenians' activity. It was always to be feared that the Irish cause might push the men who supported it on to some desperate act. Thus, thanks to the initiative of Bright before the House of the Lords and the House of Commons, one step forward was made with the bill of 1869. This bill put on equal footing the Irish and Anglican churches, awaiting a law relative to landed property that would be administered in a spirit of equity that would justify the name of United Kingdom, which England, Scotland, and Ireland bear today.

Nevertheless, the police did not relax their guard, and the Fenians saw themselves hunted down mercilessly. The former succeeded in foiling several plots, whose instigators were pursued and sentenced to deportation.

Among them, after an attempted overthrow in Dublin in 1879, were the Irishmen O'Brien and Macarthy. They both belonged to the family of that Farcy who was implicated in the affair of 1867.

Those engaged in revolt had been betrayed by informers, and the police arrested them before they had been able to execute their plans.

O'Brien and Macarthy never wanted to identify their accomplices. They alone took upon themselves the responsibility of this conspiracy. The court dealt with them with excessive severity. It condemned them to life imprisonment at hard labor, and they were sent to the penitentiary of Port Arthur.

These men, however, were not the only political prisoners. Port Arthur already had many under lock and key when Dumont d'Urville visited it in 1840. The French navigator, in the name of justice, protested against this barbarous practice when he cried out: "The penalties received by thieves and counterfeiters have not been deemed severe enough for the political prisoners, who have been judged unworthy of living among them and, as rogues deemed incorrigible, have been cast among murderers."

It was there then, in 1879, that the two Irishmen O'Brien and Macarthy had been transported and had remained for eight long years. They were subjected to the penal colony's regulations in all their rigor, in the middle of that foul peat bog.

O'Brien had been a foreman in a Dublin factory, Macarthy a longshoreman. Each of them had much initiative and some education. Family ties, memories, and certain incidents had enrolled them under the flag of Fenianism. They had risked their lives on it, and they had lost their freedom. Could they hope, after a certain length of time, that their sentence might come to an end, that a pardon would permit them to leave the penal colony? No, they were not counting on it, and no doubt this frightful existence would drag on until the end of their lives, unless they managed to escape.

Would such an eventuality come about? Wasn't all escape from this Tasman Peninsula impossible?

No, provided that help came from outside, and for several years now the Fenians from America had been putting together the means of plucking their brothers from the horrors of Port Arthur.

Toward the end of the year, O'Brien and Macarthy had been forewarned that an attempt to rescue them would be made by friends in San Francisco. When the moment arrived, they would receive a new announcement, telling them to be ready to escape.

How had they received the first notice in the penitentiary? And how would the second one be brought to their attention? And how did the prison's surveillance system fail to notice this, since all day and night, inside or out, they were under close guard by the police?

There was, among these guards, one Irishman who happened to be sympathetic toward his compatriots. Through devotion to the cause of Fenianism, in order to save the last victims sent from America to Tasmania, this Irishman—Farnham by name—had managed to get himself assigned as a guard in the penitentiary of Port Arthur, with the secret purpose of abetting the escape of the prisoners. No doubt he risked a great deal if the attempt failed, if it were discovered that he had been in league with O'Brien and his companion in the penal colony. But many a time this sort of devotion could be found among the Fenians, where there exists a solidarity that goes as far as sacrificing one's life for the cause. A few years before, had not six political deportees escaped from Australia thanks to the relays established from place to place, permitting them to reach the coast and embark on the *Catalpa,* which, after a battle with the police ship, transported them to America?

For about a year and a half, Farnham had been carrying out his duties as guard to the satisfaction of his supervisors, whereas his compatriots had been locked up there for some six years already. Soon he was assigned to be among the guards of their squad, so that they were constantly under his supervision, and he could accompany them outdoors. What gave him some difficulty, since they did not know him, was inspiring confidence in them and not to be taken for a false friend. He eventually succeeded, and a perfect understanding grew between them.

Farnham's biggest concern had been not to raise suspicions. So he had to show himself just as pitiless toward the convicts in his squad as were the other guards. No one would have noticed that he treated O'Brien and Macarthy with any indulgence. It is true, both submitted to the harsh discipline of the penitentiary without protest, and Farnham never had the need to be ruthless with them.

Furthermore, on several occasions, it had not escaped the Kip brothers' attention that this guard stood out from the others by his less common and less crude manner. And yet this observation had not led them to think that Farnham was playing a role. Besides, they had never belonged to the squad that the latter guarded, and they had scarcely encountered him from the time they were allowed to perform office work.

That they learned about the case of O'Brien and Macarthy was due to their having to consult documents concerning the personnel of Port Arthur. That is how the cause of the sentence of the two Fenians was revealed to them—a condemnation that was purely political and which forced them to live this abominable existence in the midst of the vilest criminals.

Upon discovering what O'Brien and Macarthy were, Karl Kip told his brother:

"That's why they refused the hand that we stretched out to them!"

"And I understand that," replied Pieter Kip.

"Yes, brother, all we are to them is people condemned to death, murderers who were somehow spared the gallows!"

"Those poor men!" continued Pieter Kip, thinking about the two Irishmen locked up in this penal colony.

"Whereas we're just fine here!" cried Karl Kip, making one of those angry gestures that he could not contain and for which his brother always feared the consequences.

"Of course," replied Pieter, "while we too are victims of a judicial error that will be corrected some day, these two men are condemned for life, and for seeking the independence of their country!"

Yet if the functions of Farnham at the penitentiary were of a nature to facilitate the escape of the Fenians, it did not seem that the opportunity was forthcoming in the near future. For more than a year, the two Irishmen knew, through him, that some Americans were busy preparing this escape, but no notification had yet been sent. So O'Brien and Macarthy were beginning to despair, when, on the evening of April 20th, Farnham sent the following communication to them:

He was returning from Port Arthur to the penitentiary, when an individual approached him, called him by name, gave his own name—Walter—and the agreed-upon password between the Fenians of San Francisco and himself. Then he informed him that the escape attempt was going to be carried out soon under the following conditions: before the fortnight, the steamer *Illinois*, sailing from San Francisco for Tasmania, would arrive in Hobart Town and remain in the harbor. There it would await favorable conditions to cross Storm Bay and approach the Tasman Peninsula. The day and the point along the coast where he would send his launch would be indicated in a subsequent message. This message, in case Farnham and his negotiator managed to see each other but had no opportunity to speak, would be a note wrapped in a green leaf that Walter would drop at the foot of a tree, where Farnham would be able to pick it up. There would be nothing further to do but follow the information contained in this note.

One can imagine the emotion, as well as the joy, of those two Irishmen when they received this communication. With what impatience they would await the arrival of the *Illinois* in the harbor of Hobart Town, hoping that its crossing would not be slowed down by any incident at sea. In the southern hemisphere April is not yet the month when violent Pacific storms break out. A fortnight, Walter had said, and the steamer would be there! What were fourteen days of patience after six years spent in this hell of Port Arthur!

Since Walter could not dream of entering the penitentiary, it would be outdoors that he would try to locate Farnham and have time to warn him. It was then that he would let him know the day when the fugitives should leave the penal colony and the place where the launch of the *Illinois* would go to pick them up. Perhaps even, on that day, when their squad was getting ready to return to Port Arthur, the three Irishmen could reach the shore. They would wait and

Farnham was returning from Port Arthur . . .

see—and act according to circumstances as they unfolded. The important thing was that Farnham be alerted in time, that he receive the final message one way or another. Although he had only seen Walter once, he would recognize him without difficulty. So during the days to come he should always remain on the alert, and if Walter was unable to get in direct touch with him, he should watch his approach carefully, be constantly ready to catch the slightest signal. Then, when Walter dropped his note at the foot of the tree, he would need to take great precautions in picking it up, and then to let the two Irishmen know about the contents!

"We will succeed," he added. "All the preparations have been well coordinated. The arrival of the *Illinois* will not raise suspicions. It will anchor in Hobart Town like a ship coming for a stopover, and when it returns to the open water across the bay, maritime authorities will suspect others. Once at sea . . ."

"We will be saved, Farnham," exclaimed O'Brien, "saved by you, who will return with us to America!"

"Brothers," Farnham responded, "I will have done for you what you would have done for Ireland!"

A week rolled by, and Farnham had not seen Walter again, who no doubt was watching out for the American steamer in Hobart Town.

On their side, the Kip brothers had no more news from Mr. Hawkins. They thought endlessly of the retrial that he had talked to them about; they lived only for that hope, not even daring to wonder what reasons it might be supported by! Their conviction was based on the role that Flig Balt, and probably Vin Mod, his instigator, had played in the drama of Kerawara and in the murder of Harry Gibson. But those two wretches had left Hobart Town almost a year ago already, and what had become of them, no one could say.

So, when he looked at this situation and saw how it would probably go on and on, Karl Kip sometimes became irresistibly impatient. He thought of escaping, and he proposed to his brother that they risk everything in fleeing. But without outside assistance, any escape was practically impossible.

On May 3rd a fortnight had passed since the notice given by Walter to Farnham. Those two men had not seen each other again. Unless there had been delays en route, it seemed likely that the *Illinois* should have reached the harbor of Hobart Town. But, obviously it was not there, for the two Irishmen would have been forewarned.

What a state of anxiety they were living in! And when their work squad approached the shore, with what avidity their eyes looked toward the sea, seeking among the ships at the opening of Storm Bay one that was to carry them away from this cursed land!

They stood there, immobile, looking at some smoke chased by the wind from the southeast, which signaled the approach of a steamer before it had cleared the tip of Cape Pillar. Then the ship appeared and came around the point to enter the bay . . .

"Is that it? . . . Is that it?" repeated O'Brien.

"Maybe," answered Macarthy, "and if that's the case, forty-eight hours will not go by without Farnham having been alerted."

And they remained thoughtful.

Then the rough voice of the chief guard called them to work and, in order not to awaken suspicions, Farnham did not treat them gently.

As for him, once his shift had ended, he would leave the penitentiary, walk into town, and wander through the streets along the port, in hopes of meeting Walter. All in vain. After all, it was not at Port Arthur, but at Hobart Town that Walter was to await the *Illinois,* and he would not reappear in the vicinity of the penitentiary until after the arrival of the steamer, in order to give the last instructions to Farnham.

That day, during the afternoon, several squads—among others, the one to which the Fenians belonged—were sent to a job five miles in a southwesterly direction. There, on the edge of the forest, they were clearing trees for the establishment of a farm that the administration had decided to develop only a half mile from the coast.

Now, since it was a question of laying out the placement of the farm, the Kip brothers were assigned to the squad. They had been charged with overseeing the implementation of the plans they had worked on in the office.

They stood there, immobile . . .

The convicts, whose numbers rose to about a hundred, walked to the site under the surveillance of a score of guards and their chief.

As usual, the prisoners wore a chain riveted around their foot and attached to their belt. Now since their entry into the offices of the penitentiary, Karl and Pieter Kip, exempted from that heavy constraint, wore only the yellow convict clothing from Port Arthur.

From the day they exchanged a few words and a few thanks with O'Brien and Macarthy, they had had only very rare opportunities to meet with them. Now, moreover, knowing the history of the Fenians, deported for political reasons, they forgot their own troubles in feeling pity for the fate of those Irish patriots.

As soon as the human herd was on the site of the future farm, the work began. At the end of the clearing that was planned for this part of the forest, Karl and Pieter Kip, under the leadership of one of the guards, went out to mark those trees that needed to be chopped down according to the plans.

It was a fairly cool day. Winter was approaching, and a number of dead branches already strewed the ground among the dry leaves. Only the evergreens, the holm oaks, and maritime pines had kept their foliage. The sea breeze, blowing in from the west, wafted through the chattering branches. The air was filled with the perfume of resinous species of trees mixed in with the salty marine smells. The growling of the surf against the rocks along the shore could also be heard, above which flocks of night birds darted hither and yon.

Assuredly, O'Brien and Macarthy had to believe that, under these conditions, no launch would have been able to reach the shore. As for Farnham, after hoisting himself to the top of the cliff, he had determined that not one ship could be discerned on this part of Storm Bay. So either the *Illinois* had not yet arrived or it was still out in the harbor.

For several months, in preparation for the upcoming work on this farm, a road had been opened between Port Arthur and this part of the peninsula—a route fairly well frequented, for it served a few other agricultural sites. So several passersby sometimes stopped and watched the prisoners as they labored. It was of course taken for granted that they were kept at a distance, and that they were not permitted to communicate with the convicts.

Among the passersby, O'Brien and Macarthy did notice one individual who went up and down the road several times.

Was it Walter? They did not know him at all, but Farnham recognized him, and while avoiding the least imprudence, did not lose sight of him. At the same time, a sign that he made to the two Fenians showed that he was indeed the man expected. What was he doing here and why was he trying to get close to Farnham if not to give him notice of the steamer's arrival and to agree on the time and location when the escape would take place?

The head guard who directed the squads was a brutal man, suspicious and extremely harsh. Farnham would not have been able to enter into a conversation with Walter without appearing suspect. The latter understood and after several useless attempts, he decided to proceed according to what had been already agreed to.

In his pocket, a prepared note contained the necessary directions. Having shown it to Farnham from a distance, he went toward one of the trees that bordered the route at some fifty paces from there and picked a leaf in which he wrapped the note, which he set at the foot of the tree.

Walter, making one last gesture, which Farnham understood, went quickly back down the road and disappeared in the direction of Port Arthur.

The Fenians had not missed a single movement of that man. But what could they do? They could not pick up that note without the risk of being seen.

It was therefore up to Farnham to act, not without extreme precautions. So he had to wait until the convicts had finished their work on this side of the clearing.

Now, as bad luck would have it, the head of the guards had just sent one of his squads there, and it was not the one Farnham was watching over.

One can easily imagine how great his concern was, and that of his compatriots. They were stationed at more than two hundred paces from the road, while the other convicts occupied its edge!

Among them Karl and Pieter Kip were proceeding with the marking of the trees, including the one near where Walter had stopped for an instant. There was also reason to fear that the leaf in which he had wrapped the note might allow it to be visible, which might be picked up and brought to the head of the guards.

Immediately the alarm would be sounded. When the squads returned to Port Arthur, surveillance would be on high alert both inside and outside the penitentiary. The prisoners would be confined to quarters and would not return to their work for several days. The attempted escape would fail. When the *Illinois* sent its launch to pick up the two Fenians, there would be no one at the agreed-upon location. After a wait of several hours they would have no choice but to return to the open sea.

Meanwhile the sun began to set. A mass of clouds was accumulating on the western horizon. At six o'clock, the head of the guards would give the signal to quit, so that the squads would return to Port Arthur before night. Now, it was not enough that Farnham could make his way to the foot of the tree; there had to be light enough so that he could see the leaf rolled around the note. If he did not succeed in picking it up today, it would be too late. The wind and the threatening rain would soak and blow away the leaves fallen on the ground.

The Irishmen did not take their eyes off of Farnham.

"Who knows," murmured O'Brien in the ear of his companion, "if it wasn't today that our friends planned to take us away?"

Today? No, that was not likely. Didn't Farnham require some time to make the final plans, and for the Irishmen to reach the shore at the indicated point? But in forty-eight hours at most, certainly, the ship *Illinois* would be at its appointed spot.

The last rays of the sun gleamed at ground level. If Farnham could reach the tree, there would still be enough light to pick up the leaf at its foot. He moved about so that he could approach the place where Walter had stopped, and nobody noticed, except maybe the two Irishmen, who scarcely dared turn their head in that direction.

Once near the tree, Farnham bent down. Among the dead leaves that were strewn on the ground, a single green leaf stood out, half crumpled, half torn—the same one that had been used to wrap the note that Walter had dropped.

The note was no longer there! Perhaps the wind had carried it off? Perhaps it had already been picked up and handed over to the head guard?

When Farnham rejoined his squad, O'Brien and Macarthy gave him a questioning look. They gathered that he had not succeeded. And, once back at the penitentiary, what terrible fears must have preyed on their minds when Farnham told them that Walter's note had disappeared!

The Note

This is what the note contained:

"The day after tomorrow, May 5th, as soon as the opportunity presents itself during your outdoor work detail, find your way, all three of you, to the Saint James Point on the west coast of Storm Bay, where the ship will send its launch.[1] If the weather has not permitted it to leave the harbor of Hobart Town and to cross the bay, wait until it is in sight of the Point and keep watch from sunset until sunrise.

"God protect Ireland and come to the aid of your American friends."

This note contained no names, neither of the addressees nor of those who had written the note, whose terms were as concise as they were clear. It did not even give the name of the steamer sent from America to Hobart Town, whose destination remained unknown.

However, the name of Ireland was written out in full. So there was no doubt that it was intended for the Fenians of Port Arthur. If it happened to fall under the eyes of the captain, he would certainly make no mistake: the escape plan clearly concerned O'Brien and Macarthy, and it would never be carried out.

But this note left by Walter, which contained such precise information and set up a rendezvous for fugitives in forty-eight hours on the Saint James Point, who had ended up with it?

It was the Kip brothers.

It must be remembered that they had noticed Walter's comings and goings on the road. Perhaps they thought at the time that this man was trying to make contact with one of the convicts. However, they had not kept their eyes on him to the same degree as Farnham and his compatriots. They had not seen Walter detach a leaf from the tree, roll it around a note, drop it on the ground. If the note was in their possession, it was by pure chance.

Indeed, while the squads were busy chopping down trees, Karl and Pieter Kip were going back and forth along the road to mark the trees along the edge of the clearing.

When Pieter Kip, who was ahead of his brother, found himself near the tree, he walked around it before raising his pruning knife to notch the trunk.

Now just at that moment, he noticed between its roots, a green leaf half rolled up. There, sticking out, was a little piece of paper. After picking it up he recognized that it enclosed a note bearing a few lines of writing.

In an instant Pieter Kip had read the note. Then, assuring himself, with a quick glance around, that no one had seen him, he slipped it into his pocket.

His brother rejoined him and, while they both continued their work, he told him of his find.

"It's about an escape plan . . . yes! . . . an escape!" murmured Karl Kip, "condemned men who are going to regain their freedom . . . while we . . ."

"Karl, they are neither killers nor robbers . . . ," Pieter Kip answered. "It's about the two Irishmen . . . O'Brien and Macarthy . . . Some friends have prepared their escape!"

And, in fact, this note could only have been intended for the two Irishmen deported to Port Arthur.

"But," said Karl Kip, "there are only two Fenians in the peniten-

In an instant Pieter Kip had read the note.

tiary, and, if you read it right . . . if I understand correctly . . . it concerns three fugitives."

Obviously that would be inexplicable for the two brothers, who did not know, who did not even suspect, the involvement of the guard Farnham with his compatriots.

"Three?" repeated Karl Kip. "Who's the one that's going to leave with them?"

"The third," replied Pieter Kip, "is perhaps the carrier of the note. And I wonder if this third person might be that man we saw prowling along the road? He was probably trying to contact O'Brien or Macarthy."

At that moment Peter Kip noticed the two Irishmen—who were exchanging a few quick words with one of the guards, the one who led their squad. Through his mind flashed a sudden idea. This guard, Farnham, was Irish, too . . . Could he be the third man?

It was then six o'clock in the evening. The head guard had given the signal for heading back to the penitentiary, and the entire group, organized by the guards into a column of two by two, began to march back to Port Arthur.

The Kip brothers were in the rear of this column while the Irishmen were at its head. And what dreadful worries Farnham had! No doubt the note had been dropped there by Walter, no doubt that it had been lost or taken!

It was exactly seven o'clock when the convicts reentered the penitentiary, and, after their evening meal was completed, Karl and Pieter Kip returned to their cell.

For lack of light, they would not have been able to reread the note, but that wasn't necessary. Pieter Kip had learned the sentences by heart, word for word.

Yes! An escape was imminent! Yes! It involved O'Brien and Macarthy, as well as the guard Farnham! The latter was without a doubt facilitating their escape, giving them the chance on the evening of May 5th, in thirty-six hours, to reach the Saint James Point. There, as soon as darkness permitted, a launch would come ashore, a launch from the ship that had arrived from Hobart Town. If the conditions at sea prevented it from leaving the harbor, it would have to wait a day, perhaps two, and who knows whether the fugitives would be discovered, recaptured, and returned to the penal colony?

"No matter," declared Karl Kip, "for luck is on their side. They won't have to hide themselves in the forest and risk being pursued by the station guards! They won't have to cross through the palisades on the isthmus and risk being devoured by the guard dogs! No! The shore is only five miles away. And besides, the work is bringing them closer to it. A ship will come . . . its launch will pick them up . . . in a couple of hours it will have passed Cape Pillar . . . and us, we'll just . . ."

"Brother," Pieter Kip then observed, "you forget that neither O'Brien, nor Macarthy, nor even Farnham knows anything about all this!"

"That's true, the poor fellows!"

"That someone dropped a note at the foot of that tree, they know full well, I believe, and I remember even seeing Farnham head in that direction. He couldn't find it, and now he must be afraid that it was picked up by one of the guards, and then handed over to the warden. And then precautions would be taken to prevent any escape at all."

"But," exclaimed Karl Kip, "no one has found that note except you, Pieter . . . no one knows what it contains, except us . . . and nothing can prevent the would-be escape from being carried out. ."

"Yes, Karl, provided that O'Brien and Macarthy are made aware of it, and they are not . . ."

"They will be, Pieter . . . They will be . . . We're not forgetting that they came to our defense. We can't forget that we must help to free these patriots from the penal colony. Their only crime is to have dreamed of independence for their country."

"Tomorrow, Karl," replied Pieter Kip. "Tomorrow we'll find some way of getting this note to them."

"And," said Karl Kip, seizing his brother's hands, "why shouldn't we flee with them?"

This was the proposal that Pieter Kip was waiting for. For his part, he had certainly thought about it, deeply, and weighed both sides of the question. Yes! . . . as soon as the occasion presented itself, when he gave this note to the two Irishmen, when they had knowledge of it, when they learned that all was in readiness for the escape, that the ship would approach the Saint James Point, that a launch would come for them during the night of May 5th, well! if Pieter Kip told them, "We wish to flee with you," could they refuse? . . . Would they treat them as unworthy of coming along?

And yet, for the Fenians, the Kip brothers were criminals who deserved no pity, and, associating themselves with the Irishman's flight, would that not be granting freedom to the murderers of Captain Gibson?

Pieter Kip had thought about all that, and at the same time about all the steps Mr. Hawkins had pursued, endlessly, to obtain a retrial for them. Could they simply flee? He could not get used to that idea!

But on the other hand, if he had confidence in the future, did his brother Karl share that same confidence? No, and to await a redemption that was both uncertain and remote, he just could not reconcile himself to it! And yet what Pieter Kip told him made a deep impression. His heart throbbing, he listened to it and felt himself weaken little by little.

"Brother, listen to me. I've given it a lot of thought! I admit . . . sure! . . . after what we will have done for them . . . I admit that O'Brien and Macarthy won't refuse our request to leave with them . . . though they only see us as two murderers."

"Which we aren't!" cried Karl Kip.

"Which we are in their eyes . . . and in the eyes of many others . . . maybe everyone except Mr. Hawkins! Anyway, if we manage to escape the penitentiary, to get back on board ship, to seek refuge somewhere in America, what will we have gained?"

"Freedom, Pieter, freedom!"

"And will it still be freedom when we are obliged to hide behind a false name, when we are denounced by the police in all countries . . . when we are always be under the threat of extradition? Ah! My poor Karl, when I think about what our existence will be under those conditions, I wonder if it's not better to remain in the penal colony and wait here until our innocence has been recognized . . ."

Karl Kip remained silent. A dreadful struggle was taking place within him. He understood the strength and the rightness of the reasons that his brother pointed out. Having escaped, their new life would be abominable with the seal of crime on their forehead! In the eyes of the Fenians and their companions, the Kip brothers would never have stopped being the murderers of Captain Gibson.

All night long Karl and Pieter Kip debated, and the former ended by giving in. Yes! for everyone including Mr. Hawkins, flight would only be seen as an admission of guilt.

On their side, O'Brien and Macarthy and Farnham were terribly anxious. After all, Farnham had not been wrong. The man who walked up and down the street really was Walter, from whom he received the first note. A note wrapped in a leaf had been dropped at the foot of a tree. If the note was no longer there, it had been turned over to the warden! Mr. Skirtle now knew that an escape attempt had been prepared under the conditions that the note revealed . . . that it dealt with the two Irishmen, working together with their compatriot Farnham! And so new restrictions would be imposed on them, and they would have to renounce the hope of ever recovering their freedom!

So, until daybreak, these unhappy men awaited the guards coming to shut them up in the solitary confinement cells of the penitentiary.

The next day was Sunday, when the convicts were not sent out to do hard labor. The rule required them to attend religious services, and afterward they would remain consigned to the courtyards.

When it was time to go to chapel, O'Brien and Macarthy felt their apprehensions diminish. No reprimand having been leveled against them, they concluded that the captain had no knowledge of the note.

As soon as the convicts had taken up their usual place, the minister conducted the service. No incident occurred to interrupt it. The two Irishmen were side by side in their pew, watching Farnham, whose regard clearly implied nothing new.

Mr. Skirtle attended this service as he did each Sunday by order of the higher administration. His attitude betrayed no concern, and this would not be the case if word of the escape plan had leaked out.

Besides, neither Farnham, nor O'Brien. nor Macarthy noticed that they were the object of any special attention. So, what they felt it was best to believe, was that the note had been blown away by the wind, and it would be impossible to find it now.

When the minister had finished the sermon, which concluded the service, the convicts left the chapel and returned to the dining room for the first meal. They then spread out across the courtyards or sought shelter under the inner courtyards, for the rain was starting to fall.

What Pieter intended was to find O'Brien or Macarthy in the courtyards—where the convicts formed separate groups, which would be easier than in the dining halls—and just hand over the note to them, saying:

"Here is a note I picked up. No one other than my brother and I have any knowledge of it. It's up to you to decide what to do!"

Then Pieter Kip would withdraw.

Now, since it was not forbidden for the inmates to converse with each other, it did not seem that Pieter Kip's plan would incur any risk. It was just a question of slipping that note into O'Brien's hands—or into those of his companion—and indicating its source.

Unfortunately, what would have been easy when the convicts were in groups in the courtyards, would be less so if they took shelter under the inner courtyards in the common rooms. There, eight or nine hundred prisoners were more closely grouped together under the surveillance of the guards.

And that is exactly what a succession of violent rains obliged them to do before the end of the afternoon. The rooms had to be used in common and not for one instant did Karl or Pieter Kip find the moment to approach the two Irishmen.

And yet it was important that O'Brien and Macarthy be made aware of it this very day.

It was already May 4th, and the note indicated the next day for the rendezvous at Saint James Point, where the launch would await the fugitives.

As for reaching the agreed-upon place, here is how the Kip brothers understood that it might be done. The next day the convicts were to be employed in the part of the forest that the administration was having cleared. This work usually went on until six o'clock in the evening. It would be that moment, no doubt, just before getting together the various squads for the return to Port Arthur, that Farnham, under some pretext or other, would choose to accompany the two Irishmen to the edge of the clearing. People would not suspect anything; they would not even be surprised since the prisoners would be with a guard. Then, very probably, when the squads started off, no one would notice the absence of O'Brien, Macarthy, or Farnham. It goes without saying that if, by misfortune, their absence were noticed, the head warden would give the alarm. But, thanks to night falling, in the middle of this thick forest, it would be difficult to pick up the trail of the fugitives.

On the other hand, if their flight were noticed only after the squad's return to Port Arthur, the cannon would be fired immediately. The alarm would be rung throughout the peninsula. But since the coast was located only a half mile from the clearing, the fugitives would already have had the time to reach Saint James Point. Then, if the launch was waiting for them, it would only take a few tugs on the oars to bring them safely aboard the *Illinois*. The ship would have all night to leave Storm Bay, and at sunrise it would be some ten miles beyond Cape Pillar.

However, to repeat, it was essential that the Irishmen be informed in time, by tomorrow at the latest if not this very day. So, if Pieter Kip failed to communicate with them before evening, it would be impossible to do it during the night, since his brother and he occupied a separate cell that they could not leave.

Such was their situation, anxiety for the Fenians about the missing note, impatience for themselves for not having succeeded in warning either O'Brien or Macarthy! And time was passing, the hour approaching when all the convicts would be locked up in their sleeping quarters.

At the worst, would it not be sufficient to warn the two Irishmen first thing in the morning? Would they not have time to escape toward the end of the day? In any case, they would have no chance of reaching the shore unless they were outside the penitentiary. And, the next day, during work hours, would not Karl and Pieter Kip finally have an opportunity to approach the Irishmen, since he and his brother enjoyed a certain liberty in marking the trees?

Toward six o'clock in the evening, after a rainy day, the sky became clear as the sun neared the western horizon. A brisk wind chased away the last clouds. The convicts were given permission to leave the inner courtyards for a few moments before returning to their rooms, and, under the care of the guards, they dispersed throughout the outer courtyards.

Perhaps there would finally be a moment to meet O'Brien or Macarthy? It was Pieter Kip who had the note, and he was the one who would try to take it to the Fenians.

At seven o'clock, according to regulation, the convicts would return to their barracks, with rooms of about fifty convicts each. Then, after roll call, they would be locked up until the next morning, and the Kip brothers would be returned to their cell.

Several groups had formed, here and there, in keeping with the camaraderie of the penal colony, the attraction of condemned men for each other. They did not talk about the past . . . what was the use? nor of the present . . . what could they change? . . . but rather of the future! And in that future, what did they foresee? Some softening of the penitentiary discipline, sometimes a remission of their sentence, perhaps the success of their escape?

As mentioned, the Kip brothers and the two Irishmen did not normally encounter each other. From the day when O'Brien and Macarthy had received with deliberate coldness the thanks from Karl and Pieter Kip, they had never spoken to each other. So, not being in the same work squad, they could scarcely meet any time except during the mornings or afternoons on Sundays and holidays.

Meantime, the hour was fast approaching. It was important for the Irishmen to be alone at the moment when Walter's note was exchanged, and it was just then that Farnham, prowling around them, seemed never to take his eyes off them.

No doubt there was every reason to believe that Farnham was

in on the escape and that he was probably going to accompany the prisoners in their flight. But still, if that supposition were false, if Farnham surprised the Kip brothers in conversation with the Fenians, all would be lost . . . And yet, no! . . . Pieter Kip could not be mistaken. Looks of understanding were exchanged between the three men, looks where impatience struggled with anxiety! Their deep worry permitted them no peace of mind.

At that instant, called in by the head guard, Farnham was ordered to leave the courtyard. Passing by, he had not been able to say a word to his compatriots, whose apprehensions redoubled. In this position that they found themselves, everything was suspect. What did they want of Farnham? Who had called him? Was it the captain, about the note? Had his complicity been discovered?

Prey to an emotion they could not hide, O'Brien and Macarthy took a few steps toward the door, as though to watch out for Farnham's return, wondering if they were not going to be called up in their turn.

In the somber, empty place where they stopped, it seemed there was no risk of being seen, or being heard.

Pieter Kip advanced with a rapid step, rejoined the Irishmen and with a quick movement seized O'Brien's hand that the latter at first tried to withdraw.

At that moment O'Brien felt a piece of paper slipped between his fingers, while Pieter Kip said in a low voice:

"It's a note that concerns you. Yesterday I picked it up near the road at the foot of a tree. No one has any knowledge of it except my brother and me. I could not get it to you any sooner. But there's still time. It's for tomorrow. You'll see what you are expected to do!"

O'Brien had understood, but his emotions were so stirred up he could not respond.

And then Karl Kip who had just approached the group, leaning toward Macarthy, added: "We are not murderers, gentlemen, and you can see that we are also not traitors!"

12

Saint James Point

The next evening, a little after seven, at intervals of a few minutes each, three flashes of light illuminated the high walls of the penitentiary behind Port Arthur. Three loud detonations followed. It was the alarm cannon whose sound, originating at ground level on the Tasman Peninsula, was going to stir things up like a bee's nest. The guard posts would immediately be linked to each other by patrols, and the dogs would be held at chain's length along the palisades of the isthmus at Eaglehawk Neck. No thicket or clump of trees in the forest would escape being searched by the guards.[1]

Those three cannon shots signified that an escape had just been discovered, and measures had quickly been taken to prevent the fugitives from leaving the peninsula.

Besides, the weather was so bad that it was impossible to escape by sea. No small craft could have landed on the beach; no ship could have approached the shore. So, since they would not be able to cross the palisades of the isthmus, the escapees would be forced to hide out in the forest where they would presumably soon be found and returned to the penal colony.

In fact, the wind was blowing hard from the southwest, which churned up the sea in Storm Bay and along the seaward side of the peninsula.

That evening, after the work crews had returned to the penitentiary, they had discovered the absence of the two prisoners from the fifth squad. While he was bringing them back, the chief guard, who was leading the column, had not noticed their disappearance, this fifth squad being under the surveillance of Farnham, whom no one suspected.

So it was at the evening roll call that they discovered the escape, and the captain was immediately informed.

Since it concerned the Irishmen, O'Brien and Macarthy, two political prisoners, it was probable that they had received the assistance of some outside friends. But under what conditions had this escape been worked out? Had the fugitives already been able to leave the island? Were they hiding in some prearranged location? That is what the search would perhaps uncover, now that the three cannon shots had alerted all the personnel on the peninsula.

As far as Farnham was concerned, when he had been called to the office the night before, it was only a service matter. No suspicion had surfaced about him. And even when his absence was also confirmed, it did not at first raise any questions. Mr. Skirtle and the head constable must have believed that the Irishmen had gotten rid of him before taking flight themselves.

As has been said, it was not plausible that O'Brien and Macarthy had escaped on a launch, given the turmoil of the sea. So, on the order of Mr. Skirtle, a detachment of guards went immediately to the isthmus, which they had been watching closely ever since the cannon alert. They checked to see that the guard dogs posted along the palisades were alert and that the other dogs were let loose on the shores of Eaglehawk Neck.

An attempted escape always has a considerable effect on the personnel of a penitentiary. The prisoners of Port Arthur now understood that two of their companions had just tried to escape and that it concerned the Irishmen O'Brien and Macarthy. And how that attempt excited the envy of these wretches! Condemned by common law, they considered themselves on the same plane as political prisoners. The escapees were prisoners just like them, the Fenians, and they had managed to escape! Had they succeeded in leaving the peninsula? Were they hidden somewhere in the forest, waiting for some outside help to come and pick them up?

What was said in the barracks was also said in the cell of the Kip brothers. But the latter knew what others did not: a ship was to pick up the fugitives, a launch was to pick them up at Saint James Point. But, had the launch been there at the planned moment? "No, it's impossible," replied Karl Kip in response to the questions of his brother. "The wind is blowing a gale in Storm Bay! No small craft

*The guard dogs of Port Arthur**

*Illustration from the *Voyage of the Griffin,* adapted by P.-J. Stahl (Hetzel's note).

could beach there. No ship, not even a steamer, would risk running so close to shore."

"Well," observed Pieter Kip, "are these unfortunate men going to be spending the night on the Point?"

"The night and the next day, Pieter, because escape cannot be carried out in daylight. And who knows if this storm will have ended in twenty-four hours?"

During these long hours, neither of the two brothers could sleep. While the storm lashed against the narrow window of their cell, they listened. Could they not hear a coming and going of guards, indicating that the two Irishmen, arrested in their flight, were perhaps returning to the penitentiary?

It was under the following conditions, earlier that day, that the escape of O'Brien and Macarthy had been carried out, with the complicity of their compatriot Farnham.

It was nearly six o'clock. The squads were finishing up the clearing of the trees. The forest was already becoming lost in the gloom. Five or six minutes more and the head constable would give the order to return along the Port Arthur road.

At that moment the two brothers observed that Farnham, approaching the Irishmen, said something to them in a quiet voice. Then the latter followed him to the edge of the clearing where they stopped in front of one of the trees that had been marked for cutting.

The head constable did not seem much worried about their going off in that direction under the surveillance of a guard, and they stayed under the trees until the time when the squads were formed in a column to return to Port Arthur.

As already stated, no one realized that O'Brien or Macarthy or Farnham had failed to rejoin their companions. It was only after the roll call made in the courtyard of the penitentiary that their absence was noticed.

Profiting from the growing darkness, the three fugitives had been able to sneak away. In order to avoid a patrol returning to a neighboring post, they had to lie down in the deep underbrush, taking care not to betray themselves by the clinking sound of the chain that O'Brien and Macarthy wore from their feet to their waist.

Once the patrol passed, the three stood up and moved on. Stopping periodically, with their ears cocked for the slightest sound, they managed to reach the crest of the ridge at the foot of which Saint James Point stretched out into the sea.

Darkness had enveloped the entire Tasman Peninsula, a darkness all the more profound since the clouds, very thick, pushed along by the west wind, filled the entire sky.

It was nearly six-thirty when the fugitives came to a stop to observe the bay.

"No boat," said O'Brien.

And indeed it did seem that the bay was deserted; lacking a silhouette that would be detectable in the darkness, a ship would only have been visible by its running lights.

"Farnham," Macarthy asked, "are we really on the cliff of Saint James?"

"Yes," Farnham declared, "but I doubt that a launch has come ashore!"

And how could they have dared to hope so, hearing the sea roaring in the distance while the spray from the waves, raised by the gusts of wind, rose nearly to the top of the ridge!

Farnham and his companions walked toward the left, and then descended to the beach, so as to reach the extreme end of the point.

It was a sort of narrow cape, encumbered by rocks, filled with pools, that ran along two or three hundred feet and whose curvature formed a little creek opening toward the north. A launch would have found calmer waters if it had succeeded in getting through the reefs against which the sea broke with extraordinary violence.

They reached the end after struggling against the gale, then placed themselves in the shelter of a tall rock. The note brought by Walter told them to be at that date on Saint James Point, and there they were—although they did not have much hope of being picked up, at least not that evening. Besides, the terms of the note foresaw this possible delay, and they remembered it word for word:

"If the weather has not permitted it to leave the harbor of Hobart Town and to cross the bay, wait until it is in sight of the Point and keep watch from sunset until sunrise."

They could only follow these directions.

"Let's find some shelter," said O'Brien, "some hole in the cliff where we can spend the night, and tomorrow."

"Without going too far from the Point," Macarthy observed.

"Come," said Farnham.

Foreseeing bad weather, the latter had taken care to inspect this deserted beach during his last Sunday off. Perhaps at its base the cliff might offer some sort of crevasse where the three fugitives would be able to hide until the launch arrived. Farnham had discovered just such a cavity in an angle at the very beginning of the Point and had brought down some food—dried biscuits and preserved meat, bought in Port Arthur—in addition to a bowl, which he now filled with fresh water at a nearby stream.

In the darkness, and buffeted by these blinding gusts of wind, it was not very easy to find this crevasse again, and the fugitives did not succeed in doing so until after having crossed the beach, whose slope was not very steep.

"That's where it is," said Farnham.

And in an instant all three had found their way into a cave no more than five or six feet deep, where they would be sheltered from the tempest. Only, at high tide, pushed by the wind that was beating it like a whip, perhaps the raging water could reach the opening. As for the packets of food, which would suffice for at least forty-eight hours, Farnham found them undisturbed.

Scarcely were the three compatriots settled in when they heard a gun shot, repeated three times, echoing above the fracas of the gale winds.

It was the cannon of Port Arthur.

"The breakout has been discovered!" exclaimed Macarthy.

"Yes, now they know we've escaped!" replied O'Brien.

"But we're not yet captured!" said Farnham.

"And we won't let ourselves be captured!" added O'Brien.

First off, it was necessary for the two Irishmen to remove their chains, in case it became necessary to run. Farnham had brought along a file, which was used to cut their leg irons.

Finally, after six long years spent in the penal colony, O'Brien and Macarthy were now no longer tethered to those heavy chains of the convict.

It was obvious that during the night no launch would land anywhere along the coast. And, besides, how would any ship have risked placing itself right in the middle of this dangerous series of reefs extending from Storm Bay to Cape Pillar?

Nevertheless, their excitement was intense, and the fugitives could not resist the need to observe the approaches to the point. Several times, without fear of being spotted, they left their shelter, wandered along the beach, seeking vainly in the dark the lights of a ship!

Then, returning to the cave, they discussed the situation, which, when daylight came, would be extremely dangerous.

Indeed, after having searched the environs of Port Arthur and inspected the forest as far as the isthmus, would the guards extend their exploration as far as the shore? The dogs, accustomed to following the trails of convicts, would they not discover this hole where Farnham and his companions were hiding?

And while they pondered these frightful eventualities, the name of the Kip brothers was mentioned by O'Brien. Remembering the service that the Kip brothers had rendered them:

"No," he exclaimed, "no! They are not murderers. They said so, and I believe them!"

"And they have a lot of heart," added Macarthy. "By turning us in they could have hoped for a reward, but they didn't do it."

"I've heard about the Hobart Town affair, more than once," continued Farnham, "the murder of Captain Gibson of the *James Cook*. A few individuals have taken an interest in the Kip brothers, and yet most people don't believe they were unjustly condemned."

"They are innocent! They are!" repeated O'Brien. "And when I think I refused to shake hands with them . . . Ah, the poor men! No! they're not guilty, and in the penal colony of Port Arthur, in the middle of all those criminals, they must have suffered what we have

Seeking vainly in the dark the lights of a ship!

suffered ourselves! But in our case, it was for having tried to free our country from those British vultures! And beyond that, friends have arranged to rescue us. But Karl and Pieter Kip, they are here for life! Ah, you know, when they came to us to give us that slip of paper they had found, I could've told them: 'Come along with us! Our compatriots will welcome you as brothers!'"

The night was advancing, still rainy and frigid. The fugitives suffered from the cold, and yet it was not without the keenest apprehension that they awaited the dawn. They heard the sound of barking from time to time, which indicated that the dogs had been loosed across the peninsula. Accustomed to sniff out the convicts, to recognize the garb of the penal colony, would not these animals discover the crevice where Farnham and the compatriots were hiding?

A little after midnight the beach was entirely covered by the rising tide, which was pushed higher by the fury of the west winds. The sea rose to the point that the base of the cliff was battered by the waves.[2] For a half-hour the fugitives were flooded up to their knees. Fortunately the level did not rise any further, and the ebbing tide withdrew the water despite the resistance of the storm.

Before the break of day the tempest began to diminish somewhat. Little by little the wind shifted to the north, making the bay more passable. Farnham, O'Brien, and Macarthy could thus hope that the sea would soon begin to calm. When day came, the improvement was visible. If the waves still crested beyond the reefs, a launch could without too much difficulty come ashore on Saint James Point from the reverse side.

But it would still be necessary to await the evening before venturing onto the beach.

Farnham divided the food that he had brought into three parts, bread and dried meat for each. It seemed wise not to eat much, foreseeing new delays beyond the forty-eight hours, for there was no way of replenishing the food. As for fresh water, that evening it would be easy to refill the bowl at the stream.

Part of the morning was spent in these conditions, and was not marked by any incident. The storm was definitely winding down, and the sun reappeared among the last clouds in the east.

"The ship that is in the Hobart Town harbor," said O'Brien, "is going to be able to cross Storm Bay, and it will reach the peninsula by evening."

"But, of course," responded Macarthy, "they're going to patrol the coast more carefully."

"Let's think about this logically. No one knows in Port Arthur either that a ship has arrived from America to take us aboard or that a rendezvous was given to us at Saint James Point. So from that, what are they going to suppose? We are hiding in the forest—and for the first days at least, that's where most of the search will be carried out, rather than here on the shore."

"That's what I'm thinking," Farnham observed, "but how about Walter? Just two days ago, Saturday, we met him on the Port Arthur road. Did he then return to Hobart Town? That seems likely to me. After returning to the steamer, he probably told the captain that we would be at Saint James Point on Monday evening."

"No doubt," replied Macarthy, "for if Walter had not returned to Hobart Town, he would've met us that night! In that darkness, it wouldn't have been too difficult for him to throw the patrols off the track."

O'Brien declared, "I agree. And, on Sunday, Walter must have left Port Arthur on one of the tenders used for the harbor service."

"And we are certain," added Farnham, "that he will press for the departure of the steamer. So all we have to do is wait . . . As soon as night falls, the launch will pull up to the point."

"God willing!" O'Brien replied.

Toward one o'clock in the afternoon there was a close call. Voices were clearly heard on the edge of the cliff, scarcely a hundred feet above the crevice that sheltered the three fugitives. At the same time they heard the barking of dogs that were being worked into a frenzy by their masters.

"The constables! The guard dogs!" Farnham cried out. "That's the greatest danger!"

It was indeed to be feared that these animals would come down onto the beach, where the guards would follow them along the path that Farnham had taken the day before. There, the dogs would start searching about, and their instinct would lead them to the base of the cliff, where they would end up discovering the cave. And what resistance could O'Brien, Macarthy, and Farnham put up against a dozen armed men when they had no weapons themselves? The Irishmen would be seized in a moment and brought back to the penitentiary. And they knew full well the fate that would await them! The double chain and the dungeon for O'Brien and Macarthy! Death for Farnham for having facilitated their flight!

All three remained motionless at the back of the cave. It was no longer possible to leave it without being seen. And where could they take refuge except on the last rocks of the Point? So, in order not to return to the penal colony, they would have to throw themselves into the sea! Yes, anything rather than fall back into the hands of the guards!

Meanwhile, the sound of voices reached them. They could hear words exchanged on the top of the cliff and the shouts of those pursuing them, mixed in with the furious barking of the guard dogs.

"This way! This way!" one of them repeated.

"Let loose the dogs!" said another. "And let's search the beach before we return to the post."

"And what would they have come here for?" answered the brutal leader of the squad, whose voice Farnham recognized. "They can't have saved themselves by swimming, so it's in the woods that we have to look for them!"

O'Brien had grabbed his companions' hands. After this observation by their leader, it was probable that the guards would leave. But somebody said:

"We can still take a look. Let's go down the path that leads to the beach. Who knows if all three of them aren't hiding in some hole down there?"

All three? So apparently there was no longer any doubt in Port Arthur that Farnham was an accomplice of the two Irishmen in this escape and might well be with them.

At that moment, although the conversation could be heard less distinctly, the howling of the dogs drew closer—proof that the guards were heading for the path.

"Let loose the dogs!" said another guard.

One fortunate circumstance would perhaps prevent the fugitives from being discovered. The sea, still high at this moment, flooded the beach right up to the foot of the cliff, and the backwash of the surf was still bathing the edge of the cave. It would have been impossible to see the opening unless they turned about the cliff from this side. As for Saint James Point itself, it showed only its furthest rocks under the foam of the waves. It would take two hours of ebb tide for the beach to become walkable again. So it wasn't likely that the guards would dally in this place, being in a hurry to find themselves on a better trail.

Meanwhile the dogs barked more violently, and no doubt instinct pushed them along the cliff. One of them even leaped across the rush of the waves, but the others did not follow his example.

Almost immediately, the head constable gave the order to walk back up the path again. Soon all the tumult of barking and voices faded away. All that could be heard was the roar of the sea crashing against the base of the cliff.

Escape

The danger was now less immediate, but still very real. After searching the forest, the guards would return to search the shore more thoroughly.

As mentioned, if escapes were sometimes successful from the penitentiary of Port Arthur, then they had to involve going out to sea. Either the convicts succeeded in securing a boat, or they constructed it themselves and could thus reach some other point of Storm Bay. As for attempting to cross the isthmus, that way was considered impossible. And those fugitives who hid themselves in the forest were inevitably recaptured within a few weeks. The commander was aware of this, and searches for escapees always started first in the forest when the weather prohibited flight by sea.

Since the storm was beginning to dissipate and the shore of the peninsula could soon be approached by sea, detachments of guards would no doubt closely inspect the surrounding creeks no later than the next day.

That's what O'Brien, Macarthy, and Farnham told themselves, but with what apprehensions and impatience! How the hours of that afternoon seemed to drag on endlessly, with no launch, listening to the noises from outside, believing they heard the crunch of steps on the sand, the barking of those ferocious bloodhounds, fearing at each instant to see one of those dogs leap upon them!

Then there were some moments when they felt more confident. Without risking leaving their hiding place, they had a view of a broad sector of the bay, and they could watch the passing of ships at sea. Several sailing vessels were now visible since the wind had shifted to the north as a light breeze. Several, tacking, entered the bay after clearing Cape Pillar. Farnham knew from Walter's communication that the American vessel that had arrived in the harbor of Hobart Town was the steamer *Illinois*. So it was for trails of smoke that his companions and he himself were searching on the horizon, smoke floating southward, smoke that would announce the approach of the expected ship in the midst of such perils!

And yet it was still too early. There were only some twenty miles between Hobart Town and Saint James Point. It would be enough for the *Illinois* to leave the harbor by six o'clock in the evening. It would not be too imprudent to get near the Point so long as the cover of darkness would permit the crew to send a launch to pick up the fugitives.

"But do they know on board the *Illinois* if we have managed to escape or not?" Macarthy asked.

"Don't worry," replied Farnham. "We've already been at the agreed-upon place for twenty-six hours, and by this morning the news of our escape will have reached Hobart Town. The governor must have been warned by telegram; and besides, in my opinion, Walter probably hurried back to rejoin the *Illinois*. If the steamer was unable to leave yesterday because of the foul weather, it will not be long now in making its way toward the peninsula."

"It's already five o'clock," observed O'Brien, "and in an hour and a half the darkness will make it difficult to distinguish Saint James Point. How will the captain of the *Illinois* be able to send off a launch?"

"I don't doubt," replied Farnham, "that he has taken all proper precautions! He knows, or some sailor on board knows, the whole shoreline of the peninsula. Even at night, he won't be at a loss to . . ."

"Smoke!" exclaimed Macarthy.

In the northwest direction appeared a fine stream of smoke above the horizon, whose purplish clouds veiled the sun.

"Is that it? . . . Is that the *Illinois?*" asked O'Brien, who would have immediately raced out onto the beach, if Farnham, out of prudence, had not held him back.

Storm Bay is usually frequented by a great number of ships, mostly steamers. The one that had just been pointed out, would it not turn southeast and begin to head straight out to sea? Nothing about it yet would lead one to believe that it would follow the coast.

Never had the fugitives' anxiety been greater, even when the constables descended the path from the cliff, their dogs threatening to leap out upon the beach! Never, on the other hand, had they felt greater hope! The smoke grew visibly toward the southeast. Before a half hour had gone by, while there was still daylight, they could see the ship detach itself from the line of the sky and the sea. From its smoke, which was not very heavy, it did not seem that it was forcing its speed. Indeed, if it was really the *Illinois,* there would be no reason for it to have been sailing full steam! By nightfall, it was certain of being just a few cable lengths from Saint James Point. And then the launch would be lowered with no risk of being seen.

Suddenly O'Brien let out a cry of despair:

"It's not the one! It's not the *Illinois!*"

"And why is that?" asked Farnham.

"Look!"

The steamer had just changed direction and was no longer approaching the peninsula. It was maneuvering as ships do that are trying to head toward Cape Pillar in order to leave Storm Bay.

And after that interminable waiting, a whole day, night was now falling! The hope of salvation that seemed so close at hand when the ship would take them aboard, had now vanished. It was leaving the peninsula, heading for the open sea!

So, it was not the *Illinois,* announced by Walter, whose smoke the fugitives had perceived. The American steamer had apparently remained in the harbor at Hobart Town. But there was still time. Perhaps it would arrive in the middle of the night?

Fine, they'd wait, and they'd keep watch! As soon as darkness was complete, O'Brien, Farnham, and Macarthy would cross the beach, walk out to the end of the Saint James Point, and huddle on the furthest rocks. And if a steamer approached, they would hear in the dark the throb of its engine and the roiling of its propeller. And if it sent one of its launches, they would hail it and it would come to them through the offshore reefs. And, if the surf prevented them from landing, they would throw themselves into the sea—they would be welcomed and transported at last on the *Illinois!* Yes, just as O'Brien had said, even if they were to lose their lives in the attempt, anything rather than return to the penal colony!

The sun had just disappeared behind the horizon. At this time of the year, the last shimmers of dusk would not last very long, and then the bay and the shoreline would quickly sink into the shadow of night. The moon, then in its last quarter, would not rise before three in the morning. Under a starlit sky, veiled in heavy clouds, the night would be dark.

Now, there reigned a deep silence over the sea. The breeze, having calmed toward evening, was now only intermittent puffs. Out on the bay, even at the distance of two or three miles, the fugitives would have easily heard the noise of a steamer advancing toward the shore, and even at five or six cable lengths, the sound of a launch propelled by its oars.

O'Brien, unable to remain still, tried, despite his companions' warnings, to walk out onto Saint James Point.

It was imprudent, for there was still some lingering daylight, and from the top of the cliff, guards could have made him out. But it did seem as though this part of the shore was deserted for now.

Crawling out on the sand, O'Brien reached the spot where Saint James Point met the beach. There, enormous boulders bearded with kelp were piled up, marking the beginning of the Point, which, uncovered at low tide, advanced some two to three hundred feet into the sea, curving off to the north.

At that moment, O'Brien's voice reached Farnham, who was crouched near Macarthy inside the cave.

"Off the Point! . . . Off the Point!" he cried.

Had he perceived the launch, or at least detected some sound of oars? In any case, they had to join him without hesitation. And that is what Farnham and Macarthy immediately did, crawling across the beach.

When the three of them were together at the foot of the first rocks, O'Brien said:

"I thought . . . yes . . . I think . . . A launch is coming!"

"Which way?" asked Macarthy.

"This way."

O'Brien pointed to the northwest.

That was precisely the direction that a launch would have followed in coming through the reefs to try to reach shore.

Macarthy and Farnham listened. They too caught the sound of rhythmic strokes. No doubt, a launch was coming in from the sea, slowly, as though unsure of its route.

"Yes . . . yes! . . ." repeated Farnham. "It's the pull of oars against oarlocks . . . a launch is out there . . ."

"And it comes from the *Illinois!*" added O'Brien.

Indeed, it could be none other than the launch sent from the steamer to the agreed-upon place. But in the middle of the gathering darkness, it was pointless to try to look for the ship. It was perhaps a good mile out at sea, not only so as to remain undetected close to the shore but also so as to avoid approaching unwisely this coast that was littered with reefs.

They had only to reach the end of the Point and watch for the launch, hail it if need be to indicate the direction to follow, then to jump in as soon as it reached the last of the rocks.

Suddenly there came a barking from the top of the cliff, and shouting as well!

A detachment of police accompanied by a dozen dogs soon appeared along its crest! After having searched the edge of the forest, they had returned to the shoreline.

Not far from there, the convict squads that were working on the clearing were preparing to return to Port Arthur.

From the guards' shouting, O'Brien, Macarthy, and Farnham understood that they had been discovered. The guards had seen them as they crossed over the beach! Perhaps even O'Brien's calling out had betrayed them?

Now, their only chance of rescue was the arrival of the launch, and they could do nothing to hasten it! And if they were not mistaken and the launch was indeed approaching, would they be able to reach it before the guards caught up with them at the end of the point? And then the sailors who were rowing it, would they dare come ashore when they heard the noise of a struggle? If need be, would there be enough of them to attack the guards, seize their prisoners, and take them to safety aboard the *Illinois?*

"The dogs . . . the dogs!" cried out Macarthy at that moment.

After rushing down the path along the cliff, the mastiffs were bounding across the beach—four or five of them, trained to chase down convicts, and barking furiously.

Almost at the same moment, a dozen guards, armed with revolvers, called to each other:

"This way . . . this way! . . ."

"There they are! . . . All three of them!"

"At the end of the Point . . . the end of the Point!"

"There's a launch coming in! . . ."

O'Brien had not been mistaken. A launch was attempting to come ashore. If he and his companions had not been able to see it, it is just that the launch was not visible from the foot of the cliff. But the attention of the guards, posted on the top of the cliff, had been attracted by the launch, which, after having gone along the coast, tried to slip in between the reefs. There was no doubt that they were

Almost at the same moment, a dozen guards appeared.

there to pick up the Irishmen. Then, looking out to sea, they ended up noticing the presence, very suspicious, of a ship on the other side of the bay.

It is also what two other convicts had observed, busy on the edge of the clearing and who had reached the top of the cliff.

They were Karl and Pieter Kip.[1]

One can easily imagine how preoccupied they had been throughout the whole day! They knew full well that the foul weather of the past night would not have permitted the American ship to approach the Tasman Peninsula. They had even said to each other that the three fugitives, after reaching Saint James Point, must have concealed themselves in some hollow during that night and the following day! And how had they managed to obtain a bit of food?

True, the storm had ended some fifteen hours ago, leaving the bay navigable. What could not have been done the day before would probably be done this very evening, when darkness permitted.

As usual, in the morning, the Kip brothers had left the penitentiary for their work outdoors. Approaching the cliff, with some anxiety, they sought to make out, toward the west or along the coast, some curl of smoke indicating the approach of a steamer.

The day went by, and, ten minutes before the signal to depart was given, they could hear shouts echoing from the direction of the shore.

"Those poor men . . . they've been discovered! . . . ," exclaimed Karl Kip.

At this moment ten or twelve guards, abandoning the care of the squads to their companions, ran off in that direction, and the Kip brothers were able to follow without being detected.

Arriving at the top of the cliff, they lay down flat and looked below. Yes! A launch was weaving its way in toward Saint James Point.

"There won't be enough time!" said Karl Kip.

"The poor wretches are going to be recaptured!" added his brother.

"And we can't help them!"

Scarcely had Karl Kip said these words than, seizing Pieter by the arm:

"Follow me!" he said.

A moment later both were descending the path and running across the beach.

The launch of the *Illinois* was approaching the rocks of the shore. Although they had seen the guards rushing up, the American officer and his sailors had no thought of stopping, for they no longer had any doubt that the fugitives had been there since the day before. So, pulling hard on their oars and running the risk, in this gathering darkness, of tearing their hull open on one of the reefs, they made one last effort to reach the end of the Point before the guards.

But when the launch finally landed, it was too late. O'Brien, Macarthy, and Farnham, despite their resistance, were already being dragged back toward the cliff.

"Forward, men! Forward!" cried out the launch's officer.

His sailors, armed with cutlasses and revolvers, rushed after them as soon as they landed, racing to free the fugitives.

There was a savage battle. The Americans were eight in number, the officer, helmsman, and six men. Even counting Farnham, Macarthy, and O'Brien, that made only eleven against some twenty guards—others, hearing the first shouts, having rejoined their comrades on the beach.

In addition, the ferocious mastiffs would also be adversaries that were no less dangerous.[2]

So it was that the sailors fired first at the dogs. Shots rang out. Two of the animals, struck by bullets, were killed, and the others fled, rending the air with their howls.

The two groups of combatants then fought an extremely violent battle in the midst of this semidarkness. Macarthy and Farnham, who had not been able to disengage themselves to join the fight, were being hauled off by the guards, when two men barred their route.

Karl Kip and his brother hurled themselves upon the guards and succeeded in freeing their prisoners.

More rifle shots, and some men were grievously wounded on both sides. Now, on this narrow strip of shoreline, it was impossible for the struggle to be prolonged to the advantage of the Americans.

The guards withdrew, carrying their wounded.

The officer and the sailors of the *Illinois,* constrained to give up the fight, would lose the fugitives, and who knows if they themselves might not pay with their freedom in the prisons of Hobart Town for this noble attempt on behalf of the Irishmen?

Fortunately, if the gunfire, the shouts, and the barking had been heard as far as the forest's clearing, they had also been heard out to sea. On board the *Illinois* they understood there was a bitter fight between the sailors and the guards, a fight in which it was necessary to intervene immediately.

So the commander approached to within at least two cable lengths of shore, and a second launch was lowered to the sea with a dozen sailors.

In a few moments this reinforcement reached the Point, and the situation changed instantly. The guards, no longer outnumbering the others, had to release the prisoners and withdraw, carrying their wounded. As for the officer and the sailors, they reembarked in the two launches with the three fugitives, after a last exchange of gunfire.

At that moment Karl Kip and his brother, calling out to O'Brien, said to him:

"Saved, you're saved!"

"And you, as well!" replied the Irishman.

Before they realized what was happening, the two brothers, on a sign from O'Brien, were seized by the sailors and placed in one of the launches that returned to the steamer.

Soon thereafter the *Illinois,* heading out into Storm Bay, rounded Cape Pillar and, as night settled in, cruised under a full head of steam out into the vast Pacific.

Mr. Hawkins Follows Up

At Hobart Town, for several months, the Kip affair had been the topic of intense discussion. Had there been a reversal in the public's opinion? Was there a majority who now thought that Karl and Pieter Kip were no longer the murderers of Captain Gibson? No! For these two victims of judicial error, opinion had not yet changed to that extent. But people knew that Mr. Hawkins believed in their innocence. Everyone realized that he was pursuing his own inquiries, that he had repeatedly brought the issue up with the governor of Tasmania, and that His Excellency Sir Edward Carrigan listened to him willingly. So some people were already saying:

"But yet . . . suppose Mr. Hawkins is right!"

Nevertheless—and it must be emphasized—the guilt of the Kip brothers was quite clear to the majority of the population, and certainly the affair would have been forgotten long since if the shipowner had not put so much energy into demanding a retrial.

One can easily imagine that the visit Mr. Hawkins had made to Port Arthur had only served to reinforce his conviction. His conversations with the warden, the conduct of the two brothers in the penitentiary, the act of courage that had granted them a certain easing of their situation, their dignified attitude when he interviewed them, the desire they both held of seeking out the true authors of the crime among the crew of the *James Cook,* the suspicion raised by the shady ways of Flig Balt and Vin Mod, and finally the profound gratitude that Karl and Pieter had shown him, and in which he held a certain hope—everything had contributed to strengthening his belief. Besides, how could he have forgotten his earlier relationship with the shipwrecked Dutchmen from the time of their meeting on Norfolk Island, their intervention during the attack of the Papuans, and finally what the *James Cook* owed to Karl Kip for having saved it from foundering and from the hands of Flig Balt?

No, Mr. Hawkins would not allow himself to be shaken in his resolve. He would dedicate himself to this task. Even if he had to do it alone, he would find a way to wrest from this story its last secret, to prove the innocence of the condemned, to free them from the penitentiary of Port Arthur!

Mrs. Hawkins shared the convictions of her husband, if not his hope about the how the affair would ultimately end. She encouraged him to pursue it, although public opinion was very much opposed. It pained her greatly to see him confident one day, without hope the next, passing through all these stages. And, for herself, she never stopped supporting him in their little society of friends, amid all the people in his entourage. But the majority refused to change their opinion. This frightful murder, followed by a verdict of death, had made a profound impression on them, and it even convinced those who, during the course of the trial, still had some doubts.

Now, it was clearly on Mrs. Gibson, in the intimacy of their close friendship that bound them together, that Mrs. Hawkins had the greatest influence. The unfortunate widow had at first refused to listen to her. In her immense grief, she saw but one thing, that her husband was no longer alive, whoever the murderers might have been. However, Mrs. Hawkins continued to be so affirmative in regard to the Kip brothers that she ended up listening to her. She also began to conceive the possibility that they were not the murderers and was frightened at the thought that these innocent men were being detained in that dreadful prison of Port Arthur.

"They'll be freed!" repeated Mrs. Hawkins. "Sooner or later, the truth will come out, and the true murderers will be punished!"

However, while Mrs. Gibson was subject to the influence of Mrs. Hawkins, her son was obstinately convinced of the guilt of the Kip brothers. Whatever deference he owed the shipbuilder for his habitual sureness of judgment, he had never yielded to his reasons—reasons that were purely moral. Nat Gibson clung to the material proofs brought out by the inquest, established by the pretrial investigation, in accordance with the near unanimity of the Hobart Town population. So when Mr. Hawkins spoke to him and expressed his deep suspicions about Flig Balt and Vin Mod, Nat only replied:

"Mr. Hawkins, my father's papers and money, as well as the weapon that was used to strike him down, were found in the valise and in the bedroom of the two brothers . . . It would be necessary to prove that Flig Balt or Vin Mod could have put them there, and that can't be proven."

"Who knows, my poor Nat?" Mr. Hawkins answered, "Who knows?"

Exactly . . . who knows? For that's the way things had happened. But Vin Mod had acted with such cunning that it would have been impossible to determine his presence at the inn of the *Great Old Man*.

Indeed, when Mr. Hawkins asked the hotel owner on several occasions about this, he obtained no result. The man did not even remember whether, at the time the Kip brothers were living in his house, the room next to theirs had even been occupied. In any case, Vin Mod had never been to his inn, and no one could confirm seeing him there.

Such was his state of mind and such were the steps that Mr. Hawkins pursued in trying to have the trial reopened—and he did so with a tenacity that some considered a monomania.

Then, on the morning of May 7th, a very unexpected piece of news spread through the city.

The governor had been notified that an escape had just taken place in Port Arthur. Two political deportees, two Fenians, and one guard, who was their compatriot and accomplice, had managed to flee and had been picked up by a steamer, certainly sent by their American friends. At the same time, two additional convicts, taking advantage of the opportunity, had fled with them.

These convicts, condemned for a crime of common law, were the Dutch brothers Karl and Pieter Kip.

In fact, during the struggle between the American sailors and the guards on Saint James Point, when they had come to the assistance of the three fugitives, the two brothers had been recognized. They had apparently been taken aboard the steamer against their

Mr. Hawkins asked the hotel owner about this.

will; but who could believe that they had not been in league with the Fenians, and were not part of this escape plan? . . . No . . . all that must have been agreed upon in advance.

And that is what the guards declared upon their return to the penitentiary, where the absence of Karl and Pieter Kip was already known. That is what the captain no doubt believed when he was informed of this quintuple escape. And that is what he said in his report that very day to His Excellency Sir Edward Carrigan.

The effect that this piece of news had in Hobart Town and all of Tasmania was predictable. Mr. Hawkins was one of the first to have knowledge of it, through the governor who had summoned him to his residence. The telegram sent from Port Arthur, once placed under his eyes, promptly fell from his hands. He could not believe what he had read. He looked at His Excellency, he stammered, his voice was broken:

"They have escaped . . . they have escaped! . . ."

"Yes," responded Sir Edward Carrigan, "and there is no doubt that they were in league with the two political prisoners and their accomplice."

"Those men . . . those men . . . ," exclaimed Mr. Hawkins in great agitation, "Yes . . . I understand them . . . I understand that they wanted to regain their freedom, I understand that friends came to their aid . . . that they prepared their flight . . . I approve of it even . . ."

"What are you saying, my dear Hawkins? Are you forgetting they are enemies of England?"

"That's true . . . that's true . . . and I shouldn't speak so in your presence, Mr. Governor. But, all in all, those Fenians, those political prisoners had nothing to lose! . . . They were condemned for life in Port Arthur, whereas Karl and Pieter Kip . . . no! I cannot believe that they are associated with this escape! . . . Who knows if it is not a false piece of news?"

"No," replied the governor, "the facts are only too certain."

"And yet," answered Mr. Hawkins, "Karl and Pieter Kip knew about the efforts being made on their behalf to obtain a retrial! . . .

They knew that Your Excellency was interested in their case . . . that I had devoted myself to their cause . . ."

"No doubt, my dear Hawkins, but they must have thought you would not succeed, and when a chance for escape presented itself . . ."

"We'd have to admit," Mr. Hawkins added, "that those Fenians did not consider them criminals. They would never have given their aid to the murderers of Captain Gibson . . . and the commander of the American ship would never have welcomed murderers on board his vessel!"

"I'm not sure how to explain all that!" replied His Excellency, "perhaps we will learn the answers later on . . . What is not in doubt is that the Kip brothers have left Port Arthur, and you do not have to worry about them anymore, my dear Hawkins."

"Of course I do . . . On the contrary!"

"Even after this escape, you still believe in their innocence?"

"Absolutely, Mr. Governor," replied Mr. Hawkins with the tone of unbreakable conviction. "Oh! I expect people will say I'm crazy, that I refuse to yield to the evidence, that their flight is a formal confession of their guilt, that they weren't counting on the result of a review because they knew themselves to be guilty, that they preferred to escape when the chance to do so was offered to them . . ."

"In truth," declared the governor, "it would be difficult to interpret otherwise the conduct of your protégés!"

"Well, no, no!" countered Mr. Hawkins, "This flight is no confession. In all this, I repeat, there is something inexplicable, which the future will explain. I would rather believe, yes, believe that Karl and Pieter Kip have been kidnapped."

"No one will accept that."

"No one but me, so be it! I'm satisfied with that, and I won't abandon their cause. And how, Mr. Governor, could I forget the attitude of those two unfortunate men when I visited them in Port Arthur . . . the resignation of Pieter especially, their confidence in my efforts; how could I forget what they did on board the *James Cook,* forget what Karl Kip has done in the penitentiary? I will not abandon them, and the truth will be known! No! A hundred times no! Karl and Pieter Kip did not spill the blood of Captain Gibson! They're not murderers."

Sir Edward Carrigan did not want to insist further or to say anything that would make Mr. Hawkins any more upset. He simply announced the information that he had received from the office of the port of Hobart Town:

"According to the report that was sent me," he said, "an American ship, the steamer *Illinois,* whose stopover was scarcely explained, arrived in the harbor. Everything leads to believe that, since it left yesterday morning, it picked up the prisoners at an agreed-upon spot along the peninsula. Assuredly, they are being brought to America. Now in that country, if the two Fenians and their accomplice are safe as political deportees for whom extradition is not admissible in international treaties, it will not be the same for those who are condemned by common law. If the Kip brothers are discovered, their extradition will be requested, it will be obtained, and they will be brought back to Port Arthur, where they will not escape a second time."

"Provided, Mr. Governor," concluded Mr. Hawkins, "that I will not have already succeeded in discovering the real authors of the crime!"

And what good would it serve, arguing with someone who had such a set purpose? It is certain that appearances tended to support the governor's views, despite Mr. Hawkins's refusing to agree. And that was the general opinion. Defenders of the Kip brothers became even rarer—reduced to just one. Their flight was interpreted as proof against them. Evidently they were not counting on their case being reopened or on the results that a retrial would give, since they had fled. The opportunity of recovering their freedom was offered to them; they hastened to take advantage of it.

Such were the consequences of this escape, which turned public opinion even further against the two brothers and became a new proof of their guilt.

Understanding how much Mr. Hawkins, far from reconsidering his ideas, seemed on the contrary even more attached to his convictions, Nat Gibson avoided every mention of the subject. But he could not get used to that thought, that the murderers of his father had escaped Port Arthur, that the political internees had accepted them as companions, and that America had consented to give them asylum. Extradition would return them to the penitentiary, and there they would be subject to their full punishment in all its rigor.

Some twenty days went by. The *Lloyd*[1] gave no news of the *Illinois* in its maritime correspondences. Not one ship had met it during its crossing of the Pacific. There was no doubt, however, that the American steamer had been used for the purpose of picking up the Irishmen. According to the inquiry made by order of the governor, a single ship had left the port after the storm of May 5th: it was the *Illinois,* en route to America. But toward what port of the United States was the steamer proceeding? . . . Where would the escaped prisoners land? That no one really knew. How would they arrange to have the Kip brothers arrested as they disembarked on the New Continent?

On May 25th, Mr. and Mrs. Hawkins had the very real pleasure of receiving a visit that had been announced for some time. Mr. and Mrs. Zieger, having decided to spend several weeks in Hobart Town, had left Port Praslin on the German steamer *Faust*. After a rapid crossing, they disembarked in the capital of Tasmania, where their friends were waiting for them.

As with their previous trips, Mr. and Mrs. Zieger were lodged at the Hawkinses' home, and a room had been prepared for them. Their first visit in town was to the widow of the captain and her son. Nat Gibson and his mother experienced very strong emotions in the presence of Mr. and Mrs. Zieger as they talked, with many tears, about the terrible drama of Kerawara . . .

At his arrival, Mr. Zieger did not know that the Kip brothers had escaped from the penitentiary of Port Arthur. When he learned of it, he saw—as so many others had—a new proof that justice had not committed an error by condemning them.

However, it should come as no surprise that, during the first days of their visit, Mr. Hawkins wanted to discuss this matter with his correspondent from Port Praslin. He gave him the whole story, recalling to him all the mysterious circumstances of the murder, and added:

"And first, my dear Zieger, when you found out that the two brothers had been accused of masterminding the crime, when you learned of their condemnation, could you believe it?"

"No, of course not, my friend. That Karl and Pieter Kip were murderers . . . that seemed impossible! . . . I had always seen in them, men as intelligent as they are honest, men who felt profoundly indebted to Captain Gibson and to you, not forgetting that they were shipwrecked on the *Wilhelmina,* rescued by the *James Cook.* No! . . . I never would have thought that they were guilty."

"And suppose they weren't? . . . ," responded Mr. Hawkins, who was looking directly at Mr. Zieger.

"You have some doubts on this subject . . . after all the testimony and the evidence?"

"I am convinced that they are not the authors of this crime, and waiting only until I can prove it . . ."

Faced with such an unequivocal declaration, Mr. Zieger said:

"Listen, my dear Hawkins, Mr. Hamburg in Kerawara, myself in Port Praslin and in all of New Ireland, we did the most thorough investigation. There is no tribe in the archipelago about whom we did not gather precise and verified information. Nowhere, not even in New Britain, no native could have taken part in the murder of Captain Gibson . . ."

"I do not claim, my dear Zieger, that this crime must be attributed to some native of the Bismarck Archipelago, but I do say that it was not committed by the Kip brothers."

"By whom, then?" asked Mr. Zieger. "Some colonists . . . some sailors? . . ."

"Yes . . . some sailors . . ."

"And from what crew, my dear Hawkins? At this time there were only three ships in the port of Kerawara, and not a single one at Port Praslin."

"Yes, there was one."

"Which one?"

"The *James Cook.*"

"What! . . . you think that one or two men on the *James Cook* could be the murderers?"

"Yes . . . Zieger, the very ones who found on the wreck of the *Wilhelmina* the weapon that the murderer used . . . the ones who later introduced it into the valise of the Kip brothers, where they had already placed Gibson's papers and money!"

"There were men among the *James Cook* crew capable of this?" asked Mr. Zieger.

"Indeed there were," declared Mr. Hawkins, "and among others, those men that Master Balt had taken on in Dunedin, and who revolted against the new captain."

"One of them might be the murderer?"

"No . . . I accuse Flig Balt of this crime . . ."

"The bosun?"

"Yes, the one I had named as captain of the brig when we left Port Praslin, and who, by his incompetence, would have lost the ship, with all hands, without the intervention of Karl Kip!"

And then he added that Flig Balt must have also had an accomplice, the sailor Vin Mod.

Mr. Zieger, very moved by this affirmation, pressed Mr. Hawkins further. Were his suspicions backed by some material proof? Didn't they just depend on presumptions that could not be established as reality? Would one not have to admit that the bosun, aided by Vin Mod in his desire to do away with Captain Gibson, had prepared this stratagem to have the crime fall onto the heads of the Kip brothers over a long period of time?

And, in contrast, if Flig Balt decided to have his vengeance against them, it could only be after the nomination of Karl Kip as captain, or when Karl had suppressed the mutiny inspired by him.

This indisputably logical reasoning had certainly been considered by Mr. Hawkins, but intractable in his unshaken conviction, he had thrust it aside then and still did now.

"My dear Zieger, when Flig Balt and Vin Mod first had the idea of the crime, they were already in possession of the dagger that belonged to the Kip brothers. That is when they got the idea of using it so that these unfortunate men would be accused later of murdering Captain Gibson. For you, that may seem only hypothetical . . . For me . . . it is a certainty . . ."

And, in fact, the explanation that Mr. Hawkins offered was the real one.

"Unfortunately," he added, "Flig Balt and Vin Mod have been gone from Hobart Town for nearly a year. I didn't have the time to keep track of them, to gather ironclad proof against them that could have led to a retrial. It was even impossible for me to learn what has become of them."

"But I know, yes, I know!" responded Mr. Zieger.

"You know? . . . ," cried out Mr. Hawkins, seizing his friend's hands.

"Without a doubt . . . Flig Balt, Vin Mod and the recruits of the *James Cook* . . . I have seen them."

"Where? . . ."

"In Port Praslin."

"When? . . ."

"Three months ago . . ."

"And are they still there? . . ."

"No . . . they had embarked on a three-master, a German ship called the *Kaiser,* and after a two-week stopover in Port Praslin, they left."

"For? . . ."

"For the Solomon Archipelago, and since then I have had no news . . ."

Thus Flig Balt and Vin Mod, along with Len Cannon and his comrades, had shipped out. To what port? It was not known, but they now formed a part of the crew of the *Kaiser.* This three-master had put into port a few weeks before at Port Praslin. So if the bosun and Vin Mod were the murderers of Captain Gibson, they had no fear of reappearing on this archipelago, the scene of their crime, just as Mr. Zieger observed.

And now they had left, headed for those other dangerous latitudes toward which they hoped to steer the brig, and, with the help of their companions, they would do to the *Kaiser* what they had been unable to do with the *James Cook!*

And then how could anyone find any trace of them aboard some ship whose name they would probably change? How could they be found? Did not their absence make a reopening of the Kip case virtually impossible?

Things were at this point when, a few days later, June 20th, *Lloyds* mentioned in its maritime news the arrival of the *Illinois* in San Francisco. It was on May 30th—about three weeks after its departure from Storm Bay—that O'Brien, Macarthy, and Farnham had disembarked and for whom their political brothers reserved the warmest, the most enthusiastic welcome to the land of freedom. The newspapers celebrated noisily the success of their escape and gave honor to those who had prepared it, almost like a revenge of Fenianism.

At the same time, it was learned that the two Dutchmen, Karl and Pieter Kip, had disappeared since disembarking.

Had they stayed in San Francisco to avoid falling into the hands of the American police? Had they not instead traveled to the interior of the United States? How could one know? And now, when the request for extradition arrived, it would be too late.

This information served to confirm the views of the Kips' accusers and to put an end to the doubts that this affair might still have raised. Mr. Hawkins, himself, while secure in his convictions, which nothing would be able to shatter, slowed down his activity. What use would a retrial be since the Kip brothers, having escaped from the penitentiary of Port Arthur, had now taken refuge in America, from where they probably would never return?

So they were going to concern themselves no more with the crime of Kerawara when suddenly, on the morning of June 25th, a bit of news began to spread around the town—news that, at first, no one wanted to grant much credence.

Karl and Pieter Kip, who had arrived the day before, had just been arrested and incarcerated in the prison of Hobart Town!

15

The New Fact

No! That could only be one of those rumors that nobody knows where they come from or how they are spread but that the public's common sense would soon refute.

Was it conceivable that the Kip brothers, after having had that unhoped-for opportunity to flee to America, had then returned to Tasmania? They, the murderers of Captain Gibson, had come back? Might it be that the boat on which they had taken passage when leaving San Francisco had been constrained to land at Hobart Town? And then, recognized, denounced, apprehended, they must have been led back to prison and were now awaiting their return to the penitentiary, where any new attempt at flight would be prevented. As for thinking they might have come back on their own, that they had committed such a foolish deed, that was inconceivable!

Whatever the case may be—and the most impatient could verify it as early as the next morning—Karl and Pieter Kip had been shut up in prison since the day before. Yet the chief warden would not consent to say under what conditions they had been brought there, nor in what way their arrest had been made.

Nevertheless, if this fact seemed inexplicable, there was one man whose steadfast belief in them suggested the true explanation. A revelation occurred in his mind—it would be more accurate to say in his heart. It was the solution of a problem that he had wrestled with since the incredible escape of the Kip brothers.

"They didn't flee!" exclaimed Mr. Hawkins, "they were carried off from Port Arthur! Yes! They came back of their own volition, returned because they're innocent, because they want to have their innocence revealed openly and in full daylight."

That was the truth.

Indeed, the day before, an American steamer, the *Standard* from San Diego, had arrived and moored in the harbor with a cargo for Hobart Town. Karl and Pieter Kip were on board as passengers.

During the *Illinois*'s voyage between Port Arthur and San Francisco, the two brothers had first remained extremely reserved in regard to their companions in the penal colony. They had even protested against their "abduction." Moreover, when they affirmed once again that they were not the murderers of Captain Gibson, neither O'Brien nor Macarthy nor Farnham, nor anyone else, put that affirmation in doubt. And if they regretted this escape, it was because efforts were being made to reopen and retry their case, and they might be compromised by it.

Further, although it was chance, chance alone, that had brought the Kip brothers out on Saint James Point, they had not hesitated to fight against the guards. And, from that moment on, what could be more natural than that the Fenians who had profited from this circumstance decided to pull them aboard the American ship? . . . After the favor that Karl and Pieter Kip had just rendered the Irishmen, it was out of a sense of gratitude that they did it. And could they now repent for having done it? . . . No, and anyway, what was done was done.

Upon the arrival of the *Illinois* at the port of San Francisco, the Kip brothers took leave of the Irishmen, who tried in vain to convince them to remain. Where were they going to take refuge? They did not say. But, being without resources as they were, they did not refuse the offer of several hundred dollars, to be reimbursed when possible. After one last farewell, they separated from O'Brien, Macarthy, and Farnham.

Fortunately for them, no request for extradition had yet been addressed to the American authorities by the Great Britain consul, and the police had been unable to arrest them at their disembarkation.

From that day on, two brothers could not be seen on the streets of San Francisco, and there was reason to believe they had left the city.

Truth to say, forty-eight hours after reaching land Karl and Pieter Kip were staying in a modest inn at San Diego, capital of lower California, where they hoped to find a ship departing for some port on the Australian continent.

Their firm intention was to return as soon as possible to Hobart Town to give themselves up to that justice system that had so unjustly condemned them! If their flight had been interpreted as an admission of guilt, their return would shout out their innocence to the world. No! They would not accept living on foreign soil as criminals, with the unending fear of being recognized, denounced, recaptured! What they wanted was a retrial, a public clearing of their name!

It was this plan and its implementation that Karl and Pieter Kip had discussed continually while aboard the *Illinois.* No doubt Karl at first felt a certain revulsion toward the idea. To finally be free and to renounce one's freedom? To rely on Man's court of law, on human fallibility? But he soon gave in to the arguments of his brother.

So they were in San Diego, seeking to embark, and as soon as possible, on a boat heading for Tasmania. Circumstances served them well. The *Standard* was heading directly to Hobart Town, and it was taking on passengers from various classes. Karl and Pieter Kip, content with a simple economy-class berth, held their reservations under a borrowed name. The next day the steamer left port, heading southwest. After a fairly long crossing, vexed by bad weather in the Pacific, it finally rounded Point Raoul near Port Arthur and dropped anchor in Hobart Town harbor.

The next day, the entire city was soon aware of all that had been reported via rumor. And a sudden turnabout of opinion occurred in favor of the Kip brothers, and who could be surprised by that? Were they then the victims of a miscarriage of justice? They had not fled the penitentiary voluntarily, and as soon as they found an occasion to leave America, they had returned to Tasmania! And, now, would it not be possible to establish their innocence on less fragile grounds than simple presumptions?

As soon as the news reached Mr. Hawkins, he went to the prison, the doors of which were immediately opened to him. An instant later, he found himself facing the two brothers, locked up in the same cell.

There, in front of the shipowner, they stood up, their hands joined.

"Mr. Hawkins," said Pieter Kip, "it is not for you that we returned to bear new testimony. You've known the truth for a long time, and you never believed we were guilty. But this truth we felt needed to be told to everyone, and that is why the *Standard* brought us back to Hobart Town."

Mr. Hawkins was so moved that words failed him. Tears flowed from his eyes, and finally he said:

"Yes," he said, "Yes, gentlemen . . . that's fine . . . that's wonderful what you've done . . . It's the clearing of your name that awaits you here . . . with the sympathy of all the honest people! You were not to remain the escapees of Port Arthur! The efforts I made, and those that I will make once more will succeed! Your hand, Pieter Kip! . . . Your hand, captain of the *James Cook!*"

And in returning this title again to Karl Kip, the worthy Mr. Hawkins gave him all his respect.

So, all three of them studied the affair once more, this time in light of the suspicions that the bosun and Vin Mod had aroused in them. The two brothers then learned that Flig Balt, Vin Mod, and Len Cannon and his comrades had embarked on the *Kaiser,* how, after their layover in Port Praslin, they had left for the archipelago of the Solomons. And, at the present time, who knew if, already masters of the ship, they weren't already committing piracy in this part of the Pacific where it would be impossible to find them?

"And besides," observed Pieter Kip, "even if Flig Balt and his former comrades of the *James Cook* could be brought before the criminal court, what proof would we be able to produce against them? They would accuse us again, and how could we prove that they are the ones who killed Captain Gibson, not us?"

"People will believe us!" exclaimed Karl Kip. "They'll believe us since we have come back to affirm our innocence!"

Perhaps, but what new facts were there that could justify a retrial?

No need to describe the profound effect that the return of Karl and Pieter Kip had on both the Hawkins and Gibson families. Mrs.

Gibson, who herself now harbored deep doubts about their guilt, was unable to shake her son's convictions. And this is not surprising because for such a long time, ever since the facts revealed in the trial by Flig Balt, in Nat Gibson's eyes the murderers could only be the two brothers! His mind continually returned to the theater of the crime! He saw again his unfortunate father attacked in the woods of Kerawara, struck by the very hand of those he had welcomed on Norfolk Island, murdered by the castaways of the *Wilhelmina!* Yes! All the proofs were against them, and what was the defense arguing? Vague and uncertain presumptions about the bosun and his accomplice! And yet, the Kips had returned to Hobart Town! They had returned of their own volition!

It goes without saying that Mr. Hawkins had immediately demanded an audience with Sir Edward Carrigan. The governor, very impressed, resolved to do all in his power to repair this judicial error, to convene a retrial that would permit the clearing of the Kip brothers' name. And it would be a good step forward on that path if the authorities could locate Flig Balt, Vin Mod, and their companions!

It is understandable that the population of Hobart Town, in its excitement, would have suddenly declared itself in favor of Karl and Pieter Kip. Is there any reason for surprise in this changeableness in crowds? What could be more natural? This time, moreover, didn't everything that had happened since the arrest of the two brothers justify this reversal of opinion?

Meanwhile, one of the judges of the criminal court had just been designated to take up or rather recommence an inquest, to interrogate once more the two condemned brothers, and to subpoena other witnesses if needed. Who knows if some new fact might not permit the presumption of innocence and to conclude in favor of a retrial?

On the other hand, if this inquest did not succeed in showing that persons other than the Kip brothers were the murderers of Captain Gibson, they would have to accept the court's judgment, and there would be no cause for clearing their name.

The justice system began to process the case, and the investigation would follow its course. But given the circumstances, the distance from the scene of the crime, the difficulty in tracking down

Flig Balt, Vin Mod, Len Cannon, and the others who had shipped out on the *Kaiser,* it might require considerable time.

So, in the meanwhile, the prison regulations would be softened for the prisoners. They were not put in solitary confinement. They were not forbidden visits by those who were interested in their fate, among others Mr. Hawkins and Mr. Zieger, whose encouragement had sustained them throughout these tribulations.

The lord chief justice of the United Kingdom had been informed of this fascinating affair. Since the government attached great importance to finding the *Kaiser,* orders were given to search for it in that part of the Pacific that includes New Guinea, the Bismarck Archipelago, the Solomons, and the New Hebrides. The German government, for its part, had prescribed the same measures, foreseeing that the *Kaiser* had perhaps fallen into the hands of pirates in this region where England and Germany extend their double protection.

During this time, in Hobart Town, the magistrate with the cooperation of Mr. Hawkins and knowing the steps already taken proceeded in the interrogation of new witnesses. The two brothers were interrogated on the subject of their stay in the *Great Old Man* inn. Had they noticed that the room neighboring theirs had been occupied? They had not been able to answer that question, for they left the inn each day early in the morning and only returned to go to bed.

The magistrate and Mr. Hawkins, after going to that inn, realized that the interior balcony on the courtyard gave access to the neighboring room. But the hotelkeeper, who had so many one-night residents, did not remember who occupied that second room.

Besides, when the manager of the *Fresh Fish* was called before the judge, he stated—and it was true—that Vin Mod and the others had always stayed in his establishment from the time the *James Cook* arrived in Hobart Town to the day of the Kip brothers' arrest.

It was July 20th. Nearly a month had elapsed since Karl and Pieter Kip had delivered themselves again into the hands of justice. And the inquest revealed no result . . . The new evidence on which a retrial would need to be based was still lacking. Mr. Hawkins's efforts did not weaken; but what chagrin he felt in being so powerless!

Despite the comforting words of Mr. Hawkins, Karl Kip also sometimes let himself become completely discouraged—which his brother had difficulty overcoming. Who knows if he didn't even reproach Pieter for having wanted to return from America to Tasmania to represent themselves before this justice system that had condemned them the first time?

"And which will condemn us perhaps for the second time!" said Karl Kip one day.

"No, brother, no!" cried out Pieter. "God would not allow it!"

"He certainly permitted us to be condemned to death as murderers and our name to be damned to infamy!"

"Have confidence, dear brother, have confidence!"

Pieter Kip could reply in no other way. His own confidence was so strong that nothing could shake it. It was as absolute as Mr. Hawkins's belief in their innocence!

At that time, Mr. Zieger, whose stay in Hobart Town was not to extend beyond two more weeks, was trying to find a passage on a German or English steamer heading for Port Praslin.

The two families had spent these few weeks together in the most complete friendship. Since the return of the Kip brothers, they shared the same ideas, the same hopes. As for Mrs. Gibson, the thought that these two innocent people had been victims of a judicial error troubled her deeply, and it hurt her to see the situation prolonged.

But the affair remained at the same point insofar as the demand for retrial was concerned. New information relating to the Kip brothers had been picked up in Holland, but it had only confirmed what had been known earlier. In the country where memories of their family still survived, those who had accepted the Kips' culpability at the outset were not numerous; and after their return became known in Groningen, the error of their conviction was clear to everyone.

Finally, since the German ship *Kaiser*'s departure from Port Praslin, the maritime news had had no sightings of it, neither in the Solomons nor in the neighboring archipelagoes. Impossible to know what had happened to Flig Balt, Vin Mod, and the others who might be implicated in the crime of Kerawara.

So, to the great despair of Mr. Hawkins, the magistrate was about to give up continuing the inquest. The Kips' condemnation would thereby be made definitive, and the two brothers would be returned to the penitentiary of Port Arthur, unless a royal pardon came through to put an end to this dreadful ordeal.

"I'd rather die than go back to prison!" Karl Kip exclaimed.

"Or be the object of a disgraceful pardon!" added Pieter Kip.

Such was the situation. One can understand that it was of a nature to be deeply troubling to everyone involved and even to provoke public indignation.

The departure of Mr. and Mrs. Zieger was to take place on August 5th, on board an English steamer, with a stopover in the Bismarck Archipelago. The reader may recall that, on the day following the Kerawara crime, Mr. Hawkins had made two copies of his photograph of Captain Gibson, his torso nude to the waist, his chest punctured by the Malaysian kriss.

Now, before returning to Port Praslin, Mr. Zieger wanted Mr. Hawkins to make him an enlarged reproduction of the captain's head, in order to place it in the salon at Wilhelmstaf.

The shipowner consented willingly to this desire of Mr. Zieger. There would be several copies made of the new photographic print, which would remain in the hands of the Gibson, Hawkins, and Zieger families.

On July 27th, in the morning, Mr. Hawkins proceeded to carry out this operation in his studio, which contained the best equipment and which, thanks to improved chemical accelerators, could create true works of art. Wishing to operate under the most favorable conditions, he used the negative made in Kerawara, which was only of the captain's head.

After placing this negative under the enlarger, he determined the best setting to obtain a print of natural size.

As the light was excellent, a few seconds sufficed, and the new photograph was soon in a frame and placed on an easel in the middle of the studio.

That afternoon, Mr. Zieger and Nat Gibson, who had been invited by Mr. Hawkins, went to his house.

"It's them! The murderers of my father!"

It would be difficult to describe their emotions as they stood before the faithful image of Harry Gibson, the living portrait of the unfortunate captain.

It was certainly him, his serious yet sympathetic face, imprinted with mortal anguish as he had been at the very moment when his murderers had stabbed him in the heart . . . at the instant he was looking at them, with his eyes wide open . . .

Nat Gibson approached the easel, his chest heaving with sobs, prey to a grief shared by both Mr. Hawkins and Mr. Zieger, so much did the captain seem to be alive before them.

Then the son leaned forward to kiss his father on the forehead.

Suddenly he stopped, drew closer, his eyes on the eyes of the portrait . . .

What had he seen, or imagined seeing? . . . His face was distorted . . . he seemed overwhelmed . . . He grew as pale as a dead man . . . It appeared as though he wanted to speak but could not . . . His lips were contracted . . . his voice failed him . . .

Finally, he turned and seized from a nearby table one of those strong magnifying glasses which photographers use in touching up details of a print. He held it before the photograph and then cried out in a horrified voice:

"It's them! . . . Them! . . . The murderers of my father!"

And in the depths of Captain Gibson's eyes, on his enlarged retinas, there appeared, in all their ferocity, the faces of Flig Balt and Vin Mod![1]

Conclusion

For some time now, it has been known—as a result of various interesting ophthalmologic experiments done by certain ingenious scientists, authoritative observers that they are—that the images of exterior objects imprinted upon the retina of the eye can be conserved there indefinitely. The organ of vision contains a particular substance, retinal purple, on which is imprinted in their exact form these images. They have even been perfectly reconstituted when the eye, after death, is removed and soaked in an alum bath.

Now, all that was known related to this fixing of images was going to receive in these circumstances an indisputable confirmation.[1]

At that moment when Captain Gibson drew his last breath, his final look—a look of fright and anguish—had focused on his murderers, and in the depths of his eyes were inscribed the faces of Flig Balt and Vin Mod. So, when Mr. Hawkins took his photograph of the victim, the most minute details of his physiognomy were reproduced on the camera's plate. Even with nothing but that very first proof, examining it with a magnifying glass, one could have found revealed, at the bottom of his eyes, the faces of the two murderers. And, in fact, they could still be seen there.

But, at that moment, how could that thought have occurred to Mr. Hawkins, Mr. Zieger, and Mr. Hamburg? No! It had taken the combination of these circumstances—the desire expressed by Mr. Zieger to carry to Port Praslin the enlarged photograph of Captain Gibson, and this enlargement obtained in the studio of the shipowner. And when Nat Gibson drew near to kiss the portrait of his father, he thought he saw in the depth of those eyes two shiny points. He took a magnifying glass and distinctly made out the bosun's face and that of his accomplice.

Now Mr. Hawkins and Mr. Zieger also saw and recognized after Nat that it was not Karl and Pieter Kip whose faces were imprinted on the eyes of the dead man; it was Flig Balt and Vin Mod!

So there at last was the new fact allowing for the indisputable presumption of innocence of the accused, which would permit a retrial! Could the court raise doubts about the authenticity of the original photo made in Kerawara? No, for it had already figured in the criminal file, and the enlargement they had just obtained was only the faithful reproduction.

"Ah! those poor men . . . those poor men! . . . ," Nat Gibson exclaimed. "Innocent . . . and while you believed them unjustly condemned and wanted to save them, I . . ."

"But you're the one saving them now, Nat!" replied Mr. Hawkins. "Yes, you, who just saw what perhaps none of us might have ever seen!"

Half an hour later, bearing both the large and the small photographic prints, the shipowner presented himself at the governor's residence and asked to be received immediately by His Excellency.

Sir Edward Carrigan gave the order to show Mr. Hawkins into his office.

As soon as he was fully informed, the governor declared that he drew from this fact a material proof that was absolutely indisputable. The innocence of the Kip brothers, the injustice of the conviction they had received, all that was evidence in itself, and the magistrate would not hesitate to request a retrial.

It was also the opinion of the magistrate to whose office Mr. Hawkins went upon leaving the governor's residence. He had chosen to make these two visits before going to the prison with Mr. Zieger and Nat Gibson. There was no longer any doubt; there were no longer presumptions, but certitudes. It was simply that the whole past of the two brothers contradicted the verdict of the criminal court! The perpetrators of this crime were now known. The victim himself had pointed them out! . . . The former bosun of the *James Cook* and the sailor Vin Mod!

How did this news spread through the city? Where did it begin? Who was the first to tell of the discovery in Mr. Hawkins's studio? This is not known.

But what is certain is that somehow it had become known even before the shipowner arrived at the Residence. A crowd of people, as noisy as they were passionate, soon gathered in front of the prison.

From their cell, Karl and Pieter Kip thought they heard a loud outcry, shouts rending the air, and in the middle of these cries their names were repeated a thousand times. They both went to the narrow barred window that faced onto an inside courtyard.

They listened, with great anxiety. But from this window it was impossible to see anything that was going on in the nearby streets.

"What is it?" asked Karl Kip. "Are they coming to send us back to the penal colony? Ah! before I return to that dreadful life again . . ."

Pieter Kip did not answer this time.

At that moment, the sound of running feet echoed down the corridor. The door of the cell was suddenly opened.

Nat Gibson appeared on the threshold, accompanied by Mr. Hawkins and Mr. Zieger.

Nat Gibson stopped, half bowed down, and extended his hands toward the two brothers.

"Karl . . . Pieter . . . ," he said. "Forgive me! . . ."

The two did not understand . . . they could not understand . . . The son of Captain Gibson begging them . . . imploring their pardon.

"Innocent! . . . ," exclaimed Mr. Hawkins, three times. "We finally have the proof of your innocence! . . ."

"And I, how could I have ever thought . . ." continued Nat Gibson as he fell into the open arms of Karl Kip.

This matter of a retrial took no more time than that required by legal formalities. It was now easy to reestablish the facts of the case: It was on the wreck of the *Wilhelmina* that the Malaysian dagger belonging to the Kip brothers had been found. It was Vin Mod who had stolen it and brought it on board the *James Cook*. It was that weapon which he or Flig Balt had used to commit the murder, with the intention that this crime would be attributed to the two rescued passengers. It was they who had later shown the weapon to Jim, the ship's boy, in the cabin of the two brothers. As for the papers, the money, and the dagger seized in the Kip brothers' room at the *Great Old Man* inn, they had been put there on the eve of the day when Flig Balt was to be brought before the maritime tribunal. That could only have been done by the bosun's accomplice, who had remained free, by the sailor Vin Mod.

And so now there was no longer any doubt that the man who had taken the adjacent room to that of the Kip brothers was Vin Mod. After the arrival of the *James Cook,* having assured himself that Karl and Pieter Kip were lodging in this inn, he had come to rent a room. Probably disguised in order not to be recognized, awaiting the time

"Karl . . . Pieter . . . ," he said. "Forgive me!

to execute his plan, he had slipped the papers, the piastres, and the dagger into the valise, where they were found the next day, at the time of the police raid.

And that's exactly the way this loathsome plot had been perpetrated.

Obviously, the suspicions of Mr. Hawkins had long ago fallen on the bosun and his accomplice, Vin Mod; but it was necessary to wait until his suspicions became certitudes. And it had only taken this last revelation, soon made public through the Hobart Town newspapers, to trigger a change in public opinion that was as unanimous as it was justified.

Two days later, the magistrates declared that the request for a retrial was admissible. On the basis of a new fact in the case, the retrial would allow for the presumption of judicial error, and the Kip brothers were sent before the Criminal Court again.

During the proceedings of this second trial, the throng was even greater than the first; but this time the people were entirely favorable toward the two brothers. True, there was reason to regret that certain witnesses could not be at the bar, from which they would have passed to the bench of the accused. But, in a sense, weren't Flig Balt and Vin Mod already there? . . . in the depths of those eyes, inordinately wide open, of their victim? . . .

The entire affair lasted barely an hour. It ended with the clearing of the name of Karl and Pieter Kip, which was loudly proclaimed to much applause from the audience.

Then, as soon as they had been set free, when they found themselves in Mr. Hawkins's drawing room with the Gibson and Zieger families, they were finally repaid for all their suffering and shame that had weighed so heavily upon them for so long.

No need to say that offers of help came not only from Mr. Hawkins but from all his friends. If Karl Kip wanted to return to sea, he would find a command in Hobart Town. If Pieter Kip wanted to return to business, he would find businessmen ready to come to his aid. And wasn't that the best thing for both of them to do, now that the Groningen firm had been liquidated in their favor? So, as soon as the

James Cook was outfitted, it headed out to sea under the command of Captain Kip, with the worthy sailors of his former crew.

To conclude this story, it is fitting to add that several months went by before any news was received about the *Kaiser,* on which Flig Balt, Vin Mod, and their comrades—or rather accomplices—had embarked. It was learned that this ship, which had been engaged in piracy throughout the Solomons and New Hebrides, had just been captured by an English patrol boat. The sailors on the *Kaiser,* all treacherous villains, defended themselves in the manner of wretches who face the gallows in case of defeat. A number of these criminals were killed—among them Flig Balt and Len Cannon. As for Vin Mod, he managed to reach some islands of a nearby archipelago with a few others, and no one ever knew what became of him.

And so ends this *cause célèbre*—a very rare example, moreover, of judicial error—which once created a considerable stir as "The Affair of the Kip Brothers."

THE END

NOTES

INTRODUCTION

I would like to acknowledge the members of the North American Jules Verne Society and the Société Jules Verne, whose scholarly work has informed the introduction and notes for this first English edition of *The Kip Brothers*. Agnès Marcetteau-Paul, director of the Bibliothèque Municipale in Nantes, very kindly supplied photocopies of Verne's original manuscript. Volker Dehs, drawing on his extensive knowledge of the life and works of Jules Verne, also contributed many informative details. And it was a great pleasure to work with Arthur B. Evans, who edited the translation, the introduction, and the notes. (All unattributed translations from the French are by Art Evans and me.) But my deepest appreciation goes to my wife, Anna Jean Mayhew, whose help and support has truly made this book possible.

1. Since Wesleyan University Press's publication of Verne's *Invasion of the Sea* in 2001, *The Mighty Orinoco* in 2002, and now *The Kip Brothers,* there currently remains only one of Verne's *Voyages extraordinaires* never to have been translated into English, *Bourses de voyage* (1903, Travel Scholarships). Since Verne's posthumous works were substantially modified by his son, Michel, most of the author's original manuscripts for these novels have now been published in French, and (as of this writing) some have begun to be published in English. See, for example, Jules Verne, *Magellania,* trans. Benjamin Ivry (New York: Welcome Rain, 2002), and Jules Verne, *The Meteor Hunt,* ed. and trans. Frederick Paul Walter and Walter James Miller (Lincoln: University of Nebraska Press, 2006).
2. "By 1898, political questions had become the deciding factor in whether the latest Verne book were published in English at all. The tenor of his newer works were less agreeable to English-speaking audiences, or at least their publishers, who were not prepared to faithfully present Verne's views. The censorship grew beyond simply changing or removing controversial passages until eventually entire books were suppressed by simply not translating them into English," says Brian Taves

in "Jules Verne: An Interpretation," in *The Jules Verne Encyclopedia*, ed. Brian Taves and Stephen Michaluk Jr. (Lanham, Md.: Scarecrow, 1996), 16.

3. For a wide-ranging study of Verne's English translations and the extent to which they differed from their original French counterparts, see Arthur B. Evans, "Jules Verne's English Translations," *Science Fiction Studies* 32.1 (March 2005): 80–104.
4. Herbert R. Lottman, *Jules Verne: An Exploratory Biography* (New York: St. Martin's Press, 1996), 316. Lottman also observes, "One remembers the book now only because a latter-day scholar, taking the lead from Verne's grandson Jean, thought he saw in it an allusion to the Dreyfus case. To accept the theory, one would have to believe that Verne had converted to the side of Captain Dreyfus—an odd notion in view of the evidence. For in the very years the novelist was drafting his Kip story, he was also declaring to all who would listen that Dreyfus was *guilty*" (316). But, as will be discussed shortly, it is possible that Verne may have changed his mind about Dreyfus between the period when he was writing the original manuscript of *The Kip Brothers* in 1898 and when he submitted the final reworked version to his publisher in 1901.
5. Hetzel was the publisher of such famous French authors as Hugo, Lamartine, Musset, Mérimée, Stendhal, Sainte-Beuve, Nerval, Sand, Balzac, Dumas fils, Berlioz, Nodier, and Erckmann-Chatrian.
6. Two Verne novels that are exceptions to this rule are *From the Earth to the Moon* (which was serialized not in the *Magasin d'Education et de Récréation* but in a daily newspaper, *Les Débats*, in September 1865) and *Journey to the Center of the Earth* (which was never serialized, but published instead directly in book form in September 1864).
7. Christian Porcq, "Cataclysme dans la cathédrale ou le secret des *Frères Kip*," *Bulletin de la Société Jules Verne* 107 (June–September 1993): 35–52 and 109 (January–March 1994): 36–51.
8. Olivier Dumas, *Voyage à travers Jules Verne* (Montreal: Stanké, 2000), 197.
9. Verne's composition of *The Kip Brothers* was followed by *The Stories of Jean-Marie Cabidoulin* (written in 1899, published in 1901), *Travel Scholarships* (written in 1899, published in 1903), *The Golden Volcano*

(written in 1899–1900, published posthumously in 1906), *Le Beau Danube jaune* (*The Beautiful Yellow Danube*—not yet translated into English, written in 1901, published posthumously as *Le Pilote du Danube* in 1908), *The Lighthouse at the End of the World* (written in 1901, published posthumously in 1905), *The Meteor Hunt* (written in 1901, published posthumously in 1908), *The Invasion of the Sea* (written in 1902, published in 1905), *Master of the World* (written in 1902–3, published in 1904), and *Voyage d'études* (*Journey of studies*—not yet translated into English, written in 1903, published posthumously as *The Amazing Adventure of the Barsac Mission* in 1914). Most novels published after Verne's death in 1905 were rewritten—and in some cases substantially—by his son, Michel.

10. Piero Gondolo della Riva, "Les Dates de composition des derniers *Voyages extraordinaires,*" *Bulletin de la Société Jules Verne* 119 (July–September 1996): 12–14.
11. All correspondence between Jules Verne and his publisher (Hetzel père and fils) is kept in the Bibliothèque Nationale in Paris, in the archives referenced as 17004. These two letters are listed as September 2, 1901, BNF NAF 17004, folio #389, and October 26, 1901, BNF NAF 17004, folio #395.
12. In their contracts as well as in their correspondence, Verne and Hetzel always numbered the novelist's individual works in "volumes." A single novel could have been in one, two, or three volumes. Only three novels of Verne's *Voyages extraordinaires* are in three volumes (or parts): *The Children of Captain Grant, The Mysterious Island,* and *Mathias Sandorf.* Novels in two volumes (or in two parts) include, for example, *Twenty Thousand Leagues under the Seas, Hector Servadac,* and *The Mighty Orinoco.* Novels in one volume include, for example, *Around the World in Eighty Days* and *Journey to the Center of the Earth.*
13. Of the six contracts between Hetzel and Verne, the last one is dated May 17, 1875.
14. One year after having provided Hetzel with *The Kip Brothers,* Verne wrote to him on September 28, 1902, announcing that he would mail the manuscript of *Travel Scholarships* to him the next day. Verne explained that this novel takes place in the Caribbean and that because public opinion was so focused at that time on the Caribbean—the vol-

cano Pelée had exploded a few months before, killing thousands of inhabitants of Martinique—he chose this novel rather than another that he had available.

15. Verne's manuscript is available at the Municipal Library of Nantes (MJV B 100). Many of Verne's manuscripts are now available for viewing online at <<http://www.arkhenum.fr/bm_nantes/jules_verne/_app_php_mysql/ms/recherche_alpha_cles.php>>
16. Hetzel archive in the Bibliothèque Nationale in Paris: October 7, 1901, BNF NAF 17004, folio #392.
17. Alexandre Georges Roux (1853–1891), a historical painter, worked frequently for Hetzel. He provided more than 1,200 illustrations for the Verne novels. See Dominique Choffel, "Recherches sur les illustrations des 'Voyages extraordinaires' de Jules Verne" (Mémoire de maîtrise, Nanterre, 1982). See also Edmondo Marcucci, *Les Illustrations des Voyages Extraordinaires de Jules Verne* (Bordeaux: Ed. Société Jules Verne, 1956), and Arthur B. Evans, "The Illustrators of Jules Verne's *Voyages Extraordinaires,*" *Science Fiction Studies* 25.2 (July 1998): 258–60; the latter available online at <<http://jv.gilead.org.il/evans/illustr/>>.
18. According to Charles-Noël Martin in his *La Vie et l'oeuvre de Jules Verne* (Paris: Michel de l'Ormeraie, 1978), 280.
19. Froment is the name of four different engravers who worked for Hetzel and Verne: Jacques-Victor-Eugène Froment-Delormel (1820–1900), Eugène Froment (1844–1900), Emile-Alphonse Froment (?, son of Eugène), and Ferdinand-Florentin Froment (?).
20. E. E. Morris, ed. *Cassell's Picturesque Australasia,* 4 vols. (London: Cassell, 1887).
21. Four credited to Valentine and Sons, Dundee (one of the leading postcard companies of the nineteenth century; see <<http://photography.about.com/od/collectingphotos /a/a071204.htm>>) and two credited to "M. Hess Wartegg, *Samoa, Nouvelle-Guinée, et archipel Bismarck*" (published in German as Ernst von Hesse-Warteg, *Samoa, Bismarckarchipel, und Neuguinea: Drei deutsche Kolonien in der Südsee* [Leipzig: J. J. Weber, 1902]).
22. See Terry Harpold, "Verne's Cartographies," *Science Fiction Studies* 32.1 (March 2005): 18–42.

23. Augustin Privat-Deschanel and Adolphe Focillon, *Dictionnaire général des sciences théoriques et appliquées* (Paris: Garnier, 1864–67).
24. Elisée Reclus, *Nouvelle géographie universelle,* 19 vols. (Paris: Hachette, 1876–94).
25. Louis Figuier, *Les Merveilles de la science* (Paris: Furne/Jovet, 1867–91). For an excellent study of Verne's "recycling" of Figuier's works in his *Journey to the Center of the Earth,* see John Breyer and William Butcher, "Nothing New under the Earth," *Earth Sciences History* 22.1 (2003): 36–54.
26. Camille Flammarion, *L'Astronomie populaire* (Paris: E. Flammarion, 1880).
27. Jacques Arago, *Voyage autour du monde* (Paris: Hortet et Ozanne, 1839).
28. Louis Agassiz (1807–73), Swiss naturalist, who became professor of zoology at Harvard University. His *Journey to Brazil,* originally published in Boston in 1868, was translated into French as *Voyage au Brésil* and published by Hachette in 1869. It became the basis for Verne's novel *The Jangada* (1881). See Jean-Michel Margot, "Verne et Agassiz," *Bulletin de la Société Jules Verne* 25 (April–September 1973): 62–65.
29. Jean Chaffanjon, *L'Orénoque et le Caura* (Paris: Hachette, 1889). This book was the main geographical source for Verne's *The Mighty Orinoco* (1898). See Walter James Miller, "Introduction" in Jules Verne, *The Mighty Orinoco,* trans. Stanford L. Luce (Middletown, Conn.: Wesleyan University Press, 2002), ix–xvii.
30. Edouard Charton, *Voyageurs anciens et moderne* (Paris: Hachette, 1860).
31. In an 1894 interview, Verne offered the following interesting glimpse into his research and work habits:

    I may tell you that I am a great reader, and that I always read pencil in hand. I always carry a notebook about with me, and immediately jot down, like that person in Dickens, anything that interests me or may appear to be of possible use in my books. To give you an idea of my reading, I come here every day after lunch and immediately set to work to read through fifteen different papers, always the same fifteen, and I can tell you that very little in any of them escapes my attention. When I see anything of interest, down it goes. Then I read the reviews, such as the "Revue Bleue," the "Revue Rose," the "Revue des Deux Mondes," "Cosmos," Tissandier's "La Nature," Flammarion's "L'Astronomie." I also read through the bulletins of the scientific societies, especially those of the Geographical Society, for, mark, geography is my passion and my study. I have all Reclus's works—I have a great admiration for Elisée Reclus—and the whole of Arago. I also read and re-read, for I am a most careful reader, the collection known as "Le Tour du Monde," which is a series of stories of travel. I have thus amassed many thousands of notes on all subjects, and to date, at home, have at least twenty thousand notes which can be turned to advantage in my work, as yet unused. (R. H. Sherard, "Jules Verne at Home," *McClure's Magazine* 2.2 (January 1894): 120–21.

32. Louis-Antoine de Bougainville, *Voyage autour du monde* (Paris: Saillant et Nyon, 1771).
33. Jules Sébastien César Dumont d'Urville, *Voyage au pôle sud et dans l'Océanie* (Paris: Gide, 1856).
34. Louis-Isidore Duperrey, *Voyage autour du monde exécuté par ordre du Roi sur la corvette de Sa Majesté "la Coquille," pendant les années 1822, 1823, 1824 et 1825* (Paris: A. Bertrand, 1825–30).
35. Marcel Moré, *Le Très curieux Jules Verne* (Paris: Gallimard, 1960), 140; Jean Jules-Verne, *Jules Verne: A Biography,* trans. Roger Greaves (New York: Taplinger, 1976), 207; and Pierre-Félix Lagrange and Emile Valude, *L'Encyclopédie française d'ophtalmologie* (Paris: Doin, 1903–9), 3:105–286.
36. Although this Académie des Sciences article on retinal images was purely fictional, it nevertheless suggests that experiments of this sort were already being undertaken (by photographers, among others) as early as the 1850s and 1860s. See Arthur B. Evans, "Optograms and Fiction: Photo in a Dead Man's Eye," *Science Fiction Studies* 20.3 (November 1993): 341–61.
37. See "The Tell-Tale Eye: Critical Essay" by Veronique Campion-Vincent online at <<http://www.findarticles.com/p/articles/mi_m2386/is_1999_Annual/ai_55983642>>.
38. Another rich thematic focus is the recurring interplay between the var-

ious levels of meaning in the French words *preuve* (proof or evidence—as in "c'est une preuve de sa culpabilité" [it's proof of his guilt] or "faire ses preuves" [to prove oneself, to show one's ability], as Karl Kip did during the storm at sea) versus *épreuve* (photographic proof [a *trial* print from a negative] or an ordeal—e.g., "subir des épreuves" [to suffer hardships], as the Kip brothers did in prison).

39. Oliver Dumas, "La Correspondance Verne-Nadar," *Bulletin de la Société Jules Verne* 97 (1991): 14.
40. Quoted in Porcq, "Cataclysme dans la cathédrale," 107 (1993): 43.
41. Letter reprinted in Olivier Dumas, *Jules Verne* (Lyon: La Manufacture, 1988), 466.
42. Letters reprinted in Piero Gondolo della Riva, "Du nouveau sur Jules Verne grâce à une correspondance inédite." *Europe* 58 #613 (May 1980): 130, 133–34.
43. Eugène Degrave, *Le Bagne, les frères Rorique* (Paris: Stock, 1901). Lengthy excerpts of this work, translated into English, can be found in G. A. Raper, "The Story of the Brothers Degrave," *Wide World Magazine* 7.39 (June 1901): 211–19, 365–75. Thanks to Verne scholar Steve Michaluk for sharing this latter document with me.
44. See Henri Bordillon, "Balivernes sur Jarry-Verne," *Sureau* 5 (March–June 1985): 111–15. The two most popular books in French about the Rorique Affair are René La Bruyère, *Les Frères Rorique* (Paris: Librairie des Champs-Elysées, 1934), and Henri Jacquier, *Piraterie dans le Pacifique* (Paris: Nouvelles éditions latines, 1973). The latter was published in English as *Piracy in the Pacific: The Story of the Notorious Rorique Brothers,* trans. June P. Wilson (New York: Dodd, Mead, 1976). Another, more analytical study was published in Dutch in 1992: Jan Vandamme, *De Affaire Degrave-Rorique (1892–1899): Moord & Piraterij in de Stille Zuidzee* (Antwerp: Hadewijch, 1992). Vandamme analyzes the original documents in the case and also includes an overview of the various literary works inspired by the Rorique Affair.
45. Not only are the two basic stories extremely similar—two brothers accused of murdering their captain; their arrest, trial, and (unjust?) condemnation; then their ultimate exculpation—but also a number of concrete details from the Rorique/Degrave saga found their way into Verne's novel: the names of Gibson (now used for the slain captain and

his vengeance-seeking son) and Pieter (now used as first name of one of the heroes), their claim to have been castaways (the Kip brothers become real castaways), etc.

46. In a letter to Hetzel dated March 16, 1902, Verne says, "I am sending you today chapters 11 and 12 and I am keeping chapter 13, which you will have the day after tomorrow" (BN, folio 410). Reprinted in Porcq, "Cataclysme dans la cathédrale," 107 (1993): 43.
47. Cornélius Helling, "L'Oeuvre scientifique de Jules Verne," *Bulletin de la Société Jules Verne* 1 (1935): 38.
48. Letter reprinted in Gondolo della Riva, "Du nouveau sur Jules Verne," 125.
49. Letter in the Bibliothèque Nationale: February 11, 1899, BNF NAF 17004, folio #335.
50. As personified, for example, in the distasteful character of Isac [*sic*] Hakhabut in his novel *Hector Servadac.*
51. Jules-Verne, *Jules Verne,* 198.
52. Christian Porcq, "Cataclysme dans la cathédrale ou le secret des *Frères Kip,*" *Bulletin de la Société Jules Verne* 107 (June-September 1993): 35–52, and 109 (January-March 1994): 36–51.
53. Jean-Paul Faivre, "Jules Verne (1828–1905) et le Pacifique," *Journal de la société des océanistes* 11.11 (December 1965): 135–47.
54. "Les Premiers navires de la marine mexicaine" (The First Ships of the Mexican Navy) published in the periodical *Musée des familles* in 1851 and "Martin Paz" published in the same journal the following year.
55. Jules-Verne, *Jules Verne,* 5.
56. See Jean-Michel Margot, "46 ans d'expérience maritime," *La nouvelle revue maritime* 386 (May-June 1984): 12–19.
57. Jules-Verne, *Jules Verne,* 119.
58. See René Escaich, *Voyage à travers le monde vernien* (Brussels: La Boétie, 1951), repr. as *Voyage au monde de Jules Verne* (Paris: Plantin, 1955).
59. Even the villainous Vin Mod and Flig Balt are wicked not because of their nationality, which is ambiguous at best—Verne states that, with such sailors, "It seems that their nationality changes with the ship"—but, rather, because of their criminal natures.
60. Jean Chesneaux, *The Political and Social Ideas of Jules Verne* (London: Thames and Hudson, 1972), 142–43.

61. In several other novels written toward the end of his career, Verne appears to have come back to his earlier sociopolitical ideology. Consider, for example, the final *Voyage extraordinaire* to be published during Verne's lifetime, called *Invasion of the Sea* (1905). Much like *The Kip Brothers,* this novel also "closes the circle" and reflects a kind of pro-science positivism (and a corresponding lack of concern for social and environmental problems) that characterized his earliest and most famous works. See Arthur B. Evans, "Introduction," in Jules Verne, *Invasion of the Sea* (Middletown, Conn.: Wesleyan University Press, 2001), vii–xx.
62. Jules Verne, *P'tit-Bonhomme* (Lausanne: Rencontre, 1971), 82.
63. The French provinces of Alsace and Lorraine were ceded to Germany following the Franco-Prussian War of 1870.
64. Sherard, "Jules Verne at Home," 116.
65. Letter reprinted in Dumas, *Jules Verne,* 441.
66. Dumas, *Jules Verne,* 462.
67. Ibid., 465.
68. Ibid., 472.
69. Ibid., 476.
70. Lottman, *Jules Verne,* 286.
71. Dumas, *Jules Verne,* 469.
72. Olivier Dumas, Volker Dehs, and Piero Gondolo della Riva, eds. *Correspondance inédite de Jules et Michel Verne avec l'éditeur Louis-Jules Hetzel (1886–1914),* vol. 1 (Geneva: Slatkine, 2004), 44.
73. Dumas, *Jules Verne,* 466.
74. Telegram and letter cited in Lottman, *Jules Verne,* 304.
75. Jules-Verne, *Jules Verne,* p. 194.

The Kip Brothers

PART ONE

CHAPTER I

1. The manuscript has a more precise date in the right column: 27 October 1885. In the Southern Hemisphere, it's springtime.
2. Province in the southeast part of the South Island of New Zealand.
3. Tawaï-Pounamou is the local name of the South Island of New Zealand. Verne's eccentric scientist Paganel reminds us of it in chapters 2

and 8 of *The Children of Captain Grant* (vol. 3) when he recounts to the reader the history of New Zealand.

4. County in Otago province.
5. Auckland, Napier, and Wellington are harbors on North Island; the other places are harbors on the South Island of New Zealand.
6. The original manuscript and the text published in the *Magasin d'Education et de Récréation* have "seven" and "three" sailors. Verne (or Hetzel?) changed the number of the crew members between January and June 1902.
7. In Verne's French text, the obsolete English word "taps" is used.
8. South Island is written as Tawaï-Pouna-Mou and North Island as Ika-Na-Maoui in Verne's *The Children of Captain Grant* (vol. 3).
9. James Cook (1728–1779) mapped the coasts of New Zealand during his first expedition (1768–1771) and discovered the strait named after him.
10. Jules Sébastien César Dumont d'Urville (1790–1842), French explorer of the Pacific Ocean and Antarctica from 1822 to 1840.
11. In the Jules Verne Forum, moderated by Zvi Har'El (<<http://jv.gilead.org.il/forum/>>), Jan Gunnar, from Norway, suggested that the names Flig Balt and Vin Mod could be Danish. Changing Vin into Vind, Vind Mod are two Danish words meaning gain (or win) courage. Flig means polite, which is a characteristic of the boatswain when he speaks to Captain Gibson.
12. City in Ireland, close to Cork. The manuscript has ". . . Irish harbor of the United Kingdom . . ." with the word "Irish" scratched out. Verne describes Queenstown in chapter 7 ("Seven months in Cork") of his novel *Lit'l Fellow,* published in 1893.
13. Manuscript: "to settle at empty tables."
14. Manuscript: "four."
15. For this hat, Verne uses the word "surouët"—an archaic form of "suroît"—in his French text. The same form can be found in *Frritt-Flacc, A Drama in Mexico,* and *The Lighthouse at the End of the World.*
16. "Verdax" is invented by Jules Verne, probably derived from the Spanish word "Verdad" (truth). "Gibbet" is the English word for the French "gibet." To understand Verne's play on words here, it is necessary to

know that, in French, "épouser la veuve" (marry the widow) is an old colloquial expression meaning "to be executed"—either by hanging or by losing one's head in the guillotine. "La veuve" was the old colloquial word for the guillotine.

17. Manuscript: "alone."
18. Manuscript: "Len Cannon" instead of "Sexton."

CHAPTER 2

1. At the beginning of this chapter, the manuscript has the date of October 28, 1885. The ship is named after Captain James Cook (1728–79), a renowned British seaman and explorer who made several trips to the Pacific and was killed in the Sandwich Islands (today known as the Hawai'i Islands).
2. Today known as Hobart.
3. Capital city of Queensland, on the river Brisbane, near its mouth, on the east coast of Australia. There are still several shipyards in Brisbane.
4. Capital city of New Zealand, on the Cook Strait, in North Island.
5. Was this name perhaps inspired by Thomas Hobbes (1588–1679), the materialist philosopher of the seventeenth century?
6. Hobbes, Wickley, and Burnes are common family names in the Anglo-Saxon world.
7. Anagram of "oak." Koa is the Hawaiian name for a very hard wood, and it also means a strong warrior.
8. Discussion of races (along with occasional racist comments) is common in many of Verne's novels. In this, Verne was a man of his times. For more about Verne's racism, see Jean Chesneaux, *Une Lecture politique de Jules Verne* (Paris: Maspero, 1971), translated into English by Thomas Wickeley and published as *The Political and Social Ideas of Jules Verne* (London: Thames and Hudson, 1972). When Chesneaux recently updated his book, he included the fact that the *Voyages extraordinaires* published after Verne's death were modified and sometimes completely rewritten by Michel Verne; see Jean Chesneaux, *Jules Verne, un regard sur le monde* (Paris: Bayard, 2001).
9. The archipelago of the New Hebrides is today part of the Republic of Vanuatu, northeast of New Caledonia, east of the Coral Sea. The names

of the islands have changed between Verne's time and now: the three islands of Malikolo, Merena, and Eromanga are now Malakula, Espirito Santo, and Erromango.

10. The Fiji Islands are east of Vanuatu, and the island of Vanoua Linon is today called Vanua Levu.
11. Verne includes the Bismarck Archipelago—destination of the *James Cook*—in the greater Archipelago of New Guinea, today known as Papua New Guinea.
12. Capital city of New South Wales, on the southeast coast of Australia.
13. Verne's manuscript and all the French printings have "*West Pound.*" It should probably be "*West Bound.*" The name of the ship recalls the *Great Eastern* on which Jules Verne crossed the Atlantic with his brother Paul in 1867, spending one week visiting New York and Niagara Falls. The *Great Eastern,* navigating on the Atlantic, had a sister ship, the *Great Western,* traveling mostly on the Pacific Ocean. Verne's brother Paul Verne, a captain in the merchant navy, died in 1897, just before Jules began to write *The Kip Brothers.* They were very close and naming the ship "*West Pound*" may suggest another connection with Jules's beloved brother.
14. Dunedin is located at the end of an estuary, and Port Chalmers is on the north side of the same estuary (named Otago Harbor).
15. The original French text has " . . . le service de gabiers." A *gabier* is a seaman who knows how to handle the sails. In 1851, Jules Verne wrote a song (with music by his friend Aristide Hignard) called *Les Gabiers.* See Verne's comments on it in Robert H. Sherard, "Jules Verne at Home," *McClure's Magazine* 2.2 (Jan. 1894): 120.
16. In his French text, Verne uses the English word "steamer."
17. A history and a description of this particular lighthouse can be found at <<http://www.geocities.com/nzlighthouses/cape_saunders.htm>>.
18. Actually, the *James Cook,* sailing northeast, would not be able to see Cape Saunders, which is located on the south coast of the Otago Peninsula (see map at <<http://travelplanner.ath.cx/maps/dndreg.pdf>>).

CHAPTER 3

1. In the original French text, Verne uses the word "mille." A nautical mile (abbreviated nm) is 1,852 meters. This definition was adopted in

1929 by an International Hydrographic Congress in Monaco. It's exactly the length of one minute (one sixtieth of a degree) at the equator. The related speed unit is the knot, which is one mile per hour.

2. For the next few paragraphs, Verne offers a detailed description intended to teach the rudiments of New Zealand geography to his French readers. These descriptions are based on exploration reports written by navigators like Cook, Bougainville, D'Entrecasteaux, Dumont d'Urville, and others.
3. Named after Joseph Foveaux (1766–1846), lieutenant-governor of New South Wales, who had arrived in Sydney in July 1808 to assist Governor King.
4. In 1809 the *Pegasus* (Captain S. Chase) had aboard as first officer William Stewart. While the ship was in the southeastern harbor that now bears its name, Stewart began charting the southern coasts.
5. Snares Island is known for a species of crested penguins that breeds only there. In the year 2000, the population was estimated to be 30,000 breeding pairs. Snares Island is southwest of Stewart Island.
6. Harbor about 150 km northeast of Dunedin. The height of Mount Herbert is 920 m above sea level.
7. Ta Moko is the Maori form of tattooing. For more information on this ancient Maori tradition, see <<http://www.fiu.edu/~harveyb/moko.htm>>.
8. Ironically, Verne is perhaps speaking here through the mouth of his villain Vin Mod. In several novels (*Hector Servadac, The Hunt of the Meteor, The Golden Volcano*) Verne criticizes gold fever. Every time the search for gold becomes a central theme in a Vernian story, the result is invariably disastrous: either the protagonists die or the gold is lost or suddenly has no value anymore. See the special issue of the *Revue Jules Verne* (1998) entirely dedicated to the subject of gold in Verne's works.
9. The ship's name is listed in English in Verne's French text, as are the names of the *James Cook* and *West Pound.*
10. Harbor on the south coast of the South Island of New Zealand, known as "the most centrally located South Island port." Named Te Maru, "place of shelter," Timaru was originally a haven for Maori travelers canoeing along the otherwise shelterless coastline. Timaru was sparsely populated until 1859 when the British ship *Strathallan* arrived with 120 immigrants.

11. North of Canterbury Bight (Bay) is Banks Peninsula, a volcanic steep landscape where two columns were named Pompey's Pillars after the Pompey Pillar erected in Alexandria (Egypt) to honor the Roman emperor Diocletian. Christchurch is a port city just north of the Banks Peninsula.
12. Just 85 kilometers from the city of Christchurch, Akaroa is a historic French and British settlement nestled in the heart of an ancient volcano. Akaroa means "long harbor" in Maori. The town, located well inside the long Akaroa harbor, is the largest settlement on Banks Peninsula.
13. Kaikoura is also the name of a small town. In Maori legend, Maui placed his foot on the Kaikoura peninsula to steady himself while he "fished-up" the North Island. The Maori name Kaikoura translates as "meal of crayfish" (Kai—food, koura—crayfish), and it is crayfish for which the region has traditionally been famous.
14. Northeast province of the South Island of New Zealand.
15. Ben More is the name of a river in the Marlborough province. The mountain named Ben More is at 44°39'S and 171°43'E in the middle of South Island, 70 km west of Christchurch. Verne trusted the travelers' and explorers' reports he read, and he did not catch such mistakes. Another mistake of the same kind is the displacement of the Great Eyry in his novel *Master of the World.* Verne's Great Eyry should be located in Pilot Mountain close to Mt. Airy, on the border between North Carolina and Virginia. In the novel, however, Verne places the Great Eyry close to Morganton, a hundred miles west of Pilot Mountain.
16. Town established in 1850 by the British traveler Charles Clifford (1813–93), who was made baronet of Flaxbourne in 1887.
17. Cape Campbell is situated on the eastern coast of the South Island of New Zealand and marks the southern approaches to Cook Strait. Its lighthouse (with white and black horizontal stripes) was lit for the first time on August 1, 1870. Captain James Cook named Cape Campbell after Captain John Campbell, who had made many innovations in navigational instruments.
18. Cape Palliser is the southernmost point of the North Island of New Zealand and marks the northern approaches to Cook Strait. Its lighthouse (with white and red horizontal stripes) was built in 1897. The

name was given by Captain James Cook in honor of a naval colleague and patron who held the post of comptroller of the Navy Board.

19. Named after Frederick Aloysius Weld (1823–91), who settled in New Zealand to start a sheep ranch. He became minister of native affairs and was involved in the conflicts between the Maoris and the government.
20. Town located in the Marlborough region in the northeast corner of New Zealand's South Island, capital city of the Marlborough province, with around 25,000 inhabitants today.
21. Located on the southern tip of North Island, New Zealand's capital is between the Cook Strait and the Tararua foothills. The city, some 2 km in diameter, surrounds Port Nicholson, a deep water harbor, and Mount Victoria (196 m).

CHAPTER 4

1. Abel Janszoon Tasman (1603–59), Dutch navigator and explorer, was the first European to discover New Zealand; he did so on December 13, 1642.
2. Sailing north, Tasman reached the north shore of South Island of New Zealand. At sunset on December 18, 1642, the Dutch ship anchored off the coast of Taitapu Bay (now Golden Bay). After three Dutchmen were killed, Tasman decided that he would be unable to establish friendly relations with the local population. Because of this incident, Tasman named the bay "Moordenaers Baij," Murderer's Bay. "Bay of the Massacre" is the literal translation of Verne's "Baie du Massacre."
3. Tobias Furneaux (1735–81) commanded HMS *Adventure* during the second voyage of Captain James Cook, who was aboard the HMS *Resolution*.
4. Marc Joseph "Macé" Marion-Dufresne (1724–72), born in Saint-Malo, French navigator and explorer, discovered the Crozet Islands in January 1772 and reached New Zealand in May of the same year.
5. Cf. chap. 1, n. 10.
6. D'Urville Island is the northernmost part of the South Island of New Zealand. It is separated from the South Island by the "Passage des Français" (French Pass). The island was named by the crewmen of Dumont d'Urville.
7. The correct name today is Port Nicholson.

8. This comment is typical of Verne's wry, tongue-in-cheek humor. As a rule, *The Kip Brothers* is not among Verne's most humorous stories; in fact, it is probably one of Verne's most serious. More comical Verne stories include *From the Earth to the Moon, Doctor Ox,* and *The Wedding of M. Anselme des Tilleuls* (*Le Mariage de M. Anselme des Tilleuls,* yet to be published in English).
9. With a detailed description of Wellington and its immediate area now concluded, Verne returns us to the story. Such pedagogical "asides" are frequent in Verne's prose and constitute an important part of his "science-fictional" narratological recipe.
10. Roux's illustration shows Mr. Hawkins with Captain Gibson. Mr. Hawkins is portrayed in the likeness of M. Alfred Demange, the lawyer for Captain Alfred Dreyfus. Verne scholar Christian Porcq, who made the connection, adds that, even though Jules Verne himself was schooled to be an attorney, very few lawyers are featured in Verne's novels. In *The Kip Brothers,* Mr. Hawkins will play the role of the Kip brothers' lawyer-advocate.
11. This is the first mention of photography, which will play such a key role in the novel. Verne underscores the progress made in modern photographic technology in order to provide the reader, early in the story, with a credible scientific context for later discoveries. In the 1870s, the introduction of the dry-plate process marked a turning point in the history of photography. No longer did one need the cumbersome wet-plates; no longer was a darkroom tent needed. It was getting close to the time when one could take pictures without having any specialized knowledge of the technology involved.
12. New Ireland is an island northeast of New Britain, and part of the Bismarck Archipelago. It is one of the provinces of Papua New Guinea, whose administrative center is Kavieng. The island is around 320 km long, but most of it is no wider than 6 to 10 km.
13. Port city on the south coast of New Ireland, discovered by the French navigator and explorer Jean-François de Surville (1717–79) on October 13, 1769. He named the place Port Praslin to honor the French navy minister César-Gabriel de Choiseul, duc de Praslin (1712–85).
14. Coral Island, located between New Britain and New Ireland. At the

time of the story, Kerawara was the capital of the German colony of Papua New Guinea.

15. In 1884, the first German flags were seen in the Bismarck Archipelago. The German empire was in the midst of colonial expansion and, as usual, the colony was in fact ruled by a trade company, the Neuguinea-Kompagnie. New Ireland became New Mecklenburg, New Britain became New Pommern, the Duke of York Islands became New Lauenburg, and the northeastern part of New Guinea became Kaiser-Wilhelmsland. In the 1910s, the German colony (known then as "Deutsch-Neuguinea") included not only the Bismarck Archipelago, but also the Solomon Islands, the Carolina Islands, and the Marianas. For thirty years, between 1884 and 1914, the countries known today as Papua New Guinea, the Solomon Islands, the Federated States of Micronesia, Palau (or Belau), the Marshall Islands, and the Commonwealth of the Northern Mariana Islands were under German rule. Occupied by Australian forces during World War I, they were mandated to Australia by the League of Nations in 1920 and became known as the Territory of New Guinea. Australian rule was reconfirmed by the United Nations in 1947. Papua New Guinea and the Solomon Islands became independent in 1975 and 1978, respectively. Micronesia and the Marshall Islands became independent in 1986 under a Compact of Free Association with the United States. The Republic of Palau (or Belau) has been independent since 1994 under a Compact of Free Association with the United States. In 1975 the Northern Mariana Islands were designated a commonwealth in political union with the United States.
16. This dialogue about Captain Gibson's photograph foreshadows the end of the novel, providing a chiastic "frame" to the story. French author Raymond Roussel (1877–1933) was among the first to notice such a technique in Verne's works. See Raymond Roussel, *Comment j'ai écrit certains de mes livres* (Paris: Alphonse Lemerre, 1935).
17. The encounter offers Verne another opportunity to educate the reader about the natives of New Zealand, the Maoris.
18. Today Tongatapu, a southern island of the Tonga Archipelago.
19. Cannibals and discussions of cannibalism are present in many of

Verne's novels, from the bloodthirsty Nyam-Nyam tribes of central Africa in *Five Weeks in a Balloon,* to the more cultivated but equally vicious Maoris of New Zealand in *The Children of Captain Grant* and *Twenty Thousand Leagues under the Seas,* to the starving castaways aboard *The Chancellor.* Cannibalism, in addition to its "extraordinary" exoticism, serves an ideological purpose in Verne's oeuvre: it serves as a comparative social model, showing how far modern civilization has progressed from its primitive and savage roots. Occasionally, however, Verne will treat the topic with tongue-in-cheek "black humor," as in Paganel's light-hearted explanation in chapter 6 (part 3) of *The Children of Captain Grant*—a chapter aptly titled "Where Cannibalism is Treated Theoretically." For more about Verne and cannibals, see Frank Lestringant, *Cannibals: The Discovery and Representation of the Cannibal from Columbus to Jules Verne,* trans. Rosemary Morris (Berkeley: University of California Press, 1997).

CHAPTER 5

1. Orokaiva is a native language of New Guinea, spoken by around thirty-five thousand persons. Verne's use of "Orokiva" here seems incorrect—he probably meant Otaki, located on the southwestern coast of New Zealand's North Island.
2. Next to Cape Egmont sits Mount Taranaki, a dormant volcano located in the west of New Zealand's North Island. For many centuries the Maoris called the mountain Taranaki, but Captain Cook changed its official name to Mount Egmont in honor of the earl of Egmont. Its name was changed back after Verne's time, most likely because it seemed inappropriate to have it named after a British noble who had never been in New Zealand. New Plymouth, located at the northwest foot of the volcano, was founded in the 1840s.
3. Verne's concerns for our planet's ecology and environment are increasingly visible in his later novels. He was keenly aware of the possible extinction of certain species, especially whales and elephants, due to excessive hunting. Consider, for example, the following passage from his 1901 novel *Le Village aérien* (*The Aerial Village,* a.k.a. *The Village in the Treetops*)—a passage, incidentally, that does not appear in the English translation of this work:

However, as numerous as they are, the species will someday disappear. Since each elephant can bring in around one hundred francs in ivory, they are hunted mercilessly.

Each year, according to the estimates of M. Foa, no less than forty thousand are killed on the African continent, producing seven hundred thousand kilograms of ivory that are shipped to England. Before fifty years have gone by, there will be no more elephants remaining, despite their relatively long lifespan. (Chapter 3)

4. Marking the border of the Pacific Ocean in the North, the Bering Strait separates the continents of Asia and America. The Kurile (written Kouriles in Verne's time) Islands are an archipelago of twenty volcanic islands—with a total of forty-five volcanoes—joining the Kamchatka peninsula to the north of Japan. They are between the Eurasian and the Pacific tectonic plates.
5. Ohawe is located south of Mount Taranaki (or Egmont in Verne's text) on the coast of the South Taranaki Bight.
6. This lighthouse, 42 feet high, was built in 1864. Coastal erosion made it necessary to move the lighthouse back from the edge of the cliff in 1998.
7. The Polynesian (Maori) legend of the creation of New Zealand relates that Maui (written Maoui by Verne) was a demigod who lived in Hawaiiki. He possessed magic powers. One day when he was very young, he hid in the bottom of his brothers' boat in order to go fishing with them. Once out at sea, Maui was discovered by his brothers, but they were not able to take him back to shore as Maui made use of his magic powers, making the shoreline seem much farther away than it was in reality. So the brothers continued rowing, and once they were far out into the ocean, Maui dropped his magic fishhook over the side of the waka (a Polynesian canoe). After a while he felt a strong tug on the line. This seemed to be too strong a tug to be any ordinary fish, so Maui called to his brothers for assistance. After much straining and pulling, up suddenly surfaced Te Ika a Maui (the fish of Maui), today known as the North Island of New Zealand. Maui told his brothers that the Gods might be angry about this, and he asked his brothers to wait while he went to make peace with the Gods. However, once Maui had gone, his brothers began to argue among themselves about the possession of this

new land. They took out their weapons and started to bludgeon their catch. The blows on the land created the many mountains and valleys of the North Island today. The South Island is known as Te Waka a Maui (the waka of Maui). Stewart Island, which lies at the very bottom of New Zealand, is known as Te Punga a Maui (Maui's anchor), as it was the anchor holding Maui's waka as he pulled in the giant fish.

8. The Cook Straits.
9. Two archipelagoes east of the Coral Sea, with Vanuatu in between.
10. In French, Verne used the word "Papouasie," which was more generic than the Republic of Papua New Guinea of modern times. Vin Mod is referring to the islands north and northwest of New Zealand, including today's Indonesia.
11. East coast of the South Island of New Zealand, just where the *James Cook* was two days earlier.
12. North Taranaki Bight, north of New Plymouth.
13. Verne wrote "Whare-Orino," but the name today is Whareorino, a mountain (962 m above sea level) that can be seen from Auckland. It is covered by trees, known as the Whareorino forest.
14. Kawhia and Aotea are two harbors on the west coast, south of Auckland. The name Aotea comes from Aotearoa—Land of the Long White Cloud—a Maori name given to New Zealand by its Polynesian discoverer Kupe when he sighted the islands of New Zealand, which appeared as land lying beneath a cloud.
15. Auckland is New Zealand's largest city, built on North Island where the two coasts narrow. Auckland has a harbor on the east coast as well as on the west coast of North Island.
16. Manukan is today a southern suburb of Auckland.
17. The Kaipara is the largest harbor in the southern hemisphere. Its waters have provided sustenance and shelter, as well as being an important trading route north and south, since the Maori arrived in the fourteenth century.
18. The Albertlanders was the name was given to a group of colonists who settled at Port Albert, on the Kaipara Harbour, north of Auckland during 1862–63. At the time, the provincial government in Auckland was offering Special Settlement Schemes to encourage development in the

north. This particular proposed settlement was named "Albertland" in honor of Queen Victoria's consort, who had died the previous year.

19. Hokianga Bay was the place where the Polynesian explorer Kupe settled. Today it is a resort and vacation destination. The Cape Maria Van Diemen is the northernmost tip of New Zealand. It was named by Tasman in 1643 in honor of Anthony Van Diemen's wife. Anthony Van Diemen (1593–1645) was governor-general of the Dutch East Indies.
20. The Three Kings Islands are situated forty-five miles off the northeastern tip of New Zealand. Tasman anchored there on January 6, 1643, and named the islands in honor of the biblical Three Wise Men.
21. Three archipelagoes north of New Zealand. The Hebrides are islands in Scotland. To be totally correct, Verne should have written "New Hebrides." The New Hebrides archipelago is today part of the Republic of Vanuatu.
22. Archipelago extending southwest of the island of New Guinea.
23. The discussion about steam or wind-powered ships is typical of the end of the nineteenth century when most ocean-faring vessels had an engine and sails. Jules Verne himself owned a yacht—*Saint-Michel III*—that was powered by both propeller and wind.
24. In French: "le pavillon tricolore." For French readers, this expression means exclusively the French flag.
25. Nantes was the birthplace of Jules Verne. Foucault is a common French family name, but it is also the name of the scientist—Léon Foucault—famous for demonstrating the earth's rotation by means of a huge pendulum in the Panthéon in Paris in 1851. He also invented the gyroscope. The combination of Nantes and Foucault in the same sentence suggests a glimpse back to Verne's youth.
26. Archipelago northeast of Indonesia, between the Philippines and the island of New Guinea. The capital city is Ambon.
27. Ship named after the Dutch princess Wilhelmina Helena Pauline Maria, born in 1880 in The Hague.
28. An isolated island, not part of an archipelago, between New Zealand and New Caledonia. Today Norfolk Island belongs to Australia.

CHAPTER 6

1. Captain Cook on the *Resolution* discovered the island on October 10, 1774. Two British attempts at turning the island into a penal colony (1788–1814 and 1825–55) were unsuccessful. In 1856, the island was resettled by Pitcairn Islanders, descendants of the *Bounty* mutineers and their Tahitian companions. Norfolk Island is mentioned in *The Mysterious Island* (part 3, chap. 1): Bob Harvey, captain of the *Speedy*, is a convict who has escaped from the penitentiary of Norfolk Island.
2. Today's geographic coordinates of Norfolk Island are 29°02'S and 167°57' east of the Greenwich meridian. Verne's manuscript has "165 degrees 42 East," which was misread by Hetzel's typesetter and overlooked by Verne himself during his proofreading. It is important to note that Verne used the Paris meridian as his reference for longitude degrees. France did not adopt the Greenwich meridian until 1911.
3. *Phormium tenax* (New Zealand flax) can be found from New Zealand to Hawai'i.
4. This is the first mention of the penitentiary where the Kip brothers will be imprisoned.
5. Such enumerations are often used by Verne not only to convey scientific knowledge but also to exercise a stylistic technique. See Alain Buisine, "Un Cas limite de la description: L'Enumeration—L'Exemple de *Vingt Mille Lieues sous les Mers*," in *La Description: Nodier, Sue, Flaubert, Hugo, Verne, Zola, Alexis, Fénelon* (Lille: Université de Lille III, Editions universitaires), 81–102.
6. Sets of three signals are a universal appeal for help and a response to such an appeal.

CHAPTER 7

1. The name Kip is used here for the first time in the novel. Pieter is nearly an anagram of the French "trépie(d)—trois pieds," a tripod. In German, a tripod is a "Dreifuß"—or Dreyfus, like the captain Alfred Dreyfus. The novel also begins in the tavern of the *Three Magpies* (in French: "trois pies"). Was Verne aware of these lexical correlations while initially writing or while later editing the final version of *Les Frères Kip?* Most probably. A connoisseur of cryptograms, puzzles, and secret codes, Verne often inserted underlying meanings into his texts.

See Marcel Moré, *Le Très curieux Jules Verne* (Paris: Gallimard, 1960), 116–58, along with many other studies such as Guy Riegert, "Voyages au centre des noms, ou les combinaisons verniennes" in *Jules Verne IV: Texte, image, spectacle,* ed. François Raymond (Paris: Minard, 1983), 73–94; and Olivier Dumas, "L'Envers du décor, anagrammes et sous-entendus," in his *Voyage à travers Jules Verne* (Montreal: Stanké, 2000), 133–46.

2. Maluku (today's name) lies across a transition zone between Asian and Australian fauna and flora, and also between the Malay-based cultures of western Indonesia and those of Melanesia. There are over 1,000 islands in the Province, most of which are uninhabited. Some 85 percent of Maluku is water, and it sits astride one of the world's most volatile volcanic belts. Formerly known as the Moluccas, these are the famed Spice Islands of which Indian, Arab, Chinese, and later European traders spoke. The capital city of this province of Indonesia is Ambon.
3. The same age as Captain Alfred Dreyfus when he was arrested.
4. *The Children of Captain Grant* and *The Kip Brothers* are the only novels of the *Voyages extraordinaires* that have two characters referenced in the title. Other novels just mention the hero in the title, such as *A Captain at Fifteen, Lit'l Fellow, Michel Strogoff, Claudius Bombarnac,* or *Clovis Dardentor.* Mary and Robert Grant are siblings, but Karl and Pieter Kip are brothers—like Jules and Paul Verne. The novel is a celebration of brotherhood.
5. Dutch name of the South African impala; in German, "Rehbock."
6. The shallow part of the Pacific Ocean, between the Timor and Coral seas, separating Australia from New Guinea.
7. Part of the Moluccas, a chain of islands forming an eastern prolongation of the island of Java and ending at Timor.
8. The Torres Strait is located between the northernmost point of Australia, Cape York, and the island of New Guinea. It's where Captain Nemo's *Nautilus* was temporarily caught in the coral reefs (*Twenty Thousand Leagues under the Seas,* part 1, chap. 20).
9. Northeast of Australia, between the Great Coral Reef and the islands of Melanesia.
10. The chicken cage in this scene appears to be the intersection of many underlying themes. First, the word for "chicken" in Dutch is "kip." Sec-

ond, in French slang, "cage à poules" (chicken cage) means the cage in a police van or a jail cell. Third, in his autobiography *Cinq années de ma vie* (*Five Years of My Life*), Alfred Dreyfus describes a similar wire-netted cage in which he was transported to prison. Further, Alfred Dreyfus was a Jew, and Kip is the beginning of the word "Kippur," as in Yom Kippur, the Day of Atonement. The Kip brothers leave Ambon on September 23—on or around Yom Kippur—and four weeks later find themselves shipwrecked.

11. A member of the Roman Catholic Church, Verne often portrays his heroes and heroines as having an unshakable faith in God and as being fundamentally *moral* and *good*. But Verne's oeuvre cannot be characterized as Christian—there is never a mention of Christ, and most of his *Voyages extraordinaires* seem to be built around a rather deist philosophy of "Aide-toi et le Ciel t'aidera" (God helps those who help themselves). As Jean Chesneaux once remarked: "Despite fairly frequent references to Providence, to the Supreme Being, he [Verne] is fundamentally a rationalist . . ." (*The Political and Social Ideas of Jules Verne* [London: Thames and Hudson, 1972], 82). Some evidence suggests a shift in Verne's religious views, however, from his earlier works to his later ones. In the former, Verne's explorers are frequently *aided* in their quest during moments of crisis by various deus-ex-machina interventions—a providential windstorm that saves them from dying of thirst in the Sahara Desert (*Five Weeks in a Balloon*), a subterranean echo that allows a lost expedition member to be found (*Journey to the Center of the Earth*), or a single grain of wheat with which the castaways can begin to farm (*The Mysterious Island*). Very different are the heavenly interventions in most of Verne's later novels. Here, a seemingly vengeful God strikes down hubris-filled scientists who have "crossed the line" by causing, for example, a sudden chemical spill that instantly freezes the evil Herr Schultze at the end of Verne's *The Begum's Millions* or a celestial lightning bolt that destroys a now-crazed Robur and his polymorphic flying machine in *Master of the World*. For more about religion in Verne's works, see Volker Dehs, "L'Ame de l'oncle Lidenbrock: Science et religion dans les *Voyages extraordinaires*," *Jules Verne 6: La Science en question* (Paris: Minard, 1992), 85–107.

CHAPTER 8

1. Situated 100 km off the east coast of the New Caledonian mainland, Lifou, Maré, Ouvea, and Tiga constitute the Loyalty Islands archipelago, spanning a surface area of 2,200 sq km. In 1840, Dumont d'Urville drew a map of the islands. In 1864, the Loyalty Islands became a French territory. However, unsuited to intensive colonization, they were designated as native reservations, a status that established the archipelago's history henceforth. This special status, and the interbreeding that resulted from successive native migrations, set the Loyalty Islanders apart as "different" Melanesians. Traditional Kanak customs, dating back to the dawn of time, remain very strong and continue to govern daily life even today.
2. After focusing at length the heroes of the story, the narrative now returns to the villains and their nefarious plans. This abrupt oscillation between the good and evil characters serves to enhance their difference, highlighting their contrast, and to underscore the moral stakes in the drama that will soon unfold.
3. Note the foreshadowing here, where Verne is again preparing the reader for the possibility of the captain's murder.
4. The Isle of Pines is the extension of the southeast end of New Caledonia. Like the rest of New Caledonia, it is French territory.
5. In French "balade" means an easy walk. It's the name of a New Caledonian tribe and the place where Captain Cook shipwrecked the first time he came to the island. This historical village of New Caledonia is on the north shore of the island.
6. Beaupré Island was named after Charles de Beautemps-Beaupré (1766–1854), a French cartographer who was with D'Entrecasteaux in the 1790s in the archipelago of New Caledonia. Beautemps-Beaupré invented modern hydrological methods of mapping coasts. In 1844, he published maps of the French coasts that were considered the best in the world. The Isle of Pines and the three Loyalty Islands are easy to find on Pacific Ocean maps. But Botany Island, Hohohana Island, as well as Britannia Island are not referenced on even detailed maps of the area.
7. Antoine-Raymond-Joseph Bruny d'Entrecasteaux (1737–93), a French admiral who explored the South Pacific islands and the Australian

coast between 1791 and 1792 while seeking traces of the lost expedition of La Pérouse. He died of scurvy at sea off the island of Java. It was one of most successful scientific French expeditions in the South Pacific, mainly because Beautemps-Beaupré was on board and mapped the coasts of many islands with such accuracy that all navigators, including the British, used his maps for decades. The coral reefs extending northwest of New Caledonia became known as the D'Entrecasteaux Reefs and the islands northwest of the Louisiades are named D'Entrecasteaux Islands.

8. A mountain ridge forms the spine of the main island of New Caledonia. The two highest summits are Mount Panié in the north (1,628 m) and Mount Humboldt in the south (1,618 m). Mount Arago was named after the French geographer and artist Jacques Arago (1790–1855), who visited the South Pacific between 1817 and 1820. He was a close friend of Jules Verne.
9. "Canaques" is the French word for the New Caledonian natives. According to the Oxford English Dictionary, the English term is "Kanaka."
10. A kriss is a Malaysian double-edged dagger with a wavy, curved blade usually under 18 inches in length.

CHAPTER 9

1. Rossel Island is the last island east of the Louisiades. Saint-Aignan is north of the Louisiades and northeast of the D'Entrecasteaux Islands. Trobriant (also written Trobriand) is north of the D'Entrecasteaux Islands.
2. João Serrão (the true Portuguese name of Serrano) was one of the seconds in command of Magellan's expedition. He took over as captain after Magellan's death in 1521 in the Philippines. Willem Shouten (or Schouten) was a Dutch explorer and navigator who discovered a new route to the South Pacific via Cape Horn on January 29, 1616. Schouten Island is located off the east coast of Tasmania.
3. Philip Carteret (1733–96), an English navigator who made an expedition to the South Seas in 1766–69 and discovered Queen Charlotte's Isles, Pitcairn Island, and other islands, one of which is called Carteret in Papua New Guinea. The American whaler Benjamin Morrell (1795–1839) published an account of his travels in *A Narrative of Four Voyages*

to the South Sea, North and South Pacific Ocean, Chinese Sea, Ethiopic and Southern Atlantic Ocean, Indian and Antarctic Ocean (New York, 1832).

4. Most of Verne's *Voyages extraordinaires* were published during the last decades of the nineteenth century, when the major European colonial powers of the time—England, France, the Netherlands, Portugal, and Germany—were consolidating their overseas empires. With some exceptions (as in *Propeller Island,* where he condemns the harmful influence of missionaries on certain native island cultures), Verne generally defends the "civilizing mission" of Western colonialism, especially in those locales where the indigenous natives practice cannibalism. For more on Verne's political opinions, see Jean Chesneaux, *Jules Verne, un regard sur le monde* (Paris: Bayard, 2001).
5. This paragraph, where he inserts a detailed description of the flora and fauna of New Guinea into his narrative, is a good example of Verne's "en bloc" geographical pedagogy.
6. Another example of Verne's didactic technique—*negative* exposition—where he provides information about the various locations in the region *not* visited by the protagonists. For a discussion of this and other narrative strategies used by Verne, see Arthur B. Evans, *Jules Verne Rediscovered* (Westport, Conn.: Greenwood, 1988), 109–58.
7. As the *James Cook* sails toward the Bismarck Archipelago, it is surprising that it navigates so close to Cape Rodney and the D'Entrecasteaux Islands. The reason seems more narratological than nautical: Verne makes the *James Cook*'s route deviate in order to have the opportunity to stage a savage Papuan attack in the second part of the present chapter. In almost the same location, a similar attack by native cannibals was fended off by Captain Nemo in chapter 20 of part one of *Twenty Thousand Leagues under the Seas.* Whereas Nemo used electrical power to defend his vessel, Captain Gibson uses more conventional weapons.

CHAPTER 10

1. "Abîme" (abyss) is a recurring word in many of Verne's texts, from those "leçons d'abîme" (lessons of the abyss) taught by Lidenbrock to his nephew Axel on the steeple of Vor Frelsers Kirk at the beginning of *Journey to the Center of the Earth* (1864) to the disappearance of the

shattered remnants of Standard Island into the "abîme" of the Pacific Ocean at the end of *Propeller Island* (1895). Vernian scholar Terry Harpold has proposed—in a paper titled "Des Leçons d'abîme: Intertextual Relays of the *Voyages extraordinaires*," presented at the North American Jules Verne Society annual meeting held in Tampa, Florida, on May 9–11, 2003—that the word "abîme" and its variants have a special significance in Verne's vocabulary. They seem always to be thematically and textually overdetermined, drawing on the word's multiple meanings in French and alluding implicitly to other instances of its use, including those in other novels by Verne. In French, the verb "abîmer" can mean both to sink (usually in deep water) and to be ruined or destroyed, i.e., negated. This double sense is present also in its participial forms (abîmé, etc.) and, subtly, in the noun (abîme). (The English word "abyss" is also somewhat ambiguous in this way.) Verne sometimes uses multiple variants of the word in close proximity, each with a different explicit sense, such that each also reinforces the polysemy of the other (see *The Voyages of Captain Hatteras*, part 1, chap. 32, or *Robur the Conqueror*, chap. 26). As in this passage, deep water in Verne's fiction is always marked by what might be called "abyssal negativity" (see, *Twenty Thousand Leagues under the Seas*, part 2, chap. 11, or *The Chancellor*, chap. 38).

2. Here Verne defines a weather phenomenon known as "black squalls"—"grains noirs" in the original French text, also in quotes—to prepare the reader for the *James Cook*'s encounter with one in a few pages.
3. This island name cannot be found on any map. It was probably a transcription error by Verne of Muyua Island (also known as Woodlark Island), located off the coast of Papua New Guinea in the Solomon Sea.
4. Cf. n. 15, chap. 4, part 1.
5. William Dampier (1652–1715), a famous British sea captain, explorer, and hydrographer, started his career as a buccaneer who, throughout the 1670s and 1680s, raided Spanish possessions in the Caribbean, along the western coast of South America, and in the Pacific. He subsequently led several voyages of exploration around the world and became the most respected nautical mapmaker of his time. Journals that he kept from his first expedition, published in 1697 as *New Voyage*

round the World, resulted in a commission from the English Admiralty in 1699 to explore the South Seas. He completed many new charts of coastlines and currents around Australia and New Guinea. Dampier named New Britain, and also discovered the archipelago off northwestern Australia now named for him. Dampier's most legendary associate, however, was probably Alexander Selkirk who served as a member of his crew during his 1703–7 expedition to the South Seas and who was voluntarily marooned on Juan Fernandez Island. The castaway Selkirk, whose story was retold by Daniel Defoe in *Robinson Crusoe* (1719), was eventually rescued in 1709 by the English privateer *Duke*, captained by Woodes Rodgers and piloted by none other than William Dampier.

6 St. George's Channel (4°30'S, 152°30'E) separates New Ireland from New Britain and leads into the Bismarck Sea. It is one of the major shipping lanes between Australia and Japan through the Solomon Sea.

7. Mr. Hawkins here plays the same role as Paganel in *The Children of Captain Grant*, teaching the geography and the history of the various territories they cross.

8. This footnote, written by Jules Verne himself, appears in the manuscript as well as in all published French editions. It contrasts with earlier ones in the text annotating certain illustrations—tattooed New Zealand Maori (Chapter 3), Maori canoes, arms and musical instruments (Chapter 4), New Caledonian natives (Chapter 8), and a native hut in New Guinea (Chapter 9)—that were inserted by Hetzel, alerting the reader to the existence of Verne's three-volume historical work *Great Voyages and Great Navigators* (1878–80).

9. Louis-Antoine de Bougainville (1729–1811), French navigator, explorer and mathematician, started the first settlement in the Malouines (Falkland Islands). He was commissioned by the French government in 1766 to be on the first French vessel to sail around the world. During this voyage, he discovered many islands in the South Pacific (French Polynesia, the Louisiade Archipelago, Bougainville Island, etc.). In 1771 he published a very popular book about his travels, titled *Voyage autour du monde* (Voyage around the World), whose descriptions of Tahiti helped to foster the notion of the "noble savage" in works by Rousseau and early Romantic European writers. Bougainville fought in the American

War of Independence, was elected to scientific academies, became vice admiral of the French navy, and was named senator and member of the Legion of Honor by Napoleon I.

10. Louis-Isidore Duperrey (1786–1865) joined the navy when he was sixteen years old and later served as ensign and marine hydrographer with Louis-Claude de Saulces de Freycinet during the latter's circumnavigation of the world aboard the *Uranie* from 1817 to 1820. Two years later, as captain of the corvette the *Coquille* and with Dumont d'Urville as his second in command taking responsibility for botany and entomology, he undertook another very successful expedition to the South Pacific from 1822 to 1825. Duperrey became in 1850 president of the Académie des Sciences (French Scientific Academy).

CHAPTER II

1. For the first time, a German appears in the story. There are not many German characters in Verne's *Voyages extraordinaires,* and they are most often evil (Herr Schultze of *The Begum's Millions*), sour-tempered (Baron Weissschnitzerdörfer of *Claudius Bombarnac*), or borderline insane (Dr. Johausen of *The Aerial Village*). Otto Lidenbrock of *Journey to the Center of the Earth* (published in 1864, several years before the Franco-Prussian War) and Mr. Zieger of *The Kip Brothers* (written about thirty years after the war) are among the very few exceptions to this rule.
2. In Mr. Zieger's name may lie a host of underlying meanings relating to the plot of *The Kip Brothers.* "Ziege" means goat in German, and a "Ziegenbock" is a billygoat. What was the name of the captain of the *Wilhelmina?* Roebok . . . "Bok" is billygoat in Dutch, "bouc" in French, "Bock" in German. As will soon become evident, the Kip brothers will become innocent scapegoats (in French: "boucs émissaires") for Captain Gibson's murder. Further, in ancient times, what was one of the main ceremonies during Yom Kippur? The sacrifice of a scapegoat. A scapegoat is "a goat upon whose head are symbolically placed the sins of the people after which he is sent into the wilderness in the biblical ceremony of Yom Kippur" (*Webster's New Collegiate Dictionary*). One might therefore argue that the subtext of Verne's novel is the story of a judicial error, in which a scapegoat (the "combined-in-one" Kip

brothers, or, better, Alfred Dreyfus) is found guilty and unjustly sentenced.

3. Slices of the betel nut (seeds from the betel palm, *Areca catechu*), together with lime paste and other flavorings, are sometimes smeared onto the leaf of a betel pepper plant (*Piper betle*) before chewing. Betel contains a narcotic stimulant. It has been cultivated and chewed throughout South Asia and Indonesia for hundreds of years.
4. Another touch of Verne's (occasionally risqué) humor.
5. This list recalls Conseil's similar enumerations of fish and seashells in *Twenty Thousand Leagues under the Seas*. Such noun lists in Verne's prose often seem to take on a life of their own. Legend has it that Apollinaire once said of Verne: "Quel style! Rien que des substantifs! (What a style! Nothing but nouns!)." In discussing this encyclopedic aspect of Verne's style, Andrew Martin has observed, "Grammar itself is subordinated to the demands of the noun, with the result that nominal enumeration (congeries, lists, inventories) becomes the privileged rhetorical mode" (*The Knowledge of Ignorance: From Genesis to Jules Verne* [Cambridge: Cambridge University Press, 1985], 150).

CHAPTER 12

1. Any drug or other agent that increases the flow of saliva. Comparing betel with opium and tobacco, Verne makes clear its addictive character.
2. The cuscus (in French "couscous") mentioned here by Verne is not a North African dish, but a marsupial found in Australia, Tasmania, the Solomon Islands, the Moluccas, and the Celebes. Cuscus range from about 6 to 26 inches long. Their tails are 17 to 24 inches long. They are arboreal animals, adapted for living or moving around in trees. Phalangers eat fruit, leaves, nectar, insects, and sometimes small birds. Cuscuses have dense, woolly fur and long tails. They live in hollow trees and carry their young in their pouches, like kangaroos.
3. It is interesting that Verne makes no distinction between Catholic or Protestant missionaries here. In other novels, such as *Propeller Island,* he praises the former and condemns the latter.
4. To increase the verisimilitude of his narratives (and increase their pedagogical authority), Verne sometimes includes direct quotes from an explorer's report. This particular quote is from Louis-Isidore Dup-

errey (see above n. 10 of chap. 10, part 1) and his five-volume work *Voyage autour du monde exécuté par ordre du Roi sur la corvette de Sa Majesté "la Coquille," pendant les années 1822, 1823, 1824 et 1825* (Paris: A. Bertrand,1825–30).

5. The myth of tailed men goes back to antiquity and probably before. Pliny the Elder (23–79) mentions the tailed men of Ceylon, and stories about others continued to be popular throughout the nineteenth century. Verne discusses tailed men in *Five Weeks in a Balloon* (chap. 19) and in *The Aerial Village* (chap. 1). For more information, see Alain Chevrier, "Le Mythe des hommes à queue chez Jules Verne" *Jules Verne* 28 (October-December 1993): 23–38.
6. Several small islands collectively called the Duke of York Islands. It's a group of thirteen coral islands with an area of 23 sq. mi. (60 sq km), in the Bismarck Archipelago. Containing several coconut plantations, Duke of York Island is the largest of the group, formerly called New Lauenburg.
7. The chapter finishes with a dramatic "coup de théâtre" ending. It is important to remember that *The Kip Brothers,* like many other novels in Verne's *Voyages extraordinaires,* was first published in serial format. To keep the reader in suspense (and to encourage them to purchase the next issue of *Magasin d'Education et de Récréation*), Verne often used this theatrical technique at the conclusion of his chapters.

CHAPTER 13

1. Captain Harry Gibson's death-stare will prove to be a crucial turning point in the denouement of the story.
2. During this murder scene, Jules Verne never uses the word "kriss." He refers all three times to a "poignard" (dagger). In French, the word "poignard" has a much more criminal connotation than the exotic word "kriss."
3. Note Verne's emphasis that the photograph of Harry Gibson's head was taken "with extreme precision" and that his "eyes were still wide open." As in any detective story, Verne leaves a series of clues for his readers.
4. It's a missionary who leads the service, and, somewhat curiously, he is Anglican in an island belonging to Germany.

CHAPTER 14

1. Today it is Makira Island, at the southeast end of the Solomon Islands.
2. A similar scene occurs in *The Children of Captain Grant* (part 3, chap. 14), when John Mangles takes over the *Macquarie* during a ferocious storm, saving the vessel and all aboard.
3. It should be 150<degree>17<prime> *east* longitude to be close to the Solomon Islands (not west), using the Paris meridian.
4. Tasmania, a province of Australia, is a temperate island located to the southeast of mainland Australia. It is about the size of Wales or Virginia. On its southeast coast is the Tasman Peninsula, which protects the estuary of the Derwent on its east side. Hobart (capital city of Tasmania) is at the mouth of the Derwent. The Tasman Peninsula, located east of Hobart, can be reached today by road; it is 97 km from Hobart to Port Arthur, an old penal settlement on the Tasman Peninsula. The coastline that surrounds the penal settlement is one of the most spectacular landscapes in Australia. It features tall cliffs up to over 1,000 feet high and was no doubt a fearsome sight for the convicts who were sent there and arrived by ship—a sight that reinforced their belief that it was truly the end of the world where escape would be impossible. Cape Pillar and Cape Raoul are the two capes located on the southern coast of the Tasman Peninsula (not of Tasmania, as Verne said). Cape Raoul is at the entrance of Storm Bay coming from the east (the direction of the *James Cook*), and Hobart is located at the back of Storm Bay.

PART TWO

CHAPTER 1

1. In Verne's original manuscript, the name is written correctly as "Marion," but it was misread by Hetzel's typesetters and published as "Manon"—Verne having no doubt overlooked this typo during his proofreading. Nicolas-Thomas (some sources say Marc-Joseph) Marion-Dufresne or Marion du Fresne (1724?–72) was a French navigator who discovered the Prince Edward Islands and the Crozet Islands. He also explored New Zealand, where he was killed and eaten by Maori natives on June 12, 1772. Verne is obviously mistaken here when he says Marion-Dufresne died in Tasmania—a slip that seems even more puz-

zling because, some twenty years earlier, he described in detail Marion-Dufresne's true story in his *The Great Navigators of the XVIIIth Century* (vol. 2 of *Great Voyages and Great Navigators*).

2. Today Hobart Town is called just Hobart.
3. The Bass Strait separates Tasmania from Australia.
4. As mentioned above, Verne normally uses the Paris meridian in his description of longitude. Here, his specific mention of "east of Greenwich" is exceptional.
5. In Verne's original manuscript this city is spelled correctly as Launceston. Again, Hetzel's typesetters misread this word, Verne did not notice their change of spelling during his proofing, and then it was published as Lanweeston. Launceston is located in the northern part of Tasmania.
6. The correct name is "Port Dalrymple." In his original manuscript, Verne wrote "Port-Dalrympe" with a question mark in parentheses.
7. Mr. Hawkins acts as a substitute father not only for Nat Gibson but also for the Kip brothers, recalling Verne's own relationship with his editor and publisher Hetzel père. In 1862, Verne first met Pierre-Jules Hetzel, and although they were only fourteen years apart in age, Verne immediately adopted a filial attitude toward him until Hetzel's death in 1886. In many ways, Verne found in Hetzel a "spiritual father" and a role model that the author could never find in his own father, a lawyer in Nantes. The theme of the "sublime father" is nearly omnipresent in Verne's works. It was first explored by Marcel Moré (see his *Le Très curieux Jules Verne: Le problème du père dans les "Voyages Extraordinaires"* [Paris, Gallimard, 1960]) and subsequently by many other Vernian scholars such Jean Chesneaux, Daniel Compère, Olivier Dumas, and Volker Dehs.

CHAPTER 2

1. In the previous chapter, Flig Balt, Len Cannon, and Kyle were arrested and thrown into prison where they were to be held until the day of their appearance before the maritime court. But now, Verne writes as if only Flig Balt and Len Cannon had been arrested. The editors and typesetters in Hetzel's publishing house, and Verne himself during his proofreading, appear to have overlooked this glaring inconsistency in the

story. It is probable that the error sneaked into the narrative in the following manner: while composing this early chapter of Part 2, Verne remembers that later in the story Kyle must be free to help Vin Mod with his nefarious plans to frame the Kip brothers for the crime. So, without bothering to check the details of what came before, he describes Kyle as still free and at large and only Balt and Cannon as inmates of the Hobart Town jail. Such plot oversights are very rare in Verne's novels. This one makes it quite clear that, toward the end of his life, Verne's mastery of his craft was beginning to slip a little.

2. In the Anglo-Saxon world, Ned is a common first name (e.g., the Yankee harpooner in Verne's *Twenty Thousand Leagues under the Seas* who was named Ned Land). Pat, however, is more often seen as a first name in English than a last name. In selecting this unusual alias—especially after having chosen the highly unusual monosyllabic names of Vin Mod and Flig Balt for his principal villains—one wonders if Verne is once again encoding a message in the names of these characters.
3. Arnemniden is yet another transcription error in the book (overlooked by Verne during his proofreading of the galleys); it should be written "Arnemuiden," as it appears in Verne's manuscript. Arnemuiden is a village in Zealand (a Dutch province), close to Middleburg. According to Dutch Verne scholar Garmt de Vries, Arnemuiden is not a family name, but could very well be the name of a company. "Skydnam" is not Dutch and appears to be a word invented by Verne. De Vries adds that "Skydnam" is an anagram of the Dutch name "Dykmans" or "Dijkmans." The captain of the *Skydnam* is Mr. Fork, which might suggest the Kip brothers will soon encounter a fork in the road of their lives—a place where they must decide which path to take.

CHAPTER 3

1. Nat "sees" his father before his eyes. As mentioned in the Introduction, perhaps more than any other novel in his *Voyages extraordinaires* (with the possible exception of *Michel Strogoff*), *The Kip Brothers* continually foregrounds the theme of vision, of seeing, of perceiving. And its surprise "ophthalmologic" denouement will further underscore this important thematic focus.
2. In French: "hors de lui et de chez lui" meaning "outside of himself and

outside of his home." A delightful play on words—nicely captured here in English—that is characteristic of Verne's witty humor.

CHAPTER 4

1. Another major turning point of the story. To be helpful later, Mr. Hawkins has to first change his mind about Flig Balt. Verne chooses to have him do it at the last minute.
2. Contrary to what Verne said earlier, Kyle is not described as having been arrested. See n. 1 of chapter 2, part 2.

CHAPTER 5

1. Focused on courtroom drama, judicial error, and an ongoing murder investigation, the second part of *The Kip Brothers* is thematically very different from the first. No travel here, no explanations of native customs, no lengthy nautical or geographical descriptions. The detective-story aspect of the novel has now taken center stage, and the plot moves forward at a rapid pace.
2. Flig Balt now tells his side of the story. The moral repugnance one feels when reading Flig Balt's bald-faced lies is reinforced by the date of December 25. The supposedly deus ex machina nature of Balt's (false) discovery on this day of Christian miracles—as if Providence had had a hand in helping him to see the contents of the Kips' valise (a ploy calculated to appeal to the public's religious sensitivities)—is particularly reprehensible.
3. Here begin Mr. Hawkins's patient and long-suffering efforts to prove the innocence of the Kip brothers—despite the pressures of family and friends, despite the concrete evidence to the contrary, and despite the court's official judgment.

CHAPTER 6

1. The French text ("coupables ou non coupables") includes a footnote here: "*Guilty or not guilty.*" Jules Verne, who as a young man earned a law degree in 1850, wanted his French readers to realize that the judicial system in British countries is very different from the French one inherited from the "code Napoléon."

2. As mentioned, there is some evidence to suggest that Verne's portrayal of the Kip brothers might have been based not only on the popular story of the Rorique brothers (who were convicted of murder and piracy and sent to prison) but also on that other famous example of "judicial error," the case of Captain Alfred Dreyfus. Dreyfus was not immediately sentenced to death, however, but was deported and condemned to life in prison at Devil's Island in French Guyana on December 19, 1894.

CHAPTER 7

1. Verne's comments here about the "egotism" of the British and their extreme ethnocentrism may well have contributed to why this novel was never translated into English. See Brian Taves, "Jules Verne: An Interpretation," in *The Jules Verne Encyclopedia,* ed. Brian Taves and Stephen Michaluk Jr. (Lanham, Md.: Scarecrow Press, 1996), 16. For more on the ideological and political censorship in Verne's English translations, see Arthur B. Evans, "Jules Verne's English Translations," *Science Fiction Studies* 32.1 (March 2005): 91–96.
2. At the time when he was condemned to life imprisonment on Devil's Island in 1894, Alfred Dreyfus was considered guilty by almost everybody. It was not until his case was contested from within the military by the new chief of Army Intelligence, Georges Picquart, in 1896 and from without by Emile Zola in his famous "I Accuse!" editorial in 1898 that the French public became polarized over the question of Dreyfus's guilt or innocence. Similar to Mr. Hawkins, Dreyfus's brother Mathieu believed in his innocence and did everything he could to get a new trial and have the original verdict overturned. It was not until 1906 that Dreyfus was finally cleared of all charged and reinstated in the French military.
3. The family name of Carrigan is quite common in Tasmania.
4. Although not necessarily against the death penalty per se, Verne finds the practice of public executions to be both unnecessary and uncivilized. And it is interesting to note that his disapproval is not limited to those performed by the British but by the French, Italian, and Spanish as well. France abolished capital punishment only in 1947.

CHAPTER 8

1. There are many similarities between the prisons at Port Arthur and Alcatraz. Both were used as penitentiaries and are now tourist attractions. Both are close to a big city, Hobart and San Francisco, respectively. Both are on an island or a near-island (peninsula). And both had the reputation of being especially harsh and impossible to escape from. The Port Arthur penal settlement began as a timber sawing station in 1830. When coal was discovered on the Tasman Peninsula, chain gangs of convicts were used to provide the raw materials for a growing town. The prison at Port Arthur quickly grew in importance within the penal system of the British colonies, and over 12,500 prisoners from England and Australia passed through its doors between 1830 and the 1860s. In the 1870s, the penal settlement began to enter its final years. The numbers of convicts dwindled, and the last convict was shipped out in 1877. Almost immediately the site was renamed Carnarvon, and, during the 1880s, the land was subdivided and put up for auction, with private citizens taking up residence in and around the old prison. By the 1920s and 1930s, the Port Arthur area was home to several hotels and museums, and its primary economic base became tourism. Today it is one of the most visited historic sites in Tasmania.
2. Botany Bay is located in Sydney, Australia. Aboard the *Endeavor,* Captain James Cook was the first European to visit the bay in 1770, naming it Stingray Harbour. The botanist Sir Joseph Banks, who accompanied Cook and was impressed with the many species of new plants growing in this area, had it renamed Botany Bay and recommended it to the British government as the site for a colony. Captain Arthur Philip arrived in 1788 to found a penal colony there but, because of its poor soil, moved nearby and settled along the banks of Sydney Harbour instead. Although its actual location was in Sydney, the penal colony was still referred to as Botany Bay during most of the nineteenth century.
3. The correct spelling is "Bowen." Verne's original manuscript has "Bowen," but the "e" looks like an "i" at first glance—which no doubt created, once again, a transcription error in all the French editions. John Bowen (1780–1827), lieutenant of the Royal Navy, established the first-ever British settlement in Tasmania (then called Van Diemen's Land). He arrived with 48 colonists aboard the vessels *Lady Nelson* and

Albion and settled at Risdon Cove on September 12, 1803. With its poor soil and lack of fresh water, the site was badly chosen, and the settlement struggled. In February of the following year, Captain David Collins established an alternative settlement in Sullivan's Cove (the present site of Hobart), and the site at Risdon Cove was eventually abandoned. As its first colonist, John Bowen might be justifiably described as the founder of Tasmania. Although Tasmania was discovered in November 1642 by the Dutch explorer Abel Janszoon Tasman, it was not until 161 years later that the British decided to settle the island—mostly out of fear that the French would do so before them.

4. The correct spelling is "Risdon," and in Verne's manuscript it is written as "Risdon" (another uncorrected transcription error). Risdon Cove was declared an Indigenous Protected Area in July 1999. Its area of 109 hectares is managed by the Tasmanian Aboriginal Centre.
5. In describing the British penal system, Verne clearly indicates his source: the logs of Dumont d'Urville's visit to Tasmania in 1839–40. Tasmania was the French explorer's departure point for his third attempt to reach the Antarctic mainland. See Jules Sébastien César Dumont d'Urville, *Voyage au pôle sud et dans l'Océanie* (Paris: Gide, 1856).
6. At this point in his manuscript and in the published French editions, Verne inserts a footnote stating, "Actuellement, Port-Arthur est désaffecté et l'établissement pénal n'existe plus en Tasmanie" (Currently, Port Arthur is closed down and the penitentiary no longer exists in Tasmania). Port Arthur went out of service in 1877, and the Kip brothers are supposedly transferred to the penitentiary at the end of March 1886. Verne included this footnote in his text to show his readers that this "time discrepancy" was done on purpose, that it was not due to lack of information or documentation. For the fictional story to work, it was necessary to have the Port Arthur penitentiary still in existence. Two similarly footnoted "time discrepancies" can be found in the third book of the Vernian trilogy of *The Children of Captain Grant, Twenty Thousand Leagues under the Seas,* and *The Mysterious Island.* The first appears when Ayrton tells his story (referring to *The Children of Captain Grant*), and the second appears when Captain Nemo is dying (referring to *Twenty Thousand Leagues under the Seas*).
7. Verne's manuscript also incorrectly spells this as "Panbroke" instead of

"Pembroke." Pembroke County is east of Hobart, north of the Tasman Peninsula.

8. Skirtle is the anagram of "Le Krist" (Christ); the Kip brothers will be "saved" in prison by Mr. Skirtle. For a discussion of this and many other religious (and political) undertones running through the novel, see Christian Porcq, "Cataclysme dans la cathédrale, ou le secret des *Frères Kip*," *Bulletin de la Société Jules Verne* 107 and 109 (July–September 1993, January–March 1994): 35–52, 36–51.
9. The small peninsula of Point Puer (Latin for "boy") across from the Port Arthur prison was, in fact, the site of a boys' correctional facility between 1834 and 1849, the only one outside Britain in the British Empire. Over two thousand young men passed through this facility during the fifteen years of its existence.
10. "Here, covered by the muskets of their jailers, prisoners were clad in the coarse, ugly, yellow dress, marked in black with broad arrows, which was the distinctive and detested garb of the incorrigible class of offenders." Ernst Scott, *A Short History of Australia,* London: Oxford University Press, 1937. Available online at <<http://www.nalanda.nitc.ac.in/resources/english/etext-project/history/aust_hist/chapter20.html>>.
11. In English in the French text.
12. "Cat" in the French text. Used by the British navy to maintain discipline on board sailing ships during the nineteenth century, the dreaded cat-o'-nine-tails was a round wooden baton approximately 18 inches long to which was attached nine lengths of line or cord (tails) 24 inches long, each of which was knotted 3 times at approximately 2-inch intervals, and the tips of which were bound with thread to prevent fraying.

CHAPTER 9

1. The novels of Verne's *Voyages extraordinaires* often celebrate brotherhood. In *Family without a Name,* Johann takes the place of his brother Jean in prison and is executed in his place. In the *Sphinx of the Ice,* Len Guy, captain of the *Halbrane,* is searching for his brother William Guy, captain of the *Jane,* who disappeared with Arthur Gordon Pym in Edgar Allan Poe's unfinished novel. Less dramatic but still as strong is the brotherly love between Jacques and Briant in *Two Years Vacation* or

between Marc and Henri Vidal in *The Secret of Wilhelm Storitz*. Even if the brothers are villains, their fraternal love makes them more human, like the Texar brothers in *North against South* or Balao Rao and Nana Sahib in *The Steamhouse*. The brotherly rapport can even be humorous, as is that between Sab and Sib Melville in *The Green Ray*.

2. There were several retrials during the Dreyfus Affair, but none during the Rorique Affair—yet another indication that Verne, while citing the latter as his primary source, may have also woven many aspects of the former into the storyline of *The Kip Brothers*.

CHAPTER 10

1. A secret organization, consisting mainly of Irishmen. The Fenian Brotherhood was actually founded in the United States in 1858 by James O'Mahony, Michael Doheny, and James Stephens to help gain Irish American support for armed rebellion in Ireland. O'Mahony ran operations in the United States, and Stephens was in charge of Ireland. The movement also became known as the Irish Republican Brotherhood in Ireland, and as Clan na Gael in the United States, but by the 1870s it had virtually died out. A member of the Irish Republican Brotherhood, Arthur Griffith, eventually founded the Irish nationalist party Sinn Fein in 1905. The term "Fenian" derives from the Irish *Na Fianna* or *Na Fianna Éireann,* which in Celtic mythology were a band of warriors formed to protect Ireland (see <<http://en.wikipedia.org/wiki/Fenians>>).
2. Daniel O'Connell (1775–1847), known as "the Liberator," is considered Ireland's most important political leader in the first half of the nineteenth century. As an attorney—and later mayor—of Dublin, he championed the rights of Irish Catholics and worked to repeal British laws that discriminated against them. He organized the Catholic Association, which helped to pass the Catholic Emancipation Act in 1829. That same year he was elected to the British House of Commons, where he campaigned for Irish independence and the repeal of the 1801 Act of Union forming the United Kingdom. Today O'Connell is remembered mostly as the founder of a nonviolent form of Irish nationalism and for having mobilized the Catholic community of Ireland into an effective political force.

3. Written in 1891 and published in 1893, *Lit'l Fellow* (*P'tit Bonhomme*) is one of Verne's more socially conscious novels and focuses on the horrid conditions in British orphanages in Ireland. In general, Verne's attitudes toward the British (and Americans) evolved from his early novels to his later ones. His open admiration of their courage, inventiveness, individualism, and no-nonsense character—visible in such heroes as Samuel Fergusson of *Five Weeks in a Balloon,* John Hatteras of *The Adventures of Captain Hatteras,* or Phileas Fogg of *Around the World in Eighty Days*—gradually changed into a condemnation of their political imperialism, capitalist greed, and narrow-mindedness in many of his works published in the1880s and 1890s. Consider, for example, the egotistical and contemptuous Sir Francis Trevellyan (of Trevellyan Hall of Trevellyanshire) of *Claudius Bombarnac* (1892), who incarnates his nation's contempt for other countries, or Sir Edward Turner in *Caesar Cascabel* (1890), who is described as "a haughty and arrogant bully, very infatuated with his nationality, one of these 'gentlemen' who believe themselves entitled to everything just because they are English" (chapter 8).
4. Sources about Ireland used by Jules Verne for *Lit'l Fellow* and portions of *The Kip Brothers* are discussed in Brian E. Rainey, "Jules Verne and Ireland," *Proceedings of the Annual Meeting of the Western Society for French History (Canada)* 10 (1984): 151–59.

CHAPTER 11

1. Storm Bay being west of the Tasman Peninsula, Saint James Point would actually be east of Storm Bay.

CHAPTER 12

1. The Tasman Peninsula has a surface area of 520 square kilometers, and its highest point is Mount Koonya, at 488 meters above sea level. At the time of this story, most of the peninsula was covered by forests.
2. The coasts of the Tasman Peninsula are quite spectacular. Parts of the west coast (facing Storm Bay) and the south coast near Cape Raoul and Cape Pillar feature basalt columns and vertical cliffs plunging into the ocean from a height of 300 to 400 meters.

CHAPTER 13

1. Notice how Verne builds and maintains the suspense throughout this dramatic scene and how he shifts the narrative point of view—from the fugitives, to the guards, and now to the Kip brothers.
2. A lifelong dog lover, Verne frequently included sympathetic portrayals of "man's best friend" in his novels. Note, for instance, the "dog-captain" Duk of *The Adventures of Captain Hatteras*, the brave and resourceful Top of *The Mysterious Island*, the astronaut dogs Diane and Satellite in *From the Earth to the Moon*, and the super-intelligent Dingo of *A Captain of Fifteen* who, following his feats of spelling with lettered blocks, is dubbed "canis alphabeticus." But Verne's positive portrayal of such socialized animals contrasts sharply with his depiction of non-domesticated animals, and especially those viewed as dangerous to humans. Such "wild beasts" are fit only to be hunted down and exterminated, as occurs with the jaguars of *The Mysterious Island*, the tigers of India in *The Steam House*, or the lions of *Five Weeks in a Balloon* or *Propeller Island*, among many others. The ferocious mastiffs of *The Kip Brothers*, are clearly of the latter category.

CHAPTER 14

1. Lloyd's of London, the famous British insurer. It was started in Edward Lloyd's coffeehouse in London around 1688. Ship captains, merchants, and shipowners often convened there to discuss maritime news and negotiate insurance deals. In 1871, the first Lloyd's Act was passed by the British Parliament, giving official sanction to the company. Lloyd's is the oldest insurance provider in the world and has been, since the eighteenth century, a source of reliable and up-to-date information on all internationally shipped cargoes.

CHAPTER 15

1. During Verne's time, it was commonly believed that the retina would act as a photographic plate at the time of death and would record the last image seen by the dying person. Even Scotland Yard, in its investigation of the Jack the Ripper murders in London in 1888, pried open Annie Chapman's dead eyes and photographed them, hoping to see an image of the murderer therein. For a history of this belief as well as how

it appeared in various literary and cinematic works of the nineteenth and twentieth centuries, see Arthur B. Evans, "Optograms and Fiction: Photo in a Dead Man's Eye," *Science Fiction Studies* 20.3 (November 1993): 341–61, available online at <<http://jv.gilead.org.il/evans/optogram.html>>.

CHAPTER 16

1. Verne's error here lies in his use of the phrase "conserved there indefinitely." In truth, the retina does not act as a permanent photographic plate: the light-sensitive "retinal purple" (rhodopsin) he refers to is continually renewed and the old layers simultaneously erased. Such "fixing of images" would require a highly unlikely sequence of events. Ideally, the victim would need to have been in a low-light environment (maximizing the amount of rhodopsin on the retina), to have stared at something bright at the moment of death, and then to have immediately closed his eyes, allowing no further light to enter them. Then his eyes would have to be quickly excised from his body (preferably in a darkened room), and the retinal tissue carefully removed and bathed in an alum solution. Even under these near-perfect conditions, the image produced would be extremely crude. It is likely that Verne understood these facts but decided nevertheless to use this interesting piece of new ophthalmologic science to provide a believable "surprise ending" to his tale.

BIBLIOGRAPHY

Works of Jules Verne

All works were published in Paris by Pierre-Jules Hetzel unless otherwise indicated. Most novels by Verne were first published in serial format in Hetzel's *Magasin d'Education et de Récréation,* then as octodecimo books (normally unillustrated), and finally as octavo illustrated "luxury" editions in red and gold. The date given is that of the first book publication. Many entries have been gleaned from the excellent bibliographical studies of Volker Dehs and Jean-Michel Margot, François Raymond, Olivier Dumas, Edward Gallagher, Judith A. Mistichelli, and John A. Van Eerde, and especially those of Piero Gondolo della Riva and Brian Taves and Stephen Michaluk Jr.

Works in the Series *Voyages extraordinaires* (Extraordinary Voyages)

Novels marked by an asterisk were published after Jules Verne's death in 1905. It is important to understand that most of these post-1905 works were either substantially revamped or, in some cases, almost totally written by Jules Verne's son, Michel. For each novel listed, information about its first English-language edition is provided (date of publication, publisher, and translator) as well as the alternate English titles sometimes used. Also included are recommendations about the translation quality of certain English-language editions.

Cinq semaines en ballon (1863, illus. Edouard Riou and Henri de Montaut). *Five Weeks in a Balloon* (1869, New York: Appleton, trans. William Lackland). Recommended: translation by William Lackland. Not recommended: Chapman and Hall edition (rpt. 1995, Sutton "Pocket Classics"), the Routledge edition (rpt. 1911, Parke), and translations by Arthur Chambers (1926, Dutton; rpt. 1996, Wordsworth Classics) and by I. O. Evans (1958, Hanison, "Fitzroy Edition").

Voyage au centre de la terre (1864, illus. Edouard Riou). *A Journey to the Centre of the Earth* (1871, Griffith and Farran, translator unknown). Alternate titles: *A Journey to the Interior of the Earth, Journey to the Center of the Earth*. Recommended: translations by Robert Baldick (1965, Penguin, *Journey to the Center of the Earth*) and by William Butcher (1992, Oxford University Press, *Journey to the Centre of the Earth*). Not recommended: all reprints of the Griffith and Farran ("Hardwigg") edition, which begin "Looking back to all that has occurred to me since that eventful day . . ." (1965, Airmont; 1986, Signet Classics; 1992, Tor; among many others).

De la terre à la lune (1865, illus. Henri de Montaut). *From the Earth to the Moon* (1867, Gage, translator unknown). Alternate titles: *From the Earth to the Moon Direct, in Ninety-seven Hours Twenty Minutes; The Baltimore Gun Club; The American Gun Club; The Moon Voyage*. Recommended: translations by Harold Salemson (1970, Heritage, *From the Earth to the Moon*) and by Walter James Miller (1978, Crowell, *The Annotated Jules Verne: From the Earth to the Moon*). Not recommended: translations by Louis Mercier and Eleanor King (1873, Sampson Low, *From the Earth to the Moon Direct, in Ninety-seven Hours Twenty Minutes;* rpt. 1967, Airmont; 1983, Avenel; among many others), by Edward Roth (1874, King and Baird, *The Baltimore Gun Club;* rpt. 1962, Dover), and by Lowell Bair (1967, Bantam, *From the Earth to the Moon*).

Voyages et aventures du capitaine Hatteras (1866, illus. Edouard Riou and Henri de Montaut). *At the North Pole: The Voyages and Adventures of Captain Hatteras* and *The Desert of Ice: The Voyages and Adventures of Captain Hatteras* (1874–75, Osgood, translator unknown). Alternate titles: *The English at the North Pole* and *The Field of Ice, The Adventures of Captain Hatteras*. Recommended: translation by William Butcher (2005, Oxford University Press, *The Adventures of Captain Hatteras*) and the Osgood edition (rpt. 1976, Aeonian). Not recommended: I. O. Evans "Fitzroy Edition" translation (1961, *The Adventures of Captain Hatteras: At the North Pole* and *The Adventures of Captain Hatteras: The Wilderness of Ice*).

Les Enfants du capitaine Grant (1867–68, illus. Edouard Riou). *In Search of the Castaways* (1873, Lippincott, translator unknown). Alternate titles: *The Mysterious Document/On the Track/Among the Cannibals;*

The Castaways, or A Voyage around the World; Captain Grant's Children. Recommended: Routledge edition (1876, translator unknown, *Voyage Round the World: South America/Australia/New Zealand*). Not recommended: the Lippincott edition or the I. O. Evans "Fitzroy Edition" translation (1964, Arco, *The Children of Captain Grant: The Mysterious Document* and *The Children of Captain Grant: Among the Cannibals*).

Vingt mille lieues sous les mers (1869–70, illus. Edouard Riou and Alphonse-Marie de Neuville). *Twenty Thousand Leagues under the Seas* (1872, Sampson Low, trans. Louis Mercier). Alternate titles: *Twenty Thousand Leagues under the Sea; 20,000 Leagues under the Sea; At the Bottom of the Deep, Deep Sea.* Recommended: translations by Walter James Miller and Frederick Paul Walter (1993, Naval Institute Press, *Jules Verne's Twenty Thousand Leagues under the Sea*) and by William Butcher (1998, Oxford University Press, *Twenty Thousand Leagues under the Seas*). Not recommended: translation by Louis Mercier cited above (rpt. 1963, Airmont; 1981, Castle; 1995, Tor; among many others).

Autour de la lune (1870, illus. Emile-Antoine Bayard and Alphonse-Marie de Neuville). *Round the Moon* (1873, Sampson Low, trans. Louis Mercier and Eleanor King). Alternate titles: *All Around the Moon, Around the Moon, A Moon Voyage.* Recommended: translations by Jacqueline and Robert Baldick (1970, Dent, *Around the Moon*) and by Harold Salemson (1970, Heritage, *Around the Moon*). Not recommended: translations by Louis Mercier and Eleanor King (cited above) and by Edward Roth (1874, Catholic, *All Around the Moon;* rpt. 1962, Dover).

Une Ville flottante (1871, illus. Jules-Descartes Férat). *A Floating City* (1874, Sampson Low, translator unknown). Alternate title: *The Floating City.* Recommended: translation by Henry Frith (1876, Routledge, *The Floating City*). Not recommended: I. O. Evans "Fitzroy Edition" translation (1958, Hanison, *A Floating City*).

Aventures de trois Russes et de trois Anglais (1872, illus. Jules-Descartes Férat). *Meridiana: The Adventures of Three Englishmen and Three Russians in South Africa* (1872, Sampson Low, trans. Ellen E. Frewer). Alternate titles: *Adventures of Three Englishmen and Three Russians in*

Southern Africa, Adventures in the Land of the Behemoth, Measuring a Meridian. Recommended: translation by Henry Frith (1877, Routledge, *Adventures of Three Englishmen and Three Russians in Southern Africa*). Not recommended: Shepard edition (1874, translator unknown, *Adventures in the Land of the Behemoth*) and I. O. Evans "Fitzroy Edition" translation (1964, Arco, *Measuring a Meridian*).

Le Pays des fourrures (1873, illus. Jules-Descartes Férat and Alfred Quesnay de Beaurepaire). *The Fur Country* (1873, Sampson Low, trans. N. D'Anvers). Alternate title: *Sun in Eclipse/Through the Behring Strait.* Recommended: translation by Edward Baxter (1987, NC Press, *The Fur Country*). Not recommended: I. O. Evans "Fitzroy Edition" (1966, Arco, *The Fur Country: Sun in Eclipse* and *The Fur Country: Through the Behring Strait*).

Le Tour du monde en quatre-vingts jours (1873, illus. Alphonse-Marie de Neuville and Léon Benett). *A Tour of the World in Eighty Days* (1873, Osgood, trans. George M. Towle). Alternate titles: *The Tour of the World in Eighty Days, Around the World in Eighty Days, Around the World in 80 Days, Round the World in Eighty Days.* Recommended: translation by William Butcher (1995, Oxford University Press, *Around the World in Eighty Days*). Not recommended: translations by Lewis Mercier (1962, Collier/Doubleday) and by K. E. Lichtenecker (1965, Hamlyn).

Le Docteur Ox (1874, illus. Lorenz Froelich, Théophile Schuler, Emile-Antoine Bayard, Adrien Marie, Edmond Yon, and Antoine Bertrand). *Doctor Ox* (1874, Osgood, trans. George M. Towle). Short story collection. Alternate titles: *From the Clouds to the Mountains, A Fancy of Doctor Ox, Dr. Ox and Other Stories, Dr. Ox's Experiment and Other Stories, A Winter amid the Ice and Other Stories, A Winter amid the Ice and Other Thrilling Tales.* Collection contains the following short stories and nonfiction: "Une Fantaisie du docteur Ox" (Doctor Ox), "Maître Zacharius" (Master Zacharius), "Un Hivernage dans les glaces" (A Winter amid the Ice), "Un Drame dans les airs" (A Drama in the Air), and "Quarantième ascension du Mont-Blanc" (Fortieth Ascent of Mont Blanc, written by Verne's brother, Paul). Recommended: translation by Towle cited above. Not recommended: translation by Abby L. Alger (1874, Gill, *From the Clouds to the Mountains*) and I.

O. Evans "Fitzroy Edition" translation (1964, Arco, *Dr. Ox and Other Stories*).

L'Ile mystérieuse (1874–75, illus. Jules-Descartes Férat). *The Mysterious Island: Dropped from the Clouds/The Abandoned/The Secret of the Island* (1875, Sampson Low, trans. W. H. G. Kingston). Alternate titles: *The Mysterious Island: Dropped from the Clouds/Marooned/Secret of the Island; Mysterious Island.* Recommended: translations by Sidney Kravitz (2001, Wesleyan University Press) and by Jordon Stump (2001, Modern Library).

Le Chancellor (1875, illus. Edouard Riou and Jules-Descartes Férat). *The Wreck of the Chancellor* (1875, Osgood, trans. George M. Towle). Alternate titles: *The Survivors of the Chancellor, The Chancellor.* Recommended: translation by Towle cited above. Not recommended: I. O. Evans "Fitzroy Edition" translation (1965, Arco, *The Chancellor*).

Michel Strogoff (1876, illus. Jules-Descartes Férat). *Michael Strogoff* (1876, Leslie, trans. E. G. Walraven). Alternate titles: *Michael Strogoff: From Moscow to Irkoutsk; Michael Strogoff, or the Russian Courier; Michael Strogoff, or the Courier of the Czar.* Recommended: translation by Kingston as "revised" by Julius Chambers (1876, Sampson Low).

Hector Servadac (1877, illus. Paul Philippoteaux). *Hector Servadac* (1877, Sampson Low, trans. Ellen E. Frewer). Alternate titles: *To the Sun?* and *Off on a Comet!; Hector Servadac: Travels and Adventures through the Solar System; Anomalous Phenomena/Homeward Bound; Astounding Adventures among the Comets.* Recommended: Frewer translation cited above. Not recommended: translations by Edward Roth (1877–78, Claxton et al., *To the Sun?* and *Off on a Comet!;* rpt. 1960, Dover) and by I. O. Evans (1965, Arco, *Hector Servadac: Anomalous Phenomena* and *Hector Servadac: Homeward Bound*).

Les Indes noires (1877, illus. Jules-Descartes Férat). *The Black Indies* (1877, Munro, translator unknown). Alternate titles: *The Child of the Cavern, The Underground City, Black Diamonds.* Recommended: translation by W. H. G. Kingston (1877, Sampson Low, *The Child of the Cavern*). Not recommended: I. O. Evans "Fitzroy Edition" translation (1961, Arco, *Black Diamonds*).

Un Capitaine de quinze ans (1878, illus. Henri Meyer). *Dick Sand; or a*

Captain at Fifteen (1878, Munro, translator unknown). Alternate titles: *Dick Sands, The Boy Captain, A Fifteen Year Old Captain, Captain at Fifteen.* Recommended: Munro edition cited above. Not recommended: translation by Forlag (1976, Abelard-Schuman, *Captain at Fifteen*).

Les Cinq cents millions de la Bégum (1879, illus. Léon Benett). *The 500 Millions of the Begum* (1879, Munro, translator unknown). Alternate titles: *The Begum's Fortune, The Begum's Millions, The Five Hundred Millions of the Begum.* Recommended: Stanford Luce translation (2005, Wesleyan University Press, *The Begum's Millions*). Not recommended: Munro edition cited above, W. H. G. Kingston translation (1879, Sampson Low, *The Begum's Fortune*), and I. O. Evans "Fitzroy Edition" translation (1958, Hanison/Arco, *The Begum's Fortune*).

Les Tribulations d'un Chinois en Chine (1879, illus. Léon Benett). *The Tribulations of a Chinaman in China* (1879, Lee and Shepard, trans. Virginia Champlin [Grace Virginia Lord]). Alternate titles: *The Tribulations of a Chinese Gentleman, The Tribulations of a Chinaman.* Recommended: translation by Champlin cited above. Not recommended: I. O. Evans "Fitzroy Edition" translation (1963, Arco, *The Tribulations of a Chinese Gentleman*).

La Maison à vapeur (1880, illus. Léon Benett). *The Steam House, or A Trip across Northern India* (1880, Munro, trans. James Cotterell). Alternate titles: *The Steam House, The Demon of Cawnpore/Tigers and Traitors.* Recommended: translation by Agnes D. Kingston (1880, Sampson Low, *The Steam House*). Not recommended: I. O. Evans "Fitzroy Edition" translation (1959, Hanison, *The Steam House: The Demon of Cawnpore* and *The Steam House: Tigers and Traitors.*

La Jangada (1881, illus. Léon Benett and Edouard Riou). *The Jangada, or 800 Leagues over the Amazon* (1881, Munro, trans. James Cotterell). Alternate titles: *The Giant Raft, The Jangada, The Giant Raft: Down the Amazon/The Cryptogram.* Recommended: translation by W. J. Gordon (1881–82, Sampson Low, *The Giant Raft*). Not recommended: I. O. Evans "Fitzroy Edition" translation (1967, Arco, *The Giant Raft: Down the Amazon* and *The Giant Raft: The Cryptogram*).

Le Rayon vert (1882, illus. Léon Benett). *The Green Ray* (1883, Munro, trans. James Cotterell). Recommended: translation by Mary de Hautville (1883, Sampson Low, *The Green Ray*).

L'Ecole des Robinsons (1882, illus. Léon Benett). *Robinson's School* (1883, Munro, trans. James Cotterell). Alternate titles: *Godfrey Morgan: A California Mystery, An American Robinson Crusoe, The School for Crusoes*. Recommended: translation by J. C. Curtin (1883, Redpath's Weekly, *An American Robinson Crusoe*). Not recommended: I. O. Evans "Fitzroy Edition" translation (1966, Arco, *The School for Crusoes*).

Kéraban-le-têtu (1883, illus. Léon Benett). *The Headstrong Turk* (1883–84, Munro, trans. James Cotterell). Alternate titles: *Kéraban the Inflexible: The Captain of the Guidara* and *Kéraban the Inflexible: Scarpante, the Spy*. Recommended: translation by J. C. Curtin (1883, Redpath's Weekly, *The Headstrong Turk*).

L'Archipel en feu (1884, illus. Léon Benett). *Archipelago on Fire* (1885, Munro, translator unknown). Alternate title: *The Archipelago on Fire*. Recommended: Sampson Low edition (1885, translator unknown).

L'Etoile du sud (1884, illus. Léon Benett). *The Southern Star* (1885, Munro, translator unknown). Alternate titles: The *Vanished Diamond: A Tale of South Africa, The Southern Star Mystery, The Star of the South*. Recommended: translation by Stephen Gray (2003, Protea Book House, *The Star of the South*). Not recommended: I. O. Evans "Fitzroy Edition" translation (1966, Arco, *The Southern Star Mystery*).

Mathias Sandorf (1885, illus. Léon Benett). *Mathias Sandorf* (1885, Munro, trans. G. W. Hanna).

L'Epave du Cynthia (1885, illus. George Roux). *Waif of the "Cynthia"* (1885, Munro, translator unknown). Alternate title: *Salvage from the Cynthia*. Recommended: Munro edition cited above. Not recommended: I. O. Evans "Fitzroy Edition" translation (1964, Arco, *Salvage from the Cynthia*).

Robur-le-conquérant (1886, illus. Léon Benett). *Robur the Conqueror* (1887, Munro, translator unknown). Alternate titles: *The Clipper of the Clouds, A Trip round the World in a Flying Machine*. Recommended: the Sampson Low edition (1887, trans. anon., *The Clipper of the Clouds*). Not recommended: the Munro edition cited above and the I. O. Evans "Fitzroy Edition" translation (1962, Arco, *The Clipper of the Clouds*).

Un Billet de loterie (1886, illus. George Roux). *Ticket No. "9672"* (1886, Munro, trans. Laura E. Kendall). Alternate title: *The Lottery Ticket*. Recommended: translation by Kendall.

Le Chemin de France (1887, illus. George Roux). *The Flight to France, or The Memoirs of a Dragoon* (1888, Sampson Low, translator unknown).

Nord contre Sud (1887, illus. Léon Benett). *Texar's Vengeance, or North versus South* (1887, Munro, translator unknown). Alternate titles: *Texar's Revenge, or North against South; North against South: A Tale of the American Civil War; North against South: Burbank the Northerner/Texar the Southerner.* Recommended: Sampson Low edition (1887, trans. anon., *Texar's Revenge, or North against South*). Not recommended: I. O. Evans "Fitzroy Edition" translation (1965, Arco, *North against South: Burbank the Northerner* and *North against South: Texar the Southerner*).

Deux ans de vacances (1888, illus. Léon Benett). *A Two Years' Vacation* (1889, Munro, translator unknown). Alternate titles: *Adrift in the Pacific; Adrift in the Pacific/Second Year Ashore; Two Years' Holiday; A Long Vacation.* Recommended: Munro edition cited above. Not recommended: I. O. Evans "Fitzroy Edition" translation (1965, Arco, *Two Years' Holiday: Adrift in the Pacific* and *Two Years' Holiday: Second Year Ashore*) and translation by Olga Marx (1967, Holt, Rinehart and Winston, *A Long Vacation*).

Sans dessus dessous (1889, illus. George Roux). *The Purchase of the North Pole* (1890, Sampson Low, translator unknown). Alternate title: *Topsy-Turvy.* Recommended: Sampson Low edition cited above. Not recommended: Ogilvie edition (1890, trans. anon., *Topsy-Turvy*) and I. O. Evans "Fitzroy Edition" translation (1966, Arco, *The Purchase of the North Pole*).

Famille-sans-nom (1889, illus. Georges Tiret-Bognet). *A Family without a Name* (1889, Munro, Lovell, translator unknown). Alternate titles: *A Family without a Name: Leader of the Resistance/Into the Abyss; Family without a Name.* Recommended: translation by Edward Baxter (1982, NC Press, *Family without a Name*). Not recommended: I. O. Evans "Fitzroy Edition" translation (1963, Arco, *Family without a Name: Leader of the Resistance* and *Family without a Name: Into the Abyss*).

César Cascabel (1890, illus. George Roux). *Caesar Cascabel* (1890, Cassell, trans. A. Estoclet). Alternate title: *The Travelling Circus/The Show on Ice.* Recommended: translation by Estoclet cited above. Not recommended: I. O. Evans "Fitzroy Edition" translation (1970, Arco,

César Cascabel: The Travelling Circus and *César Cascabel: The Show on Ice*).

Mistress Branican (1891, illus. Léon Benett). *Mistress Branican* (1891, Cassell, trans. A. Estoclet). Alternate titles: *Mystery of the Franklin, The Wreck of the Franklin*. Recommended: translation by Estoclet cited above.

Le Château des Carpathes (1892, illus. Léon Benett). *The Castle of the Carpathians* (1893, Sampson Low, translator unknown). Alternate title: *Carpathian Castle*. Recommended: Sampson Low edition cited above. Not recommended: I. O. Evans "Fitzroy Edition" translation (1963, Arco, *Carpathian Castle*).

Claudius Bombarnac (1893, illus. Léon Benett). *The Special Correspondent, or The Adventures of Claudius Bombarnac* (1894, Lovell, translator unknown). Alternate title: *Claudius Bombarnac* (same translation).

P'tit-Bonhomme (1893, illus. Léon Benett). *Foundling Mick* (1895, Sampson Low, translator unknown). A more accurate translation of this title would be *Lit'l Fellow*.

Mirifiques aventures de Maître Antifer (1894, illus. George Roux). *Captain Antifer* (1895, Sampson Low, translator unknown).

L'Ile à hélice (1895, illus. Léon Benett). *The Floating Island* (1896, Sampson Low, trans. W. J. Gordon; rpt. 1990, Kegan Paul). Alternate title: *Propeller Island*. Recommended: none.

Face au drapeau (1896, illus. Léon Benett). *Facing the Flag* (1897, Neely, translator unknown). Alternate titles: *For the Flag, Simon Hart: A Strange Story of Science and the Sea*. Recommended: Cashel Hoey translation (1897, Sampson Low, *For the Flag*). Not recommended: I. O. Evans "Fitzroy Edition" translation (1961, Arco, *For the Flag*).

Clovis Dardentor (1896, illus. Léon Benett). *Clovis Dardentor* (1897, Sampson Low, translator unknown).

Le Sphinx des glaces (1897, illus. George Roux). *An Antarctic Mystery* (1898, Sampson Low, trans. Mrs. Cashel Hoey). Alternate titles: *The Sphinx of the Ice, An Antarctic Mystery*. Recommended: Hoey translation cited above. Not recommended: Basil Ashmore "Fitzroy Edition" translation (1961, Arco, *The Mystery of Arthur Gordon Pym by Edgar Allan Poe and Jules Verne*).

Le Superbe Orénoque (1898, illus. George Roux). *The Mighty Orinoco* (2002, Wesleyan University Press, trans. Stanford Luce).

Le Testament d'un excentrique (1899, illus. George Roux). *The Will of an Eccentric* (1900, Sampson Low, translator unknown).

Seconde patrie (1900, illus. George Roux). *Their Island Home* and *The Castaways of the Flag* (1923, Sampson Low, trans. Cranstoun Metcalfe).

Le Village aérien (1901, illus. George Roux). *The Village in the Treetops* (1964, "Fitzroy Edition," Arco, trans. I. O. Evans).

Les Histoires de Jean-Marie Cabidoulin (1901, illus. George Roux). *The Sea Serpent: The Yarns of Jean-Marie Cabidoulin* (1967, "Fitzroy Edition," Arco, trans. I. O. Evans).

Les Frères Kip (1902, illus. George Roux). *The Kip Brothers* (2007, Wesleyan University Press, trans. Stanford Luce).

Bourses de voyage (1903, illus. Léon Benett). *Travel Scholarships.* No published English translation yet available.

Un Drame en Livonie (1904, illus. Léon Benett). *A Drama in Livonia* (1967, "Fitzroy Edition," Arco, trans. I. O. Evans).

Maître du monde (1904, illus. George Roux). *The Master of the World* (1911, Parke, translator unknown). Recommended: translation by Cranstoun Metcalfe (1914, Sampson Low). Not recommended: Parke edition cited above and I. O. Evans "Fitzroy Edition" translation (1962, Arco).

L'Invasion de la mer (1905, illus. Léon Benett). *Invasion of the Sea* (2001, Wesleyan University Press, trans. Edward Baxter).

**Le Phare du bout du monde* (1905, illus. George Roux). *The Lighthouse at the Edge of the World* (1923, Sampson Low, trans. Cranstoun Metcalfe).

**Le Volcan d'or* (1906, illus. George Roux). *The Golden Volcano: The Claim on the Forty Mile* and *The Golden Volcano: Creek Flood and Famine* (1962, "Fitzroy Edition," Arco, trans. I. O. Evans).

**L'Agence Thompson and Co.* (1907, illus. Léon Benett). *The Thompson Travel Agency: Package Holiday* and *The Thompson Travel Agency: End of the Journey* (1965, "Fitzroy Edition," Arco, trans. I. O. Evans).

**La Chasse au météore* (1908, illus. George Roux). *The Chase of the Golden Meteor* (1909, Grant Richards, trans. Frederick Lawton). Alternate title: *The Hunt for the Meteor.*

**Le Pilote du Danube* (1908, illus. George Roux). *The Danube Pilote* (1967, "Fitzroy Edition," Arco, trans. I. O. Evans).

**Les Naufragés du Jonathan* (1909, illus. George Roux). *The Survivors of the*

Jonathan: The Masterless Man and *The Survivors of the Jonathan: The Unwilling Dictator* (1962, "Fitzroy Edition," Arco, trans. I. O. Evans). A translation of the original manuscript of this novel was published as *Magellania* (2002, Welcome Rain, trans. Benjamin Ivry).

**Le Secret de Wilhelm Storitz* (1910, illus. George Roux). *The Secret of Wilhelm Storitz* (1963, "Fitzroy Edition," Arco, trans. I. O. Evans).

**Hier et demain* (1910, illus. Léon Benett, George Roux, and Félicien Myrbach-Rheinfeld). *Yesterday and Tomorrow* (1965, "Fitzroy Edition," Arco, trans. I. O. Evans). Short story collection. Original French collection contains the following short stories: "La Famille Raton" (The Rat Family), "M. Ré-Dièze et Mlle Mi-Bémol" (Mr. Ray Sharp and Miss Me Flat), "La Destinée de Jean Morénas" (The Fate of Jean Morénas), "Le Humbug" (The Humbug), "Au XXIXème siècle: La Journée d'un journaliste américain en 2889" (In the Twenty-ninth Century: The Diary of an American Journalist in 2889), and "L'Eternel Adam" (The Eternal Adam). The 1965 Arco English translation does not contain the same stories as the original French edition: "La Famille Raton" (The Rat Family) and "Le Humbug" (The Humbug) were omitted and replaced with "Une Ville idéale" ("An Ideal City"), "Dix heures de chasse" ("Ten Hours Hunting"), "Frritt-Flacc" ("Frritt-Flacc"), and "Gil Braltar" ("Gil Braltar").

**L'Etonnante aventure de la mission Barsac* (1919, Hachette, illus. George Roux). *The Barsac Mission: Into the Niger Bend* and *The Barsac Mission: The City in the Sahara* (1960, "Fitzroy Edition," Arco, trans. I. O. Evans).

Novellas and Short Stories

In the octavo illustrated editions of Verne's *Voyages extraordinaires*, some novels were supplemented with a novella or a short story, which had often been previously published in a periodical journal (e.g., *Musée des familles*) or a newspaper (e.g., *Le Figaro*). Only two short story collections were published as part of the *Voyages extraordinaires*—*Le Docteur Ox* (Doctor Ox) and *Hier et demain* (Yesterday and Tomorrow)—and most of the stories contained therein also had appeared earlier. The latter collection was published only after Verne's death in 1905, and many of the short stories in it were either significantly revamped or entirely written by Jules Verne's son, Michel.

"Un Drame au Mexique. Les premiers navires de la marine mexicaine" (1876, illus. Jules-Descartes Férat) with *Michel Strogoff*. First published as "L'Amérique du Sud. Etudes historiques. Les premiers navires de la marine mexicaine" in the *Musée des familles* (July 1851, illus. Eugène Forest and Alexandre de Bar): 304–12. "The Mutineers: A Romance of Mexico" with *Michel Strogoff, the Courier of the Czar* (1877, Sampson Low, trans. W. G. Kingston). Alternate titles: "A Drama in Mexico," "The Mutineers, or A Tragedy in Mexico," "The Mutineers."

"Un Drame dans les airs" (1874, illus. Emile-Antoine Bayard) in *Le Docteur Ox*. First published as "La science en famille. Un voyage en ballon" in the *Musée de familles* (Aug. 1851, illus. Alexandre de Bar): 329–36. "A Voyage in a Balloon" in *Sartain's Union Magazine of Literature and Art* (May 1852, trans. Anne T. Wilbur): 389–95. Alternate titles: "A Drama in the Air," "Balloon Journey," "A Drama in Mid-Air." This was the first Verne story to be translated into English.

"Martin Paz" (1875, illus. Jules-Descartes Férat) with *Le Chancellor*. First published as "L'Amérique du Sud. Moeurs péruviennes. Martin Paz, nouvelle historique" in the *Musée des familles* (July–Aug.1852, illus. Eugène Forest, Emile Berton): 301–13, 321–35. "Martin Paz" in *The Survivors of the Chancellor; and Martin Paz* (1876, Sampson Low, trans. Ellen E. Frewer). Alternate title: "The Pearl of Lima."

"Maître Zacharius" (1874, illus. Théophile Schuler) in *Le Docteur Ox*. First published as "Maître Zacharius, ou l'horloger qui avait perdu son âme. Tradition génèvoise" in the *Musée des familles* (Apr.–May 1854, illus. Alexandre de Bar and Gustave Janet): 193–200, 225–31. "Master Zacharius" in *Dr. Ox and Other Stories* (1874, Osgood, trans. George M. Towle). Alternate titles: "Master Zachary," "The Watch's Soul."

"Un Hivernage dans les glaces" (1874, illus. Adrien Marie) in *Le Docteur Ox*. First published in the *Musée des familles* (Apr.–May 1855, illus. Jean-Antoine de Beauce): 161–72, 209–20. "Winter in the Ice" in *Dr. Ox and Other Stories* (1874, Osgood, trans. George M. Towle). Alternate titles: "A Winter amid the Ice," "A Winter among the Ice-Fields," "Winter on Ice."

"Le Comte de Chanteleine." Published as "Le Comte de Chanteleine. Episode de la révolution" in the *Musée des familles* (Oct.-Nov. 1864, illus. Edmond Morin, Alexandre de Bar, and Jean-Valentin Foulquier): 1–15, 37–51. No English translation available.

"Les Forceurs de blocus" (1871, illus. Jules-Descartes Férat) with *Une Ville flottante.* First published in the *Musée des familles* (Oct.-Nov. 1865, illus. Léon Morel-Fatio, Evrémond Bérard, Fréderic Lixe, and Jean-Valentin Foulquier): 17–21, 35–47. "The Blockade Runners" in *The Floating City, and the Blockade Runners* (1874, Sampson Low, translator unknown).

"Le Docteur Ox" (1874, illus. Lorenz Froelich) in *Le Docteur Ox.* First published in the *Musée des familles* (Mar.-May 1872, illus. Ulysse Parent and Alexandre de Bar): 65–74, 99–107, 133–41. "Doctor Ox's Experiment" in *Dr. Ox and Other Stories* (1874, Osgood, trans. George M. Towle). Alternate titles: "A Fancy of Doctor Ox," "Dr. Ox," "Dr. Ox's Hobby."

"Les Révoltés de la Bounty" (1879, illus. S. Drée) with *Les Cinq cents millions de la Bégum.* First published in the *Magasin d'Education et de Récréation* (Oct.–Dec. 1879, illus. S. Drée): 193–98, 225–30, 257–63. "The Mutineers of the Bounty" in *The Begum's Fortune, with an account of The Mutineers of the Bounty* (1880, Sampson Low, trans. W. H. G. Kingston).

"Dix heures en chasse" (1882, illus. Gédéon Baril) with *Le Rayon vert.* First published in the *Journal d'Amiens, Moniteur de la Somme* (Dec. 19–20, 1881): 2–3. "Ten Hours Hunting" in *Yesterday and Tomorrow* (1965, "Fitzroy Edition," Arco, trans. I. O. Evans).

"Frritt-Flacc" (1886, illus. George Roux) with *Un Billet de loterie.* First published in *Le Figaro illustré* (1884–85): 6–7. "Dr. Trifulgas: A Fantastic Tale" in *Strand Magazine* 4 (July–Dec. 1892, translator unknown): 53–57. Alternate titles: "Fritt-Flacc," "The Ordeal of Dr. Trifulgas," "Fweeee—Spash!"

"Gil Braltar" (1887, illus. George Roux) with *Le Chemin de France.* "Gil Braltar" (1938, Hurd and Walling, trans. Ernest H. De Gay).

"Un Express de l'avenir." Written by Verne's son, Michel, and first published in *Le Figaro* (Sept. 1, 1888). Translated and published (under his father's name) as "An Express of the Future" in *Strand Magazine* 10 (July–Dec. 1895): 638–40.

"La Journée d'un journaliste américain en 2889" (1910, illus. George Roux) in *Hier et demain.* Written by Verne's son, Michel, and first published in English (under his father's name) as "In the Year 2889" in *The Forum* 6 (Sept. 1888–Feb. 1889, illus. George Roux): 662–77. Later modified by Jules Verne and published as "La Journée d'un journaliste américain en 2890" in *Mémoires de l'Académie d'Amiens* 37 (1890): 348–70. The latter version was then published as "Au XXIXème siècle: La Journée d'un journaliste américain en 2889" in *Hier et demain* (Paris: Hetzel, 1910). It was then translated and reprinted as "In the Twenty-ninth Century: The Diary of an American Journalist in 2889" in *Yesterday and Tomorrow* (1965, "Fitzroy Edition," Arco, trans. I. O. Evans).

"La Famille Raton" (1910, illus. Félicien Myrbach-Rheinfeld) in *Hier et demain.* First published as "Aventures de la famille Raton. Conte de fées" in *Le Figaro illustré* (Jan. 1891): 1–12. *Adventures of the Rat Family,* trans. Evelyn Copeland (1993, Oxford University Press).

"La Destinée de Jean Morénas" (1910, illus. Léon Benett) in *Hier et demain.* Written by Verne's son, Michel, from his father's unpublished short story "Pierre-Jean" (see under "Rediscovered Works"). "The Fate of Jean Morénas" in *Yesterday and Tomorrow* (1965, "Fitzroy Edition," Arco, trans. I. O. Evans).

"Le Humbug" (1910, illus. George Roux) in *Hier et demain.* "Humbug, the American Way of Life" (1991, Acadian, trans. William Butcher) and "The Humbug" in *The Jules Verne Encyclopedia,* ed. Brian Taves and Stephen Michaluk Jr. (1996, Scarecrow, trans. Edward Baxter).

"Monsieur Ré-Dièze et Mademoiselle Mi-Bémol" (1910, illus. George Roux) in *Hier et demain.* First published in *Le Figaro illustré* (Dec. 25, 1893): 221–28. "Mr. Ray Sharp and Miss Me Flat" in *Yesterday and Tomorrow* (1965, "Fitzroy Edition," Arco, trans. I. O. Evans).

"L'Eternel Adam" (1910, illus. Léon Benett) in *Hier et demain.* Written by Verne's son, Michel, as "Edom" from his father's unfinished short story (see under "Rediscovered Works") and first published in *La Revue de Paris* (Oct. 1, 1910): 449–84. Translated as "Eternal Adam" in *Saturn* 1.1 (Mar. 1957, trans. Willis T. Bradley): 76–112.

Rediscovered Works: Unpublished Early Novels, Short Stories, and Original Manuscripts

Un Prêtre en 1835 (A Priest in 1835, written 1846–47). Published as *Un Prêtre en 1839* (1992, Cherche Midi, illus. Jacques Tardi).

"Jédédias Jamet" (Jedediah Jamet, written 1847). Published as "Jédédias Jamet" in *San Carlos et autres récits inédits,* 177–206 (1993, Cherche Midi, illus. Jacques Tardi).

"Pierre-Jean" (written ca. 1852). Published as "Pierre-Jean" in Olivier Dumas, *Jules Verne,* 205–34 (1988, La Manufacture). Original manuscript of "La Destinée de Jean Morénas."

"Le Siège de Rome" (The Siege of Rome, written ca. 1853). Published as "Le Siège de Rome" in *San Carlos et autres récits inédits,* 81–146 (1993, Cherche Midi, illus. Jacques Tardi).

"Le Mariage de Monsieur Anselme des Tilleuls" (The Marriage of M. Anselme des Tilleuls, written ca. 1855). Published as "Le Mariage de M. Anselme des Tilleuls. Souvenirs d'un élève de huitième" (1991, Olifant, illus. Gérard Bregnat) and as "Le Mariage de M. Anselme des Tilleuls. Souvenirs d'un élève de huitième" in *San Carlos et autres récits inédits,* 47–80 (1993, Cherche Midi, illus. Jacques Tardi).

"San Carlos" (San Carlos, written ca. 1856). Published as "San Carlos" in *San Carlos et autres récits inédits,* 147–76 (1993, Cherche Midi, illus. Jacques Tardi).

Voyage en Angleterre et en Ecosse—Voyage à reculons (written 1859–60). Published as *Voyage à reculons en Angleterre et en Ecosse* (1989, Cherche Midi). Translated by William Butcher as *Backwards to Britain* (1992, Chamber).

Paris au XXème siècle (written 1863). Published as *Paris au XXème siècle* (1994, Hachette, illus. François Schuiten). Translated by Richard Howard as *Paris in the Twentieth Century* (1996, Random House, illus. Anders Wenngren).

L'Oncle Robinson (Uncle Robinson, written 1870–71). Published as *L'Oncle Robinson* (1991, Cherche Midi). Original manuscript of *L'Ile mystérieuse.*

Le Beau Danube jaune (The Beautiful Yellow Danube, written 1896–97). Published as *Le Beau Danube jaune* (1988, Société Jules Verne). Original manuscript of *Le Pilote du Danube.*

En Magellanie—Au bout du monde (In the Magellanes—At the End of the World, written 1896–99). Published as *En Magellanie* (1987, Société Jules Verne). Original manuscript of *Les Naufragés du Jonathan,* published in English as *Magellania* (2002, Welcome Rain, trans. Benjamin Ivry).

Le Volcan d'or—Le Klondyke (The Golden Volcano—The Klondyke, written 1899–1900). Published as *Le Volcan d'or. Version originale* (1989, Société Jules Verne). Original manuscript of *Le Volcan d'or.*

Le Secret de Wilhelm Storitz—L'Invisible, L'Invisible fiancée, Le Secret de Storitz (The Secret of Wilhelm Storitz, written 1901). Published as *Le Secret de Wilhelm Storitz* (1985, Société Jules Verne). Original manuscript of *Le Secret de Wilhelm Storitz.*

La Chasse au météore—Le Bolide (The Hunt for the Meteor—The Bolide, written 1901). Published as *La Chasse au météore. Version originale* (1986) and as *La Chasse au météore (Version originale) suivi de Edom* (1994, Société Jules Verne, illus. George Roux). Original manuscript of *La Chasse au météore.*

"Voyage d'études" (Study Trip, written 1903–4). Unfinished manuscript, completed and published by Michel Verne as *L'Etonnante aventure de la mission Barsac* (1919). Original version published in *San Carlos et autres récits inédits,* 207–60 (1993, Cherche Midi, illus. Jacques Tardi).

"Edom." (Edom, written 1903–5). Unfinished manuscript, rewritten and published in *Hier et demain* by Michel Verne as "L'Eternel Adam." Proofs published in the *Bulletin de la Société Jules Verne* 100 (1991): 21–48.

Theater Plays and Operettas (Performed or Published, in Chronological Order)

Les Pailles rompues (Broken Straws, 1849). First performed at the Théâtre Historique on June 12, 1850. Published by Beck (Paris) in 1850.

Monna Lisa (Mona Lisa, 1852). Published posthumously in *Jules Verne,* ed. Pierre-André Touttain (Paris: Cahiers de l'Herne 1974.

Les Châteaux en Californie (Castles in California, 1852). Published in the *Musée des familles,* June 1852.

Le Colin-Maillard (Blind Man's Bluff, 1852). First performed at the Théâtre Lyrique on April 28, 1853. Published by Michel Lévy (Paris) in 1853.

Les Compagnons de la Marjolaine (The Companions of the Marjolaine, 1853). First performed at the Théâtre Lyrique on June 6, 1855. Published by Michel Lévy (Paris) in 1855.

Monsieur de Chimpanzé (Mister Chimpanzee, 1857). First performed at the Bouffes-Parisiennes on February 17, 1858. Published in the *Bulletin de la Société Jules Verne* 57 (1981).

L'Auberge des Ardennes (The Ardennes Inn, 1859). First performed at the Théâtre Lyrique on September 1, 1860. Published by Michel Lévy (Paris) in 1860.

Onze jours de siège (Eleven Days of Siege, 1854–60). First performed at the Théâtre du Vaudeville on June 1, 1861. Published by Michel Lévy (Paris) in 1861.

Un Neveu d'Amérique, ou Les Deux Frontignac (A Nephew from America, or the Two Frontignacs, 1872). First performed at the Théâtre Cluny on April 17, 1873. Published by Hetzel (Paris) in 1873.

Le Tour du monde en 80 jours (Around the World in Eighty Days, 1874). First performed at the Théâtre de la Porte Saint-Martin, November 7, 1874. Published in *Les Voyages au théâtre* by Jules Verne and Adolphe d'Ennery (Paris: J. Hetzel, 1881).

Les Enfants du capitaine Grant (The Children of Captain Grant, 1878). First performed at the Théâtre de la Porte Saint-Martin on December 26, 1878. Published in *Les Voyages au théâtre* by Jules Verne and Adolphe d'Ennery (Paris: J. Hetzel, 1881).

Michel Strogoff (Michael Strogoff, 1880). First performed at the Théâtre de Châtelet on November 17, 1880. Published in *Les Voyages au théâtre* by Jules Verne and Adolphe d'Ennery (Paris: J. Hetzel, 1881).

Voyage à travers l'impossible (Journey through the Impossible, 1882). First performed at the Théâtre de la Porte Saint-Martin on November 25, 1882. Published by Jean-Jacques Pauvert (Paris) in 1981. Published in English as *Journey through the Impossible,* trans. Edward Baxter, ed. Jean-Michel Margot (Amherst, N.Y.: Prometheus, 2003).

Kéraban-le-têtu (Keraban the Stubborn, 1883). First performed at La Gaîté-Lyrique on September 3, 1883. Published in the *Bulletin de la Société Jules Verne* (1988): 85–86.

Mathias Sandorf (Mathias Sandorf, 1887). First performed at the Théâtre de l'Ambigu on November 26, 1887.
(For an anthology of Verne's plays, see Jean-Marc Ayrault, ed., *Jules Verne: Théâtre inédit* [Paris: Cherche Midi, 2006].)

Poetry and Song Lyrics

Collected in *Poésies inédites,* ed. Christian Robin (Paris: Cherche Midi, 1989) and in *Textes oubliés,* ed. Francis Lacassin (Paris: UGE, "10/18," 1979).

Literary Criticism, Nonfiction, Speeches, and Other Prose

"A propos du 'Géant'" (Concerning the "Giant"). *Musée des familles* (Dec. 1863): 92–93. Rpt. in *Textes oubliés,* ed. Francis Lacassin (Paris: UGE, "10/18," 1979).
"Edgard Poë [*sic*] et ses oeuvres" (Edgar Poe and His Works). *Musée des familles* (Apr. 1864): 193–208. Rpt. in *Textes oubliés,* ed. Francis Lacassin (Paris: UGE, "10/18," 1979). Translated by I. O. Evans as "The Leader of the Cult of the Unusual" in *The Edgar Allan Poe Scrapbook,* ed. Peter Haining (New York: Schocken, 1978).
Géographie illustrée de la France et de ses colonies (Illustrated Geography of France and Its Colonies, 1866, illus. Edouard Riou and Hubert Clerget), coauthored with Théophile Lavallée.
"Une Ville idéale" (An Ideal City). *Mémoires de l'Académie des sciences, belles-lettres, et arts d'Amiens* 22 (1874–75): 347–78. Rpt. in *Textes oubliés,* ed. Francis Lacassin (Paris: UGE, "10/18," 1979). Translated by I. O. Evans as "An Ideal City" and included in *Yesterday and Tomorrow* (London: Arco, 1965).
Histoire des grands voyages et des grands voyageurs: Découverte de la terre (1878), *Les Grands navigateurs du XVIIIème siècle* (1879, illus. Léon Benett and Paul Philippoteaux), and *Les Voyageurs du XIXème siècle* (1880). Translated by Dora Leigh as *The Exploration of the World: Famous Travels and Travellers, The Great Navigators of the Eighteenth Century, The Exploration of the World* (New York: Scribners, 1879).

"The Story of My Boyhood." *The Youth's Companion* (Apr. 9, 1891): 221. Verne's original autobiographical essay, "Souvenirs d'enfance et de jeunesse" (Memories of Childhood and Youth), was published in French for the first time in *Jules Verne*, ed. Pierre-André Touttain (Paris: Cahiers de l'Herne, 1974).

"Discours de distribution des prix au Lycée de Jeunes Filles d'Amiens" (July 29, 1893). Rpt. in *Textes oubliés*, ed. Francis Lacassin (1979, "10/18"). Translated by I. O. Evans as "The Future for Women: An Address by Jules Verne," in *The Jules Verne Companion*, ed. Peter Haining (London: Souvenir, 1978).

"Future of the Submarine." *Popular Mechanics* 6 (June 1904): 629–31.

"Solution of Mind Problems by the Imagination." *Hearst's International Cosmopolitan* (Oct. 1928): 95, 132. Written in 1903.

Selected Interviews

Belloc, Marie A. "Jules Verne at Home." *Strand Magazine* (Feb. 1895): 207–13.

Compère, Daniel, and Jean-Michel Margot. *Entretiens avec Jules Verne, 1873–1905*. Geneva: Slatkine, 1998.

De Amicis, Edmondo. "A Visit to Jules Verne and Victorien Sardou." *Chautauquan* (Mar. 1897): 702–7.

Jones, Gordon. "Jules Verne at Home." *Temple Bar* 129 (1904): 664–70.

Sherard, Robert H. "Jules Verne at Home." *McClure's Magazine* (Jan. 1894): 115–24.

———. "Jules Verne Revisited." *T.P.'s Weekly* (Oct. 9, 1903): 589.

Correspondence and Other Autobiographical Writings

Bottin, André. "Lettres inédites de Jules Verne au lieutenant colonel Hennebert." *Bulletin de la Société Jules Verne* 18 (1971): 36–44.

Dumas, Olivier, Piero Gondolo della Riva, and Volker Dehs. *Correspondance inédite de Jules et Michel Verne avec l'éditeur Louis-Jules Hetzel (1886–1914)*. Vol. 1: 1886–1896. Geneva: Slatkine, 2002.

———. *Correspondance inédite de Jules Verne et de Pierre-Jules Hetzel (1863–1886)*. Vol. 1 (1863–1874). Geneva: Slatkine, 1999.

———. *Correspondance inédite de Jules Verne et de Pierre-Jules Hetzel (1863–1886)*. Vol. 2 (1875–1878). Geneva: Slatkine, 2001.

———. *Correspondance inédite de Jules Verne et de Pierre-Jules Hetzel (1863–1886)*. Vol. 3 (1879–1886). Geneva: Slatkine, 2002.

Martin, Charles-Noël. *La Vie et l'oeuvre de Jules Verne*. Paris: Michel de l'Ormeraie, 1978.

Parménie, A. "Huit lettres de Jules Verne à son éditeur P.-J. Hetzel." *Arts et Lettres* 15 (1949): 102–7.

Parménie, A., and C. Bonnier de la Chapelle. *Histoire d'un éditeur et de ses auteurs, P.-J. Hetzel (Stahl)*. Paris: Albin Michel, 1953.

Turiello, Mario. "Lettre de Jules Verne à un jeune Italien." *Bulletin de la Société Jules Verne* 1 (1936): 158–61.

Verne, Jules. "Correspondance." *Bulletin de la Société Jules Verne* 49 (1979): 31–34.

———. "Correspondance avec Fernando Ricci," *Europe* 613 (1980): 137–38.

———. "Correspondance avec Mario Turiello." *Europe* 613 (1980): 108–35.

———. "Deux lettres à Louis-Jules Hetzel." In *Jules Verne,* ed. Pierre-André Touttain, 73–74. Paris: Cahiers de l'Herne, 1974.

———. "Deux lettres inédites." *Bulletin de la Société Jules Verne* 48 (1978): 253–54.

———. "Jules Verne: 63 lettres." *Bulletin de la Société Jules Verne* 11–13 (1938): 47–129.

———. "Lettre à Nadar." *L'Arc* 29 (1966): 83.

———. "Lettre à Paul, à propos de Turpin." In *Jules Verne,* ed. Pierre-André Touttain, 81–82. Paris: Cahiers de l'Herne, 1974.

———. "Lettres à Nadar." In *Jules Verne,* ed. Pierre-André Touttain, 76–80. Paris: Cahiers de l'Herne, 1974.

———. "Lettres diverses." *Europe* 613 (1980): 143–51.

———. "Quelques lettres." *Livres de France* 6 (May–June, 1955): 13–15.

———. "Sept lettres à sa famille et à divers correspondants." In *Jules Verne,* ed. Pierre-André Touttain, 63–70. Paris: Cahiers de l'Herne, 1974.

———. "Souvenirs d'enfance et de jeunesse." In *Jules Verne,* ed. Pierre-André Touttain, 57–62. Paris: Cahiers de l'Herne, 1974.

———. "Spécial Lettres No. 1." *Bulletin de la Société Jules Verne* 65–66 (1983): 4–50.

———. "Spécial Lettres No. 2." *Bulletin de la Société Jules Verne* 69 (1984): 3–25.

———. "Spécial Lettres No. 3." *Bulletin de la Société Jules Verne* 78 (1986): 3–52.

———. "Spécial Lettres No. 4." *Bulletin de la Société Jules Verne* 83 (1987): 4–27.

———. "Spécial Lettres No. 5." *Bulletin de la Société Jules Verne* 88 (1988): 8–18.

———. "Spécial Lettres No. 6." *Bulletin de la Société Jules Verne* 94 (1990): 10–33.

———. "Trente-six lettres inédites." *Bulletin de la Société Jules Verne* 68 (1983): 4–50.

———. "Vingt-deux lettres de Jules Verne à son frère Paul." *Bulletin de la Société Jules Verne* 69 (1984): 3–25.

Secondary Sources on Jules Verne and His Works

Bibliographies and Bibliographical Studies

Angenot, Marc. "Jules Verne and French Literary Criticism, I." *Science Fiction Studies* 1.1 (1973): 33–37.

———. "Jules Verne and French Literary Criticism, II." *Science Fiction Studies* 1.2 (1973): 46–49.

Butcher, William. "Jules and Michel Verne." In *Critical Bibliography of French Literature: The Nineteenth Century*, ed. David Baguley, 923–40. Syracuse: Syracuse University Press, 1994.

Compère, Daniel. "Le Monde des études verniennes." *Magazine Littéraire* 119 (1976): 27–29.

Decré, Françoise. *Catalogue du fonds Jules Verne.* Nantes: Bibliothèque Municipale, 1978. Updated by Colette Gaillois in *Catalogue du fonds Jules Verne (1978–1983)*. Nantes: Bibliothèque Municipale, 1984.

Dehs, Volker. *Bibliographischer Führer durch die Jules-Verne-Forschung / Guide bibliographique à travers la critique vernienne, 1872–2001.* Wetzlar: Phantastische Bibliothek, 2002.

Dumas, Olivier, et al. "Bibliographie des oeuvres de Jules Verne." *Bulletin de la Société Jules Verne* 1 (1967): 7–12. Additions and updates: *BSJV* 2 (1967): 11–15; *BSJV* 3 (1967): 13; *BSJV* 4 (1967): 15–16. Rpt. in Dumas, *Jules Verne,* 160–67. Lyon: La Manufacture, 1988.

Evans, Arthur B. "A Bibliography of Jules Verne's English Translations." *Science Fiction Studies* 32.1 (Mar. 2005): 87–123.

Gallagher, Edward J., Judith A. Mistichelli, and John A. Van Eerde. *Jules Verne: A Primary and Secondary Bibliography.* Boston: G. K. Hall, 1980.

Gondolo della Riva, Piero. *Bibliographie analytique de toutes les oeuvres de Jules Verne.* Vols. 1 and 2. Paris: Société Jules Verne, 1977, 1985.

Margot, Jean-Michel. *Bibliographie documentaire sur Jules Verne.* Amiens: Centre de Documentation Jules Verne, 1989.

Raymond, François, and Daniel Compère. *Le Développement des études sur Jules Verne.* Paris: Minard, Archives des Lettres Modernes, 1976.

Biographies

Allott, Kenneth. *Jules Verne.* London: Crescent Press, 1940.

Allotte de la Fuÿe, Marguerite. *Jules Verne, sa vie, son oeuvre.* Paris: Simon Kra, 1928. Published in English as *Jules Verne,* trans. Erik de Mauny. London: Staples, 1954.

Avrane, Patrick. *Jules Verne.* Paris: Stock, 1997.

Born, Franz. *The Man Who Invented the Future: Jules Verne.* New York: Prentice-Hall, 1963.

Butcher, William. *Jules Verne: The Definitive Biography.* New York: Thunder's Mouth Press, 2006.

Clarétie, Jules. *Jules Verne.* Paris: A. Quantin, 1883.

Costello, Peter. *Jules Verne: Inventor of Science Fiction.* London: Hodder and Stroughton, 1978.

Dehs, Volker. *Jules Verne.* Hamburg: Rowohlt, 1986.

Dekiss, Jean-Paul. *Jules Verne, l'enchanteur.* Paris: Editions du Félin, 1999.

———. *Jules Verne, le rêve du progrès.* Paris: Gallimard, 1991.

Dumas, Olivier. *Jules Verne.* Lyon: La Manufacture, 1988.

———. *Voyage à travers Jules Verne.* Montreal: Stanké, 2000.

Dusseau, Joëlle. *Jules Verne.* Paris: Perrin, 2005.

Jules-Verne, Jean. *Jules Verne.* Paris: Hachette, 1973. Published in English

as *Jules Verne: A Biography,* trans. Roger Greaves. New York: Taplinger, 1976.
Lemire, Charles. *Jules Verne.* Paris: Berger-Levrault, 1908.
Lottman, Herbert R. *Jules Verne: An Exploratory Biography.* New York: St. Martin's Press, 1996. Published in French as *Jules Verne,* trans. Marianne Véron. Paris: Flammarion, 1996.
Lynch, Lawrence. *Jules Verne.* New York: Twayne, 1992.
Martin, Charles-Noël. *La Vie et l'oeuvre de Jules Verne.* Paris: Michel de l'Ormeraie, 1978.
Robien, Gilles de. *Jules Verne, le rêveur incompris.* Neuilly-sur-Seine: Michel Lafon, 2000.
Soriano, Mark. *Jules Verne.* Paris: Julliard, 1978.
Teeters, Peggy. *Jules Verne: The Man Who Invented Tomorrow.* New York: Walter, 1992.
Vierne, Simone. *Jules Verne.* Paris: Balland, 1986.

Other Selected Critical Studies

Alkon, Paul. *Science Fiction before 1900.* New York: Twayne, 1994.
Angenot, Marc. "Jules Verne: The Last Happy Utopianist." In *Science Fiction: A Critical Guide,* ed. Patrick Parrinder, 18–32. New York: Longman, 1979.
———. "Science Fiction in France before Verne." *Science Fiction Studies* 5.1 (Mar. 1978): 58–66.
L'Arc 29 (1966). Special issue devoted to Jules Verne.
Arts et Lettres 15 (1949). Special issue devoted to Jules Verne.
Barthes, Roland. "Nautilus et Bateau Ivre." In Barthes, *Mythologies,* 90–92. Paris: Seuil, 1957, 1970. Published in English as "The Nautilus and the Drunken Boat," trans. A. Lavers, in Barthes, *Mythologies,* 65–67. New York: Hill and Wang, 1972.
———. "Par où commencer?" *Poétique* 1 (1970): 3–9. Rpt. in Barthes, *Nouveaux essais critiques,* 145–51. Paris: Seuil, 1972.
Bellemin-Noël, Jean. "Analectures de Jules Verne." *Critique* 26 (1970): 692–704.
Benford, Gregory. "Verne to Varley: Hard SF Evolves." *Science Fiction Studies* 32.1 (Mar. 2005): 163–71.

Berri, Kenneth. "*Les Cinq cents millions de la Bégum* ou la technologie de la fable." *Stanford French Review* 3 (1979): 29–40.

Boia, Lucien. "Un Ecrivain original: Michel Verne." *Bulletin de la Société Jules Verne* 70 (1984): 90–95.

———. *Jules Verne: Les paradoxes d'un mythe*. Paris: Belles Lettres, 2005.

Bradbury, Ray. "The Ardent Blasphemers." Foreword to Jules Verne, *Twenty Thousand Leagues under the Sea*, trans. Anthony Bonner, 1–12. New York: Bantam Books, 1962.

Bridenne, Jean-Jacques. *La Littérature française d'imagination scientifique*. Lausanne: Dassonville, 1950.

Buisine, Alain. "Circulations en tous genres," *Europe* 595–96 (1978): 48–56.

———. "Repères, marques, gisements: A propos de la robinsonnade vernienne." *Revue des Lettres Modernes* 523–29 (Apr.–June 1978). Special issue devoted to Jules Verne.

Bulletin de la Société Jules Verne (1967–2000). Edited by Olivier Dumas. The official publication of the Jules Verne Society in France and one of the best sources for up-to-date and reliable information on Jules Verne.

Butcher, William. "Crevettes de l'air et baleines volantes." *La Nouvelle Revue Maritime* 386–87 (May–June 1984): 35–40.

———. "Graphes et graphie." In Butcher, *Regards sur la théorie des graphes*, 177–82. Lausanne: Presses polytechniques romandes, 1980.

———. "Hidden Treasures: The Manuscripts of *Twenty Thousand Leagues*." *Science Fiction Studies* 32.1 (Mar. 2005): 132–49.

———. "Long-Lost Manuscript." *Modern Language Review* 93.4 (Oct. 1998): 961–71.

———. "Mysterious Masterpiece." In *Jules Verne: Narratives of Modernity*, ed. Edmund J. Smyth, 142–57. Liverpool: Liverpool University Press, 2000.

———. "La Poésie de l'arborescence chez Verne." *Studi Francesi* 104 (1992): 261–67.

———. "Le Sens de *L'Eternel Adam*," *Bulletin de la Société Jules Verne* 58 (1981): 73–81.

———. "Le Verbe et la chair, ou l'emploi du temps." In *Jules Verne 4: Texte, image, spectacle*, ed. François Raymond, 125–48. Paris: Minard, 1983.

———. *Verne's Journey to the Center of the Self: Space and Time in the*

Voyages Extraordinaires. London and New York: Macmillan and St. Martin's, 1990.

Butor, Michel. "Homage to Jules Verne." Trans. John Coleman. *New Statesman* (July 15, 1966): 94.

———. "Le Point suprême et l'âge d'or à travers quelques oeuvres de Jules Verne." *Arts et Lettres* 15 (1949): 3–31. Rpt. in Butor, *Répertoire I*, 130–62. Paris: Editions de Minuit, 1960.

Cahiers du Centre d'études verniennes et du Musée Jules Verne (1981–96). Edited by Christian Robin.

Carrouges, Michel. "Le Mythe de Vulcain chez Jules Verne." *Arts et Lettres* 15 (1949): 32–48.

Chambers, Ross. "Cultural and Ideological Determinations in Narrative: A Note on Jules Verne's *Cinq cents millions de la Bégum*." *L'Esprit créateur* 21.3 (Fall 1981): 69–78.

Chesneaux, Jean. "L'Invention linguistique chez Jules Verne." In *Langues et techniques, nature et société 1*, ed. J. M. C. Thomas and Lucien Bernot, 345–51. Paris: Klincksieck, 1972.

———. *Jules Verne: Un Regard sur le monde*. Paris: Bayard, 2001.

———. *Une Lecture politique de Jules Verne*. Paris: Maspero, 1971. Published in English as *The Political and Social Ideas of Jules Verne*, trans. Thomas Wikeley. London: Thames and Hudson, 1972.

Compère, Daniel. *Approche de l'île chez Jules Verne*. Paris: Lettres Modernes, 1977.

———. "Le Bas des pages." *Bulletin de la Société Jules Verne* 68 (1983): 147–53.

———. "Fenêtres latérales." In *Jules Verne IV: Texte, image, spectacle*, ed. François Raymond, 55–72. Paris: Minard, 1983.

———. *Jules Verne, écrivain*. Geneva: Droz, 1991.

———. *Jules Verne: Parcours d'une oeuvre*. Amiens: Encrage, 1996.

———. "Poétique de la carte." *Bulletin de la Société Jules Verne* 50 (1979): 69–74.

———. *Un Voyage imaginaire de Jules Verne: Voyage au centre de la Terre*. Paris: Lettres Modernes, 1977.

Compère, Daniel, and Volker Dehs. "Tashinar and Co.: Introduction à une étude des mots inventés dans l'oeuvre de Jules Verne." *Bulletin de la Société Jules Verne* 67 (1983): 107–11.

Costello, Peter. *Jules Verne: Inventor of Science Fiction*. London: Hodder and Stroughton, 1978.

Davy, Jacques. "A propos de l'anthropophagie chez Jules Verne." *Cahiers du Centre d'études verniennes et du Musée Jules Verne* 1 (1981): 15–23.

———. "Le Premier Dénouement des *Cinq cents millions de la Bégum*." *Bulletin de la Société Jules Verne* 123 (1997): 37–41.

De la Cotardière, Philippe, and Jean-Paul Dekiss, eds. *Jules Verne: De la science à l'imaginaire*. Paris: Larousse, 2004.

Diesbach, Ghislain de. *Le Tour de Jules Verne en quatre-vingts livres*. Paris: Julliard, 1969.

Dumas, Olivier. "La Main du fils dans l'oeuvre du père." *Bulletin de la Société Jules Verne* 82 (1987): 21–24.

Dupuy, Lionel. *En relisant Jules Verne*. Dole, France: La Clef d'Argent, 2005.

Escaich, René. *Voyage au monde de Jules Verne*. Paris: Plantin, 1955.

Europe 33 (1955). Special issue devoted to Jules Verne.

Europe 595–96 (1978). Special issue devoted to Jules Verne.

Evans, Arthur B. "The Extraordinary Libraries of Jules Verne." *L'Esprit créateur* 28 (1988): 75–86.

———. "Le Franglais vernien (père et fils)." In *Modernités de Jules Verne*, ed. Jean Bessière, 87–105. Paris: PUF, 1988.

———. "The Illustrators of Jules Verne's *Voyages Extraordinaires*." *Science Fiction Studies* 25.2 (July 1998): 241–70.

———. "Jules Verne, visionnaire incompris." *Pour la Science* 236 (June 1997): 94–101.

———. "Jules Verne and the French Literary Canon." In *Jules Verne: Narratives of Modernity*, ed. Edmund J. Smyth, 11–39. Liverpool: Liverpool University Press, 2000.

———. "Jules Verne et la persistence rétinienne." *Cahiers du Centre d'études verniennes et du Musée Jules Verne* 13 (1996): 11–17.

———. *Jules Verne Rediscovered: Didacticism and the Scientific Novel*. Westport, Conn.: Greenwood, 1988.

———. "Jules Verne's English Translations." *Science Fiction Studies* 32.1 (Mar. 2005): 62–86.

———. "Literary Intertexts in Jules Verne's *Voyages Extraordinaires*." *Science Fiction Studies* 23.2 (July 1996): 171–87.

———. "The 'New' Jules Verne." *Science Fiction Studies* 22.1 (Mar. 1995): 35–46.

———. "Science Fiction in France: A Brief History and Select Bibliography." *Science Fiction Studies* 16.3 (Nov. 1989): 254–76, 338–68.

———. "Science Fiction vs. Scientific Fiction in France: From Jules Verne to J.-H. Rosny Aîné." *Science Fiction Studies* 15.1 (1988): 1–11.

———. "Vehicular Utopias of Jules Verne." In *Transformations of Utopia*, ed. George Slusser et al., 99–108. New York: AMS Press, 1999.

Evans, Arthur B., and Ron Miller. "Jules Verne: Misunderstood Visionary." *Scientific American* (Apr. 1997): 92–97.

Evans, I. O. *Jules Verne and His Works*. London: Arco, 1965.

———. "Jules Verne et le lecteur anglais." *Bulletin de la Société Jules Verne* 6 (1937): 36.

Fabre, Michel. *Le Problème et l'épreuve: Formation et modernité chez Jules Verne*. Paris: Harmattan, 2003.

Foucault, Michel. "L'Arrière-fable." *L'Arc* 29 (1966): 5–13. Published in English as "Behind the Fable," trans. Pierre A. Walker, *Critical Texts* 5 (1988): 1–5; also as "Behind the Fable," trans. Robert Hurley, in *Aesthetics, Method, and Epistemology*, ed. J. Faubion, 137–45. New York: New Press, 1998.

Frank, Bernard. *Jules Verne et ses voyages*. Paris: Flammarion, 1941.

Gilli, Yves, and Florent Montaclair. *Jules Verne et l'utopie*. Besançon: Presses du Centre Unesco de Besançon, 1999.

Gilli, Yves, Florent Montaclair, and Sylvie Petit. *Le Naufrage dans l'oeuvre de Jules Verne*. Paris: Harmattan, 1998.

Gondolo della Riva, Piero. "A propos des oeuvres posthumes de Jules Verne." *Europe* 595–96 (1978): 73–82.

———. "A propos d'une nouvelle." In *Jules Verne*, ed. Pierre-André Touttain, 284–85. Paris: Cahiers de l'Herne, 1974.

Guillaud, Lauric. *Jules Verne face au rêve américain*. Paris: Michel Houdiard, 2005.

Haining, Peter. *The Jules Verne Companion*. London: Souvenir, 1978.

Huet, Marie-Hélène. *L'Histoire des Voyages Extraordinaires: Essai sur l'oeuvre de Jules Verne*. Paris: Minard, 1973.

Jensen, William B. "Captain Nemo's Battery: Chemistry and the Science Fiction of Jules Verne." *Chemical Intelligencer* (Apr. 1997): 23–32.

Jules Verne écrivain. Nantes: Bibliothèque Municipale de Nantes, 2000.

Jules Verne et les sciences humaines. Colloque de Cerisy. Paris: UGE, "10/18," 1979.

Jules Verne—filiations, rencontres, influences. Colloque d'Amiens II. Paris: Minard, 1980.

Jules Verne: Le Roman de la mer. Paris: Seuil/Musée national de la Marine, 2005.

Harpold, Terry. "Verne's Cartographies." *Science Fiction Studies* 32.1 (Mar. 2005): 18–42.

Hernández, Teri. J. "Translating Verne: An Extraordinary Journey." *Science Fiction Studies* 32.1 (Mar. 2005): 124–31.

Ketterer, David. "Fathoming *20,000 Leagues under the Sea.*" In *The Stellar Gauge: Essays on Science Fiction Writers,* ed. Michael J. Tolley and Kirpal Singh, 7–24. Carlton, Australia: Nostrillia Press, 1981.

Klein, Gérard. "Pour lire Verne (I)." *Fiction* 197 (1970): 137–43.

———. "Pour lire Verne (II)." *Fiction* 198 (1970): 143–52.

Lacassin, Francis. "Du Pavillion noir au Québec libre." *Magazine Littéraire* 119 (1976): 22–26.

———. *Passagers clandestins.* Paris: UGE, "10/18," 1979.

———, ed. *Textes oubliés.* Paris: UGE, "10/18," 1979.

Lengrand, Claude. *Dictionnaire des "Voyages Extraordinaires" de Jules Verne: Cahier Jules Verne, I.* Amiens: Encrage, 1998.

Livres de France 5 (1955). Special issue devoted to Jules Verne.

Macherey, Pierre. "Jules Verne ou le récit en défaut." In Macherey, *Pour une théorie de la production littéraire,* 183–266. Paris: Maspero, 1966. Published in English as "The Faulty Narrative," in Macherey, *A Theory of Literary Production,* trans. G. Wall, 159–240. London: Routledge and Kegan Paul, 1978.

Magazine Littéraire 119 (Dec. 1976). Special issue devoted to Jules Verne.

Marcucci, Edmondo. *Les Illustrations des Voyages extraordinaires de Jules Verne.* Bordeaux: Société Jules Verne, 1956.

Margot, Jean-Michel. *Jules Verne en son temps.* Amiens: Encrage, 2004.

———. "Jules Verne, Playwright." *Science Fiction Studies* 32.1 (Mar. 2005): 150–62.

Martin, Andrew. "Chez Jules: Nutrition and Cognition in the Novels of Jules Verne." *French Studies* 37 (Jan. 1983): 47–58.

———. "The Entropy of Balzacian Tropes in the Scientific Fictions of Jules Verne." *Modern Language Review* 77 (Jan. 1982): 51–62.

———. *The Knowledge of Ignorance from Cervantes to Jules Verne.* Cambridge: Cambridge University Press, 1985.

———. *The Mask of the Prophet: The Extraordinary Fictions of Jules Verne.* Oxford: Clarendon, 1990.

Mellot, Philippe, and Jean-Marie Embs. *Le Guide Jules Verne.* Paris: Les Editions de l'Amateur, 2005.

Miller, Ron. *Extraordinary Voyages: A Reader's Guide to the Works of Jules Verne.* Fredericksburg, Va.: Black Cat, 1994.

Miller, Walter James. "Afterword: Freedom and the Near Murder of Jules Verne." In Jules Verne, *Twenty Thousand Leagues under the Sea,* trans. Mendor T. Brunetti, 448–61. New York: New American Library, 2001.

———. *The Annotated Jules Verne: From the Earth to the Moon.* New York: Crowell, 1978; rev. ed., New York: Gramercy, 1995.

———. *The Annotated Jules Verne: Twenty Thousand Leagues under the Sea.* New York: Crowell, 1976.

———. "Jules Verne in America: A Translator's Preface." In Jules Verne, *Twenty Thousand Leagues under the Sea,* trans. Walter James Miller, vii–xxii. New York: Washington Square, 1965.

Miller, Walter James, and Frederick P. Walter, eds. and trans. *Jules Verne's Twenty Thousand Leagues under the Sea.* Annapolis, Md.: Naval Institute Press, 1993.

Minerva, Nadia. *Jules Verne aux confins de l'utopie.* Paris: Harmattan, 2001.

Modernités de Jules Verne. Edited by Jean Bessière. Paris: PUF, 1988.

Moré, Marcel. *Nouvelles explorations de Jules Verne.* Paris: NRF, 1963.

———. *Le Très curieux Jules Verne.* Paris: NRF, 1960.

Moskowitz, Sam, ed. *Science Fiction by Gaslight.* Cleveland: World, 1968.

Noiray, Jacques. *Le Romancier et la machine: L'Image de la machine dans le roman français (1850–1900).* Paris: José Corti, 1982.

Nouvelles recherches sur Jules Verne et le voyage. Colloque d'Amiens I. Paris: Minard, 1978.

Picot, Jean-Pierre, and Christian Robin, eds. *Jules Verne: Cent ans après.* Actes du Colloque de Cerisy. Rennes: Terre de Brume, 2005.

Pourvoyeur, Robert. "De l'invention des mots chez Jules Verne." *Bulletin de la Société Jules Verne* 25 (1973): 19–24.

Raymond, François. "Jules Verne ou le mouvement perpétuel." *Subsidia Pataphysica* 8 (1969): 21–52.

———, ed. *Jules Verne 1: Le Tour du monde*. Paris: Minard, 1976.

———, ed. *Jules Verne 2: L'Ecriture vernienne*. Paris: Minard, 1978.

———, ed. *Jules Verne 3: Machines et imaginaire*. Paris: Minard, 1980.

———, ed. *Jules Verne 4: Texte, image, spectacle*. Paris: Minard, 1983.

———, ed. *Jules Verne 5: Emergences du fantastique*. Paris: Minard, 1987.

———, ed. *Jules Verne 6: La Science en question*. Paris: Minard, 1992.

Renzi, Thomas C. *Jules Verne on Film: A Filmography of the Cinematic Adaptations of His Works, 1902 through 1997*. Jefferson, N.C.: McFarland, 1998.

Revue Jules Verne (1996–2005). Founded by Jean-Paul Dekiss. A scholarly journal sponsored by several Verne-related organizations located in Amiens and Nantes, including the Centre international Jules Verne (Amiens) and the Musée Jules Verne (Nantes). As of the summer of 2006, twenty-one issues have been published.

Robin, Christian. *Un Monde connu et inconnu*. Nantes: Centre universitaire de recherches verniennes, 1978.

———, ed. *Textes et langages X: Jules Verne*. Nantes: Université de Nantes, 1984.

Rose, Mark. "Jules Verne: Journey to the Center of Science Fiction." In *Coordinates: Placing Science Fiction*, ed. George E. Slusser, 31–41. Carbondale: Southern Illinois University Press, 1983.

———. "Filling the Void: Verne, Wells, and Lem." *Science Fiction Studies* 8.2 (1981): 121–42.

Schulman, Peter. "Eccentricity as Clinamen: Jules Verne's Error-Driven Geniuses," *Excavatio* 16, nos. 1–2 (2002): 274–84.

———. Introduction and notes to Jules Verne, *The Begum's Millions*, ed. Arthur B. Evans. Middletown, Conn.: Wesleyan University Press, 2005.

———. "*Paris au XXème siècle*'s Legacy: Eccentricity as Defiance in Jules Verne's Uneasy Relationship with His Era." *Romance Quarterly* 48 (Fall 2001): 257–66.

Serres, Michel. "India (The Black and the Archipelago) on Fire." *Sub-stance* 8 (1974): 49–60.

———. *Jouvences sur Jules Verne*. Paris: Editions de Minuit, 1974.

———. "Le Savoir, la guerre, et le sacrifice." *Critique* 367 (Dec. 1977): 1067–77.

Slusser, George E. "The Perils of Experiment: Jules Verne and the American Lone Genius." *Extrapolation* 40.2 (1999): 101–15.

———. "Why They Kill Jules Verne: Science Fiction and Cartesian Culture." *Science Fiction Studies* 32.1 (Mar. 2005): 43–61.

Smyth, Edmund J. "Jules Verne, SF and Modernity: An Introduction." In *Jules Verne: Narratives of Modernity*, ed. Edmund J. Smyth, 1–10. Liverpool: Liverpool University Press, 2000.

———. ed. *Jules Verne: Narratives of Modernity*. Liverpool: Liverpool University Press, 2000.

Stableford, Brian. *Scientific Romance in Britain, 1890–1950*. London: Fourth Estate, 1985.

Suvin, Darko. "Communication in Quantified Space: The Utopian Liberalism of Jules Verne's Fiction." *Clio* 4 (1974): 51–71. Rpt. in Suvin, *Metamorphoses of Science Fiction*, 147–63. New Haven: Yale University Press, 1979.

Taves, Brian. "The Novels and Rediscovered Films of Michel (Jules) Verne." *Journal of Film Preservation*, no. 62 (Apr. 2001): 25–39.

Taves, Brian, and Stephen Michaluk Jr. *The Jules Verne Encyclopedia*. Lanham, Md.: Scarecrow, 1996.

Terrasse, Pierre. "Jules Verne et les chemins de fer." *Bulletin de la Société Jules Verne* 14 (Apr.–June 1970): 116–21.

Touttain, Pierre-André, ed. *Jules Verne*. Paris: Cahiers de l'Herne, 1974.

Unwin, Timothy. "The Fiction of Science, or the Science of Fiction." In *Jules Verne: Narratives of Modernity*, ed. Edmund J. Smyth, 46–59. Liverpool: Liverpool University Press, 2000.

———. *Jules Verne: Journeys in Writing*. Liverpool: Liverpool University Press, 2005.

———. *Jules Verne: Le Tour du monde en quatre-vingts jours*. Glasgow: Glasgow University Press, 1992.

———. "Jules Verne: Negotiating Change in the Nineteenth Century." *Science Fiction Studies* 32.1 (Mar. 2005): 5–17.

———. "Technology and Progress in Jules Verne, or Anticipation in Reverse." *AUMLA* 93 (2000): 17–35.

Vierne, Simone. "Hetzel et Jules Verne, ou l'invention d'un auteur." *Europe* 619–20 (1980): 53–63.

———. *Jules Verne, mythe et modernité*. Paris: PUF, 1989.

———. *Jules Verne, une vie, une oeuvre*. Paris: Ballard, 1986.

———. *Jules Verne et le roman initiatique: Contribution à l'étude de l'imaginaire*. Paris: Editions du Sirac, 1973.

Weissenberg, Eric. *Jules Verne: Un Univers fabuleux*. Lausanne: Favre, 2004.

Additional Materials Relating to Jules Verne's *The Kip Brothers*

Bonnefis, Philippe. "Clair-obscur." *Littérature* 26 (May 1977): 10–23.

Bordillon, Henri. "Balivernes sur Jarry-Verne." *Sureau* 5 (Mar.–June 1985): 111–15.

Bridenne, Jean-Jacques. "Jules Verne, père de la science-fiction? III: Edgar Poe et Jules Verne." *Fiction* 2.8 (July 1954): 113–17.

Burke, Keast. "Jules Verne and Australia." *Bohemia, the official organ of the Bread and Cheese Club* 11.4 (Oct. 1955): 15.

Ceccarelli, Jean. "Jules Verne et la piraterie des mers du Sud." *Neptunia* 237 (Mar. 2005): 42–45.

Chesneaux, Jean. "Les Illustrations des romans de Jules Verne." *Bulletin de la Société Jules Verne* 38 (Jan.–June 1976): 114–15.

Chevrier, Alain. "Le Mythe des hommes à queue chez Jules Verne." *Jules Verne* 28 (Oct.–Dec. 1993): 23–38.

Courville, Luce. "Au nom du père . . ." *Bulletin de la Société Jules Verne* 45 (Jan.–Mar. 1978): 132–36.

Degrave, Eugène. *Le Bagne, les frères Rorique*. Paris: Stock, 1901.

Duc, Thierry. "Jules Verne et sa justice." Mémoire de maîtrise, Université de Bordeaux III, 1988.

Evans, Arthur B. "Optograms and Fiction: Photo in a Dead Man's Eye." *Science Fiction Studies* 20.3 (Nov. 1993): 341–61. Published in French as "Jules Verne et la persistance rétinienne." *Cahiers du Musée Jules Verne* 13 (1996): 10–17.

"Une Extraordinaire affaire dans les mers du Sud." *Tribune de Genève* (Dec. 1965): 27.

Faivre, Jean-Paul. "Jules Verne (1828–1905) et le Pacifique." *Journal de la société des océanistes* 11.11 (Dec. 1965): 135–47.

Faligot, Roger. "Jules Verne and Ireland." *Irish Times* (Aug. 11, 1978): 15.

Goracci, Serge. "De quelques rapports entre les romans verniens et le roman populaire." *Bulletin de la Société Jules Verne* 50 (Apr.–June 1979): 60–68.

Grivel, Charles. "Kip Optogramme, le roman du crime et de la vue." In *Jules Verne: Cent ans après* (Actes du Colloque de Cerisy), ed. Jean-Pierre Picot and Christian Robin, 63–86. Rennes: Terre de Brume, 2005.

Grojnowski, Daniel. "Optogrammes." *Voir* 21 (Nov. 1999): 28–36. Rpt. in Grojnowski, *Photographie et langage*, 223–43. Paris: Corti, 2002.

Helling, Cornélius. "L'Oeuvre scientifique de Jules Verne." *Bulletin de la Société Jules Verne* 1 (Nov. 1935): 32–42.

———. "Les Personnages réels dans l'oeuvre de Jules Verne." *Bulletin de la Société Jules Verne* 2 (Feb. 1936): 68–75.

Hermès, Frédéric. "Autres bourdes et lapsus verniens." *Bulletin de la Société Jules Verne* 107 (July–Sept. 1993): 32–34.

Jacquier, Henri. *Piraterie dans le Pacifique*. Paris: Nouvelles éditions latines, 1973. Published in English as *Piracy in the Pacific: The Story of the Notorious Rorique Brothers*, trans. June P. Wilson. New York: Dodd, Mead, 1976.

La Bruyère, René. *Les Frères Rorique*. Paris: Librairie des Champs-Elysées, 1934.

Lacassin, Francis. "Le Coeur à gauche." *Les Nouvelles Littéraires* 55.622 (Feb. 16, 1978): 17.

———. "Jules Verne et le roman policier." In Jules Verne, *Le Pilote du Danube*, 5–18. Paris: UGE, "10/18," 1979.

———. "Jules Verne ou le socialisme clandestin." In Jules Verne, *Famille-sans-nom*, 7–36. Paris: UGE, "10/18," 1978.

———. "Jules Verne ou le socialisme inattendu." In *Passagers clandestins 1*, ed. Francis Lacassin. 99–162. Paris: UGE, "10/18," 1979.

Martin, Charles-Noël. "Préface." In Jules Verne, *"Clovis Dardentor" et "Les Frères Kip,"* 7–15. Lausanne: Rencontre, 1970.

Milani, Raffaele. "Iconografia di un naufragio." In *Viaggi straordinari attorno a Jules Verne*, ed. Franco Pollini and Loretta Righetti. 75–81. Milano: Mursia. 1991.

Milner, Max. *La Fantasmagorie*. Paris: Presses Universitaires de France, 1982.

Moré, Marcel. *Le Très curieux Jules Verne*. Paris: NRF, 1960.

Porcq, Christian. "Cataclysme dans la cathédrale ou le secret des *Frères Kip* (1)." *Bulletin de la Société Jules Verne* 107 (July–Sept. 1993): 35–52.

———. "Cataclysme dans la cathédrale ou le secret des *Frères Kip* (2)." *Bulletin de la Société Jules Verne* 109 (Jan.–Mar. 1994): 36–51.

Raper, G. A. "The Story of the Brothers Degrave." *Wide World Magazine* 7.39 (1901): 211–19, 365–75.

Righetti, Loretta. *Quando il Nautilus era una conchiglia*. Cesena: Commune di Cesena. 1988.

Robillard, Serge. "Un Dénouement extraordinaire: Réhabilitation des frères Kip." *Bulletin de la Société Jules Verne* 111 (July–Sept. 1994): 42–44.

"La Terrible histoire des frères Rorique." *Journal de Tintin* 20 (May 15, 1947).

Vandamme, Jan. *De Affaire Degrave-Rorique (1892–1899): Moord & Piraterij in de Stille Zuidzee*. Antwerp: Hadewijch, 1992.

Weissenberg, Eric. "Le Coin du bibliophile—Trois types de cartonnages Hetzel 'aux initiales.'" *Bulletin de la Société Jules Verne* 127 (July–Sept. 1998): 45–53.

Zukowski, Henri. "Boîtes." *La Revue des Lettres Modernes* 5 (Sept. 1987): 101–16.

JULES GABRIEL VERNE: A BIOGRAPHY

Jules Gabriel Verne was born on February 8, 1828, to a middle-class family in the port city of Nantes, France. His mother, Sophie, née Allotte de la Fuÿe, was the daughter of a prominent family of shipowners, and his father, Pierre Verne, was an attorney and the son of a Provins magistrate. Jules was the eldest of five children. In addition to his three sisters—Anna, Mathilde, and Marie—he had a younger brother, Paul, to whom he was very close. Paul eventually became a naval engineer.

As a child and young man, Jules was a relatively conscientious student. Although far from the top of his class, he apparently did win awards for meritorious performance in geography, music, and Greek and Latin, and he easily passed his *baccalauréat* in 1846. But his true passion was the sea. The shipyard docks of nearby Ile Feydeau and the bustling commerce of the Nantes harbor never failed to spark Jules's youthful imagination with visions of far-off lands and exotic peoples. Legend has it that he once ran off to sea as a cabin boy aboard a schooner bound for the Indies, but his father managed to intercept the ship before it reached the open sea and retrieved his wayward son. According to this story, Jules (probably after a good thrashing) promised his parents that he would travel henceforth only in his dreams. Although this charming tale was most likely invented—or at least heavily embroidered—by Verne's family biographer, Marguerite Allotte de la Fuÿe, it nevertheless exemplifies the author's lifelong love for the sea and his yearnings for adventure-filled journeys to distant ports of call.

Young Jules also loved machines. During an interview toward the end of his life, he reminisced about his early formative years: "While I was quite a lad, I used to adore watching machines at work. My father had a country-house at Chantenay, at the mouth of the Loire, and near the government factory at Indret. I never went to Chantenay without entering the factory and standing for hours watching the machines. . . . This penchant has remained with me all my life, and today I have still as much pleasure in watching a steam-engine or a fine locomotive at work as I have in contemplating a picture by Raphael or Corregio" (qtd. in Robert H. Sherard, "Jules Verne at Home," *McClure's Magazine* [Jan. 1984]: 118).

Intending that Jules follow in his footsteps as a lawyer, Pierre Verne sent him to Paris in 1848 to study law. The correspondence between father and son during the ensuing ten years shows that Jules took his studies seriously, completing his law degree in just two years. But his letters home also make quite it clear that Jules had renewed his lifelong passion for literature. Inspired by such authors as Victor Hugo, Alfred de Vigny, and Théophile Gautier and introduced (via family contacts on his mother's side) into several high-society Parisian literary circles, the young Romantic Verne began to devote himself as never before to his writing. From 1847 to 1862, he composed poetry, wrote several plays and a novel titled *Un Prêtre en 1839* (A Priest in 1839, unpublished during his lifetime), and penned a variety of short stories that he published in the popular French journal *Musée des familles* to supplement his meager income: "Les Premiers navires de la marine mexicaine" (1851, The First Ships of the Mexican Navy), "Un Voyage en ballon" (1851, A Balloon Journey), "Martin Paz" (1852, Martin Paz), "Maître Zacharius" (1854, Master Zacharius), and "Un Hivernage dans les glaces" (1855, Winter in the Ice). Some of his plays were performed in local Parisian theaters: *Les Pailles rompues* (1850, Broken Straws), *Le Colin-Maillard* (1853, Blind Man's Bluff), *Les Compagnons de la Marjolaine* (1855, The Companions of the Marjoram), *Monsieur de Chimpanzé* (1858, Mister Chimpanzee), *L'Auberge des Ardennes* (1860, The Inn of the Ardennes), and *Onze jours de siège* (1861, Eleven Days of Siege). During this period, Verne also became close friends with Alexandre Dumas père and Dumas fils and, through the former's intervention, eventually became the secretary of the Théâtre Lyrique in 1852 (he left this post in 1855).

In 1857 Verne married Honorine Morel, née de Viane, a twenty-six-year-old widow with two daughters. Taking advantage of his new father-in-law's contacts in Paris and a monetary wedding gift from Pierre Verne, Jules decided to discontinue his work at the Théâtre Lyrique and to take a full-time job as *agent de change* at the Paris Stock Market with the firm Eggly et Cie. He spent his early mornings at home writing (at a desk with two drawers—one for his plays, the other for his scientific essays) and most of his days at the Bourse de Paris doing business and associating with a number of other young stockbrokers who had interests similar to his own.

When not busy writing or working at the stock exchange, Verne spent his time either visiting old theater friends (he took trips with Aristide Hignard to Scotland and England in 1859 and to Norway and Denmark in 1861—the former resulting in a travelogue called *Voyage en Angleterre et en Ecosse* [Journey to England and Scotland]) or going to the Bibliothèque Nationale, where he would collect scientific and historical news items and copy them onto note cards for future use, a work habit he would continue throughout his life. As at least one biographer has noted, the long weekend sessions he spent in the reading rooms of the library may well have been partly motivated by a simple desire for peace and quiet: in 1861 Verne's son, Michel, had just been born and greatly annoyed his father with his incessant crying.

It was during this time that Verne first conceived of writing a new type of novel called a *roman de la science*. It would incorporate the large amounts of scientific material that Verne accumulated in his library research, as well as that gleaned from essays in the *Musée des familles* and other journals, to which he himself occasionally contributed. It would combine scientific exploration and discovery with action and adventure and be patterned on the novels of Walter Scott, James Fenimore Cooper, and Edgar Allan Poe. Poe's works in particular, which had recently been translated into French by Charles Baudelaire in 1856, strongly interested Verne for their unusual mixture of scientific reasoning and the fantastic (he later wrote his only piece of literary criticism on Poe in 1864). Verne's efforts eventually crystallized into a rough draft of a novel-length narrative, which he tentatively entitled *Un Voyage en l'air* (A Voyage through the Air).

In September 1862, Verne was introduced to Pierre-Jules Hetzel through a mutual friend of the publisher and Alexandre Dumas père. Verne promptly asked Hetzel if he would consider reviewing for publication the rough draft of his novel—a manuscript that, according to his wife, the author had very nearly destroyed a few weeks earlier after its rejection by another publishing house. Hetzel agreed to the request, seeing in this narrative the potential for an ideal "fit" with his new family-oriented magazine, the *Magasin d'Education et de Récréation*. A few days later, Verne and Hetzel began what would prove to be a highly successful author-publisher collaboration.

It lasted for more than forty years and resulted in over sixty scientific novels collectively called the *Voyages extraordinaires—Voyages dans les mondes connus et inconnus* (Extraordinary Voyages—Journeys in Known and Unknown Worlds).

Shortly after the publication and commercial success of Verne's first novel in 1863—now retitled *Cinq semaines en ballon, Voyage de découvertes en Afrique par trois Anglais* (Five Weeks in a Balloon, Voyage of Discovery in Africa by Three Englishmen)—Hetzel offered the young writer a ten-year contract for at least two works per year of the same sort. Not long after, Verne quit his job at the stock market and began to write full time.

Following Verne's historic meeting with Hetzel, his life and works fell into three distinct periods: 1862–86, 1886–1905, and 1905–25.

The first, from 1862 to 1886, might be termed Verne's "Hetzel period." During this time, he wrote his most popular *Voyages extraordinaires,* settled permanently with his family in Amiens, purchased a yacht, collaborated on theater adaptations of several of his novels with Adolphe d'Ennery, and ultimately gained both fame and fortune.

Other notable events in Verne's life during this period include:

- Hetzel's rejection of his second novel, *Paris au XXème siècle* (Paris in the 20th Century), in 1863 as well as an early draft of *L'Ile mystérieuse* (The Mysterious Island) called *L'Oncle Robinson* (Uncle Robinson) in 1865;
- the publication of his nonfiction books *Géographie de la France et de ses colonies* (1866, Geography of France and Its Colonies, coauthored with Théophile Lavallée) and the three-volume *Histoire des grands voyages et des grands voyageurs* (1878–80, History of Great Voyages and Great Voyagers);
- the unparalleled success of the novels *Voyage au centre de la terre* (1864, Journey to the Center of the Earth), *De la terre à la lune* (1865, From the Earth to the Moon), *Autour de la lune* (1870, Around the Moon), *Vingt mille lieues sous les mers* (1870, Twenty Thousand Leagues under the Seas), *Le Tour du monde en quatre-vingts jours* (1873, Around the World in Eighty Days), and *Michel Strogoff* (1876, Michael Strogoff), among others;

- a brief trip to America in 1867 on the *Great Eastern,* accompanied by his brother, Paul, with visits to New York and Niagara Falls—subsequently fictionalized in his novel *La Ville flottante* (1871, A Floating City);
- receipt of the *Légion d'honneur* just after the outbreak of the Franco-Prussian War in 1870;
- the death of his father, Pierre Verne, on November 3, 1871;
- the purchase of his third yacht, the *Saint-Michel III,* in which he sailed to Lisbon and Algiers in 1878, to Scotland in 1879, to Holland, Denmark, Germany, and the Baltics in 1881, and to Portugal, Algeria, Tunisia, and Italy in 1884 (and, while in Italy, was invited to a private audience with Pope Leo XIII);
- in 1879, the publication of *Les Cinq cents millions de la Bégum* (The Begum's Millions) in collaboration with Paschal Grousset, a.k.a. André Laurie, Verne's only combination utopia/dystopia, which featured his first "mad scientist," Herr Schultze;
- in 1882, his move to a new, larger home at 2 rue Charles-Dubois, Amiens—the famous house with the circular tower, which is today the headquarters of the Centre de Documentation Jules Verne d'Amiens.

The second phase, from 1886 to 1905, might be called Verne's "post-Hetzel period." During this time, Verne worked with Hetzel's son, Louis-Jules, who succeeded his father as manager and principal editor of the Hetzel publishing house. Verne also entered into politics: he was elected to the municipal council of Amiens in 1888, a post he would occupy for fifteen years. But this period is especially notable because of a gradual change in the ideological tone of his *Voyages extraordinaires.* In these later works, the Saint-Simonian pro-science optimism is largely absent, replaced by a growing pessimism about the true value of progress. The omnipresent scientific didacticism, a trademark of Verne's *roman scientifique,* is more frequently muted and supplanted or replaced by romantic melodrama, pathos, and tragedy. And the triumphant leitmotif of the exploration and conquest of nature, which seemed to undergird most of Verne's earlier novels, is now most often abandoned—replaced by an increased focus on politics, social issues, and human morality. This dramatic change of focus in Verne's later works appears to parallel certain personal adversities experienced by the author during this period of his life. For example:

- serious problems with his rebellious son Michel (e.g., repeated bankruptcies, costly amorous escapades, divorce from his first wife, difficulties with the law, etc.);
- severe financial worries, forcing Verne to sell his beloved yacht in 1886;
- the successive deaths of three individuals who were very close to him: his longtime mistress and friend Mme Duchesne (Estelle Hénin) in 1885, his editor Hetzel in 1886, and his mother in 1887;
- an attack at gunpoint on March 9, 1886, by his mentally disturbed nephew Gaston, who shot Verne in the lower leg, leaving him partially crippled for the rest of his life.

Verne's personal correspondence from this period also reflects his growing pessimism. In a letter dated December 21, 1886, to Hetzel fils, for example, Verne confides: "As for the rest, I have now entered into the blackest part of my life." A few years later, in 1894, the author tells his brother Paul: "All that remains to me are these intellectual distractions. . . . My character is profoundly changed and I have received blows from which I'll never recover."

Whatever the underlying reasons may have been for this change—the absence of Hetzel père's editorial supervision, Verne's awareness of certain disturbing trends in the world at large (e.g., the growth of imperialism and the military-industrial complex), or the sudden flood of tragedies in his personal life—it is evident that many of Verne's post-1886 *Voyages extraordinaires* tend to portray both scientists and scientific innovation with a heavy dose of cynicism and/or biting satire. And, in contrast to the intrepid "go where no man has gone before" scientific explorations, which characterized most of his earlier and most popular works, the later novels now often foreground, in whole or in part, a broad range of political, social, and moral concerns: among other themes, the potential dangers of technology in *Sans dessus dessous* (1889, Topsy-Turvy), *Face au drapeau* (1896, Facing the Flag), and *Maître du monde* (1904, Master of the World); the cruel oppression of the Québécois in Canada in *Famille-sans-nom* (1889, Family without a Name); the evils of ignorance and superstition in *Le Château des Carpathes* (1892, The Castle of the Carpathians); the intolerable living conditions in orphanages in *P'tit-Bonhomme* (1893, Lit'l Fellow); the destructive influence of religious missionaries on South Sea island cultures in *L'Ile à hélice* (1895, Propeller Island); the imminent extinction of whales in *Le Sphinx des glaces* (1897, The Sphinx of the Ice); the environmental damage caused by the oil industry in *Le Testament d'un excentrique* (1899, The Last Will of an Eccentric); and the slaughter of elephants for their ivory in *Le Village aérien* (1901, The Aerial Village).

During his last years, despite increasingly poor health (arthritis, cataracts, diabetes, and severe gastrointestinal problems) as well as continuing family squabbles because of his son, Michel, Verne continued diligently to write two to three novels per year. But, with a drawer full of nearly completed manuscripts in his desk, he suddenly fell seriously ill in early March 1905, a few weeks after his seventy-seventh birthday. He told his wife, Honorine, to gather the family around him, and he died quietly on March 24, 1905. He was buried on March 28 in the cemetery of La Madeleine in Amiens. Two years later, an elaborate marble sculpture by Albert Roze was placed over his grave, depicting the author rising from his tomb and stretching his hand toward the sky.

The third and final phase of the Jules Verne story, following the author's death and extending from 1905 to 1925, might well be called the "Verne fils period." During these years Verne's posthumous works were published, but most of them were substantially modified—and, in some instances, authored—by his son, Michel.

In early May 1905, Michel, as executor of his father's estate, published in the Parisian newspapers *Le Figaro* and *Le Temps* a list of Jules Verne's surviving manuscripts: eight novels (titled and untitled, in various stages of completion), sixteen plays, several short stories (two unpublished), a travelogue of his early trip to England and Scotland, and an assortment of historical sketches, notes, and the like. Hetzel fils immediately agreed to publish six of the novels that were originally intended to be part of the *Voyages extraordinaires* as well as Verne's short stories, which were grouped in the collection published in 1910 as *Hier et demain* (Yesterday and Tomorrow). Another remaining novel in the series, *L'Etonnante aventure de la mission Barsac* (The Amazing Adventure of the Barsac Mission), was published first in serial format in the newspaper *Le Matin* and later as a book by the publishing company Hachette, which had bought the rights to Verne's works from Hetzel fils in 1914.

In recent years, these posthumous works have become the topic of heated controversy among Verne scholars: how much and in what ways did Michel alter these texts prior to their publication? After a close examination of the available manuscripts (now housed in the Centre d'études verniennes in Nantes) by Piero Gondolo della Riva, Olivier Dumas, and other respected Vernian researchers, it now seems indisputable that Michel had a much greater hand in the composition of Jules Verne's posthumous works than had ever been suspected:

- *Le Volcan d'or* (1906, The Golden Volcano): fourteen chapters by Jules; four more chapters added by Michel as well as four new characters;
- *L'Agence Thompson and Co.* (1907, The Thompson Travel Agency): in all probability, almost entirely written by Michel;
- *La Chasse au météore* (1908, The Hunt for the Meteor): seventeen chapters by Jules; four added by Michel;
- *Le Pilote du Danube* (1908, The Danube Pilot): sixteen chapters by Jules; three added by Michel as well as at least one new character and a new title;
- *Les Naufragés du Jonathan* (1909, The Survivors of the Jonathan): sixteen chapters by Jules; fifteen added by Michel, along with many new characters, episodes, and a new title;
- *Le Secret de Wilhelm Storitz* (1910, The Secret of Wilhelm Storitz): rewritten by Michel to take place in the eighteenth century instead of at the end of the nineteenth; a different conclusion was also added;
- *Hier et demain* (1910, Yesterday and Tomorrow): most of the short stories appearing in this collection had been substantially altered by Michel; one of them, "Au XXIXème siècle: La Journée d'un journaliste américain en 2889" (In the 29th Century: The Day of an American Journalist in 2889), attributable mostly to Michel, and another, "L'Eternel Adam" (The Eternal Adam), mostly by him as well;
- *L'Etonnante aventure de la mission Barsac* (1919, The Amazing

Adventure of the Barsac Mission): the supposedly "final" novel of the *Voyage extraordinaires* was written entirely by Michel from his father's notes for a novel to be called *Voyages d'études* (Study Trip).

Scholarly reaction to Michel's rewrites of his father's manuscripts has been somewhat mixed. Some have called Michel's intervention in Verne's posthumous works an inexcusable betrayal of trust and a financially motivated scam that dealt a damaging blow to the integrity of Verne's *Voyages extraordinaires*. In an attempt to set the record straight, from 1985 through the 1990s, the Société Jules Verne in France arranged for the publication of Verne's original manuscripts of several of these works. Other scholars disagree and have pointed out that Jules Verne encouraged Michel to publish his own fiction under his father's illustrious name; that during the final decade of his life when his eyesight was rapidly failing, Jules reportedly asked Michel to "collaborate" with him (as secretary-typist) to help bring several of his later novels to publication; and that Michel's sometimes radical modifications of Verne's posthumous works often improved their readability—an enhancement that would assuredly have received his father's wholehearted approval. The debate continues to this day.

With Michel's death in 1925, the final chapter of Verne's literary legacy was (for better or worse) now complete. Ironically, in April of the following year, a pulp magazine called *Amazing Stories* first appeared on American newsstands. It published tales of a supposedly new species of literature dubbed "scientifiction"—defined by its publisher, Hugo Gernsback, as a "Jules Verne, H.G. Wells, and Edgar Allan Poe type of story"—and its title page featured a drawing of Verne's tomb as the magazine's logo. The popularity of *Amazing Stories* and its many pulp progeny, such as *Science Wonder Stories* and *Astounding Stories*, was both immediate and long lasting. As the term "scientifiction" evolved into "science fiction," the new genre began to flourish as never before. And the legend of Jules Verne as its patron saint, as the putative "Father of Science Fiction," soon became firmly rooted in American cultural folklore.

ABOUT THE CONTRIBUTORS

ARTHUR B. EVANS is professor of French at DePauw University and managing editor of the scholarly journal *Science Fiction Studies*. He has published numerous books and articles on Verne and early French science fiction, including the award-winning *Jules Verne Rediscovered* (Greenwood, 1988). He is general editor of Wesleyan University Press's "Early Classics of Science Fiction" series.

STANFORD L. LUCE is professor emeritus of French at Miami University in Ohio and author of the first American Ph.D. dissertation on Jules Verne (Yale, 1953). He has published extensively on Céline and has previously translated Verne's *The Mighty Orinoco* and *The Begum's Millions* for Wesleyan's "Early Classics of Science Fiction" series.

JEAN-MICHEL MARGOT is an internationally recognized specialist on Jules Verne. He currently serves as president of the North American Jules Verne Society (NAJVS) and has published several books and many articles on Verne and his work. His most recent include a study of Verne's theatrical play *Journey through the Impossible* (Prometheus, 2003) and a volume of nineteenth-century Verne criticism titled *Jules Verne en son temps* (Encrage, 2004).